I0902198

PENGUIN BOOKS

THE DAWN OF RECKONING

Leslie W is the pen name of Kayce Teo.

Born and bred in Singapore, she graduated with a BA in English Literature from the National University of Singapore. She was one of six mentees selected for the Fiction category of the Mentor Access Project, an annual programme initiated by the National Arts Council to develop young and emerging writers in Singapore's four official languages.

Her debut fantasy novel, *The Night of Legends*, was written under the mentorship of award-winning writer, Dave Chua.

Sign up for her newsletter at kayceteo.com for writing and life updates.

OTHER BOOKS IN THIS SERIES

The Night of Legends (2019)
The Light of Stars (2022)

PRAISE FOR *THE NIGHT OF LEGENDS* TRILOGY

'A wickedly fun conclusion to an amazing trilogy. Wildly entertaining and packed with cinematic, gripping action.'

—Dave Chua,
award-winning author of *Gone Case*

'Leslie W weaves magic into her words to make each action scene as vivid as if you were watching a movie. The world she's built is foreign yet familiar in its themes, with compelling characters that will stay with you long after you've turned the last page.'

—Catherine Dellosa,
author of *Of Myths and Men*

'*The Light of Stars* is an electrifying YA fantasy rich in suspense, action, and tender moments. Leslie W's evocative prose, exceptional worldbuilding, and compelling characters drew me in from the get-go. A praiseworthy sequel to *The Night of Legends*!'

—Vivian Teo,
author of the *My BFF is an Alien* series

'With a razor-sharp plot and strong emotional arc, the sequel to Leslie W's *The Night of Legends* raises the stakes and makes for a dangerously compelling read that is impossible to put down and hard to forget.'

—Joyce Chua,
author of *Land of Sand and Song*

'Keix, an awakened soldier trying to find her own way, is the perfect foil to guide us through the *1984*esque *Star Wars* setting—paper thin trapezoidal buildings, mystical creatures like haagis and shihs, and shady organizations trying to control magic for the "public good". I highly recommend!'

—Nabeel Ismeer,
author of *The Hunter's Walk*

'A page-turner at every chapter. Riveting, action-packed, and full of exciting plot twists, I couldn't put it down. The worldbuilding is stupendous, peopled by relatable characters that I rooted for. Leslie W's storytelling prowess and prose left me wanting more.'

—Eva Wong Nava,
author of *The House of Little Sisters*

'I loved *The Night of Legends,* book one of *The Night of Legends* young adult coming-of-age fantasy trilogy. *The Light of Stars,* the second book, beats it hands down. In the first book, our team of six heroes discovered everything they'd been taught was a lie. Now, in *The Light of Stars,* they have to find their own truths. And what a journey they must make to do so. This is a gripping read, with many unexpected plot twists as kick-ass girls Keix and Vin fight unexpected enemies in a city that changes its configuration every dusk and dawn. Be prepared for self-discovery, loss, love, and a dramatic changing of loyalties as the two young women and their six companions journey on towards their destinies. A must read. Can't wait for #3.'

—Audrey Chin,
award-winning author of *The Ash House*

The Dawn of Reckoning

Leslie W

PENGUIN BOOKS
An imprint of Penguin Random House

PENGUIN BOOKS

Penguin Books is an imprint of the Penguin Random House group of companies whose addresses can be found at global.penguinrandomhouse.com

Published by Penguin Random House SEA Pte Ltd
40 Penjuru Lane, #03-12, Block 2
Singapore 609216

Penguin Random House SEA

First published by Penguin Random House SEA 2026

10 9 8 7 6 5 4 3 2 1

ISBN 9789815144567

Typeset by MAP Systems, Bengaluru, India

www.penguin.sg

For the stubborn ones, fuelled by spite to prove naysayers wrong.
You're the true star.

YURKORDU
TILSOR
WOODS
LAKE HOUSE
SECTOR
L
B
G
C
M
CITY CENTRE
H
F
D
A
I
K
E
J
N
ATROS
SEWAGE PLANT
N

Contents

1

Keix | Uninvited

This is it, Keix thought to herself. *This is Yurkordu.*

Jagged outlines of cliffs that reached endlessly into the sky had come into sight. By her estimate, it was almost noon. Hours ago, the warmth of the rising sun had chased away the foggy night and gradually illuminated a barren-looking landscape painted in a monochrome palette of grey.

Keix eyed the distance to the foot of the rocky mountains, where she assumed the entrance to Yurkordu was located. A jolt of apprehension mixed with a hint of thrill ran through her. Turning to her travelling companion, she said, 'Jūn, let's hurry.'

Since the two of them left Tilsor for Yurkordu a couple of weeks ago, they had been keeping a brisk, steady pace throughout their journey, resting at regular intervals; Jūn didn't want to risk tiring themselves out in case they ran into ExA (short for ex-Atrossian) soldiers. Decades ago, this group used to govern Atros, the place where Keix had grown up. In their bid for absolute power, they experimented with building and bonding machine parts to their own bodies so they could become literal fighting machines. ExA's greed caused the citizens of Atros to suffer immeasurable hardship under their rule. A group of commoners then banded together to drive those exploitative soldiers out of their homeland. While ExA was regrouping to take back their city, the portal between the living and the dead was opened; the electromagnetic waves emitted by the ghosts caused the machine parts in the soldiers' bodies to malfunction, foiling their plans for revenge. As ExA lay in wait, their need and want for revenge simmered and intensified. And when the Ifarls closed the portal recently, ExA's festering hatred erupted.

The ex-Atrossians returned with a vengeance, more bloodthirsty than ever, with new troops who had honed their battle instincts all their lives for this one moment—to take back what they felt the world owed them.

While Keix was confident that she and Jūn could easily take down a handful of these ExA soldiers, getting ambushed by a hoard of them might spell trouble and put a dent in their own plans. But considering that they were this close to Yurkordu and it was an open field ahead . . .

'We'll be able to see any attackers coming from afar,' said Keix in her most convincing tone. 'And I'm sure you'll be able to hear them.' She was certain of this because Jūn was a Kulcan, a race known to have exceptional hearing, as well as impeccable physical control over their bodies. Keix was only half-Kulcan on her father's side, but her senses were considered pretty exceptional by Atrossian standards.

Brows furrowing, Jūn met Keix's hopeful gaze. 'It's harder to hear anything in detail in an open space. And there are clusters of trees nearer to the foot of the cliffs . . .'

As he trailed off, Keix bit her tongue. He was worrying needlessly. They hadn't run into *any* living soul during the entire journey here. That was why Keix had managed to ignore the unsettling feeling in the pit of her stomach even as it grew with each passing day. There were too many volatile variables, and they were racing against time to take ExA by surprise.

But it seemed like Iv't killing every single one of the ExA soldiers who had infiltrated Tilsor was the right move. He was, by all accounts, the most powerful Ifarl who had ever lived. The story goes that around seventy years ago, ExA was hunting him for reasons unknown. One day, they lured him out of his home and attacked his family, killing his beloved wife and causing his infant daughter to go missing. Iv't then opened the portal between the living and the dead in a bid to find his loved ones, and the event subsequently led to ExA's downfall and Iv't's self-imprisonment.

The news that Iv't had resurfaced must have been contained, since it was peaceful thus far. It was a small blessing for Keix's little group of friends, who were now scattered in different places, working to stop ExA from taking over the world.

When the knot between Jūn's brows loosened, Keix knew he had given in. The next second, she took off, giggling. 'Race you!' she shouted without looking back. Jūn could overtake her in an instant if he wanted to, but he seemed content to let her sprint ahead.

Keix's hair, which had grown to a shoulder-grazing length, was pulled into a low ponytail. She let it down now, allowing the wind to tease the strands apart. Feeling lighter and a little more unrestrained, she ran through her mission in her head again. She had to convince the Kulcans to join her side to thwart ExA's world-domination scheme. There was no way to go up against these part-machine, part-human fighters and expect to win otherwise. The sad excuse of an 'army' that she and her friends had gathered comprised mainly Tilsorians, who were either traders or bandits. That's why Maii and Iv't were tasked with getting the Ifarls out of hiding to beef up their numbers—though the strength of their mysterious race lay more in being on the sidelines rather than on the frontlines of a battle. That's why Zej and Dace, together with Dace's father and Seyfer, had to head back to Atros to get intel about ExA and to see if they could round up any Atrossian troopers for their cause; it was highly likely that Atros's soldiers were being held captive by ExA in their own city.

No matter how strategic a battle plan Keix and her friends had formulated—using the ever-shifting layout of Tilsor to their advantage, among other things—everyone knew deep down in their hearts that without the help of the Kulcans, the outcome of the war was pretty much decided. Even Iv't, whose Ifarl powers seemed limitless, had admitted he wasn't confident of eradicating ExA once and for all. His thirst for revenge put him on the same side as Keix and her friends, but Keix would be stupid to trust him because of this. So, she pinned her hopes on the Kulcans' help, believing that every step she took towards Yurkordu was one step nearer to victory in this seemingly impossible-to-win war.

Keix slowed to a brisk walk as clusters of trees came into view. She wiped her sweaty palms on her thick outer robe. The garment that she had thrown on to ward off the increasingly strong and freezing winds felt too heavy and suffocating after her run. But the biting cold on her heated cheeks told her that it would be unwise to remove it. Everywhere she looked, looming slate grey rock faces taunted her every move.

Jūn stopped, cleared his throat and gestured to a well-trodden path. 'We're here.'

Keix found his formality amusing, but she was vibrating with nerves and from the cold, so she couldn't crack a smile. She eyed the wide path, marked with white and grey gravel, shimmering under the blazing sun. It sloped upward and led to a rather large gap in the cliffs.

This is Yurkordu, she repeated to herself. *The Kulcans' homeland. Jūn's home.*

Once, for a very short period of time, Keix had hoped it could be her home too. It seemed like only yesterday when she had first left Atros in search of her Kulcan father. He was a mystery to her because she had never met him. All the information that she could cobble together on him was from stories told by her mum. But if he were a good person, like her mum insisted, why had he not come for Keix when she died?

The death of the only family Keix knew had planted a seed of immeasurable grudge in her. For the longest time after that, she had banished her father's existence from her memory. If he didn't want to be in her life, she would gladly return the sentiment.

But fate didn't seem to want to let Keix stew in her resentment. Her entire value system was overturned and she lost all sense of self-identity when she was dealt one betrayal after another. The first was when Atros, the organization to which she had sworn her life, imprisoned her and carried out all sorts of twisted experiments to turn her into a hybrid—a human host for paranormal beings—because they needed a hybrid army to 'protect' themselves and innocent Atrossians against ExA should the latter launch an attack.

Thankfully, her friends—Zej and Pod—broke her out of her coma-induced imprisonment. But she never anticipated that the next betrayal would strike even closer to heart when Zej turned his back on her and let the Ifarls put her up as sacrifice for their ritual to close the portal between the living and the dead. Keix was supposed to die during the rites, and it was only by a miraculous stroke of luck that she had survived. The impact of the ritual knocked her out, and in her semi-conscious state, she had seen Jūn riding a shih towards her and telling her that he could bring her to meet her father. And what was initially a journey to see her absentee father—a desperate attempt to find a sense of belonging in life, really—transformed into a matter of life and death where the fate of the entire world was at stake.

Keix didn't have it in her to just sit back and watch ExA kill people senselessly in their aim to conquer the world—not when Pod had been murdered in cold blood by an ExA soldier right in front of her . . .

Tears stung her eyes at the memory. She didn't want to cry right now, so she craned her head back and squinted at the white-tipped cliffs.

'Don't look up at the sun directly,' said Jūn in a soft, chiding tone. He cradled the back of her head and got her to tilt her head back down gently. Then, he stood wordlessly next to her. He had, as usual, caught on to her mood and sensed that she needed some time to organize her emotions before heading into Yurkordu.

After Keix blinked away the remnants of her tears and the sunrays that had been seared onto her eyelids, she asked, 'Is that s-snow on the peaks?'

Jūn had told Keix about the existence of such a thing on their way to his homeland. But why did he sound so fascinated by something so commonplace to him?

'White, soft, and fluffy, floating down from the skies like'—Jūn had tried to search for an appropriate word—'confetti? Every snowfall is different, and every one of them will tease out a part of you that you were perhaps not aware of,' he had elaborated wistfully.

Keix had never seen this 'snow' before. Atros, where she had grown up and lived in for the past eighteen years of her life, was hot and humid. Rainy days were few and far between. No one spared much thought about their environment. Why would they, when it was an indisputable, unchangeable fact? But the look of wonderment in Jūn's eyes told her everything about this phenomenon that his inadequate vocabulary couldn't. 'It sounds intriguing,' she had replied. 'I'd like to see it.'

At present, as if recalling their conversation from before, Jūn said, 'You'll have to go further and climb up the mountain ranges to see it. I'll take you there once you've settled in.'

Keix turned to him and their eyes met. The word of thanks that was at the tip of her tongue was snatched away with her breath. There it was again. The smile that crinkled the corners of his eyes; the way he behaved as if she mattered—as if she were *all* that mattered; and the certainty that she felt in her gut (a certainty that she was rationally inclined to reject) that this was all real, that his feelings for her were genuine, and that he had no other agenda besides letting her know that he liked her.

But *why*? They barely knew each other. Technically speaking, they had first met that fateful night of the ritual, and all that Jūn had said to her was, 'If you want to look for your father, head north out of Atros. I'll meet you at the woods that's a two-day ride outside Sector L.' Then, their second encounter was when he had saved her from a group of ExA soldiers at some wooded area outside Atros. Since then, they had been practically joined at the hip, no thanks to their special circumstances. Yet, when Jūn was addled after getting slashed with a poisonous blade, he had let slip that he had first met her when he was fourteen. If that was the case, why couldn't she remember anything? Keix had wanted to ask him about this numerous times, but she simply couldn't bring herself to raise the question. Everything that she had uncovered in the past months—especially Atros's lies about using black-hole bullets to capture their own citizens to turn them into hybrids—had worn her down. Truth, it seemed, was all dependent on one's knowledge or beliefs.

'Overthinking again, I see,' teased Jūn.

Keix couldn't suppress a smile. Jūn had a knack for deciphering her every minute expression and move. Of course, he couldn't read her exact thoughts, but his attentiveness towards her moods made her more aware of both herself and her surroundings, as well as him. She noticed how he had become less reticent and more animated after leaving Tilsor, how she would always feel a tingling warmth in the depths of her heart when he smiled at her, how they had both frozen every time they drew too close to each other. At these times, Keix had an inkling that he was thinking of *that* moment—*that* kiss that had almost happened—between them.

Jūn was right. Keix had never had to slow down and make decisions—nor consider the ripple effect of her actions—until she got a second chance at life. And now that she had extracted herself from Atros's vice-like grip—both physically and mentally—she'd had to learn to think for herself. She second-guessed herself at every turn and with every move she made, because she knew she needed to reconfigure her viewpoint and select her own values.

Having grown more introspective, she also had to face the tangled mess in her heart labelled 'feelings and emotions'—concepts that she used to ignore. She was wary of romantic entanglements, especially after putting an end to her ambiguous relationship with Zej, whom she had a semi-crush on since she was fourteen. She couldn't deny her attraction to Jūn, but did she really want to take their relationship to the next level? *Urgh*. She was getting a splitting headache. Taking the cowardly way out, she brushed off Jūn's comment half-jokingly. 'Me? Hardly. Unless the thinking's done with my fists. Or sword.'

'Your swordsmanship *is* improving,' he said with a genuine laugh.

Keix blushed and beamed at his praise. Though they wanted to reach Yurkordu as quickly as they could, Jūn had insisted that they take an hour out every day to do combat training before they turned in for the night. His dedication to teaching her how to use a sword was part of the reason why her heart kept gravitating towards him.

'So,' continued Jūn, sucking in a deep, noisy breath as if he was nervous. 'What do you think?' He gestured to the cliffs.

'First impressions?'

Jūn gave an earnest nod. His bid for affirmation was endearing. Even though Keix had asked about his hometown umpteen times—what was it like, the Kulcans and their culture—his replies had always been vague and measured as he insisted he didn't want to influence her perception.

'Breathtaking,' replied Keix. After a beat, she added, 'And intimidating.'

'Yeah? I'm glad we feel the same way,' breathed Jūn, as a complex play of emotions crossed his face.

'Are you sure there's nothing you want to tell me before we head in? Nothing you need to prep me for—like packs of shihs lurking in the shadows that we'll have to take down?' Keix tried her best to look stern. She would never admit that she was stalling. Despite Jūn's reservations, she *had* managed to coax some information out of him about the Kulcans. He had said that no matter how dire the situation with ExA seemed, the Kulcans in authority could be stubborn and hard to convince. 'If there are two things we Kulcans actively avoid, it's'—Jūn had then held up his forefinger—'one: fights we can't win, and'—another finger shot up—'two: fights that don't concern us.'

'So, you guys are not meddlers,' Keix surmised.

Jūn grimaced. 'That's one way to put it. But we need to help stop ExA when they are going around slaughtering innocent people . . .'

Keix's heart had squeezed at his words then because the image of Pod getting skewered through his chest with a bloodied blade, his life seeping out of him, crossed her mind.

Sensing her distress, Jūn had fallen silent. Neither of them had broached the topic again until now.

'There's one more thing, actually,' said Jūn hesitantly. 'I kind of . . . broke a couple of rules in my hurry to get to you, so I might get punished when I get back.'

Keix's eyes widened. Jūn was a rule breaker? She filed that piece of information away. 'In your hurry to get to me?' she asked, tilting her head in confusion.

'You know, the night of the ritual.'

Wait . . . so Jūn hadn't chanced upon her the night the Ifarls closed the portal between the living and the dead? He had given a vague 'I was in the vicinity' explanation when she last asked him about it. She understood his evasiveness then; they were strangers, and she was purposefully interrogating him. Things were different now, however, so she boldly asked, 'How did you find me, anyway?'

Jūn's ears reddened. He looked like a small boy who had been caught red-handed doing something embarrassing. He cleared his throat. 'Er . . . I'll tell you everything once you've settled in, okay?'

'Tomorrow.' Keix was letting him off easy because she was dealing with her own tumultuous emotions. 'You'll come clean with me tomorrow. Everything.'

After Jūn nodded, she asked, 'So, what's the punishment?'

'It's nothing I can't take,' he hedged again. 'I promise. So, are you ready?' he asked, steering the conversation away clumsily.

Am I ready? For what? To finally enter Yurkordu? To meet my father for the first time? To see Jūn get punished? To face the Kulcans in charge to get them to fight a war they never asked for? Keix inhaled deeply and squared her shoulders, willing that knot of discomfort in her gut to disappear. 'As I can ever be.' She reassessed the trail in front of her. There wasn't much to see, to be honest, because once it led into the cliffs and got flanked on both sides by equally craggy rock faces, it disappeared past a bend. 'Are you sure that this is how we get into Yurkordu?'

Jūn raised an eyebrow at her.

'All right, that was a stupid question,' admitted Keix with a laugh. 'But you said we'd need our pendants to get into Yurkordu; there's nothing around that indicates we're stepping through a threshold or gate, or something . . . unless . . . this gap in the cliffs can be considered some sort of an open gateway?'

Jūn looked thoughtful. 'I've actually never considered that. I only ever left Yurkordu after I got my charm and I've never taken it off—except when I passed it to you for safe keeping.'

Back then, Jūn had just saved Keix and her best friend, Vin, from some ExA soldiers. He wanted to leave them at an abandoned hut to head to Tilsor to get some food for Keix, who was close to fainting from starvation at that time. He said he would return soon. But Keix wouldn't take his word for it, so she demanded him to hand over his sword as collateral. Instead of acquiescing, he took off the thin chain around his neck and passed it to her. He reassured her that it was more valuable than his sword, and that he would definitely come back for it.

Keix had accepted the necklace, which had an onyx charm strung on it, because she herself had received a similar charm from her mother on her eleventh birthday. With it came a handwritten card from her father that said,

> It is customary for us to gift our descendants with a family heirloom when they reach the age of eleven. The number has great significance in Kulcan culture. Perhaps one day you will find out why.

So, was the number eleven important to Kulcans because that's when they received the 'key' to leave and enter Yurkordu at will? If Jūn had also received his pendant when he was eleven, it would mean that he had never taken it off in a decade except for that one time when he handed it over to Keix . . .?

Trying to hide how flustered this new piece of information made her, Keix started, 'I mean . . . I just imagined stepping through a doorway or archway. You know, like the one in . . .' Keix felt herself silenced by an invisible force. Right. They couldn't talk about the Taavar tournament. It was one of the rules, enforced by an Ifarl charm, that they had been subjected to when they joined the contest in Tilsor to help Seyfer find Iv't. *Looks like the enchantment still works*, thought Keix.

Jūn, who caught the drift of her thoughts, gave her an understanding nod. 'I've been told that the boundary of Yurkordu is a short distance from where the cliffs end. I suppose crossing the threshold is similar to entering Tilsor. There, you need to know the name of the place for it to materialize. For Yurkordu, you just need to be wearing the charm.'

'What happens if we don't have our charms with us?'

'Why don't you try?' Jūn smirked.

'You're trying to trick me into an embarrassing situation, aren't you? I'm going to run into an invisible wall and get thrown back and land on my bum. I won't fall for it.' Keix crossed her arms to underscore her resistance.

'All right,' confessed Jūn, holding up his hands in mock surrender. 'You got me. You need to do this'—he put two fingers on his forehead then frowned—'as you step through the invisible wall.'

Keix regarded him sceptically as he held her gaze, then snorted in amusement. 'It never crossed my mind to question if I could leave or enter Yurkordu if I didn't have my charm.'

'All right. You try now then. Try entering Yurkordu without your pendant,' said Keix as she took a step back.

'Me?' asked Jūn, turning to face her. He sounded like he thought her suggestion was absurd, but he still reached for his chain and looped it off his head. Then, he paused, mild surprise registering in his features.

'What is it?'

'Ah, nothing,' he said non-committally and deposited the accessory into her outstretched palm.

Keix's breath hitched. Jūn's implicit trust in her was disorienting, more so because she knew that he didn't expect the same in return. *Tomorrow*, she swore to herself. *I'll make him tell me everything tomorrow. When exactly did we first meet? Why do I not remember it? How did he find me on the night of the ritual? What isn't he telling me? I'll get the whole truth and decide once and for all if I should throw all caution to the wind.*

Jūn, turning back to the cliffs, hesitated for a moment and tilted his head as if he was confused. Then, walking briskly forward, he said, 'I don't know exactly where the threshold is, but it should be somewhere near . . .'

Keix watched him veer a little off the centre of the path, pause for a split second, then run headlong into an invisible wall a short distance from the cliffs.

'Ouch,' he said, rubbing his forehead. 'So, that's what happens.' He turned back to her with a bemused smile. 'You try going through with both charms.'

Keix nodded, glad that this little 'experiment' of theirs was taking some edge off her apprehension of arriving at Yurkordu. She stalked towards the path and easily crossed over the barrier that Jūn had encountered. There wasn't any indication that she had passed a threshold. She remembered when she had entered Tilsor for the first time and the curious feeling that had blanketed her like a draught of caution. Had Jūn faked the collision? She turned and looked at him with suspicion. 'You're not pulling my leg, are you?'

On the other side of the supposed barrier, Jūn was staring at her—or rather, through her—in astonishment. He raised a hand and touched the unseen barrier. 'Oh, wow. You just vanished,' he breathed.

'What?' Keix pulled a face and moved sideways, but Jūn's gaze remained fixed on where she had been standing.

Cocking his head to the side, he asked, 'Can you hear me?'

'Yeah, I can. Can *you* hear me?' When Keix received no reply, she extended her hand towards his outstretched one. A current ran through her when their fingertips touched.

Jūn's eyes became as round as saucers at the contact but in an instant, a mischievous smile replaced his look of shock. He curled his long fingers, trapping Keix's hand firmly and pulled her towards him.

Taken unawares, she stumbled forward and knocked her forehead into his shoulder.

'Are you all right?' asked Jūn hurriedly. 'I'm so sorry—I didn't mean to do that. But, wow. You just disappeared. Could you hear me?'

'Yes. Could you?'

Jūn shook his head.

'You aren't messing with me, right?'

'Why would I do that? Here, you try.'

Keix unclasped her necklace and handed both charms to Jūn. Then, she gasped when she saw that both the path and the gap in the cliffs had vanished. The cliffs had also moved closer to her. 'Wow. This is so bizarre.' She walked up to the mirage and touched the rock face. Instead of the craggy texture of a real rock wall, the barrier felt like a solid, cool, and smooth wall. She pushed against this mind-boggling illusion, but it didn't budge. 'Can you step through?' she asked.

Without hesitation, Jūn walked forward and stepped through the illusion. A faint ripple outlining his body appeared, and then he disappeared into the rock wall.

'Can you hear me?'

Absolute silence met Keix's question. She couldn't sense a rustle even with her Kulcan hearing turned up to maximum sensitivity. 'What if we both have our necklaces, but are on different sides of the barrier?'

Jūn's disembodied hand appeared, holding out her charm.

The moment Keix touched her necklace, the illusion vanished and Jūn magically materialized again.

'Say something?' asked Keix, feeling silly.

'What do you want me to say?' asked Jūn. 'Can you hear me?'

'Yes,' replied Keix with a laugh. 'Thanks for indulging me.'

'Anytime,' said Jūn with a bright smile. Then his gaze softened, and he added, 'The pleasure's all mine.'

Anytime, thought Keix as heat rushed back to her ears. Could she ever get used to this kind of treatment?

Since the two of them had wasted enough time, they proceeded into Yurkordu without any more shenanigans. They had barely started up the path when Jūn's demeanour turned serious. In an even tone, he said, 'Someone's coming down the mountains.'

Keix knew Jūn well enough by now to know that he wasn't happy to have company this early, so she perked up her ears as they continued up the trail. After they entered the gap in the cliffs, she made out several sets of approaching footsteps. She squared her shoulders. If Jūn had heard these people, it would mean that the opposite was true too. The group sounded pretty far away, but after rounding only two corners along the twisty path, three Kulcans—two males, one female—appeared.

One of the guys was lean, while the other had a stocky build. Both were equally tall—though, as far as Keix could tell, Jūn was still the tallest Kulcan she had met. All three newcomers had on thick robes lined with fur and were regarding Keix with half-wary, half-sinister expressions.

The female Kulcan, whose eyes were a shade lighter than Jūn's, were fixed on him with an unreadable expression.

The lean Kulcan spoke first. His voice was raspy as he said something in what Keix assumed was the Kulcans' native language. Though she didn't understand him, it was clear from his tone and expression that he was mocking Jūn. Noticing Keix's confused look, the offensive Kulcan's eyes lit up maliciously and he drawled out his next words in the Atrossian language, keeping his eyes on Keix although he was addressing Jūn. 'I thought you were afraid of the punishment awaiting you.' His lilt was a little stronger compared to Jūn, but it grated on Keix's nerves in a way that Jūn's never had.

'Get out of my way, Mujin,' said Jūn in a cold and commanding tone that he had never used with Keix. She appreciated that he didn't switch back to whatever language Mujin was using, but Mujin seemed hell-bent on frustrating them both. He said something else to his friends in their native language, then clicked his tongue and grinned. His male companion smirked in response, but the female Kulcan side-eyed him.

'I see that you still have a distasteful sense of humour, going around calling full-grown women "little girl",' said Jūn. He jerked his chin in the direction of the female Kulcan. 'Sandom's unimpressed.'

Mujin's eyes flashed but he turned towards Sandom, who looked as if she was dealing with two kids' petty squabble. She replied in the Kulcan language, her tone matter-of-fact, staring right into Mujin's eyes as if to drive her point home.

Keix decided that she disliked Sandom the least out of the group when Mujin huffed, looking chastised. He appeared to be on the verge of muttering an apology but decided to redirect his attention to Jūn and retorted, 'I see that you've gotten addicted to breaking rules.'

Keix's glare at Mujin turned piercing. What rules exactly had Jūn broken? Was it illegal to bring her into Yurkordu? If so, why had her father given her the charm that would allow her to enter his hometown?

'She's one of us,' said Jūn, his simmering anger barely contained.

Keix could hear another set of footsteps approaching now; surely these Kulcans in her company knew that too.

Mujin's smile faltered but he regained his cocky bearing quickly enough. 'Doesn't mean a thing,' he said. 'You rode your shih out of Yurkordu without permission. I saw it with my own eyes. And I have orders from my dad to capture you once you return. Bakuro, Sandom, take him and the intruder back.'

In the blink of an eye, Jūn, Mujin, and Bakuro had their weapons drawn. Keix's hand had only just landed on the hilt of her own sword, but Jūn already had the tip of his sword pointed at Mujin's throat, while Bakuro and Mujin were holding Jūn at swordpoint too. Sandom, meantime, hadn't moved a muscle.

Keix was deciding if she should pull out her sword when a shout rang through the air.

'Jūn!'

The deep, gravelly voice belonged to a figure who was descending rapidly down the path in the most composed rush Keix had ever seen.

'What do you think you're doing?' asked the new joiner, who was frowning at the sight that greeted him, emphasizing the deep creases between his thick, overgrown brows.

'Basch . . . I . . .' murmured Jūn, lowering his blade reluctantly. Then, he turned to Keix with a meaningful gaze, as if directing Basch's attention to her.

When Basch's eyes met Keix's, something registered in the middle-aged Kulcan's face, and he said, 'I'll take it from here, Mujin.'

Mujin sneered, but he put his sword back in its scabbard. Bakuro followed suit. Then, smoothing a facade of indifference over his anger but not succeeding, Mujin insisted, 'We'll escort you back, since we're already here. But how about the girl? She has no business being here.'

Basch didn't respond to Mujin. Instead, he held Keix's defiant gaze for a length of time. Finally, he said, 'She's my guest.'

2

Keix | Yurkordu

Keix stared at the Kulcan named Basch. His hair was cropped short and he had thrown on a thick cloak over his robes, just like Mujin and his gang. The layers of clothes not only added to his height and build, but they also accentuated his impeccable and commanding bearing. The oppressiveness in the air was palpable due to his no-nonsense attitude, although his sword wasn't even drawn.

Keix eyed the weapon slung over Basch's shoulder. It would be unwise to let her own sword out of sight. The Kulcans seemed to be constantly prepared for battle. But her concern for this detail was fleeting because what had Basch just said? She was his guest? That could mean only one thing . . . He was her father?

She scanned the middle-aged Kulcan from head to toe, searching for any hint of similarities between this man and herself. His eyes were long, narrow, and proportionate to his angular face; Keix's round eyes tended to overwhelm her other features. But the telltale signs were there, in the shape of their nose tips and the curve of their upper lips.

Tongue-tied, Keix turned to Jūn. What should she do now? Was there a greeting or a particular way to address one's father in Kulcan culture? She was about to spiral into panic mode when her memories and sanity returned. Why should she worry about *her* manners when *he* was the absentee parent? Throughout her entire life, he had given her nothing more than a letter and the charm with which to enter Yurkordu. Even after her mother's demise, he had never come back for her.

He sent Jūn for you, reminded a niggling voice at the back of her head.

You don't know that for certain, argued another.

Keix silenced the anxiety and doubts within herself, as she suppressed a frustrated sigh. Now that she had emerged from the fog of nervousness at meeting her father for the first time, she was able to assess him in a clearer light. Like the quartet of younger Kulcans present, Basch carried himself with self-assuredness and exuded a tangible air of lethality. All of them were blades cut from the hardest metal, sharpened to perfection, quiet, merciless threats lying in wait within their scabbards for the opportunity to draw blood, to cut through their opponents the moment they were unsheathed.

Basch spoke, breaking through the tension. 'The chiefs are gathering in the hall as we speak. Let's not keep them waiting.' The way he turned on his heel immediately and started back up the path told Keix that this man was used to being obeyed.

Mujin sniggered softly and turned to Keix. 'After you,' he said. As if he was afraid she wasn't aware that he was being factitious, he bowed.

In Atrossian culture, one only exposed their nape, lowering their defences, to someone whom they felt was harmless. Keix would bet her sword that Mujin had insulted her on purpose. She could also have sworn that in her peripheral vision, she saw Sandom rolling her eyes.

Keix ignored Mujin's childish actions and fell in line behind Basch. These 'chiefs' sounded like important people. She had better make a good impression if she wanted to convince them to join forces against ExA. The fate of the world was balancing precariously on the flimsiest game plan that a bunch of young adults—Keix included—had come up with. Well, technically, there were three full-grown adults present when all the strategizing was taking place. The first was Ma.erdene, the Tilsorian who seemed to be tight with Jūn and the Kulcans. But she was clearly getting on in years and could only stay put in Tilsor as the rest of them scrambled off in different directions to prep for the inevitable and ultimate battle. Then there was Iv't. Not much more could be said about him; Keix could only hope that Maii was holding her own as the two of them headed home to engage the other Ifarls. And the last of the lot: Alric, Dace's father, whom they had managed to rescue from the clutches of ExA. Alric was probably the only one they could trust, seeing as he was also an Atrossian whose goal was to chase ExA out of his city—again. But Keix knew that the relationship between Dace and his dad was strained. Still, she had faith that Dace would be able to focus on their end goal. His apathetic attitude notwithstanding, Dace was someone whom she would trust with her life. Plus, Zej and Seyfer—arguably the most cool-headed ones in the group—should be able to mitigate any disagreements and keep them on track.

Each part of their plan was like a domino placed one after another in a circle. The fall of any one of the pieces would cause the rest to topple. Keix was shouldering the biggest role, so she had to be the most stable piece in the configuration. Not simply a domino, but an unmovable brick. She *must* succeed.

Subconsciously, she straightened out her robe and adjusted her sword.

The path was growing narrower now. Rock faces closed in on both sides, and soon, their party of six had to line up in a single file behind Basch to proceed through the pass. Keix was second in line, followed by Jūn, Mujin, and Sandom, with Bakuro bringing up the rear. Less and less light was making it through the narrowing crack above them. During sunset, this path would probably be too dark and difficult to navigate for those who were not familiar with the route.

'How long till we reach the chiefs?' Keix asked Jūn after a while. Sweat was dampening her back despite the cold. The climb must be to blame.

'Now, don't you go telling an outsider all our secrets, Jūn,' drawled Mujin in a faux joking tone.

'Buzz off, Mujin,' retorted Jūn. 'I've said it before, and I'll say it again. Keix isn't an outsider. She's a Kulcan.'

Mujin's comeback was immediate. In a voice sharp with contempt, he said, 'Even if she has Kulcan blood, it doesn't make her one of us.'

Keix's ears started burning. She didn't need Mujin to tell her what she knew. But his words still felt like a gut punch. She wanted to retort that she couldn't care less about being one of them and ask him to shut up, but Basch was a step ahead of her.

'Enough,' he said in his rumbling voice, shooting them a stern look over his shoulder that effectively zipped all their lips up.

Jūn, living up to his role as a true rebel, took the opportunity to whisper his reply to her original question. 'We're just at the base of the mountains. It might take a while longer.'

Keix gave him a nod of acknowledgement while she tried to ignore the lingering feeling of discomfort that was settling in right at home in her heart.

With the path to Yurkordu getting increasingly steep and windy, she forced herself to take measured breaths and tried her hardest to not pant. Her pride wouldn't allow her to show any sign of weakness; not when the rest of her company looked like they were on a leisurely stroll.

It was telling that Jūn, who could probably hear her heart racing in exertion, didn't utter a word to check on her when he had done so constantly on the journey from Tilsor to Yurkordu. He did, however, keep his hand on the small of her back every step of the way. The reassuring gesture also seemed to serve as a reminder to Mujin and his minions of Jūn's protectiveness of her.

When Keix turned around to give Jūn a small, grateful smile, she caught Mujin eyeing her with an unpleasant smirk. He was like a pesky pest she wanted to squash but couldn't. There was also the matter of not wanting to create a commotion—especially when she hadn't sussed out the situation. There was something peculiar about the power dynamic within this small group of Kulcans that she couldn't quite figure out. She listed out mentally what she knew and what she had observed thus far.

One: Jūn said Basch held a rank equivalent to an Atrossian general.

Two: Basch's status would likely be below the chiefs, whom he was bringing her to meet.

Three: Jūn, as well as Mujin and his friends, deferred to Basch.

Four: Mujin had mentioned when they first met that his father had ordered him to capture Jūn.

So . . . was Mujin's father one of the chiefs? If so, shouldn't Mujin be all cocky and irreverent in front of Basch too? Unless respect came with age for the Kulcans . . .

Too many nuances were flying over Keix's head. And she was certain that it wasn't because she had never been the brightest spark in the room. It was simply due to the fact that it was impossible to distil the entirety of the Kulcan culture into bite-sized nuggets. No wonder Jūn was averse to giving oversimplified summaries or replies whenever she had a question about the Kulcans. The richness and layers that made them unique couldn't—and shouldn't—be condensed into soundbites. It dawned on Keix that this was the case for any community.

Ifarls are mysterious. Kulcans are great fighters. These were useless, sweeping statements, concluded Keix.

'You shouldn't waste your breath, you know?' Mujin's voice cut through her epiphany and burnt through the last vestiges of her patience.

Stopping in her tracks and rounding back on Mujin, she snapped, 'Why don't you heed your own advice?'

'We know what you're here for. And the answer's no,' he said, looking stunned at the fire in Keix's tone.

Keix was baffled at Mujin's split personality. How could his attitude be so cocky one moment, then so blundering the next? Also, what did he know, exactly? Keix looked to Jūn for answers, but he looked equally dumbfounded.

'Whatever you think you know, you don't,' said Keix through gritted teeth. She wouldn't back down. 'And who are you to speak on behalf of the chiefs?'

Mujin stuttered but couldn't come up with a response.

'She's right,' came Basch's voice from behind Keix. She whipped her head around to see him glowering at them.

'It is tradition that we let those who come to Yurkordu with requests state their ask. The chiefs will then discuss and make a decision. There are—and will be—no exceptions,' continued Basch. Steadying his gaze on Keix, he added, 'But feel free to continue chattering if you think keeping the chiefs waiting is the best way to get them to say yes to any of your requests.' Then, once again, he turned his back on them without waiting for a response and continued on the path.

Chastised, Keix clamped her mouth shut and lengthened her strides to catch up with Basch. Her thoughts turned inwards. Throughout her life, she had been indifferent about her heritage. All she knew—and cared about—was that she had never lost a fight in her life because of the superior Kulcan reflexes she had inherited. But when Atros took her loyalty and tore it to shreds, her sense of identity and belonging had been decimated, awakening in her a burning curiosity to find out more about the Kulcans. It seemed like crucial information that would help her get out of the pit of despair into which she had fallen. But the events at Tilsor, especially the Taavar tournament, made it clear as day that she was the only one who could define herself. She found a new perspective. Who and what made a Kulcan a Kulcan was no longer significant to her because she knew who she wanted to be: someone who juggled selflessness and selfishness with finesse, someone who wasn't afraid to embrace the full spectrum of her emotions, someone who was worthy of having the second chance that fate had bestowed upon her.

When the pass opened into a dense forest, Keix was pulled out of her musing.

Rows upon rows of trees, impressively tall, with thick trunks and lush crowns that seemed to reach as high as the sky, surrounded them. The base of the crowns almost skimmed the tops of the Kulcans' heads, but because Keix was a good head shorter than them, she would have to stretch her arm up to touch the luscious leaves. How did the Kulcans get the trees to grow so . . . uniformly?

It reminded her of the maze-like woods that the ExA soldiers had driven her and Vin into when she left Atros, and how Jūn had come to their rescue. Those who weren't familiar with this area in Yurkordu would definitely lose their way here. Besides, Keix didn't have the best sense of direction; she had gotten lost in the woods outside of Atros even though the trees didn't look like they had been replicated thousands of times over. But the Kulcans moved without hesitation and she just followed along. The terrain was flat here—probably to aid the disorientating layout—so she took the chance to catch her breath too.

The mossy grass that covered the ground snatched up the sounds of their footfalls. Even though the air felt still, there was a hollow, ambient quality to it that resembled a hum when Keix turned up her sense of hearing to the highest sensitivity. What was even more surprising was that she couldn't hear any sound coming from the Kulcans at all—not their breathing, not their footsteps, not even any flapping or rustling of the layers of their thick coats against their robes. Keix knew first-hand how silently Jūn could move. But it was surreal to witness this in an entire group of Kulcans; they were in such close proximity to her too!

If not for how loud Keix noticed she herself was being, she would have thought that their surroundings were enchanted to swallow up the sound of their every movement.

A relatively short walk through the dense forest brought them to another crack in the rocky cliffs. Another dim, winding path. Another similar forest. Another short walk through it. Yet another gap in the rock face that loomed over them.

It would be a gross understatement to say that Keix was mind-blown. She was once a soldier; she knew a natural fortress when she saw one. Yurkordu was more than that. It was impenetrable. If, instead of her original plan, she tried convincing the Kulcan chiefs to take her and her friends in, and then make Yurkordu their main battlefield, their victory against ExA would be guaranteed; Keix was sure of that. Regardless of the strength of ExA's army, it would be impossible for them to swarm Yurkordu. With only one person being able to make it through the rock crevice at any one point in time, all Keix and her comrades had to do was to stand guard at the narrow opening and skewer their enemies one at a time. It would be a bloodbath for ExA and the Kulcans might not even need to lift a finger. Wouldn't that be more palatable, loaning out a piece of land rather than precious Kulcan lives?

The rest of the journey flashed by as Keix's brain went into overdrive crafting this new plan. Even the exhaustion setting in and burning sensation in her legs that was intensifying with every step she took soon became an afterthought as a seed of hope started germinating in her heart.

* * *

The first signs of civilization appeared in the form of familiar stomping noises, the clanging of swords, and stern shouts of what sounded like commands ringing through the air.

Keix deduced, from the unconcerned expressions on the rest of the Kulcans' faces, that the commotion was likely a typical training session rather than a raging battle. Curious to see what the Kulcans' exercises were like, she perked up her ears and kept her eyes peeled for any signs of movement.

What turned out to be the last winding path between the rocks soon led them to an open landscape with an unobstructed view of the clear, blue sky. Keix blinked as her eyes adjusted to the sudden brightness. A handful of short, polygonal buildings were lined along a small body of water. Connecting all of them was a gentle sloping path that led to higher grounds.

Keix was certain they had come a long way up the mountains. The sun was hanging much lower in the sky now. But even at this elevation, there was an absence of snow, the thing that Jūn was most excited to show her. How far up was the peak? Where were the chiefs gathered?

Keix had no answers. Right now, her gaze was drawn to a large field where dozens of Kulcans were paired up, their brows scrunched in concentration as they fought one another.

The seriousness of these drills was on a whole different level from the ones that Keix had done when she was a cadet at the Atros

Training Institute, more commonly known by its acronym, ATI. Nonetheless, the scene brought back memories of her trainee days where the morals of the world only existed in black and white, where hidden agendas were tucked so well out of sight and mind that no one questioned their non-existence, where following orders was the sensible thing to do. The world was wild now. Correction: The world had *always* been wild, except Keix was blind to this fact in the past. She had been shaken to the core when the thick shroud was lifted. But at this moment, to her surprise, she found that the lingering feelings of longing and disappointment that she had held on to since leaving Atros had subsided into something less than a dull ache. There was only one explanation for this. She had gotten over Atros's betrayal. Truly. The realization brought a genuine smile to her face.

As Keix's party drew closer to the field, she was struck by how sharp and forceful the Kulcans' movements were. 'Are your combat practices always so intense?' she whispered to Jūn. The answer was obvious, but the lack of conversation was making her antsy, so she had said the first thing that came to her mind.

Jūn nodded in reply. 'We start training every day once we turn eight, but these sessions are only for those fifteen and older.'

Keix made a quick mental calculation. Jūn had been doing this for almost two-thirds of his life. That explained his monster-level stamina, among other things. To get on par with him, she would have to train extra hard moving forward. She tried her darnedest to make her footfalls lighter and less noisy as she asked, 'Are there other sorts of training?' Stealth training was likely in the Kulcans' core curriculum, considering the way they could move so quickly and noiselessly.

Then, before Jūn could answer, Keix blurted, 'Hold on . . . is this the entire Kulcan army?' Yurkordu seemed vast, but it didn't look like it had much liveable space so far. What if the chiefs didn't have enough Kulcans to spare even if they agreed to help her take down ExA? But surely, Jūn would have warned her before they left Tilsor if this was the case?

'This is just a small part of our drills,' replied Jūn with a laugh when he caught the drift of her thoughts. 'There are many other groups training elsewhere throughout the mountains.'

Mujin gave a derisive snort and asked in a purposely sharp and loud tone, 'What are you? A *spy*? Why are you asking so many questions?'

Mujin's outburst sucked every last decibel out of the air. The Kulcans, who had clearly ignored the inconspicuous arrival of her party in favour of focusing on their training, halted their moves in a split second as they turned their eyes to Keix in unison. Embarrassed at the sudden attention, she remained mum while she glared at the culprit who had put her on the spot. How many of the Kulcans here would believe her even if she denied Mujin's accusations?

Basch's commanding voice rang out then, adding to the list of surprises Keix was getting today. He addressed the trainees in what Keix had come to identify as their native language, and the soldiers immediately straightened their arms at the sides of their bodies and inclined their heads at Basch. Then, they went back to sparring as if their session had never been disrupted.

Keix picked her jaw off the ground. Basch held *this* level of power over the Kulcan army? Getting on his good side—as well as getting confirmation that he was her father—was imperative now. She tried to catch his eye as she asked in her most polite tone, 'Are the chiefs at the peak of the cliffs?'

Basch looked taken aback that Keix was addressing him directly. But he shook his head and answered without hesitation, 'They're at the Council Hall.'

'Just a little further up,' supplemented Jūn.

Keix gave a nod of thanks to the both of them, and the group fell silent again as they continued walking. They passed by more buildings that were variations of the ones near the training field and, eventually, reached the largest plain that Keix had encountered in Yurkordu so far. It didn't take a genius to tell which building was the Council Hall because there was only one structure that stood out like a sore thumb, cylindrical instead of polygonal, and completely painted in black. It also posed a stark contrast against the backdrop of slate-grey cliffs and greenery.

Even the entrance doors—glass-panelled, wide arches that doubled as both doors and windows—were designed to intimidate.

It was only when Jūn looped his fingers through Keix's that she realized she was shivering. The cold was a contributing factor. But mainly, it was her nerves that had finally gotten to her. Her knees almost buckled when she stepped through the arches because of the sense of foreboding that washed over her. She gripped Jūn's hand tighter and reassured herself, *I can do this. Basch said the Kulcans will listen to those who came here to seek help. They can be reasoned with. The fate of the world is at stake, after all. I can convince them.*

I must.

3

Keix | A Contentious Request

'That is all?' Keix's outburst echoed through the Kulcans' Council Hall. She had just presented her case to the chiefs. Standing in the middle of the circular space, spotlighted by the bright sunlight filtering in through a series of windows in the conical roof right above her, she felt like a performer after her act, scanning the audience for a semblance of response—positive or negative, it didn't matter.

Seconds passed but still, no one moved or made a sound.

Keix couldn't bear it any longer, so she continued railing, 'That's the only thing you have to say? That you'll *discuss* and *think* about what I've said?' She had tried to contain her frustration. She really had. And it wasn't like she had come into this meeting without managing her expectations; she knew the Kulcan chiefs weren't going to say yes to her immediately. She just hadn't predicted that this 'willingness' to let her state her case would turn out to be a sham.

Throughout her recount about how dangerous ExA's agenda was, the Kulcan chiefs had all but listened to her pleas with expressions that could only be described as bored. Not one of the five of them seated on the raised platforms in the hall showed any signs of concern.

Keix wanted to be angry at Jūn for not preparing her for this chilly reception. But it didn't seem like he had any idea this would happen either. His face had blanched, then turned to varying shades of red and back as he relayed his own account to supplement hers. He spoke mostly in Atrossian, for her benefit, but lapsed into his native language when he got agitated. Yet, even then, the chiefs never bothered to look less disinterested.

'We said we will hear what you have to say, and we've done that,' said the Kulcan chief sitting on the high-backed chair with the most elaborate design. At least he had the decency to have conducted the entire 'listening' session in Atrossian, even if he hadn't bothered to introduce himself. Jūn had addressed him as Daman, but Keix didn't know if it was his actual name or the Kulcan word for chief.

Mujin, who was on Daman's left, couldn't look smugger. He had proceeded without hesitation to stand beside Daman's chair upon entering the hall—an action that had intensified Keix's dread as a puzzle piece clicked into place. Daman, who was probably *the* chief of the chiefs, must be Mujin's dad. His throne was on a waist-high dais, while the other four chiefs—two on each of his sides—were on knee-high platforms. These other chiefs were perched on equally intimidating but less-intricately carved thrones which were arranged in a semi-circle. Beside each of these chiefs was a guard. All the Kulcans had on equally stoic expressions, and were tall and lean. Only one of the five chiefs was female.

Keix opened her mouth to protest again, but her father (Keix had come to terms with the deduction that Basch was her father because, all things considered, it was highly unlikely there was another suitable candidate for this role) interrupted her again. She would have thought that being a highly ranked commander of the Kulcan army, Basch's designated spot would be to the right of Daman, or any of the other chiefs present. But he had, instead, stationed himself beside her this entire time.

What Basch said, despite his measured tone, must have been outrageous because it caused an uproar. Even the guards, who could have been mistaken for statues, seemed offended. Mujin, of course, had to have the most dramatic reaction. He pointed to Keix and exclaimed in Atrossian, 'Who do you think we are? We're not Odats!'

Confused at the turn of events, Keix blurted, 'I never said you were!'

She had no intention of going near any Odats—at all. Those foul creatures with dark-mustard skin and squat faces were not only repulsive, but also mercenaries with no loyalty to anyone except the highest bidder. 'You're not expecting me to pay you to fight for us, are you?' she gasped. She had left Atros and Tilsor with nothing but the bare necessities. Even if she wanted to, there was nothing on her person that could possibly be of a value sufficient to hire a troop of Kulcans.

Another outcry rippled through the Kulcans at her words. This time, they looked thoroughly incensed and scandalized, although the female Kulcan chief was eyeing her with interest.

All right, so besides Daman, all the other Kulcans understood Atrossian just fine. Keix had suspected that they didn't—what with their lack of reaction to her speech just now. But she didn't get why the chiefs were all so riled up now. Frowning at Jūn, she mouthed, 'What's going on?'

Instead of a proper reply, he gripped her hand and gave a small shake of his head. His eyes were crinkled in amusement, and he looked like he was trying his best to hold back his laughter.

Daman shouted something that cut through the hubbub and everyone settled back down immediately.

Turning to Keix and switching back to Atrossian, he said, 'I think we're done here—for today.' His tone brooked no argument as he continued, 'We still have the matter of Jūn's punishment, and I would like to speak to Basch privately after that. Bakuro and Sandom are going to escort you back to Basch's house. You will wait there until we have an answer to your request, which shouldn't take long. But you are free to leave Yurkordu if you are in a hurry. Just leave your . . . charm behind.'

It took a second for Keix to realize that not only had Daman dismissed her, but he had also obliquely revoked her access to Yurkordu. Bakuro and Sandom marched her out of the Council Hall before she could put up any resistance. Besides her momentary confusion, two other reasons contributed to why she didn't kick up a fuss. One, Sandom had squeezed her hand firmly, as if asking for her trust; at the same time, Jūn had given an imperceptible jerk of his head towards Sandom, which Keix took to mean that he wanted her to go with Sandom for the time being.

With these bewildering signals, Keix couldn't help but wonder, *Do I have more allies than I believe?*

* * *

The building to which Sandom and Bakuro brought Keix was a little farther up the mountain. Located at the end of a short path that forked off from the main road, Basch's house stood alone and was tucked into an alcove in the rock cliffs. It looked similar to one of the many mid-sized, polygonal structures that they had bypassed on their way here.

After leading Keix into the home through a flap (there were no doors to be found), Sandom said in Atrossian, 'Stay *here*.'

Keix thought that it wasn't far-fetched to assume that all Kulcans understood and spoke Atrossian to some degree; they just pretended to not know the language whenever it suited their needs or mood.

As though worried that Keix hadn't understood her, Sandom repeated herself and pointed to the floor.

Keix wanted to know where exactly she stood with Sandom, so she decided to be direct. 'What exactly is going on? And whose side are you on?' she asked.

Bakuro, who was still holding the door flap open, raised an eyebrow at Keix's sharp tone.

'It's—' Sandom paused, then continued, 'complicated.' Crossing her arms, she added, 'Wait for Jūn or Basch to come back. To explain.'

'When will they be back? Will Jūn be fine?' Keix pressed, desperate for a more specific answer.

'I don't know.' Yet another pause. 'Yes, they will be fine.'

The odd rhythm of the exchange brought back memories of Keix's interrogation of Jūn when they had first met outside Atros. And it suddenly struck her how much Sandom's eyes resembled Jūn's. 'Are you, by any chance, related to Jūn?' she blurted.

'Sister,' Sandom said with the shadow of a smile. Then, while Keix was still processing this revelation, Sandom inclined her head at Bakuro and the two of them stepped out of Basch's house swiftly, letting the door flap fall with a resounding slap.

By the time Keix registered that they were gone, her disorientation had peaked. Her first thought was to follow Sandom and Bakuro, since they weren't guarding the house. But what if she was mistaken for a spy because she blatantly disobeyed Daman's orders? And what if the chiefs decided to use this a pretext for rejecting her request for aid?

Resigned, Keix started pacing the large, heptagonal room. Basch's home was more spacious than it looked on the outside. Huge, boxy pieces of furniture—whose functions she couldn't determine—filled the space. The most distinctive feature in the room was a tapestry depicting a man riding on a shih. After giving the abstract painting a once over, Keix deduced that it must be a depiction of Basch on his shih. She scrunched her nose and walked away.

How long would she take to get accustomed to this strange land? Was there even any *need* to? Now that the Kulcans seemed dead set on not agreeing to her request, what was the point of staying on in Yurkordu? On top of these hard questions, she was thrown a mind-boggling mystery that was as pointless as it was irksome.

Jūn has a sister. His sister is Sandom. Why didn't she bat an eye when two other Kulcans had drawn their swords on her brother? thought Keix, as she continued walking around Basch's house. Answers eluded her and by the time Basch returned, she had almost worn a trail into the floor.

'Where's Jūn?' she asked without preamble, striding towards the stern-looking Kulcan the second he stepped into the room.

Basch's eyes were tired, but there was a softness in them that she hadn't noticed before. He unslung his sword and placed it on a long, arc-shaped stand situated to one side of the door flap. Sitting down on the platform beside his weapon, he gestured to the empty space beside him. 'Sit. I'm sure you're exhausted from the journey,' he said.

Keix threw a suspicious glance at him (and also the platform that looked nothing like a couch). She repeated her earlier question, then added, 'How is he?'

'Jūn's been sent to reflect on his actions.'

'You mean he's been locked up? Where is he?' She couldn't contain her agitation. 'I want to see him now.'

'He'll live,' Basch said mildly, putting his hands on his lap. 'Besides, I thought you were here to see me.'

It took Keix a full second to wrap her head around the fact that there was a hint of envy in Basch's tone, and that he had indirectly confirmed her assumption that he was her father indeed. Despite the handful of times Basch had come up in her conversations with Jūn, he had never referred to her father by name.

'Who are you?' asked Keix in as even a tone as she could manage. While she didn't want to let Basch off the hook so easily, she was still acutely aware of the level of authority he held over the Kulcan army—which meant that she should care just a little about his opinion of her, as she might need his help later on.

'I am Basch. Basch Gaalgash. Your father.'

Keix almost gaped at the matter-of-fact manner with which he said those words. How shameless could he be, claiming a role that he had never assumed?

Taking her silence as encouragement, Basch continued in a warmer tone, 'I would like to get to know you, Keix. Would you allow me to do so, or would you feel better if you could beat me up first?' He gestured to her hands.

Keix looked down and realized she was clenching her fists so hard that they were shaking. 'Why does it matter? You've never bothered to look for me all these years. Even when mother d-died, you never came.' It was no longer possible to ignore the suffocating feeling that had taken hold of her. She took a deep breath and tried to loosen the knot in her throat.

Basch's lips parted, as if he were considering his next words.

'You know what?' Keix interrupted him before he could say anything. 'This was a mistake. I shouldn't have come to Yurkordu. I *wouldn't* have, if Jūn had told me right from the start that you guys are selfish and cowardly creatures. Fearless fighters?' She snorted. 'It's clear the Kulcans have no intention of joining forces against ExA, so there is no reason for me to stay here any longer. Bring me to Jūn and I'll let him know I'm leaving of my own accord. This'—she reached for her charm and took it off—'is yours. You can have it back.'

She threw her accessory to Basch, who caught it with impeccable accuracy. Refusing to back down, she held her chin high as he silently assessed her haughty stance.

Eventually, he sighed. 'I'll have someone take you to Jūn later. But in exchange, I want you to hear my side of the story.'

Keix considered Basch's request. It seemed like a fair exchange. Besides, he was right. She was exhausted—or rather, she was on the verge of an adrenaline crash. She would make use of his story time to rest for a bit. Then, she would say her goodbye to Jūn before heading back to Tilsor to work out another plan with the rest of her gang. She didn't want to give up so easily. But she had to cut her losses. Another day spent in Yurkordu meant having the balance tip another degree in ExA's favour—especially if the chances of getting the Kulcans to join them was zero to none. Still, the thought of having to separate from Jūn sent a jolting pain through her heart. Even if she was sure he would choose to come with her, she had to steel herself against potential disappointment.

'This had better not take long,' she said huffily and sat down on the platform, as far from Basch as possible.

Basch hesitated at Keix's hostility, but he started his tale all the same. Of all places to begin, he had to talk about how he met her mother. 'Layne and I first met twenty-three years ago in Atros. It was my third time visiting the city. She was assigned to keep me—'

'Okay, okay. Hold up now,' Keix cut in. As fascinating as it would be to hear about her parents' 'love story', it felt uncomfortably intimate. This was also the first time in ages that someone had referred to her mother by name. Hearing it made her realize she wasn't ready to talk about Layne. Despite the fact that Layne had died years ago, Keix had held her grief buried within the darkest depths of her being and only came to terms with this loss when she was forced to confront her feelings during the Taavar trials—in other words, very recently.

'Can we skip past the sappy parts? Because we both know full well that you left her to fend for herself. And me.'

Basch flinched at the acid in Keix's tone. 'I know what it looks like, but that's not the truth.'

'No,' snapped Keix. 'You don't get to twist the facts or rewrite the narrative here just because there's no one to corroborate or refute your story.'

'I sent Jūn for you. And Layne. Around your eleventh birthday.'

Basch's words shook Keix to her core. Her eleventh birthday? That was the year that her mum passed. Now it made sense why Jūn had said he met her when he was fourteen. But if he had come for them, how was it possible that she had no recollection of this significant event?

'Jūn reached Atros on the day Layne died,' elaborated Basch, as if he sensed her next question. Voice cracking with emotion, he continued, 'He was supposed to invite the both of you to Yurkordu. But unfortunately, he was too late.'

Keix would have staggered backwards if she hadn't been sitting down. The regret in Basch's voice was palpable. She didn't have to be able to read his mind to know what he was thinking. Because she was having the same thought. If Jūn had arrived a day earlier, and Layne had accepted this invitation, she might still be alive . . . The knot in Keix's throat tightened back up and grew even bigger.

'Jūn didn't know what to do since he was instructed to contact only Layne. After he returned to Yurkordu to break the news to me, I decided to let you stay in Atros instead of bringing you here. That is on me. So, in a way, your hatred for me is not unjustified.' Basch paused to let his words sink in. 'If you don't believe what I'm saying, you can ask Jūn about it. I requested him to withhold this from you until I spoke to you first.'

Tears welled up in Keix's downcast eyes. She blinked rapidly to clear them, but it only made the huge, fat teardrops fall on her clenched fists. 'Why?' she croaked. Her voice was softer than a whisper. She wasn't sure what kind of answer she wanted or needed to hear. Her life after her mother's death could have been completely different if Basch had not left her alone in Atros. She could have trained as a Kulcan instead of an Atros trooper. She could have had a family to lean on. The possibilities were endless. But Basch never gave her the option.

'It was better for you,' said Basch quietly.

'That wasn't for you to determine.'

'You don't know the Kulcans, Keix. You don't know *us*. I was in love with Layne, but I couldn't bring her back here. Not when we had so much internal turmoil. The chiefs whom you saw today? Less than five years ago, all of them were at each other's throats because of petty squabbles. You couldn't go anywhere without constantly looking over your shoulder, worried that you might get kidnapped and taken as hostage so that the chief who had locked you up could use you to make demands of *your* chief.' Basch's distaste for what he was describing was clear.

'But you sent Jūn for me and Mum!'

'Yes, I did. Because it just so happened that during that time, there was a short period of ceasefire among the chiefs, and I was hopeful that everyone would have the good sense to crave for peace. Or at least some semblance of it.' He sighed again, more deeply and wearily this time. 'But by the time Jūn returned, it was obvious that they preferred the status quo before.'

'So, you're saying you left me in Atros because it was safer?' Keix didn't bother to hide her incredulity. Basch must have known what Atros had done to her. How could he sit there now and turn her whole world upside down with just his words?

'I *thought* it was safer.' Basch's brow was furrowed in anguish. 'We knew all along that Atros was looking for ways to beef up their defences. That they had engaged the Odats. What we hadn't predicted was that they would resort to something even more unethical, which was creating a hybrid army in order to guard against ExA. They kept asking us to train their soldiers and join forces with them. But no one except the Kulcans knew that we were equally up to our necks in the messes we kept creating for ourselves. This is what happens when you live in a literal bubble and are secretive about what's going on inside it. Whatever makes it out is usually how you want people to know or see you.'

Keix, who knew all about living in a bubble, snorted at how much truth there was in what Basch had said. Still, she didn't see where he was going with this. 'What are you trying to tell me? That the Kulcans are resistant to sending help to fight ExA because the peace that you have right now hasn't come by easily? That I should just give up and leave Yurkordu? Or do you want me to hide here like you Kulcans?' Keix paused for effect, then continued before Basch could get a word in, 'Makes sense since I'm half-Kulcan—that I should be half as cowardly as the rest of you.'

Shaking his head empathetically, Basch said something that Keix would have least expected. 'I'm trying to tell you to give me some time to convince them to join your war. *Our* war. There is no way that we can remain here and live unbothered by what's happening outside Yurkordu. Already, we're getting worrying signs that someone—likely ExA—is moving towards us—'

'Wait—what do you mean by that?' Keix couldn't contain her shock. She and Jūn had not encountered anything out of the ordinary on their way here . . . How could it be that ExA troops were nearing Yurkordu?

'I'll tell you more when I can. But before we get any concrete news that it's really safe out there, I'd advise you against leaving Yurkordu at the moment.'

Basch's cryptic words sent a chill down Keix's spine. Her heart plummeted when she thought of how Vin and the rest could be in danger right now.

'Those in Tilsor are safe right now,' Basch reassured Keix. 'I promise, if we receive news that an attack on them is imminent, I'll gather what I can of the Kulcan army—and trust me when I say that I have much sway over them—and march there with you right away.'

'But that would be too late!' And Zej and Dace . . . Keix's stomach churned. She shouldn't have let her guard down. She should have travelled at the fastest pace she could because whatever perceived risks there were paled in comparison to the thought that her friends could die because she had taken her own sweet time.

With conviction, Basch said, 'It won't. We have our means of getting our information. And I know this doesn't look like it, but Daman *will* join the war. He'll come around to it. Because if ExA wins, they'll find a way to breach the magical barrier that we have in place. And if you hadn't caught the drift of what I've been saying so far, I'm laying it out for you. We, Kulcans, are a warring race. All that physicality, our well-honed senses, the propensity for fighting . . . They turn inwards when we don't have a common enemy.

'You're right to say that the peace we have now is hard-fought. But it's not here to stay. The only way to make sure this peace lasts is to make them—us, Kulcans—see that there are bigger things worth fighting for out there. Only then will we be able to create an enduring bond,' concluded Basch.

Keix wasn't sure if she should be hopeful or disgusted that Basch was using this war against ExA as a rallying cry for the Kulcans. And she couldn't quite grasp his logic. This 'bond' he was aiming for still seemed temporary, no matter how she dissected it. Because the way he put it, it seemed like the Kulcans would turn on each other once—*if*—ExA was eliminated. But she supposed that now, for her at least, there was everything to gain and not a thing to lose. If Basch could be trusted, she didn't have to abandon all hope of banking on the Kulcans' help—yet. But how were the Kulcans getting their news? And what kind of news were they getting that had Basch so convinced that things would turn in her favour?

Not one to sit back and rely on others' help, Keix thought she ought to negotiate the terms that Basch had set. 'Now that I've heard your side of the story,' she started, 'it seems like you and the Kulcans are getting much more out of this little arrangement.'

'What do you mean? Are you going back on your word?'

Keix gave Basch the side-eye. 'I'm just saying that your goal clearly isn't to get me to listen to your excuses for not doing your job as a father in the past eighteen years. Your goal is to unite the Kulcans under a cause that I just so happen to bring to the table.'

'So, what do you want in exchange?'

Keix thought for a long while, but Basch didn't rush her. Finally, in a hard voice, she said, 'I want to meet the rest of the chiefs individually, and Sandom's going to be my interpreter. If you think

I'm going to trust your word that you're my best bet in trying to get Daman to agree to my requests, you're sorely mistaken.'

Basch cast his eyes downwards and didn't move for a very long while. Was he weighing the advantages and downfalls of letting Keix get her way? Eventually, he raised his head, levelled his gaze with Keix, and said, 'All right, then.'

Keix, who hadn't anticipated that Basch would agree to her terms so quickly, decided to push her luck. 'So, whom should I start talking to first? Who's the next in line to become the chief?' When Basch answered that it was him, Keix didn't know if he was joking. So she ignored him and prodded, 'And after that?'

'Del.'

'Which one's Del?'

'The female chief,' replied Basch with a half-smile.

Nodding in acknowledgement, Keix then said, 'Shall we go now?'

Basch couldn't resist chuckling at her presumption. 'First thing tomorrow morning. You've had a long day, so you'd best rest up.' He stood up, picked up his sword, and turned to leave.

Add that to the list of things that I'm going to not *feel guilty about today—Basch having to leave his own house because I'm here,* thought Keix. To Basch's retreating back, she said firmly, 'And after that, you'll let me meet Jūn.'

At this, Basch turned and gave her a last appraising look (Keix thought she caught a glint of pride in his eyes) before nodding in acquiescence. 'You're going to do just fine with Del tomorrow.'

4

Keix | Negotiations

After Basch's departure, the tension left Keix's body in an instant. She let her spine, which she had been holding ramrod straight, collapse as she slumped over sideways on the platform where she was seated. Out of the corner of her eye, she spotted her charm, which Basch had left behind. She picked it up and stared at it while she thought about her next move.

For the time being, she was stuck in this awkward status between being a guest and a prisoner at Yurkordu. Even if she wanted to explore this foreign land, there were too many misunderstandings that could arise should she step out of Basch's home without an escort. Deciding that her best course of action was to remain where she was and heed Basch's advice to rest, she moved into a more comfortable position on the platform. Still, she was too high strung to fall asleep, so she turned her hearing up to its maximum sensitivity to figure out what was going on outside.

Basch's house was secluded, but it wasn't fully enclosed. Just a heavy flap of material covered its entrance archway, which meant that noises from outside could still filter through into its interiors. Keix couldn't differentiate the medley of sounds that she was hearing in the beginning, but after much focusing, she could make out snatches of conversations and some clanging of weapons being struck together. There were also bits of laughter scattered in the mix, which made Keix nostalgic for her trainee days in Atros.

The noises gradually died down as the Kulcans settled in for the night, and Keix decided she would try to sleep too, if not for anything other than to regain her energy and wits for her talks with the other chiefs tomorrow. She thought her slumber would be fretful, since she was spending the night in this strange land and without Jūn's comforting presence. But she had clearly misjudged her exhaustion because she fell asleep the moment her eyelids slid shut. The next thing she knew, someone was nudging her to wake up.

A semi-familiar voice called, 'Hey, do you want to eat something and wash up before you meet the chiefs?'

Keix sprung up and blinked rapidly to clear the sleep from her eyes. It took her a moment to reorientate herself. A soft glow was spilling through an opening in one of the polygonal walls of Basch's home, and the person talking to her was . . . 'Sandom?'

'It's me, yes. The chiefs start their day early. You should look presentable when you meet them.' Sandom was wearing a set of robes in a much lighter shade today, and she looked more approachable. In her arms was a neatly folded pile that looked like a clean set of clothes.

If not for the fact that Sandom was implying that Keix wasn't looking her best, Keix would have chuckled at the staccato way in which Jūn's sister was trying her best to speak in the Atrossian language. Instead, Keix stood up immediately, trying to smooth her wrinkled and dusty robes, only to stop short when she saw that she was sending dirt flying everywhere. Could that be the reason why the Kulcan chiefs were looking at her in disdain yesterday? Surely, they wouldn't be so superficial? Regardless, Keix wasn't going to take chances today. She followed Sandom back to the main path and headed farther up the mountain. Along the way, Keix chowed down on the bland pieces of bread that Sandom had brought for her. They also met many Kulcans who were starting their day. While everyone nodded at Sandom in greeting, they stole glances or stared outright at Keix, with a whole spectrum of expressions ranging from curiosity to hostility.

About ten minutes after they set off from Basch's house, Sandom and Keix arrived at a fork in the path. They took the path on the right and walked for a fair distance before entering a clearing. Situated in the open area was a spring with gentle, bubbling waters. The size of the spring and the wisps of smoke being emitted from its still, turquoise-coloured water reminded Keix of the baths in Ma.erdene's establishment in Tilsor. But Keix still turned to Sandom with a querying look. This was where she was supposed to wash up? In the freezing cold outdoors? But Sandom only jerked her chin in the direction of the pond in response. When Keix didn't move, Sandom said, 'You'd better hurry if you want to catch Del.'

At the reminder, Keix gritted her teeth and chased away all thoughts of discomfort from her head. She considered just rubbing her face clean and washing her hair to get the grime out of it, but she decided that she might as well take a bath, even if it meant running the risk of freezing to death—an unlikely scenario because she was pretty sure Sandom wouldn't allow it to happen. The last thing Keix wanted was to throw away or affect her chances of changing Del's impression of her. She hurried to take off her clothes and plunged into the water while Sandom stepped away to give her some privacy.

Keix didn't know if it was because Sandom was Jūn's sister, but there was a familiarity to her quiet presence that set Keix at ease. Also, to Keix's surprise, the water in the spring was hot, which was perfect for Yurkordu's weather. The warm bath did more to chase away her fatigue than the undisturbed sleep she just had. If the circumstances were different, she would have loved to while her entire day away here. But there were Kulcan chiefs to be convinced, so she bathed quickly and thoroughly. Then, she reached for the clothes that she had discarded just now (she had left the only other set of clothes that she had brought with her in Basch's home).

Sandom interrupted Keix, holding out the pile of folded robes and saying, 'Here.'

'These are . . .?'

Sandom looked at Keix as if she was addled. 'Robes. For you.'

'Er, thanks. These are yours?' asked Keix. She hadn't expected such a kind gesture from Sandom, who nodded in reply to her question.

Keix quickly put on the garments and was surprised to find that they fit her well, since Sandom was at least half a head taller than her. The hems of the clothes grazed her ankles instead of dragging on the ground, so Keix deduced that she must be wearing one of Sandom's old sets of robes. Keix repeated her thanks, which Sandom waved away and replied, 'We'd better get going now.'

As they headed back to the main path, Keix decided to push her luck. 'What's Del like?' she asked. 'Is there anything you can share with me, so I have a better chance of persuading her?'

Quirking up an eyebrow, Sandom sized Keix up as she kept walking. 'Reasonable,' was her reply that came after a beat.

'So, does that mean I have a better chance of convincing her compared to Daman? But Daman's the one who calls the shots, right?'

'You'll do just fine,' said Sandom with an inscrutable expression. Then, she gestured for Keix to stop talking as the main path came into sight. She probably didn't want to appear to be on friendly terms with Keix in front of other Kulcans.

Still, Keix thought it was weird that Sandom had said the same thing as Basch about her being able to 'do just fine'. But she didn't probe further. Falling silent, she tried to commit to mind the different routes in Yurkordu. There appeared to be only one main path, which forked into narrower pathways at different intervals. Compared to Tilsor, this place was a breeze to navigate.

Just as Keix was starting to wonder how far Del's house was, Basch approached them from behind. He was dressed in more casual-looking robes today, and Keix took the flush in his cheeks to be a telltale sign that he had just exerted himself physically. Had he just returned from combat training? Keix kept her query to herself as she didn't want to appear to be concerned about Basch.

Minutes later, the three of them reached their destination. Del's house, like Basch's, was also located at the end of a path that led off from the main route. It had a similar structure too, except it was twice as big. Keix thought that since the space was bigger, it would be partitioned in some way, like how apartments in Atros were divided into different rooms. However, just like in Basch's house, pieces of furniture were clustered in groups and arranged in unique combinations to form distinctive, tiny 'spaces'.

Del gestured for Keix to take a seat on one of two rectangular platforms set at an angle to each other, while she herself sat down on the other piece of furniture. Even without her high-backed seat, Del looked more intimidating than bored. Basch and Sandom, on the other hand, stood behind Keix, as if guarding her from the Kulcan chief's stern and unwavering gaze. Or, they could just be worried that Keix might attack Del if the talk went south.

'So, what else do you have to say to me?' asked Del without preamble once she settled down.

'Er . . .' started Keix. The first thought that came to her mind was that she must have looked infinitely silly to have asked for Sandom's 'translation' services. Del's fluency in Keix's native language was impeccable. She must have also understood every word that Keix had said yesterday. Otherwise, she wouldn't have added the word 'else' to her question.

What *else* was there to say that she hadn't already said? Keix was stumped. She took a slow, deep breath and looked around. Somehow, her gaze landed on a piece of tapestry hanging behind Del. Unlike the one that she had seen in Basch's house, this piece of art didn't depict a Kulcan, though it was similarly abstract-looking. Keix thought she could make out four creatures arranged in a circle, set against a gradient, red-to-orange-to-white background.

The image reminded Keix of a story that her mum used to tell her when she was a child, and suddenly, the words came to Keix. Matching Del's unwavering gaze, Keix cleared her throat and began, 'I've already said what I wanted to when we gathered at the Council Hall. I have nothing more to add to that.

'But,' continued Keix, disregarding Del's raised eyebrow, 'I have a story to share. It's titled, "Those That Lived".'

A flicker of emotion flashed in Del's eyes.

'Do you know it?' asked Keix.

Del pursed her lips. 'It's the title of a Kulcan fable. But go ahead.'

Keix's heart started racing. It was entirely possible that Basch had shared a Kulcan fable with her mum, who had, in turn, transformed it into a bedtime story for her. She fought the urge to turn back to look at her father. Instead, she launched into her tale, mimicking the way in which her mother used to tell the story, in a low, shaky voice that resembled that of an elderly person.

'Stories of how the world was formed are one aplenty. This is our version. The one that generations before us have told to their descendants. The one that our ancestors passed down, the one that you'll pass down to your descendants. If you ever have any.'

Keix paused and searched Del's face. The Kulcan chief had schooled her expression into one of disinterest, but Keix hoped she wasn't imagining the quiet spark she saw in Del's eyes. Continuing her tale, Keix didn't stop her narration this time around.

'Like all creation myths, it starts simply enough—with a higher being getting bored of their existence.

'Because, somehow, we all know that living a life that never ends is possibly the worst punishment one could ever have, right?

'Everything just ceases to be. Things that used to be interesting lose their novelty, and it gets harder to derive the same level of excitement with something else that is equally fresh. Emotions are numbed as we get used to them, even as they increase in intensity. And the list goes on. It's just natural, don't you agree?

'But I digress.

'Where was I?

'Ah, yes. The higher being.

'No one knows how or why they did it: create our world. Because the story just goes that the higher being was bored and thus, created two creatures out of their pure imagination. The first was the qiue, a tiny creature that could sit on the tips of the higher being's fingers. The animal had wings to propel it through the air and it sang beautiful melodies. The second was the oka: A beast whose head reached past the waist of the higher being as it stood on all fours. This oka had a tail, a muscular, furry body, and powerful legs that carried it swiftly wherever it wanted to go on land.

'Don't ask me why these traits, in particular, were imparted to these creatures. We can only assume that it was done out of preference. The higher being simply liked something that could fly or move nimbly, because they themself could do so, too? And this creator likely enjoyed music and wanted pets that they could summon to their side in an instant.

'So, anyway . . . this creator enjoyed watching the two critters at first. They were fascinated by the difference between the qiue and the oka. The animals inhabited the same environment. But because one cruised through the air and the other cantered across the land, their interactions were few and far between.

'Occasionally, when they did run into each other, nothing particularly interesting happened either. At least, nothing that the creator would consider as interesting.

'Very soon, the higher being grew bored. Again. So, they concluded that having more copies of these two "prototypes", so to speak, would kick things up a notch. The more, the merrier. Two became four. Four, eight. And so on. With countless copies of the qiue and the oka, two separate communities were formed.

'But that wasn't enough for the creator. Boredom struck again, and they decided to imbue a wild factor into each and every one of the creatures. This factor created individuality. It led each qiue and each oka to behave differently—sometimes, erratically—from those around them.

'And, my dear, you can imagine why this is where it gets complicated. Fast.

'Let me draw the comparison of juggling balls. You have two balls. You pass them from one hand to another. It's relatively easy, isn't it? What if you double the number of balls? Four. You just need a little more skill, you say? It gets challenging. Eight, sixteen . . . You can see how easily it's going to get out of hand, right? The number of balls keeps doubling, but the number of hands you have remains at two.

'Yet, you start to enjoy the chaos even as you drop the balls. It's no longer about the juggling, but watching the balls bump into each other, steer each other off their originally "intended" path.

'Then, a particularly experimental mood strikes you. You come up with a bunch of other traits that cannot be discerned at a glance—not by anyone but yourself; traits like indifference, greed, the need to do the right thing, and more. You materialize and capture these traits separately into balls of water, swirling about within their invisible cocoons. You toss the spheres upward and vaporize them. The mist falls on the qiues and okas, and clings to them, infusing them with a mix of the qualities they had come in contact with.

'Soon after, you notice differences in the interactions. The separate communities are mingling more. Some qiues and okas even start banding together and forming their own groups.

'You've observed enough. You've grown tired of this project. You move on to another thing that catches your eye because you think that's the end of it.

'But it's not. If you had stayed to observe, you would have noticed that those infused with higher levels of "undesirable" traits have started to move in on the more passive groups, to take over their land, influencing them to their advantage. Some even start massacring others.

'The leftover creatures scatter in fear. They go into hiding. Some of them band together to try to prevent the "undesirables" from advancing on the others, the more vulnerable communities. But the number of this group of do-gooders, somehow, is few and far between. They fall, eventually.

'Those in hiding stay hidden. They think it's the only way to survive. Even as some of them try to convince the rest otherwise, nothing moves.

'A status quo is reached.

'What happens next? Oh, nothing at all. No one breaks the equilibrium. But the undesirables, because of their bloodthirsty nature, turn on each other and wipe each other out. When no more "undesirables" remain, the survivors emerge from the shadows to lead a peaceful life once again.

'How long does it take for this peace to return, you ask? Hm . . . that has not been asked before. If it had been, then there was no answer. Because I simply do not know.

'And yes, that is the end of the story.

'Is the story true?

'Well, I suppose that like all myths, it is mostly fictional. But it carries sprinkles of truth too, doesn't it? Yes, sprinkles of truth like the sprinkles of traits that the higher being bestowed upon the qiues and okas.

'How about the moral of the story? Hm . . . Perhaps if we go back to the very beginning, it would be that one shouldn't bite off more than what they can chew, right? Yes, I suppose that would have been the simple solution. To keep thinking simply and prevent the narrative from getting too complicated. But, no. That isn't the answer I've been told.

'The moral of the story, my little one, is that everyone is different. And that it isn't what we appear as physically that makes us bond with each other. Who we are—the qualities that aren't apparent to the naked eye—is what matters.

'The "undesirable" qiues and okas banded together because they were scheming enough to know that everyone had their own strengths and weaknesses. By exploiting this knowledge, they could play to one another's strengths and be stronger together. And this "strength" that they gathered could let them conquer and enslave the rest of the creatures.

'Why did they want to do that, you ask? Well . . . yes, greed could very well have been the motivating trait for this group of creatures . . . Fear, perhaps. But we'll never know, since the traits were visible to no one else except for the higher being, who had moved on from this little scenario that they created.

'In any case, some of the qiues and okas who didn't have the "undesirable" traits tried to get everyone to band together. They thought if the rest of the community worked together, they might have been able to combat the evil. But not everyone agreed. Many refused to join the alliance, because of reasons that only they themselves knew. And because they didn't offer their help, evil was able to triumph.

'Which brings us to the true moral of the story—that unless you're the aggressor, you need to hide from the "undesirables" of the world until it is safe enough, peaceful enough to return. There is no point leading the charge because you won't be able to succeed in getting the rest on your side of the fight.

'Going into hiding is the only way to protect ourselves.'

As Keix concluded her story, it struck her how condescending and one-sided the pauses and the digressions sounded to her now. When she was younger, she had always thought that they were engaging. Beyond the fact that she found the story strange, she didn't think very much of it. Now, she felt a hint of savage satisfaction when she saw Del looking at Basch, her gaze sharp, as if silently reprimanding him for his daughter's impudence. But Keix kept her eyes trained on Del. When the Kulcan chief finally shifted her gaze back to Keix, she asked pointedly, 'Is this story similar to the Kulcan fable that shares its title?' She knew the answer to her question, but she wanted to get Del's acknowledgement.

The Kulcan chief's eyebrow twitched before she countered, 'Why does it matter? And how does this help your cause?'

'Because fables always have a moral and I want to know how the Kulcans interpret the story,' replied Keix.

After a length of time, when Del remained mum, Keix said, 'It's in the concluding line, isn't it? "Going into hiding is the only way to protect ourselves." Laying low is the solution, because evil will eradicate itself. But I beg to differ. I think the fact that it took the "undesirables" so long to eliminate the rest shows that if the others banded against them, they would have been outnumbered, and peace would have arrived sooner. And those who had gone into hiding only to get tracked down and killed might not have lost their lives—if they had chosen to fight with the rest.'

Del's eyes glinted dangerously at the hidden meaning in Keix's words, and she said, 'It is far-fetched to make this complicated assumption from such a simple story—especially when the conclusion had been laid out for you.'

'You're not wrong. But sometimes, the simplest stories have the most complex takeaways, don't you think? Especially when the moral of the story is presented so blatantly, it seems to be mocking the audiences' ability to analyse and think for themselves,' said Keix, stretching the tension in the air to its breaking point.

Del's lips thinned and she stood up, signalling a clear end to this discussion, and said to Keix, 'That is open to debate.'

* * *

'How did you know the Kulcan tale?' asked Sandom, who was leading Keix to where Jūn was locked up.

After they had left Del's house, Basch brought them to the other three chiefs' houses. Keix repeated what she had told Del to these other chiefs, only to be met with looks of ridicule. In fact, Keix had felt increasingly demoralized with each meeting, because they made her talk with Del seem the most successful, even if the female chief had still appeared unconvinced at the end of it.

Then, Basch told Keix that he had gotten approval from Daman for her to visit Jūn. Basch went on to confiscate Keix's sword because he said no weapons were allowed where Jūn was banished. Subsequently, Basch left Keix in Sandom's care and the two of them made a detour to Sandom's home where she re-emerged lugging a huge bag over her shoulder. Keix had been about to ask Sandom what was in the bag, but was silenced by a look from the Kulcan. So, she kept her lips zipped while they trekked up the main path, farther and farther up the mountains, until sounds of the Kulcan civilization faded away behind them.

'Are we finally out of earshot of the rest of the Kulcans?' asked Keix. 'Can I speak now?'

'Yes, we are,' replied Sandom finally. 'And yes, you may speak, though I'd prefer you not to.'

Keix ignored Sandom's preference and continued, 'How did you gauge that? If you're within earshot of someone else?'

Sandom looked mystified. Still, she obliged with a halting reply. 'You just tune up your hearing to the highest alertness and observe the ambient sounds. When you can't hear them, it's likely they can't hear you either.'

Keix was taken aback by the simplicity of the logic in Sandom's explanation and felt suddenly embarrassed. 'But my physical abilities . . . as half-Kulcan, aren't at your level,' she said.

Sandom frowned. 'Train more,' she said, as if Keix was dense. 'Natural talent is nothing if you don't hone it.'

Chastised, Keix pursed her lips and decided to stop asking Sandom stupid questions.

The air was turning thinner as they ascended the slopes, and even though Keix couldn't spot a single fleck of snow anywhere, she could sense that the peak was near. The chilliness was biting now.

Sandom suddenly stopped in her tracks and said, shoving her bag into Keix's hands, 'Here. Pass this to Jūn. Just continue along this path and you'll reach him in another hour.'

Keix squeezed the bag. It was lighter and softer than she had expected. She looked at Sandom, confused. 'Another hour?' she repeated. 'You're not coming with me?'

Sandom shook her head. 'I can't stand the cold. Get going. Jūn's probably going to rush down to meet you before you're even halfway there. You don't have to worry about getting lost. There's only one path up.'

Keix's eyes widened in disbelief. Just how cold exactly was it going to get? She could already feel the chill seeping in through the layers of clothes she was wearing, even though the sun was blazing overhead. Also, what did Sandom mean when she said Jūn was going to meet her halfway? Wasn't he locked up?

'Oh, and one more thing,' said Sandom to an increasingly bewildered Keix. 'You know the way back to the village, right?'

Keix nodded. The path was straightforward enough.

'Just head back down when you're ready . . . whenever that is,' said Sandom. She turned to leave, jogging down the path as if she couldn't wait to get out of there.

Staring at Sandom's retreating back, confounded at the vagueness of her parting words, Keix stood still for a moment, unsure of how to proceed. Then, she gathered herself and continued making her way up to the peak. She lengthened her strides and prepared to bombard Jūn with all the questions she had had for him, and new ones that had risen since they entered Yurkordu. Be it coaxing or threatening, she was going to get all the answers this time.

5

Keix | Equilibrium

Even before Keix could make it halfway up the slope, her teeth had started chattering so violently that she couldn't even string two coherent thoughts together. With every step that she took, the temperature dipped even further. The wind was gusting now, tugging her hair, her robe—as well as Sandom's bag—away from her, then whipping them back against her. What was worse was that the snow that Jūn had described as such a magical sight was storming down from the sky, lowering the visibility of her surroundings. Pretty soon, she would be unable to see her fingers even if she held them out in front of her. She might even get buried alive if the snowstorm got heavier—that is, if she didn't freeze to death first.

Magical. Yeah, right. She was seriously doubting Jūn's judgement now. How could anyone speak so fondly of these innocent-looking yet deadly white flakes? Keix continued placing one foot in front of the other as she fought to keep her eyes open against the biting cold. After an indeterminate amount of time, she suddenly heard a familiar voice calling, 'Keix?'

'J-j-j—' Keix started. But something solid engulfed her before she could get a word out. Her senses had been frozen to a state of incapacity by this point, so it felt like she was having an out-of-body experience. She knew instinctively that this figure was Jūn, and that he was wrapping his arms around her, but she couldn't feel his body heat, so she thought she was hallucinating. The next thing she knew, her vision had fogged over, and with her sight went the last shred of her consciousness.

By the time Keix came to, the nerve endings on her body had warmed up. She was at a flat, open plain carpeted in snow. Scattered around were trees similar to the ones that she had seen on the trek to the Council Hall. She was seated down under one of them, bundled in a large, thick, and furry cloak. This must have been what was in Sandom's bag, Keix deduced, when she saw the empty bag strewn to one side.

'Feeling better?' Jūn's gentle voice sounded next to Keix's ear, scaring her just-recovered wits out of her. What she had initially thought was a tree trunk that she was leaning on turned out to be the person whom she came for. And this person was practically hugging her from the back! Her body suddenly felt like it was on track to spontaneously combusting.

Keix's first reaction was to scoot away from Jūn, who let her go without resistance, as she coughed to cover up her embarrassment. To calm her racing heart, she made a show of adjusting herself to find a comfortable seating position facing Jūn. Straightening her back as she got ready to 'interrogate' him, she asked, 'You carried me all the way here?'

Jūn nodded serenely. 'The workout warmed me up,' he said with a chuckle.

Keix couldn't believe that he could still crack a joke. How could anyone be in such a good mood despite being punished? Keeping her expression stern, she scolded him. 'I could have died halfway up the mountain! And how can you laugh when you're . . . stuck here?' She gestured to the barren surroundings, knowing full well that she was being dramatic. But she couldn't think of any other way to impress upon him the fact that she was here for a serious conversation. To emphasize her point, she tried to punch his shoulder, but Jūn stopped her manoeuvre effortlessly, wrapping his icy hand around her clenched fist and lowering it.

'I wouldn't have let you. Never,' he said with conviction. 'And I'm just happy to see you. I thought they wouldn't let you come up here.'

Keix's flush, which looked set to subside just a second ago, crept back up her neck. She wasn't going to let Jūn's flirtatious tone distract her. 'Basch got Sandom to take me halfway up here on the condition that I listen to his side of the story.'

Jūn let go of her hand then. He cast his eyes downward, and his voice quavered as he stated, 'You've spoken to Basch.'

'Yes,' said Keix. She didn't want to mention that she had also spoken to the other Kulcan chiefs yet, because her first order of business was to resolve the question that had been bugging her since she met Jūn. So, she continued, 'He was certain that Daman will join the war. He also asked me not to leave Yurkordu now because it seems like ExA could be approaching. But how would he know that? The two of us didn't encounter anything out of the ordinary when we were headed here. Just how are you Kulcans getting your intel?' Keix figured that it might be a long shot asking Jūn about this, since he wasn't in the good graces of Daman or the chiefs. But he was the only person in Yurkordu she could trust.

'It's true that we didn't come across anything peculiar on our way back,' replied Jūn, frowning. 'But after Sandom and Bakuro escorted you out of the Council Hall and I was getting an earful from the chiefs, one of our Kulcan scouts burst in and announced that there were small groups of people heading in this direction. It's concerning because these groups seem to be moving rather stealthily.'

Keix met Jūn's eyes. She knew he was thinking about the attackers that they had encountered outside Atros and how quietly they moved.

'I wouldn't rule out the possibility that it's those ExA soldiers, but they don't stand a chance against our scouts, so I wouldn't be alarmed. And don't forget Yurkordu's protective barrier.'

Keix was impressed by Jūn's confidence, but at the same time, she couldn't help but feel uneasy about these new revelations. 'Your barrier doesn't seem particularly protective. Anyone with the charm could come in anytime they like.'

'You're not wrong. But getting the charm off any Kulcan would prove to be a challenge. We'd die before letting any of them land in the hands of our enemies.'

'What do you mean? If anyone manages to kill a Kulcan, won't they just be able to rip the charm off the corpse?'

'We've been taught to destroy it when we're dying. And even if someone manages to get through the barrier, they would have a long way to go to reach us. By that time, most, if not all, of the intruders would be dead.'

Keix couldn't refute Jūn's words. Yurkordu *was* a fortress defended by the best fighters. But she couldn't stay here in this hideout—not when her friends were out there risking their lives. Now that she had gotten one agenda item off her list, she moved on to the next one. 'I've also spoken to the rest of the Kulcan chiefs individually.'

Jūn's eyes widened at her revelation. 'How did you manage to do that? And how did it go?'

Shaking her head, Keix admitted, 'I got Basch to set up the meetings, but they didn't seem convinced. Whether or not the Kulcans decide to join the war, I'm leaving Yurkordu in two days to head back to Tilsor. That's the amount of time I'm willing to spare Basch and the rest of the Kulcan chiefs.'

Jūn paused for a moment, then nodded. 'Daman has sent more Kulcans out to gather information. They should be back before then. And you've spoken to Del too, right?'

'Yes, but she doesn't seem inclined to help. Basch said Del's reasonable, and you seem to have faith in her too. Why is this so?'

'She is respected by the other chiefs because she has influence that she chooses not to wield in order to maintain the peace that we have now. Ironic, isn't it? Many Kulcans feel that Daman is wary of her because if she gets ambitious, she could overthrow him. Perhaps that's why she maintains as low a profile as she can. If you've managed to convince her, she might swing the vote in our favour.'

Keix tried to wrap her head around this complicated explanation but failed; she probably wouldn't fare that well in Yurkordu even though she had boasted to Del about getting complex interpretations from simple stories.

'But if he still refuses to help,' continued Jūn. 'I'll leave with you.'

Jūn's words untangled a knot in Keix's heart. He was set on being on her side even if it meant leaving his home. But why? If Keix couldn't understand from where and when his affections for her stemmed, she didn't think that she would be able to accept his feelings readily. She gritted her jaw in determination, ready to confront the topic that she had been avoiding all this time. 'Basch also told me that he had asked you to keep certain things from me because he wanted to speak to me first. So now that I've heard his side of the story, I want to hear yours.'

At Keix's words, Jūn's expression turned hopeful and vulnerable.

'From the beginning,' she added sternly. 'And I'd better get the full story from you.'

Jūn took a deep breath. 'It's going to sound bad.'

'Why?'

'Because you're going to think I'm a stalker,' he admitted after some hesitation. 'But I swear I had no ill intentions.'

'Had? So, you mean you have ill intentions now?' Keix raised an eyebrow, eliciting a nervous gulp from him. There was a part of her that wanted to get back at him for keeping the story of how he had first met her in the dark all this while. But there was another part that was equally ready to cave and tell him that she was just teasing him.

After Atros's betrayal, she had never felt safe trusting anyone other than Vin. But somehow, after everything they had gone through in Tilsor, Keix knew deep down in her heart that Jūn would rather let himself get hurt than allow any harm to come to her.

'No, I didn't mean that!' he hurried to clarify. 'It's just . . . Okay, if you've spoken to Basch, you would know that he sent me on an errand to Atros when I was fourteen.'

Keix nodded, making sure to keep her expression neutral.

'I was supposed to drop by Ma.erdene's to exchange some intel, then head to Atros to invite you and your'—Jūn paused for a split second—'your mother to Yurkordu. But because it was my first time heading to Tilsor, I ran a little behind schedule. That was why I didn't manage to reach Atros on your eleventh birthday or the day after that . . .' Jūn's voice became smaller with every sentence he uttered; he knew how distressing this topic was for Keix, so he had tried to avoid broaching it.

Keix had cast her eyes to the ground at the mention of her mother and her eleventh birthday. There was still a dull ache at the core of her being whenever she replayed in her head the fateful scene that she encountered during the third trial of Taavar. It was seared onto her soul. How hopeful, disappointed, and frustrated she had felt when she saw the 'ghost' of her mother appear. How, without a care, she had rushed forward to embrace the illusion. How the form of her mother had acknowledged her, and how the words that her 'mother' uttered had resounded through her being. Keix had never let herself admit that she missed her mother because it was just easier to avoid confronting her feelings.

But the acceptance of her fears had made her less afraid to be in touch with her feelings now. For the first time, she decided to state the facts out loud. This felt like the right time to do it, like how it had felt right during the trial to confront her feelings head on.

'My mother died a few days after my birthday,' she recalled. 'Two Atros troopers came to my home that day and took me to an orphanage.'

The gentle breeze that had been caressing her face stilled, as if it were afraid to let time move on from this moment.

Jūn's whisper broke through its magic. 'I know . . . I was there . . .' he confessed. 'I saw you returning home hours before that because I'd arrived much earlier. But I was supposed to speak to Layne, so I didn't approach you directly. I just lingered at the stairwell because I thought it was better to wait until she was back. I didn't even know if you knew about Basch. And when the troopers came . . . I heard them breaking the news to you.'

Keix drew a stuttering breath. She had prepared herself mentally for Jūn to corroborate Basch's account. Even if they had agreed to deceive her, there was no real value in gaining her trust. She was but an ex-Atros trooper trying to do right by a world that seemed content to sit back and watch with disinterest as its people set out to slaughter each other in a bid to gain power. But what she hadn't expected was for Jūn to tell her that he had witnessed one of the lowest points in her life. Her memory of the event was hazy at best, but the feeling of shock and loss had left a deep and lasting scar.

'I didn't know what to do,' said Jūn, sounding genuinely anguished. 'So, I did the next thing that I thought I ought to do. I followed you to see where the troopers were taking you. I wanted to make sure that you were safe before I headed back to report to Basch what had happened. I tried to change his mind about leaving you in Atros, at the institution, but he was adamant that it would be better if you remained there until you were older and the situation in Yurkordu stabilized.

'It just felt like all the forces in the world wanted to keep you in Atros. It was never the right time. Complications surfaced one after another.'

'Complications?' asked Keix, her voice almost a whisper.

'When Basch sent me to get you and Layne, there was a temporary truce called between the tribe leaders. But by the time I came back to Yurkordu, we were back to square one. The tribe leader who managed to get all the Kulcans on the same page was assassinated and everyone started pointing fingers at each other. We . . . we went back to sleeping with our swords by our sides.'

'That's the reason why the two of you just decided to leave me there?' Keix couldn't eliminate the tremor from her voice. She didn't want to make the conversation about her. She didn't want to make it sound like she was placing blame on Jūn and Basch. But she needed to press on to fill in the gap between when Jūn left her at Atros and when he found her the night of the ritual. Still, Keix was reminded of her observation of how everyone in Yurkordu seemed to be ready for battle. Even during these supposedly peaceful times, no one had forgotten the need to be prepared for a war. Just how bad had the fighting gotten in the past?

'Yes. But I went back to Atros every year to check on you and report back to Basch on how you were doing,' said Jun, guilt creeping into his voice.

'Spy on me, you mean?'

'I'm sorry,' said Jūn. The guilt and self-reproach in his voice was evident. 'If only I'd arrived a day earlier . . .'

Keix let the silence stretch. There were limitless ifs in life. If Jūn had arrived a day earlier, her mum might have never died. Keix herself might have never joined Atros as a trooper. Then, she would never have met Zej, nor Vin or Pod. And she would never have experienced Atros's betrayal. And the list went on. And she would not be the person she was right now. And would that be something good? No one could say for sure, because everyone only had one shot in life. Time only moved forward. That's why she had concluded that it was pointless to dwell on these things. Of course, she felt regretful about the things that could have been. But it just wasn't in her to mope about it. It made no sense to do so.

Still, as much as she wanted to put a hand over Jūn's clenched fists and tell him that no one could undo the past, she couldn't bring herself to do so at this moment—not when she had just found out that their relationship seemed to have started off on an uneven footing, with him knowing so much about her so early on, when she hadn't even been aware of his existence.

'Is that why you're . . . you treat me the way you do?' asked Keix. 'Because you feel responsible for my plight?'

Jūn shook his head and protested vehemently, 'That was never in consideration!' He grasped Keix's hands and exhaled deeply, as if he was on the verge of confessing to her his deepest secret.

'Then why do you treat me as if I'm . . . I'm something . . . more?' Keix cringed at her own question. But she *had* to know.

Words failed Jūn as he opened and closed his mouth a couple of times. Eventually, he said, 'You don't understand, Keix. You exude this . . . I don't know how to explain it. But it draws people to you. In the beginning, I was just worried about you. I have seen what grief does to a person. But when I went to Atros every year to see how you were doing, I saw your resilience. How you remained optimistic despite what happened to you.'

Keix didn't know what to make of that. She'd never seen herself in that light before. The only thing she knew was that life went on. Somehow.

'I was a walking shell,' she admitted—more to herself than to Jūn. 'I didn't dare to face my feelings or grief. I don't think there's anything admirable about that.'

Jūn shook his head again. 'You were just processing your grief in your own way. No two people deal with the death of their loved ones in the same way.'

The certainty with which he said that swayed Keix's long-held belief that there was something wrong with her, since she hadn't sobbed her eyes out after her mother's passing. Almost everyone else who had ended up in the institution—no matter how strong a front they put up—cried themselves to sleep at night. Keix knew that because of her superior sense of hearing. She gave a half-nod, half-shrug because she wasn't sure how to respond. Her gut was telling her that Jūn was reassuring himself too. *I have seen what grief does to a person*, he had said. But whom was he talking about? It must be someone he cared a lot for. Would he ever open up to her? She debated if she should ask him outright, but it felt a bit too personal for now. She also wasn't sure if she really wanted to know the answer, so she kept mum instead.

Mistaking the reason for her silence, Jūn said, 'I'm sorry, I was being presumptuous. I—' He paused mid-sentence, then gestured awkwardly to the sky in a sudden change of topic. 'It's going to get even colder when night falls. I'll walk you back down and come back here once you can find your way back.'

Surprised, Keix blurted, 'You can leave the peak if you want to? I thought you were supposed to be locked up here. But'—she looked around—'that doesn't seem to be the case.'

Something sparked in Jūn's eyes, as if Keix's concern afforded him some hope that all was not lost in this relationship that he valued. He rushed to explain, 'I could leave, if I wanted to. But I'd just be escorted up here again, and my stay here would be extended. To leave in the shortest time possible, I need to serve out my entire sentence. It's just two weeks.'

Add that to the list of Kulcan things I can't comprehend, thought Keix. In Atros, being locked up meant bars and cages. No one would voluntarily stay put, like what Jūn was doing now. While still trying to make sense of the Kulcans' way of life, Keix noticed that the sky had gotten significantly darker over the course of their conversation. Either the sun set early here, or she must have been unconscious for longer than she had thought; the sun had still been blazing overhead when she was trekking up to the peak with Sandom. *Sandom . . . Oh, yes.* Now that Keix had gotten most of the answers she wanted, she was reminded of how Sandom had casually dropped the shocking fact that Jūn was her brother. 'I have one last question. Sandom's your sister?'

Jūn's reply was a tentative smile. 'Yes, Sandom's my sister. But that's a long story, and I don't think I can finish telling it if you want to get back to Basch's house before it's dark. Come on, we should go now. I don't want to risk you getting lost on your way down.' He stood up and extended his hand to Keix to help her up.

But Keix didn't take it. It felt as though she had broken down many invisible walls between Jūn and herself today, and she needed to keep that momentum going if she really wanted to get to know him as well as he did her. He actually seemed relieved to have the truth out in the open, and Keix could tell that he had become even less guarded now.

'I'm staying here tonight,' she said, wrapping the cloak around herself tighter.

Jūn's smile vanished, and his expression became one of barely constrained longing mixed with uncertainty and hope. His voice was husky when he asked, 'You're not upset with me?'

Keix's cheeks warmed up at his intense gaze and she decided to be honest with him. 'No,' she sighed. 'I'm not upset with you.'

Jūn reached for her exposed fingers and pulled her upright. 'You're staying here tonight. And you're not upset with me. In that case, we'd better move to somewhere else.' For some reason, his words sent a shiver down Keix's spine.

'Where are we going?'

'Away from the elements.'

Keix didn't resist when he led her towards a cliff beyond a sparse cluster of trees. They walked a couple dozen steps along the length of the rock face, then he took a left turn into a crevice in the wall. The gap opened into a path much narrower than the ones that she had traversed through when she first entered Yurkordu.

As they made their way down the path, the howling of the wind, blocked out by the cliffs, got quieter. But a faint whistling remained in the background. The narrow path became tighter and harder to navigate, and it also got dimmer as traces of dusk fled from the rapidly darkening sky. By the time they came to a stop, darkness had descended.

Keix's breath hitched. The complete absence of light brought to mind her previously recurring nightmare where she had confronted the image of her mother's ghost. But things were different now. Had her nightmares ceased because she had finally overcome her fears and accepted that her mother would never begrudge her? Or was it because Jūn had never left her side after that, which gave her a sense of security and acceptance?

'Can you see anything?' Keix muttered, trying to fill the silence that was getting increasingly stifling. Her other senses were sharpened in the dark. Besides the persistent whistling noise, the only sounds she could hear were that of Jūn and herself breathing, and their footfalls. Jūn's hand, which was still clasping hers firmly, felt burning hot—a far cry from how freezing cold it was when he had first grabbed her hand.

'Not exactly, but I know the way around.'

Keix was reminded of how Jūn had led them through Tilsor and its ever-shifting Sectors. 'Is there a map for these . . . tunnels? Have you memorized it like how you committed to memory all the different Sectors in Tilsor?'

Jūn gave a soft laugh. 'There's no map, but I've been here enough times to know the area.'

'I was under the impression that Kulcans only come up here when they get punished. Or is this a *recreational* area too?' Keix couldn't keep the confusion out of her voice.

Jūn laughed again, this time louder, as he tugged at her hand, indicating that she should sit down. Lowering herself down slowly, she fought the urge to reach out to feel her way around because she didn't want to accidentally grope Jūn.

'How can you be sure that I wasn't punished often when I was younger?'

Keix's brows furrowed. What he said was true. The only reason why she couldn't be certain was because she didn't know him well enough.

'I used to run into a lot of trouble.'

'So, you were brought up here to freeze in the cold?'

'It's just a long-standing tradition. And I got used to it.'

Jūn's shoulder brushed against Keix's, as if he had shrugged.

'What kind of elders send kids to freeze to death for breaking the rules?' Keix was appalled. The immense dislike she harboured against Daman and the rest of the chiefs for how they had behaved at the council meeting was obvious.

His voice raw with regret, Jūn said, 'I'm sorry. I should have told you more about Daman and the rest of the chiefs.'

'Yes, you should have,' said Keix with a sigh. 'You should have told me about Daman and the rest. If I had known better, I would never have been caught unawares yesterday. I know you said that I should see things for myself, learn to figure things out myself rather than listening to others, but there are times when things need to be told to me! To let me have time to process these thoughts, feelings.

'You're afraid of tainting my views or perspective of certain people but when I go into a situation like this blind, I don't know what to do. I'm not intelligent enough to think on my feet. My first reaction to anything is always to resist and to fight my way through obstacles. And I've learnt the hard way that using your fists doesn't always solve problems. Why do you not trust me to be sceptical of the things that are said to me, after all the lies I've been told?' Keix's outburst came as fast as a gathering storm and blew itself out just as quickly. In fact, it was the last bit of anger and frustration that she had held in.

A long silence ensued.

Finally, Jūn said, 'I'm sorry. It was all my fault.'

Keix thought for a long moment before replying, 'I know you're sorry. But it's not all on you.' Then, she sighed and added, 'Just don't do it again.'

Jūn swallowed audibly before he promised, 'I won't.'

It was only now that Keix felt a weight, held close to her heart, that she'd never noticed being lifted. The imbalance in the relationship between Jūn and herself was, at long last, rectified. Or at least, that was what it felt like to her. She wanted to make sure that Jūn was on the same fresh page with her, so she took a deep breath and said, 'Can we get to know each other properly again?'

6

Keix | Hearth

'My name is Jūn Gantulga. You can call me Jūn.'

Keix opened her mouth to speak but words failed her. The only sound that made it past her lips was a choked laugh. Of all the things that Jūn could have said in reply to her question, he chose this. It was like the first time when they had met all over again, when Keix asked him who he was. At that time, she had been equal parts irritated and baffled. Now, she was more amused and confounded.

'It's just . . . I've always wanted us to start on the right foot.' The self-consciousness was obvious in Jūn's voice.

And in an instant, everything fell into place for Keix. This self-introduction was a rite for Jūn. For some inexplicable reason, it was his way of giving their relationship a fresh start.

He started to elaborate, 'I wish we could have—'

But Keix interrupted him. 'I'm Keix. And I'm half-Kulcan, half-Atrossian,' she said, trying to keep a straight face. She really shouldn't laugh since she knew how much this meant to him, but a muffled giggle still escaped her. The sound broke through the awkward uncertainty that had been hanging in the air and the two of them burst out in uncontrollable laughter. As absurd and cheesy as it sounded, this out-of-nowhere reintroduction, it felt right. And by the time the guffaws subsided, they were both out of breath.

Keix muttered the first thing that came to her mind once she regained her ability to speak. 'You're cute, you know?' she said, shaking her head.

A beat passed before Jūn said, sounding bemused, 'No one's ever called me that before.'

If there was enough light for her to catch a glimpse of him, Keix was certain she would see that he was blushing. 'Well, I guess not. Since Kulcans are huge, tall, and scary.'

'Is that how you see me?' Jūn asked, surprised.

'Hm? Well, I guess so . . . at least in the beginning.' When Jūn didn't say anything, Keix somehow felt the need to explain herself. 'You did come out of nowhere to . . . save me. That was a very cool entrance, by the way. Very impressive,' she said, referring to the way he had appeared in front of her to stop the black hole bullet speeding towards her. She expected him to chortle at her comment, but Jūn's reply was unexpectedly remorseful.

'I almost lost you that day,' he said.

'Okay. Let's just stop right there because we're not going to circle back when we are—were—are. When we *are* making progress.'

Jūn inhaled deeply. 'Then what do you want to talk about?'

'You. I want to talk about you,' said Keix resolutely.

'Okay . . . what do you want to know?'

'How about we start with your childhood? From your first memory.'

'My first childhood memory . . .' murmured Jūn.

Keix didn't rush him as he sorted through his memories. Instead, she tried to imagine baby Jūn, with gold, intensely mesmerizing yet innocent eyes staring at her and she couldn't help but smile.

'I think I was about four? Just running around the house with a wooden sword that many Kulcan children play with.'

'A sword? At four?' Keix knew she shouldn't sound so judgemental. After all, the earliest memory she had was of how badly she cried after her favourite food stall that sold the most delicious candy shut down for good. She was six then.

'I grew up in a rather turbulent time,' confessed Jūn. 'In case you haven't noticed, the Kulcans aren't at all as harmonious as they appear.'

'So I've heard,' she said, recalling what Basch had said to her about the Kulcans being a warring race.

'The memory I have . . . is not a happy one.'

Keix swallowed at Jūn's confession. 'You don't have to tell me if you're not ready. I'm sorry for bringing it up.' She had only meant to tease him; she regretted that the first question she had posed had forced him to relive his bad memories.

'There's nothing to be sorry about. I just . . . my dad died when I was four, during one of the raids conducted by one of the other tribe leaders.'

Keix froze. 'I—I'm sorry for your loss,' she said in a quiet voice.

There was a soft rustling noise, as if Jūn had shrugged. 'I don't remember much of it,' he said in a mild tone. 'And Basch took me in after that, so I grew up under his care.'

Keix squinted, trying to get a glimpse of Jūn's expression in the complete darkness. The moon seemed to have sensed her need to check if he was okay, because at that moment, a wisp of illumination filtered in from the sliver of an opening in the cliffs above them. The yellow orb had made its way across the sky and was peeking at them, as if it wasn't bothered about getting found eavesdropping on their conversation.

There was a thoughtful look on Jūn's face, and a glimmer of sadness in his eyes. But there was also a softness in them when he met Keix's eyes, although neither of them spoke for a long while.

When an echoey, sinister howl sounded in the distance and the temperature seemed to dip even further, Keix shivered involuntarily. 'What's that sound? A shih?' she asked.

The corners of Jūn's eyes crinkled at her question. 'I've never heard a shih howl. But that sound's not uncommon here in the highlands at night. Legend has it that it's from someone who got lost after getting sent here for committing a heinous crime.'

'Have many Kulcans gotten lost here?' asked Keix, throwing Jūn a look of mild disbelief even though she was pretty sure that she'd be utterly, hopelessly lost if she was here alone.

Jūn shrugged. 'Enough, I guess, to make us think twice about wandering off too far every time we're sent here.'

Keix shuddered again. It then occurred to her that she had been hogging the cloak which Sandom got her to bring for Jūn. She tried to take it off to hand it back to him. 'Are you cold?'

'It's all right. You can have it,' said Jūn hastily.

'Come, let's share,' said Keix, scooting closer towards him. It was clear that he would reject her outright if she offered the cloak to him, so this was the best compromise. Also, Keix was reluctant to give up the only piece of clothing that was preventing her from getting frozen into a walking corpse again. She slung the cloak over Jūn's broad shoulders despite his protests and it felt like the outerwear, which had enveloped her, had suddenly shrunk. She even had to huddle closer to Jūn to make sure that it covered them both. Because Jūn was so tall, the hem of the cloak couldn't reach the ground. The gap formed kept letting in a draft, making it harder for them to stay warm.

Jūn repositioned himself from her side to her back. He took care to not make any physical contact, except when he adjusted the cloak to cover them completely in order to stop the air from entering this tiny space which they had created for themselves.

Keix's self-consciousness returned, and her heart thumped rapidly. She was cognizant of the fact that, if not for that thin layer of air between then, Jūn would be hugging her from behind. There was no way that Jūn was comfortable in this position, having to keep this distance from her. Keix herself wasn't; she was going to get a cramp if she continued to hold her back straight. In the end, the tension was too much to bear, and emboldened—or should she say muddled—by the cold, she decided to throw all caution to the wind. She leaned back against Jūn's chest.

At the contact, Jūn drew in a sharp breath and stiffened his back, but he didn't pull away.

Keix could feel the steady beat of his heart now, and she was glad that it was pounding as quickly as hers.

Clearly disconcerted, Jūn cleared his throat and said, 'Er, perhaps I can tell you a bit more about the history of Yurkordu?'

Keix played along and answered jokingly, 'Wow, look at you volunteering information about the Kulcans. How far we have come in such a short time!'

Jūn's laugh was short and still sounded a little awkward. But he launched into his story right away. 'This is a story passed down by word of mouth, but the Kulcans have always believed that there is some truth in it because of how realistic and practical it sounds.'

Keix nodded in encouragement as a faint layer of clouds moved to obscure the moonlight. But there was still enough illumination for her to see the jagged outline of the alcove they were in.

'Well,' came Jūn's voice from beside her ear, as his breath skimmed past it, 'if you've spoken to Basch, then he might have told you that peace between the tribes has always been tenuous, because we just can't seem to get along.' Jūn sighed, his frustration and resignation clear.

Basch had blamed the Kulcans' inclination towards violence on their gift of physical abilities, but Keix's take was that the excuse made them sound no better than the Odats, who had no qualms about exploiting their psychopathic love for killing by becoming mercenaries.

'Fights and raids among tribes were common occurrences,' continued Jūn. 'But it used to be much less bloody in the past, apparently. It is said that the tribe leaders of the past—whom we call chiefs now—treated these surprise attacks more like sport than an actual battle, because they held a grudging sense of respect for each other. But all bets came off when one of the tribe leaders was fatally poisoned. While the tribes didn't get on spectacularly, there were certain lines that were never crossed—until then.

'It was also around that time that rumours about a Kulcan extending help to the Ifarls started floating around. This was unprecedented. We were supposed to keep to ourselves and not let outsiders know too much about us.

'Everyone was shocked beyond words, to say the least. All the evidence then pointed to this other tribe leader, but he denied having anything to do with either of these crimes. Eventually, a joint trial—the first of its kind where the remaining tribe leaders came together with the same goal in mind—was held, and the alleged culprit was sent into exile.'

Keix frowned. The relationship between the tribe leaders was so convoluted. She turned her head to face Jūn and asked, 'If they could come together to persecute this person, why couldn't they live harmoniously with each other after that?'

Jūn half-shrugged and shook his head. 'The incident only made things worse. It was as if the last bit of trust that they had in each other was completely obliterated. The raids and attacks resumed shortly after, but they soon grew in viciousness. Many more Kulcans started getting killed. And that only angered the rest even more. Violence begets violence.'

Even with Jūn's explanation, Keix found it hard to visualize a Yurkordu where the Kulcans were at war with each other for no good reason at all. 'What happened to the Kulcan who was exiled?'

'Rumour has it that he never left these peaks. Because they didn't provide him with any food or drink after sending him away, they estimated that he died after a week of being here. The extreme cold might have made him lose consciousness, and he might have wandered off and gotten lost in the mazes formed by the cracks in the rock cliffs here. But the thing is, no one ever found his body. There are Kulcans who prefer darker stories—as if this isn't dark enough—who say that he haunts these cliffs as a half-alive phantom, waiting for justice to be served because he maintained his innocence, right until the end.'

Jūn paused for a moment before adding, 'Remember the Kulcan that I said was rumoured to have gotten lost here?'

At Keix's look of realization, he confirmed, 'It's the same tribe leader.'

Right on cue, the hair-raising howl sounded once again.

'Most of us know it's just a cautionary tale for younger Kulcans. But yeah, this howling doesn't help,' said Jūn. 'It's just the way the wind sounds when they weave through the cliffs. But it does bring on the goosebumps, doesn't it?'

Keix nodded and shivered again. But this time, it wasn't due to the cold or the creepy story that Jūn had just told. It was just an involuntary reaction because with the conclusion of the story, her awareness of the proximity between Jūn and herself had returned.

'Cold? If . . . if you don't mind, I can try warming you up by'—Jūn cleared his throat—'by holding you a little tighter.'

Kei didn't know how to tell him that even though it felt like her extremities were getting frozen off, the parts of her body which were in contact with him were on the verge of combusting into flames. She opened her mouth, even though she wasn't sure what she wanted to say, but her teeth ended up chattering from the cold. 'I . . .' She started, but her mind drew a complete blank when Jūn tightened his embrace, drawing her closer.

Keix's eyes widened at his boldness, but she clamped her lips shut. Jūn's hug was driving her heart to overexertion because she was fighting against her instinct to melt into his arms.

'I'm sorry. I was of no help in convincing Daman,' said Jūn in a dejected voice. He lowered his chin to Keix's shoulder, causing her to turn into a statue because his breath was skimming across the crook of her neck, causing all sorts of wild thoughts—none of which had any relation to the topic he was talking about—to surface. Otherwise, she might have turned around to pat Jūn's head comfortingly because it was something that he liked doing to her whenever she was gloomy. Instead, she sighed and said, 'It's not your fault. We came here knowing that we might not succeed, although I'm still miffed at him and the other chiefs. But it was worth a shot. And I got to see Yurkordu too.'

'That, you did. Does it live up to your expectations?'

'Well, not all parts, I guess. The snow would have been more impressive if I hadn't been at the risk of freezing to death or getting buried alive.'

Jūn chuckled and Keix could have sworn that there was something eerie about the way the environmental elements in Yurkordu seemed to understand their conversations, because the moment the complaint left her lips, snowflakes started drifting down leisurely from the sky. Well, this sight was definitely and infinitely more romantic. Was this what Jūn meant when he said that she'd feel different with every snowfall?

'You know, you can tell me if Kulcans are descended from sorcerers who can control the weather, right?'

She could hear Jūn's smile in his voice when he said, 'It is quite magical—Yurkordu. That, at least, is something you've got to admit.'

Keix made a noise that sounded like she agreed with Jūn, and a companionable silence fell again.

After a length of time, Jūn spoke up, his voice resolute. 'Stay with me until the Kulcan scouts come back with news? It's going to be a few days, or a week, tops. Basch will keep his word to send someone up here to convey any information to you. And when that happens, I'll leave Yurkordu with you.'

'How about your punishment?'

'Well, now that I've decided to leave, there doesn't seem to be any point in following their rules, right?'

Keix didn't reply, but as she pondered Jūn's words, she kept feeling light touches on her hair. When she couldn't take it any more, she let go of the coat, wiggled out of Jūn's embrace and turned back to fix a querying gaze on him. The soft moonlight was hitting his face now, and it seemed to make his golden eyes glow.

'Snowflakes,' said Jūn sheepishly. 'I was trying to brush them off.' Letting the cloak fall to a heap behind him, he reached out to flick off what Keix supposed was another snowflake from above her ear. Then, without warning, Jūn had swept the pad of his thumb over her lower lip, all while staring intently at it.

Beyond doubt, Jūn was making a move on her. She needed to decide now if she wanted to reciprocate his feelings, but the electrifying touch had sent her thoughts into a jumble. The scene of their almost-kiss flashed in her head again. Why was she hesitating? The last time that Jūn had taken the initiative to draw this close to her, she had held back because of Zej. But with Pod's death, she had realized that Zej's priorities were far from hers. She had given Zej a chance after he betrayed her by sending her to be sacrificed during the Ifarl ritual; so why couldn't she afford Jūn, who had done nothing except showed her genuine care and concern, and protected and helped her, a chance? Even if she disregarded all that, the physical attraction she had felt since the first time she met him was undeniable.

On impulse, she placed her hand on Jūn's cheeks and closed the negligible distance between them. His skin felt warm beneath her fingers, and shock registered in his eyes as she pressed her lips to his.

Jūn froze for a split second before letting out a low groan. Then, he placed one hand on the back of Keix's head as his other hand circled her waist and pulled her towards him, moulding each and every curve of her body to him.

They softened against each other and Keix slid her hands towards his ears, tracing featherlight touches along them.

Shuddering, Jūn pulled back from her, a dark fire burning behind his eyes. 'What are you doing to me . . .' His husky voice, thick with desire, ignited a thrill within Keix.

'I've never . . .' she stopped short mid-confession. Back when she was studying at Atros, she had walked past broom closets or empty classrooms and heard moans coming from within. It wasn't hard to hazard a guess as to what was happening inside these spaces. When Vin was with her, they would always exchange funny looks and struggle to contain their giggles as they ran quietly past these spots to avoid disturbing their inhabitants.

Jūn's laugh interrupted her reflection. 'I shouldn't have asked that question. You're overthinking now,' he said.

Keix couldn't help but chuckle at his accurate assessment. 'I don't know what I'm doing to you. I don't know what to do now. I've only ever kissed—' Keix stopped herself just in time. It was probably bad manners to talk about Zej now.

'Look at me,' said Jūn reassuringly. 'Focus on me. Right now, it's just us two. What do you want to do to me?' His thumb began tracing a line from her earlobes to the crook of her neck, and back again.

Keix's breath caught even as she wanted to ask him how he could look so composed now, asking such a question? But she didn't want to back down. She touched his lips, now a little swollen from their kiss, with her fingertips and found herself letting out an involuntary whimper at their softness.

The sound seemed to have triggered something in Jūn, as he pulled her back into a deeper kiss. Keix's senses exploded like bursts of dark fire. Her hands found their way to Jūn's shoulders, and she pushed him from his sitting position to lie on the floor, breaking the kiss.

He didn't resist her administration, but his eyes were burning with a want so intense, he looked like he was on the verge of devouring her. Emboldened by his reaction and the foreign yet pleasurable feelings coursing through her body, she adjusted herself to straddle him before leaning forward to resume their kiss. All she could hear was the pounding of their hearts and their ragged breaths as they surrendered to the all-consuming fires that they had ignited in each other. The heat engulfed Keix seductively, bewitchingly, coaxing forth a sense of contentment that she had never felt in her life.

Was it because she was away from Atros, or the fact that she had already met her father, or because of how otherworldly Yurkordu was, which made her feel like she'd been teleported to a different world—one that was far removed from the trauma that she had been through in the past months?

How long had it been since she had felt at peace with the world? She couldn't remember.

For a moment, Keix considered ditching the ridiculous mission that she had undertaken to try to save the world. But a howl rang through the air again, as if reminding her of the realities of her situation.

Lulled by Jūn's strong heartbeat and the feel of his skin against hers, Keix refused to resurface into the real world just yet. She wished with all her heart that there was no war, and that they didn't have to go back to Tilsor or Atros. She was being selfish, yes. But she was going to give herself the leeway to put away her worries for now—until the Kulcan scouts came back.

She'd face the music then.

Interlude I

The afterlife is a strange world.

Time stops. But only for me. I am suspended in time even though everything else moves on around me. But it doesn't matter. The sense of peace and calm from the chanting that brought me here is all that matters—all that I need in this endless world that I am in now.

I don't remember much. But I know I am dead.

Between my consciousness and my body exists a gulf that can never be bridged. I see through absent eyes. My soul is not mine. I—it—floats aimlessly through this dimension.

There are other souls in varying degrees of translucency. I wonder if I'm the same. But I can't see myself. I can see them. Their eyes all convey the same thing. The sense of loss, of being lost, of not knowing where the end is—all coexisting with an opposing awareness that this will continue beyond the end of time.

I wonder if I'm the same.

No one speaks. Do they *have their voices? Do* I *still have my voice? I'm not sure. We exchange glances in the silent acknowledgement that we have the same unspeakable dream we're waiting to realize. We've left something important behind. We can't move on. We are held captive in this strange dimension.*

7

Zej | Break

'Looks like it's deserted,' whispered Zej. He was leading his party of four—Dace was right behind him, followed by Alric, and then Seyfer—to the sewage plant outside of Atros's Sector M.

Zej was sure that every one of them was dealing with their own mixed feelings about returning to Atros after all that had happened in the past couple of months. Alric, Dace's father and a high-ranking member of Atros, had been thrown in a cell for defending his son's involvement in a crime; Dace had broken into one of Atros's most secure facilities with a group of rebels and foiled the organization's plans to build a human-ghost hybrid army. After a series of messy events, where Alric had been used as leverage over his son, he was incidentally saved by Iv't's massacre of the ExA soldiers in Tilsor. When Zej and his friends had come up with a plan for a group of them to head back to Atros to spy on ExA's advancement—so that they wouldn't be going into this 'save the world from ExA' war blind—Alric had volunteered to join them. In response to Dace's protests that he would only be delaying their progress, Alric had countered that he held sway over the Atrossian leadership. If Atros hadn't fallen to ExA, he could convince the Atros leaders that Zej and Dace, both of whom had been labelled as wanted criminals by Atros, were on their side.

Then there was Seyfer, the elite Atros soldier and a reluctant ally whose history with Keix and her friends was complex, to say the least. He was one of the first hybrids Atros had created, and he had been sent after Keix and her friends. But fate turned the tables on him and he was captured together with the rest of the hybrids and put up as sacrifice for the ritual to close the portal between the living and the dead. After the rites concluded, Seyfer had escaped and only resurfaced to ask (or rather extort, since he was holding Alric and Lana, who was Dace's girlfriend, as hostages at that point in time) Zej and his friends to help him get to Iv't; Atros was certain that getting the powerful Ifarl on their side was crucial in defeating ExA. Now that everyone had banded together to stand up against ExA, Zej couldn't tell how Seyfer felt about all of this; the elite soldier had remained mostly expressionless and quiet throughout their journey from Tilsor to Atros.

Even Dace, who was the chattiest of the group, hadn't spoken much in the past weeks. Although his father had managed to escape ExA's clutches, Lana had not. She had been killed in cold blood by ExA along with Zej's best friend, Pod.

Zej, who desperately wanted to block out the bloody image of Pod's death because he couldn't process why or how it had happened so suddenly, had shut his emotions down. He hadn't even put up a fight when Keix had broken up with him—if he could call it breaking up, since they had never been together in the first place—and told him to trust Dace's instinct on this mission. How had Dace earned Keix's trust in such a short time? The two of them had only first met at this abandoned sewage plant that Zej's group was currently entering. Zej had brought Keix to this temporary hideout after he had rescued her from the underwater prison in Atros's Paranormal Electromagnetic Energy Research Centre (or PEER for short).

At least Dace had never betrayed Keix the way you had, first joining a rebel group without telling her, then allowing the Ifarls to put her up as sacrifice for the ritual, said a disdainful voice inside Zej's head. He brushed the criticism aside and let the mental walls that he had built up around himself rise a little higher. His self-reproach was brought to a temporary halt when the subject of his ire spoke.

'Let's go in by this side door,' said Dace, gesturing to the left of where Zej was heading. He cast a glance behind him and explained to Alric, 'This was one of Oka's meeting places. I was stationed here to monitor Atros's surveillance feeds and would alert someone whenever I spotted abnormalities.'

Alric nodded and said, 'We know.'

We, thought Zej. Atros knew about this rendezvous point for Oka—which wasn't surprising, considering how their troopers had descended on the plant with Odats in tow to recapture Keix and take down Oka members. Zej had always assumed that Atros launched an attack on the plant because they had tracked Keix down, but Alric's tone implied that the information that Dace had volunteered wasn't new. *How long had they known, then?* Zej wanted to ask, but he held back, because the last thing he wanted to do was to butt into this awkward exchange. Alric and Dace had barely spoken to each other on the way to Atros. Zej knew Dace didn't have the best relationship with his father because of Alric's role in Atros and Dace's previous involvement with Oka—the rebel group that Zej had joined when he found out that Atros wasn't as righteous as they made themselves out to be—but the animosity seemed to be one-sided on Dace's end so far. Alric had been cooperative, even if he felt like a weird addition to the team—a huge, benign tumour that wasn't causing anyone any pain, but whose presence was apparent every step of the way.

'We knew about this place way back,' continued Alric. 'But there was never any need to interfere or to clamp down on what you guys were doing. Until . . .'

'Until Atros found out that we had Keix and were working with the Ifarls,' interrupted Zej.

Alric nodded. 'Keix's escape made us realize how vulnerable we were to attacks. We couldn't risk having the Ifarls close the portal because we knew that once there were no ghosts left to disrupt ExA's machines, they would advance on us rapidly.'

Just how much did Atros know, exactly? wondered Zej. Reflexively, he looked to Seyfer for answers. But the elite soldier's face was unreadable, as usual.

'Here,' interrupted Dace. 'Let's head in to talk.'

Zej made his way down the familiar spiral staircase. He had been here a handful of times. Dace was the one who knew this place like the back of his hand, having been assigned here on a longer-term basis.

Dust had settled in the control room situated at the bottom of the stairs. The chairs and coffee table had been knocked over from the Atros attack. Half of the screens mounted on the walls had fallen to the ground. The only pieces of furniture that had made it out relatively unscathed were the couch, which had been placed flush against one of the walls, and the tables at which Dace used to sit to monitor the surveillance footage.

'Let's talk about what we should do next, and if we should fire up the generators,' said Dace. 'Because once we do that, we run the risk of getting discovered by ExA, who seem to have taken over the city.' He was moving around and setting the furniture right, behaving as casually as if he were tidying up his house for some friends whom he had invited over. 'But if we don't, we will have no way of finding out what's happening inside Atros unless we sneak in.'

Alric, who looked exhausted, walked over to sit on the couch. Meanwhile, Zej parked himself at the foot of the stairs as he considered Dace's words. If this was a couple of months ago, Zej would have bristled at Dace's tone because he wouldn't have followed the lead of someone whom he felt had questionable morals—in other words, someone like Dace. But recent events had made him re-evaluate his own sense of self-superiority. Perhaps he himself was the one with skewed morality. The thought threatened to bring him to a new low again.

'Since we set off from Tilsor, we've not run into any ExA soldiers,' said Seyfer, taking a seat in the only chair that he had righted. 'But the boundary of Atros is crawling with them. And *Odats*.'

Zej shared Seyfer's disgust for the Odats. He had come across these mercenaries previously when he was working for Atros, which had hired them secretly to make up for the dwindling number of Atros soldiers. Now, these Odats were on the side of ExA, Atros's sworn enemy. The revulsion was clear in Zej's voice when he said, 'We can't stay holed up here forever. The best way to get into Atros might be through the underground sewage system, but we don't know if ExA has sent their soldiers or Odats to patrol the pipes or the areas where the manholes are located.' He was more than familiar with the network of pipes that ran through every Sector in Atros. Because heat signatures were hard to detect in these tunnels, he had used them often to get in and out of the city undetected when he was spying on Atros for Oka.

Come to think of it now, the reason why Atros left the network unguarded was because they didn't have enough troopers to cover the exits. But ExA was clearly different. Zej didn't even want to imagine how much resources they had to be able to employ so many Odats to patrol the boundary of Atros.

'If we can't get into Atros,' started Seyfer, whose brows were snapped together in concentration, 'we won't be able to get any information, which means this trip is basically wasted. Not to mention, if we don't get any intel beforehand, by the time ExA decides to move towards Tilsor, or anywhere else for that matter, we'll be too late.'

'Even if we manage to get our hands on a hovercar, we might not be able to get to Tilsor in time either,' agreed Zej.

'But if using the underground pipes to sneak into Atros is out of the question, it might be an even bigger challenge to get past the guards at the borders,' piped up Dace. 'We've observed their patrols for the past few days, and there is no lapse or gap that we can take advantage of to get into the city centre. That's where most of the action is taking place, I would presume.'

Zej nodded. 'The patrols are even tighter than the ones I've seen during Atros's rule,' he said as he racked his head for a workaround or solution.

'There's something you haven't tried,' came Alric's deep, gravelly voice from the side of the room. 'One of you can pretend that you've captured me, and that should get you into—'

'No!' interrupted Dace. 'It's too dangerous. We don't know what ExA will do to you if . . .'

Zej took a deep breath and bit his lower lip as the crease between Seyfer's brows deepened. From a purely objective point of view, Zej thought that Alric's suggestion not only made sense, but it might also be their best course of action right now. ExA would be looking to eliminate the leaders of the previous government now that they had taken over the city. And the old Zej, the one who prioritized mission goals over everything else, would have taken Alric up on his suggestion in a heartbeat. But Keix's last words to him before they parted ways were still ringing in his head . . . *Trust Dace's instincts.* Zej glanced towards the subject of his conundrum, who had taken a seat on one of the chairs too, and saw that his gaze was filled with a mixture of panic, anger, and resignation. Dace's response was probably born out of an instinctual fear of losing another loved one instead of a desire to take down ExA, but Zej decided to take his side anyway. 'Dace is right,' he said firmly. 'We don't know what ExA would do to you if you were to fall into their hands. We'll find another way in.'

'Actually,' interrupted Seyfer tentatively, 'there might be another way in—that doesn't require any of us to be bait.' He stood up and stalked towards the table that was right next to the couch. On it was a small container filled with gum, which had miraculously survived the violent confrontation that had happened here. He picked up a few pieces of the candy and scattered it across the dust-covered table. Then, he repeated the action with another batch of candies.

Alric remained in his seat but turned his body slightly so he could see Seyfer better.

Dace made his way to stand beside Seyfer and picked up a piece of gum. 'Ah, fond memories. Kaplan used to hate it whenever I popped gum while we were on duty together,' he reminisced, unwrapping the candy and popping it into his mouth. 'Wonder how he's doing now . . . if he's still alive.'

Zej, in the meantime, had moved from his spot at the staircase to get a better view of what Seyfer was doing. He wasn't the most familiar with Kaplan. They had crossed paths several times, but Zej never knew how to interact with him because Kaplan was one of the most awkward people Zej had met in Oka. Kaplan also lacked combat skills, so Zej didn't think that he would have survived the raid that day. He couldn't be sure though, because he hadn't seen any bodies on their way in. There was no way there had been no casualties; someone—likely Atros or ExA—must have cleaned up this place after.

Seyfer, who paid no heed to Dace's blabbering, clustered the pieces of gum on the table into four groups. 'Security is tight, as you guys have said, but I think there may be a gap that we can take advantage of,' he said, shifting the gum around.

Zej leaned forward, intrigued to know what Seyfer had discovered that he and Dace had not managed to.

'Security changes shifts four times a day, every six hours,' continued Seyfer. 'The transitions happen pretty smoothly, but have you noticed that there tends to be a little more talking and handover going on when the two night shifts swop duties?' He put two groups of gum together, then split them again and moved them around in a manner that reflected the movement of the soldiers that they had observed so far.

'But that's not the best time to take them unawares. Because the night shift guards are more vigilant compared to the ones on the morning shifts . . .'

Zej's eyes widened. Now that Seyfer had pointed this out . . . 'And there's this particular pair of guards who tends to linger in the security post for longer than the others!' said Zej in a rush.

Seyfer nodded, but Dace looked sceptical as he asked, 'How do you know that it's always the same pair? The guards are wearing helmets now, and the Odats look pretty much the same.'

'We can't be sure,' replied Seyfer. 'But if we get the systems up and running to access the surveillance footage, we might be able to confirm our suspicions and see if there's really a gap in the patrol that we can take advantage of. Perhaps we can even create a distraction to buy ourselves enough time to get into the city. But in case this option doesn't pan out, we should be able to check if the entrances to the underground pipe system are really guarded. If they aren't, Zej could lead us into Atros through the pipes. Of course, the best-case scenario is that we're able to get all the information that we need from accessing this footage, and we can head back to Tilsor to share with the rest what we found without having to step foot into Atros.'

Zej and Dace exchanged glances, then nods. They were too far along in their mission to head back to Tilsor empty-handed.

* * *

The tapping sounds of keyboards filled the air as Zej, Seyfer, and Dace tried to focus on breaking back into the system. Despite the noise, Alric, who had fallen asleep on the sofa, didn't move a muscle at all. His chest rose and fell steadily as his breathing remained measured and deep. The breakneck pace at which they had travelled back to Atros must have taken a toll on the middle-aged man.

Dace had managed to power up one of the smallest generators in the plant. It was enough to operate the machines in the control room to minimize the disturbance so that they could stay off ExA's radar for as long as possible.

As it turned out, ExA had the good sense to reconfigure parts of Atros's systems, so the previous method of tapping into the surveillance feeds of the borders no longer worked. They had to find another way to access the footage they needed.

Dace grunted in frustration. 'If only Pod—' he started before he stopped short.

Zej's fingers froze over his keyboard. If only Pod was here . . . Zej wished he had the right to voice out this thought too. Hearing his friend's name dredged up all the thoughts that Zej had fought hard to keep buried. Pod. His best friend whom he had unwittingly sent to his death. It had all happened so fast that even now, Zej couldn't fully comprehend how things had spiralled out of control back in Tilsor.

After they escaped from the ExA soldiers who had held them captive, they had found that all the paths were being routed into a particular Square. There, they saw Keix and the rest, and before they knew it, they had been outnumbered and captured by ExA.

Vin and a woman with a mussed-up ponytail had then thrown something at the soldiers that made some of them catch fire, and caused some others to scream and claw at their skins in pain. The next second, one of the ExA soldiers had impaled Lana through her chest with the blade that was attached to their hand. Dace was the first to react, kicking out at his captor, but that triggered the ExA soldier holding on to Pod to kill him in the same gruesome way.

Seeing the blade protruding from Pod's chest had brought Zej's world crumbling down in slow motion. He had always subscribed to logic in every aspect of his life. That was why he could understand why Atros was doing experiments on the people they had captured, even if he didn't agree with it; to Atros, everything that they did was a step towards their goal of creating a hybrid army. Their destination couldn't be clearer. Things were done systematically, and no one was killed needlessly. They were sacrificed when they had to be, but no one was ever murdered in spite—or at least that's what Zej used to believe.

But Atros seemed tame next to the ExA soldiers, who had no qualms about hurting anyone who got in their way.

No, don't you try to push the blame to ExA. Pod's no longer around because of you. Because you chose to put everyone's life on the line. Because, to you, Atros's survival was more important than the individual lives of your friends and the people you pretend to care about, an anguished voice in his head lambasted him. He tried to shake off the guilt, but he couldn't stop his breathing from becoming shallow and rapid.

Yes, if Pod were around, they might have gotten the information they needed and more, just seconds after the generator was powered up. Pod was *that* good.

'Look,' said Seyfer breathlessly. 'It seems that ExA hasn't reworked too much of the system's security or managed to go that deep into Atros.' His fingers flew over his keyboard, and even though he had none of Pod's practised ease, the fact that he was able to gather this much information was a testament to his skills.

'How do you know that?' asked Zej, wondering what kind of training Atros's elite soldiers really went through. He wasn't sure that without Seyfer, they would have made it this far.

'Here.' Seyfer pointed to two of the screens which were still mounted on the wall in front of him as he pulled up surveillance footage of the entrance to PEER. The all-white interiors of the corridors that weren't supposed to be on the system officially showed up on the screen. Zej remembered these passages all too well. He used to walk through them every single day when he was a trooper. It was in one of these sterile tunnels that he saw Keix, who had been declared dead. That incident prompted him to dig deeper into what Atros was doing, which subsequently led to him joining the rebel group Oka. To gain entry to these levels, ExA would first need to know of their existence. But judging from the deserted feed, ExA either hadn't managed to get access to these places, or they didn't know that this part of the institute existed.

'Is this live?' asked Zej.

Seyfer nodded. 'But the connection's not that great, as you can tell from the flickering,' he said. As if to substantiate his statement, the image flickered into nothing except static. This breakthrough seemed to have reinvigorated him as he continued banging away at the keyboard. 'I'm going to comb through every bit of surveillance footage starting from the city centre to see if I can find anything,' he explained.

But as expected, many feeds were no longer available. ExA must have killed all the cameras or created another system to host these streams. The only footage Seyfer managed to get were of deserted alleyways in the other Sectors that looked to be abandoned now. Where was everyone? It seemed like all the Atrossians had vanished into thin air. If that was the case, why was ExA guarding an empty city?

Zej fell silent, trying to work through the possibilities in his head. His thoughts were interrupted when Dace stood up abruptly and declared to no one in particular, 'I'm going to take a breather.'

Alric didn't stir from his slumber and Seyfer, who was so focused on his task, ignored Dace too.

Zej watched Dace leave the room and felt a sudden burst of panic. The incessant clicking of Seyfer's keyboard pounded away at Zej's skull, threatening to tear the composure that he'd tried to hold together apart. He stood up abruptly and said, 'I'm gonna . . .' before trailing off. It wouldn't sound right to say that he was going after

Dace. To his surprise, Seyfer stopped typing and turned back to cast an inscrutable glance at him.

Then, Seyfer's gaze flicked to the sleeping Alric and then back to Zej. 'Yeah, go ahead,' he said mildly. 'Keep an eye on him just in case he does something unpredictable and dangerous.'

As Zej turned on his heel to head down the corridor, he thought he heard Seyfer sigh in resignation. By the time he regained sight of Dace's retreating back, they were halfway up a flight of stairs. The steps led to a watchtower situated at the northeast end of the compound.

When Dace reached the top of the stairs and walked over to the area overlooking Atros, Zej strode up right next to him and crossed his arms. They were at the highest spot in the sewage plant, and it offered an unobstructed view of a large portion of Sector M's borders.

Zej would have been worried about getting seen by ExA soldiers if not for the fact that it was the deepest point of the night and the sky was overcast. There was barely any illumination for anyone to see them. Similarly, they also couldn't see into the Sector, which was dark, either. It was only because of his familiarity with the city that Zej managed to catch sight of a couple of soldiers—barely larger than specks of dust at this distance—patrolling the dimly lit borders.

After a length of time where neither of them spoke, Dace said, 'I don't need a babysitter.' When Zej didn't reply, he asked, 'What's the point of all this?'

What's the point of all this? The question echoed in Zej's head. It was something that he hadn't dared to ask himself. He wanted to say that this was all to save the innocent lives that were caught in the middle of the struggle for power between ExA and Atros. That this was all for freedom. For the freedom to live without fear. But . . . was it really? Sacrificing one innocent life to save many other innocent lives—the math used to make sense to him. But recently, he had been rethinking the logic. What was it that Dace had said to him previously?

It hits differently, doesn't it? When the person whose life is on the line is someone so close to your heart.

Pod's death scene made its way into Zej's head again, and he felt as if he was the one who was getting skewered through the heart.

Dace was right. Dace had been right all this time.

It was Zej's fault. It was his fault that Pod had died. He tried to shake away the image of Pod's final moments, but it was seared in his mind's eye. His chest heaved as he gulped down air, but it still felt as if he were suffocating. Panicking, he tried to conjure up another image of Pod, laughing and joking. Pod was always happy, amicable. Zej wanted—no, needed—Zej *needed* to see the Pod he knew. He had to see that Pod again. Not the Pod who looked shocked, bloodied. Not Pod dying. Dead. No.

'It's survival, isn't it?' Dace said.

Was Dace answering a question? Or posing one to Zej?

Zej couldn't, for the life of him, follow this conversation. Was it even supposed to be a dialogue?

Dace, who hadn't sensed Zej's lack of comprehension, continued, 'It's always been survival! First, we were trying to survive ExA's greed. Then, we were trying to survive the opening of the portal because of Iv't's anger. Now, we're back to trying to survive ExA's quest to take over the world again!' Dace paused, then let loose a humourless laugh.

None of what was happening registered in Zej's mind. His vision turned dark and blurry. He was panting even harder now. His eyelids slid shut and he fell forward onto his knees. There was a shrill ringing in his ears that drowned out everything. Someone tugged him up by his shirt collar and shook him, as if trying to pull him to his feet and get him to cooperate. His cheeks smarted. Wait . . . did someone just slap him? He had to fight back. He couldn't see a thing, but he was pretty sure that he could still throw a punch. And that was exactly what he did. He didn't know what or whom he was aiming at, but by instinct, he swung his fist. It made contact with something hard, and pain shot up his arm at the impact, clearing his vision for a moment, bringing him back to his senses. That's when he saw that he had punched Dace in the jaw. He hadn't meant to do that. He was about to apologize when Dace muttered a curse and returned the favour. This time, the pain, which originated from Zej's jaw, was intense enough to really pull him out of his head. The horrifying image of Pod was driven out, but the guilt remained. And because of this, he didn't resist when Dace punched him again. The force sent him flying to the ground, where he lay unmoving, his eyes burning with tears.

'Get up,' Dace bit out.

Zej ignored him. No. He wasn't going to get up. He refused to.

'I. Said. Get. Up.' Dace tried to haul him to his feet once more. When the attempt failed, Dace shook him like a rag doll. 'You have no right to wallow in self-pity! You brought this on yourself!'

A crack sounded through the air when Dace slapped Zej again, snapping his head to the side. A burning sensation engulfed Zej's right cheek, and he tasted blood in his mouth. Good. He deserved it. He craved the punishing pain. A couple of hits wasn't enough to drive away this debilitating feeling intensifying within him. That's why he let Dace straddle him and grab both his shoulders, to shake him while yelling, 'Fight back! Come on!'

Zej closed his eyes. If he could anger Dace enough, Dace might just kill him right here and now. Then, he wouldn't have to live out the rest of his life being remorseful.

Dace let go of his shoulders and gave him another slap. And another. And another . . .

All Zej did was smile and revel in the pain. But after a while, the blows gradually became lighter, until . . . something wet landed on Zej's burning cheek. Before he could register that Dace was crying, Dace's weight had collapsed fully on him.

'Why?' Dace's choked sob sounded right beside his ear.

'Why?' Zej repeated in a whisper.

Even though the both of them uttered the same word, the answers they were seeking couldn't be more different.

Zej let Dace's heaving cries wash over him. He had no idea when he himself started crying, shedding tears that he didn't even know he had been bottling up.

Dace had lost his lover.

Zej had lost his treasured friend.

Lana and Pod had died within seconds of each other because of someone else's vendetta and greed.

Enveloped in this cocoon of remorse and self-pity that they had spun for themselves, Zej and Dace couldn't hear anything but the reproaching voices in their heads. They were only jolted back to reality when they heard Seyfer's disapproving voice.

'Any time the two of you are done feeling sorry for yourselves, I've got something to show you,' he said.

In an instant, Dace scrambled to get himself off Zej. The two of them stood up, embarrassed and perplexed.

Zej rubbed his tear-stained face with his shirt and cast his gaze around to see that the clouds had dispersed. Dawn was approaching. How long had he and Dace been here, at the rooftop? And how loud a racket had they made? Could any of the ExA soldiers patrolling the borders have heard them?

Wordlessly, Dace brushed past Seyfer to head down the stairs.

Zej followed suit and came face to face with an unsmiling Seyfer. When he walked past Seyfer, the elite Atros trooper hissed in disgust, 'You're in this state because you lack conviction. If you were committed enough, you wouldn't feel this way.'

8

Zej | Infiltration

When Zej and Dace returned to the control room, Alric was already sitting at the desk typing away at the keyboard. He still looked a bit worse for wear, but the short rest that he had taken had put some colour back into his face.

At Zej's questioning gaze, Seyfer explained, 'Alric's clearance level is higher than mine. We decided to try to see if it could help us get into more systems that the ExA hasn't managed to reconfigure yet.'

'Did it work?' asked Zej.

Seyfer didn't answer his question directly. Instead, he stepped right up to Alric's side and said, 'Come and see what we found.'

Alric spun around in his chair to face Zej and Dace while he started, 'What ha—' He stopped short when he took in the sight of both Dace and Zej's sullen expressions and swollen eyes.

Zej worked his jaw and grimaced in pain. Spectacular bruises were going to appear on his cheeks soon, if they hadn't already. It was a miracle that Dace hadn't knocked his jaw loose.

'Er . . . what was I going to say?' stuttered Alric as he cleared his throat. 'Right. ExA. ExA has shut down most of the surveillance feeds. But like Seyfer found out, they still haven't managed to get into the lesser-known systems such as the labyrinths within ATI and other important buildings—probably because they haven't figured out how to get into these places . . .'

'Or they don't need to,' chimed in Seyfer. 'Because the main parts of the buildings—we haven't managed to access the cameras in these areas—are sufficient for their purposes.'

Zej's eyes widened. He had never heard of the laboratories, where the experiments to turn humans into hybrids were conducted, being referred to as labyrinths. What was even more surprising was finding out that the underground facility that he had always thought was unique to PEER was also built into other buildings.

'So, while we gained access to these surveillance cameras in the labyrinths and other "secretive places" in Atros, we still can't ascertain what's happening in the city right now,' said Seyfer.

Dace, whose eyes were still puffy, asked in an exasperated manner, 'You mean we're back to square one after going through all this trouble?'

Alric and Seyfer exchanged a significant look. When Alric gave Seyfer the slightest nod, the elite Atros soldier said, 'No, not exactly. We managed to hack back into the feeds of the surveillance cameras that Atros had on the street levels of the different Sectors and . . . everywhere else looks deserted too.'

'Everywhere?' exclaimed Zej as he frowned in confusion. 'Why aren't the streets crawling with ExA soldiers and Odats like the borders?'

Seyfer shook his head. At the same time, Alric tapped on the keyboard and brought up a series of videos. At the top left corner of every frame was a timestamp that was familiar to all of them.

With his gaze moving from one screen to another, as if he were trying to decipher a puzzle, Dace asked, 'Could these live streams be faked?'

'Yes, but it's unlikely,' replied Alric. 'There doesn't seem to be a point to fake them. Seyfer and I went through many of them just now, and although there's no obvious movement, there are telltale signs such as a change in lighting, as if the clouds obscuring the moon have moved away or vice versa. Look at this screen right here'—he pointed at one of the bottom screens—'you can see the reflection of the rising sun in some of the buildings' windows.'

Zej tried to wrap his head around this new revelation. Atros's population had been steadily declining from as far back as he remembered because people kept dying during the ghost attacks, but the city had never reached a point where it looked as uninhabited as this. 'How about the city centre?' he asked. That used to be the highest-trafficked area in Atros.

Seyfer shook his head and pulled up more footage that showed a handful of figures walking along the streets. If not for their attire and the weapons they were carrying, they could have been mistaken for Atrossians who were out on an early-morning stroll. 'There's a healthy number of ExA soldiers, as well as Odats, patrolling the streets in the city centre—though the frequency of patrols isn't as high as the one at the borders,' supplemented Seyfer.

'But the thing is, there are no signs of any Atrossians on the streets. Alric and I tried to access other systems to see if we could glean any clues as to what's happening in Atros. And the only thing we found is that ExA is generating at least quadruple the amount of electricity and energy that Atros used to,' said Seyfer.

Alric jumped in to continue, 'And this is getting channelled to Atros's main buildings such as PEER and ATI—which makes sense if they're setting up bases in these places. But what we can't figure out is why the bulk of this energy is being sent to abandoned factories situated in the different Sectors.'

'Wha—w-why?' Zej's confusion intensified with the sudden deluge of information.

'Could ExA be manufacturing more machines in these factories? If that's the case, what kinds of weapons are they making?' asked Dace evenly.

'Any guesses that we make will just be a stab in the dark because we can't access the cameras in and around those abandoned factories,' replied Seyfer. 'But from what we've seen and encountered of ExA, it's not a long shot to say that they are manufacturing weapons to be embedded in the soldiers' bodies.'

Having finally sorted out his thoughts and caught up with the flow of the conversation, Zej asked, 'Why would they need so much energy to create those blades and machine parts?'

Alric's expression was solemn as he answered, 'It's unlikely those are the only weapons they are making. You guys remember droids, right?'

Dace and Zej nodded. Droids were humanoid machines that ExA used to produce to do all sorts of manual work. But ghosts unleashed into the world after the portal between the living and the dead was opened caused these machines to malfunction and fatally harm Atrossians. Thus, Atros's new leaders had dismantled all of them and put them out of commission after they chased ExA out of the city.

After a long silence, Zej said, 'So, ExA is manufacturing a robot army? But this is all only conjecture. We won't know unless we see it for ourselves. And going back to Tilsor with this information doesn't seem useful at all.'

'Agreed,' said Seyfer. 'Which is why we should try to get into the city to confirm our suspicions. Back in Tilsor, we've already discussed the different ways in which things could unfold, and this is the worst-case scenario—ExA having taken over the city and preparing for some sort of huge battle plan to enslave everyone. It would be counterintuitive for us to head back to convey a message that everyone had seen coming.' He looked at Dace, then Alric, and added, 'But Alric could—'

'I'm going with you,' Alric interrupted Seyfer with a firm rejection. 'I'm not as young and spry as you youngsters, but my experience might come in handy. Besides, we'll likely have a better chance of surviving if we stick together.'

Both Zej and Seyfer looked to Dace, but when he shrugged as if to imply that Alric was his own man, the two outsiders didn't deem it appropriate to say more.

'So, what's the best way to get into Atros? Through Zej's sewage pipes?' asked Dace.

'Yes, that is most likely it, seeing as security within the Sectors isn't that tight,' said Seyfer, tapping on the keyboard to bring down all the footage from the screens. Then, he turned back to Zej and Dace, looking more serious than ever. 'But we need to act fast, because of what I'm going to show you next.' As he spoke, he tapped a key, and all the functioning screens flashed to black. White text appeared against the dark background.

Alric explained as Zej and Dace frowned at the screen. 'I decided to access this outdated system that Atros used to send confidential, encrypted messages to each other. It hasn't been used in almost a decade, but I thought I'd check on it because I didn't want to miss out on anything.'

The room fell silent and Zej's eyes grew rounder as he deciphered the mass—and mess—of messages. Even Dace looked shocked as his eyes rapidly tracked through the texts, his thorny attitude forgotten.

The correspondences were arranged in a chronological order, even though the contents read like the messages had been sent intermittently. After half a minute, Zej finally tracked down the earliest message of consequence. He pointed to it in case Dace was still searching for it.

Team 271: Odats have increased in numbers in the past two days in Sector D.

Team 174: ExA just rounded up the last group of citizens in Sector K. It's all emptied out. I would say it's a ghost town here except there'd actually be more activity if the ghosts were around.

Team 341: Would take on a ghost army over ExA and Odats combined any day.

Team 228: Sector J's empty now too.

Team 271: They're keeping the people in the production plants, making more weapons. Those are the only buildings that are hives of activity. But they're so heavily guarded no one knows what goes on inside them.

Team 228: Sorry for the radio silence. We almost didn't make it out of the building when ExA raided it. Met three other people, but they didn't want to join us. They said that moving around in a bigger group would draw more attention.

Team 271: Do they know about us?

Team 228: They do now. I told them how to access this system, but it's getting harder to find terminals within the Sectors. Took us ages to find this one and we'll be on the move soon.

These messages, as well as the dozens that followed, corroborated Alric and Seyfer's findings. A handful of these teams were clearly more active than the rest, but whatever resistance these people had put up, it wasn't going well.

Zej took a deep breath and continued scanning through the messages.

Team 271: Haven't heard from Team 341 in a while . . . Two possibilities. One, they escaped and are on their way to look for backup. Two, they haven't been able to find a terminal.

Team 174: Three, they got caught and we can assume that they're dead.

Team 271: Thanks for the optimism.

Team 174: We're running out of food supplies. It's do or die now.

Team 228: We're also running out of places to hide.

The messages got increasingly darker as Zej read on. Soon, he saw Team 174 telling everyone to check this space at a certain date and time, and his blood froze when he came to the very last line of text on the screen.

Team 174: Sector A. Tomorrow night. 0400 hours. Teams ending with odd numbers will surface and create a distraction in Sector A, and one half of the rest will try to escape from Sector L. The other half will try to escape from Sector M.

'Wait . . . this . . .' said Zej, pointing to this message and asked, 'When was this sent?'

Looking directly into his eyes, Seyfer said, 'Three days ago.'

Zej blanched. They hadn't encountered anyone on their way here, and from the footage that they had seen, ExA was operating as if nothing major had happened in the past couple of days. If those who were planning to escape from Sector M had been successful, there was a very small chance that it would be so peaceful right now. The sudden surge of anger within himself took him by surprise and he blurted out, 'How did they plan on going up against ExA? They were outnumbered and the only thing they managed to do was send themselves straight into death's jaws!'

'They were desperate. Otherwise, why would anyone take such a drastic step?' said Dace quietly.

Ever the practical elite Atros soldier, Seyfer said, 'This also means that ExA is more concerned about people leaving Atros than anyone entering. That's what the patrols at the borders are for—to keep people in rather than out.'

Alric's voice was measured as he said, 'And if this rebellion—regardless of its scale—really happened yesterday, ExA would be focusing on rounding up any stragglers. Which means that this is the perfect time to infiltrate into the city.'

Seyfer crossed his arms and nodded in agreement.

Zej didn't know why, but Dace suddenly seemed more determined than ever.

'So, what's the plan?' asked Dace. 'We enter the underground pipe system from the entrance that's nearest to this sewage plant?'

'It's one of the most obscure entrances to the underground pipes,' replied Zej. 'But it's a risk getting there because there's no cover around the area. And it's light now.' He frowned in concentration as he ran through different possibilities in his head. 'How about the one outside Sector J? We can get to its vicinity under the cover of the woods from here, and the open area it's set in is much smaller.'

'We'll need time to travel there, and it's also a lot nearer to the Atros border,' said Alric, shaking his head. He took down the depressing messages on the screens and drew up some more surveillance footage. 'Look. It's crawling with Odats and ExA soldiers. The risk of getting caught is the same—if not higher—comparing both options.'

'Should we wait till night since it's already daybreak now?' asked Dace.

Both Seyfer and Alric shook their heads. 'The longer we drag this out, the less of an advantage we have.'

Zej, who was deep in thought, was silent for a while before he finally said, 'In that case, we should leave immediately. Because if we're going in through the pipes, it's going to take us seventeen hours, at least, to get into Atros from here.'

* * *

'This way up,' said Zej, gesturing to one of the exits leading out of the sewage pipes. They had reached Sector A, one of the closest Sectors to Atros's city centre.

Their fourteen-hour-long trek had been uneventful. As they had predicted, ExA wasn't really taking much notice of what was going on outside their borders. Zej's two main concerns—one, ExA had noticed the ruckus from the fight that he and Dace had had, and two, that the journey to the entrance of the sewage pipes was too exposed—turned out to be unfounded.

'Are you sure about this?' Seyfer's voice was pinched. This was one of the few times that Zej had seen the elite soldier huffing—probably because all of them were trying their darnedest to breathe in as little of the revolting air in the underground tunnels as possible.

Seyfer was the one who had suggested that they enter Sector A through the pipes. The Sectors just next to the city centre, where they suspected ExA had set up base, were home to not only more buildings, but also taller ones compared to the outlying Sectors. These structures could provide better cover from ExA soldiers.

When Zej's group opened the manhole cover to enter the pipes, there was a rotten stench that had gushed out from within. The sewage pipes smelled unpleasant—that was a foregone conclusion. But they had never smelled of death. Zej had only managed to prevent himself from regurgitating the contents of his stomach because he hadn't eaten much to begin with. And when he looked at the rest of his company, especially Seyfer, he knew that the same thing was running through their minds. There must be corpses in the underground pipes. *A lot* of them. No one said a word when they climbed down the ladder. Their worst suspicions were confirmed when they saw a bunch of bodies floating in the shallow waters. At first glance, a niggling voice at the back of Zej's head had told him that there was something off about the corpses. It was only when the tracking lights lining the inside of the pipes flickered a bit brighter that he saw that all of them were missing their hands and feet.

What was ExA doing?!

'Yeah, he's sure,' interjected Dace in answer to Seyfer's question. 'Zej knows these pipes like the back of his hand. Needed the knowledge to sneak in and out of Atros to deliver information to Oka. He's a great spy.'

Zej's nape prickled. He had gotten used to Dace's digs at him, but after being caught sobbing together yesterday—an incident that neither of them had brought up again—something in their relationship seemed to have shifted. Now, even though Dace's words sounded sarcastic, it was almost like the sarcasm was directed at Seyfer instead of Zej.

'Well, I'm glad for his knowledge, then,' replied Seyfer formally. He looked at Zej, then back at Dace, and added in a measured tone, 'We may have been on opposite sides previously, but we're working towards a common goal, so I'd appreciate it if you'd tone down the hostility towards me.' Getting stuck in the pipes must have gotten on Seyfer's nerves because Zej had never seen him act this way before. Finding out that ExA had taken over the city probably hadn't lifted his spirits either.

'What can I say? I'm good at holding grudges,' said Dace.

'The enemy of my enemy is my friend,' intoned Alric, who was bringing up the rear. He sounded like he was chastising his son.

'Yeah, yeah. I know. My *friends*,' drawled Dace in reply.

Since Zej was leading the way, he was the first to reach the top of the ladder. He tried to use one hand to shift the manhole cover to the side, but it refused to budge. The rungs were narrow and could only fit one person at a time. Even though the covers were heavy, he used to be able to move them from the inside without much trouble. The past few months of being on the run and not eating proper meals, coupled with the light-headedness that he was feeling right now, must have made him weaker.

'Do you want me to do it instead?' called Seyfer from below him.

'Let me try again,' insisted Zej. This time, he bent his knees slightly, then straightened his legs to use the momentum generated to lift the cover.

A loud scraping noise echoed through the tunnels as the manhole cover edged to the side from the sudden force.

Everyone froze, expecting ExA to rush towards the cause of the disturbance. But after a minute passed with no signs of movement from the outside, a little bit of the tension left Zej's shoulders.

'Move to the side just a little,' came Seyfer's voice from below Zej.

When Zej did as requested, Seyfer made his way up the rungs to stand shoulder to shoulder with him. It was a squeeze, but they both managed to get a hand each on the manhole cover.

'Right. On the count of three. One, two, three,' counted Zej.

With Seyfer's help, the cover was lifted and moved to the side with minimal noise this time around.

The quartet exited the pipes and emerged into a ghost town. It was exactly like what the messages had described and what the footage had shown. Sector A was deathly quiet. Its proximity to the always-bustling hub, which was the city centre, had meant that there was always some kind of activity going on throughout the day, and even deep into the night.

It was night now, and the glare from the street lamps spotlighted the lack of action. Windows painted black by the absence of light in the apartment buildings were like soulless eyes. And vehicles lay like neatly lined corpses at the sides of the roads. Using the buildings as cover, the four of them made their way in the direction of the city centre. Once in a while, as Zej and his group moved from one side of the road to the other, he would catch a glint of light reflected in the panes, and the structure would come alive for a split second, like a menacing monster stirring in the midst of its deep slumber.

'Should we keep going?' whispered Seyfer after they crossed yet another road junction. After this street, there would barely be any cover for them as they approach the invisible line that divided Sector A from the city centre.

'Let's keep going,' said Zej.

'We can find an empty unit in one of the high-rises if there's still time,' suggested Seyfer, gesturing to a cluster of tall buildings in the distance. 'It'll give us a better vantage point to observe what's going on.'

Everyone nodded in agreement. Fatigue was apparent in their eyes, but so was determination. There really was no turning back once they made a run for it.

Dace glanced in his dad's direction. 'You sure you want to come along?'

'Worry about yourselves.'

Zej could tell that Alric was pleased by Dace's concern even as he waved it off.

'I'll go first,' said Seyfer.

'Right behind you,' confirmed Dace.

'I'll be the last,' said Zej, indicating that Alric should be between Dace and him.

Once they stepped out of the shadows, Seyfer lengthened his strides and picked up his pace. Zej couldn't help but feel a little envious of the speed at which Seyfer sprinted despite having just trekked for almost an entire day. Dace, who was as tall as Seyfer, also lagged behind the elite trooper.

Zej adjusted his pace, so he was on Alric's heels. He could hear the man's laboured breathing as he tried to keep up with his son.

The open field wasn't huge, and within minutes, the four of them had covered about two-thirds the distance to the city centre.

Just as Zej considered their next course of action, now that they looked to be able to make it into the city centre without a hitch, he heard a series of hisses. Alric, who was right in front of him, stumbled and fell over.

'Alric!' Zej gasped as he immediately bent over to help Dace's father. But when he grabbed Alric's arm and tried to haul him up, he realized that Alric hadn't tripped over but was instead, out cold. Yet, he wasn't bleeding and didn't have any visible wounds on him.

Dace, who had heard the commotion, turned and ran back. 'What happened? Dad?' he asked anxiously, huffing as he helped Zej pull Alric to his feet.

Seyfer, who was way ahead of them, caught up to what was happening and was about to turn around too when Zej hissed at him, 'No! Don't!'

There was no way Zej and Dace would leave Alric behind, but if Seyfer was also held back, their chances of ever succeeding in their mission would be forfeited too. 'Just keep going!' shouted Zej. He didn't see any point in keeping a low profile now that ExA had zeroed in on them. Working together to carry an unconscious Alric, Dace and Zej continued to move in an erratic manner to avoid the tiny, unidentifiable ammunition being shot at them while searching for the nearest cover and escape route.

From his peripheral vision, Zej could see that Seyfer was running towards the city centre on their originally planned route.

'Left,' yelled Dace when they came to a crossroad.

Zej followed his directions without hesitation.

But when they took the turn, they came face to face with a squarish machine that was hovering in mid-air. Immediately, it started spitting out bullets at them.

Dace, who had slowed down in shock, was hit by a couple of the flying objects.

In a split second, both Alric and Dace had become dead weight, dragging Zej down as his knees buckled. Finally, it dawned on him what the 'bullets' were: syringes containing sedatives that Atros used. But his realization had come too late as something pierced through the skin on his neck. Before he fell unconscious, he saw Seyfer, who was about to cross into the city centre, stumbling forward too.

9

Zej | Captive

Zej woke up in an eerily familiar environment. Blinding fluorescent white light. White walls. White ceiling, except for a little silver circle that was the air-circulation vent. The smell of disinfectant in the air. His entire body ached and his shoulder hurt like hell. He looked down at himself. He had been stripped of all his clothes. Both his wrists and ankles were weighed down by something cool—metal bracelets about two fingers wide encircled each of his wrists and ankles. The contraptions seemed custom-made, fitting snugly without biting into his skin.

A deep chill set into his bones.

Everything that he had seen in the underground pipes made sense now. His new 'accessories' must contain some sort of retractable blades; that was why the bodies in the pipes had stumps for their wrists and ankles . . .

'Dace . . .' Zej's throat burned as the word escaped him.

Dace had been caught together with him. So had Alric and Seyfer. Where were they now? Had they been sent to this facility too? Zej had to find out. He looked around and saw that he was in a cell simply furnished with a bed, a toilet, and an overhead shower. He staggered to the shower, turned on the faucet, and gasped as ice-cold water rained on him. In record time, he had scrubbed off the grime on his body with the small bar of soap provided. Now, he smelled just like his cell.

After he pulled on the bright orange outfit—short-sleeved shirt with matching pants—that had been left for him, he heard some scuffling sounds coming from one of the walls. He walked towards it and a door that he hadn't noticed before—because it was the same exact shade of white as the walls—slid open.

Wait . . . his cell was unlocked?

He shook his head to clear his confusion. Whatever the case, one fewer locked door meant one step closer to freedom—or so he thought.

Zej stepped out into a long and wide corridor, and his jaw dropped at the sight that greeted him. At every ten-step interval was a wall-mounted screen playing footage of a man wearing a similar bright orange outfit; the man was strapped to one of the narrow benches that Atros used to keep people from thrashing around as they experimented with them.

The video had no narration, but its warning was clear. And Zej, having already put two and two together, could predict what would happen next.

True enough, without warning, the man let out a high-pitched scream, wide-eyed and shocked, as the metal contraptions activated with a loud click, and both his hands and feet detached from his body and dropped to the ground; the metal bracelets and anklets followed soon after, with the loudest squelches and clunks Zej had ever heard in his life.

Zej's mind blanked and he didn't even react when someone bumped his shoulder and whispered next to his ear, 'Hey, you new here?'

Even though Zej didn't reply, the man continued as if Zej had answered him. 'That's just to scare people to prevent them from trying to escape. I've watched it millions of times and it still gives me goosebumps.'

The man's frankness grounded Zej's thoughts as he pulled himself out of the abyss that kept beckoning to him. He blinked rapidly to get his vision back into focus and sized up the person in front of him. The man, who looked to be in his late twenties, gave off vibes that reminded Zej of Seyfer. He had wavy, black hair that was pushed back from his face, accentuating a pair of long, narrow eyes and high cheekbones. His smile made him look friendly enough, but it didn't mask the air of intimidation he exuded.

When Zej finally found his voice, he asked, 'How does it . . . activate?'

The man cast a furtive look around, then jerked his head, indicating that Zej should follow him. 'From what I gathered,' he whispered, 'every guard has a controller to make them'—he snapped his fingers and clicked his tongue to illustrate the snapping of the blades.

'So, they just point the controller at the person they're looking to . . .' Zej couldn't complete his sentence. 'What if someone else gets in the way?'

The man gave a half-shrug as several people dressed just like the two of them, complete with the deadly bracelets and anklets, filed into the corridor. When the man moved closer to the wall to make room for this group to pass, Zej did likewise. Once the group was out of earshot, the man continued, 'We figured that they punch our numbers'—he jabbed a finger at the string of digits embroidered on a tag affixed to the left of his uniform—'into the remote, then hit the kill switch.'

Zej glanced down at his shirt.

2827049.

He hadn't noticed the number tag before. *I suppose they number us as they imprison us*, he thought, since his number was larger than the man's, which was only three digits. Zej did a quick estimation. If the counter started from one, it would mean that almost two-thirds of the entire population of Atros had been imprisoned!

'It's also printed on the back of your uniform,' supplied the man helpfully.

Was that the reason why people who were shuffling past us did a double take? Zej thought. He was the newbie on the block. Yet, no one, other than this man, dared to look him in the eye. Instead, they kept him at a berth and some of them even conversed in low murmurs as they snuck glances at him.

'How long have you been here?' Zej couldn't help asking. He tried to shake off the unwelcome gazes.

'Long enough.' The man's laugh was bitter. 'Come on, I'll introduce you to the rest.'

'The rest?' repeated Zej.

'Yeah. I hang out with a group of friends and ex-colleagues. We all came in around the same time. Not all of us are still here, though.' He sighed, his eyes darkening in sadness and resignation.

It suddenly occurred to Zej that he didn't know the man's name, so he asked, 'How do I address you?'

The man didn't miss a beat as he continued leading Zej down the corridor, moving in the same direction as the other prisoners, and answered, 'Rett.'

'I'm—'

'Zej,' said Rett, flashing Zej a wider smile without halting his steps.

Zej grounded to a stop. 'How—?'

Rett turned to the flabbergasted Zej and gave a genuine chuckle. 'Recognized you the moment I saw you. Would be blind if I hadn't, after seeing your mugshot sitting on the "Wanted" list for months.'

'You're a trooper?' asked Zej, picking up his legs once more to catch up with Rett.

'You could say that,' replied Rett with an air of mystery. At Zej's look, he added smugly, 'Elite trooper.'

Zej gaped. He was right about this man having similar vibes to Seyfer. 'So you know—'

'Seyfer. Yes, I know him, though we served in different units. How did the errand to Tilsor go? Though seeing as you're here, I'm inclined to believe that you guys failed.'

Zej bit his tongue. He wasn't sure he should be spilling everything to someone he had just met.

At Zej's reluctance, Rett continued, 'How is he? Surely, he's not . . .'

Dead . . . Zej completed Rett's question in his head, and he recalled how Seyfer had fallen to the ground after getting struck by the sedative needle. He answered tentatively, 'I don't think so. W-we were discovered by some ExA drones as we were trying to make our way into the city centre, and we got hit by sedative needles. If . . . I mean, he should have been brought here like me.'

'Hm,' said Rett as they made another turn and entered a spacious hall with rows upon rows of long tables spaced out neatly. Uniformed prisoners, like them, were milling about, holding trays for food, and sitting down for a meal. 'Let's get our breakfast first,' he continued and gestured for Zej to join the line with him.

Still feeling out of place, Zej observed everyone around him, though he tried to be less obvious about it by shifting his gaze around every other second. Despite the fact that every one of the prisoners had on the metal contraptions, the mood was surprisingly light.

Zej followed along as Rett picked up two trays and passed one to him. Then, they joined the queue and Zej's mouth watered when he got served two slices of bread, a generous serving of mixed vegetables and processed meat, a bottle of water, and another bottle of a sugary energy beverage that he used to drink when he was a trooper-in-training at Atros Training Institute. If not for the killer bracelets and anklets, he would have thought that he was dreaming of his days at ATI.

Thinking of his trainee days brought back memories of Pod, and Zej's throat closed up.

Mistaking his reaction for revulsion for the food, Rett said, 'I hadn't pegged you for a spoiled brat.'

Zej shook his head. He wanted to tell Rett that it was a misunderstanding. But why should he care what Rett thought about him? He wasn't here to gain anyone's approval. He was here to collect information. *Information that I don't even know if I will be alive to convey*, he thought. He pushed away the depressing thought. This was not the time to be a self-defeatist. *I'll figure it out one step at a time*, he promised himself.

'I was just thinking why they would feed us so well. This is a standard meal at ATI, isn't it?' Zej remembered that the meal portions back at ATI had always been generous. Atros said that troopers needed to eat well in order to protect the city well. He also recalled the message from Team 174 about how they were running out of food supplies.

Rett nodded and said, 'Got to feed us well so we can carry out the job that they want us to do. Anyway, come, let's get to our table and I'll fill you in.' He ushered Zej to one of the tables at the side of the hall.

'Guys, look who I found,' said Rett when he stopped between two long tables, which sat ten and eight people respectively.

The triumph in his voice made Zej feel like a prey that had walked straight into its predator's open jaw as all eighteen pairs of eyes swivelled towards him.

Zej's nape prickled when everyone's eyes widened in recognition. Were all of them elite troopers like Seyfer and Rett? They definitely looked the part. The same level of intensity in their stares. Tense lips that held back unspeakable secrets. Eyebrows snapped together, judging everything and everyone with suspicion. Uncanny. Was it possible to put a bunch of people through a regimen and expect them to emerge on the other side as clones? Even Rett's mask of joviality wasn't good enough a disguise.

Someone let out a low whistle. Someone sniggered. Someone said, heaping on the sarcasm, 'A rebel. Impressive.'

'Hey, hey, hey. There's no need for hostility. We're all in the same boat here,' said Rett. He put down his tray and gestured to an empty spot at the table. 'Sit.'

Zej wondered if he should leave. But where would he go? Everyone else seemed to know the rest of the people sitting at the same table, lowering their heads as they ate, occasionally conversing in low whispers. He set his tray down and took a seat, ignoring the urge to shift his weight around. He picked up the bottle of water on his tray and twisted the cap open.

'So . . . Zej, tell us how spectacularly you and Seyfer failed the mission,' said the person next to him without preamble. It was a girl with an explosion of light brown curls that framed a small, oval face. She put down her fork, which she had been using to pick at the food in her tray, and turned to give him her full attention.

Zej couldn't determine if her greeting was meant to be rude or if she was really curious, because she had this air of superiority about her. Minus the fact that her sharp, narrow eyes were trying to bore holes into his, she reminded him of a doll. A cute, but snobbish-looking doll. There was a faint smattering of freckles over her pert nose and cheekbones, and a pair of—what he supposed was—larger-than-average front teeth peeking out from between full lips. Even though she looked like a teenager, Zej was willing to bet one of his limbs that she was likely his age or older.

Zej took a gulp of water so he didn't have to respond immediately.

Rett tsk-tsked. 'Not you too, Sif.'

'Excuse me?' said Zej after he had taken his time to screw the cap back on his bottle. He looked straight at this woman called Sif and held her gaze to let her know that he was not intimidated.

Sif repeated herself, then elaborated, 'You guys were supposed to bring back someone who could help us chase out . . . these'—her eyes darted to a pair of guards patrolling the perimeter of the dining hall—'droid-like people. If you're here, it obviously means that you've failed, right?' She let out a sigh, and when her gaze dropped in disappointment, Zej almost felt sorry that he was choosing to keep his cards close to his chest.

'Hey, Sif,' interrupted Rett. His gaze had softened, and he spoke as if he was comforting a child. 'It's not the end of the world. Remember? Seyfer's mission was Plan C. We still have a ton of backup plans. We just need to wait for the time to be right, ya?'

Zej watched as Sif took a deep, calming breath and nodded. Then, Rett started eating and Sif returned to picking at her food.

Atros still had tricks left up its sleeves? thought Zej. For the life of him, he couldn't imagine what these backup plans that Rett was talking about were. Acting as indifferently as he could, he asked, 'What other plans are you talking about?' Then, he took a bite of his food, pretending as if he were just engaging Rett in a casual conversation of no consequence. But the moment Zej tasted the food, he choked and started coughing. The vegetables and meat tasted like they had been soaked in brine. His reaction earned him a laugh from Rett and a grimace from Sif.

'The cooks can be a little heavy-handed with the salt,' said Rett, his eyes still crinkling with amusement. He unscrewed Zej's bottle of water and handed it to him. 'But it's best to finish up the food. It'd be a pity to die of starvation before we kick these bastards out of our home, eh?' Rett had bent forward and whispered that last sentence conspiratorially.

Nodding and taking the bottled water from Rett, Zej took a huge gulp of it to wash down the overwhelmingly salted food. 'Thanks,' he said, still teary from having choked on his food.

'Don't mention it. And as for your question, I'll share more when you're ready to trust us, ya?' Rett's smile was wide, but there was an obvious, calculative look in his eyes.

Trust? thought Zej. *Easier said than done.* But he wasn't going to reject Rett's overture outright. As Alric had said, 'The enemy of my enemy is my friend.' And even if Zej didn't want to consider Rett and the rest of the elite troopers as friends, they could still be potential allies. He reconsidered divulging the fact that he and Seyfer *had* gotten Iv't out of his self-made prison in Tilsor—*if* Rett and his gang were open to sharing their secrets too. Returning Rett's smile, he said, 'Vice versa.'

For the rest of the meal, Zej kept quiet as he sorted out his thoughts. He was hoping Rett's group would be chattier, so he could eavesdrop on their conversations to see what information he could glean. But the elite troopers had little to say to each other, despite their rapport, which was apparent from the way they exchanged glances. Perhaps included in an elite trooper's training was how to communicate silently, not unlike the Ifarls' mindspeak abilities. *Wouldn't that be handy now,* he thought, scoffing to himself.

* * *

Zej had to remind himself to keep his mouth closed as he and Rett filed into another hall several corridors down from where they had just finished their meal. A buzzer had sounded when Zej was returning his tray, as instructed by Rett, and people started moving towards the same exit unanimously and without being instructed to do so.

It was mind-numbing to see people reacting to these cues as if they had been programmed to do so.

When he threw Rett a questioning look, the elite trooper just shrugged again.

Sif, who caught his look, chimed in with a huff, 'It's just easier to fall into line. You'll see—or you won't, if you're lucky.'

Besides Rett, Sif was the only one who deigned to speak to Zej. The rest of the group seemed to prefer to treat Zej as a pest—his presence almost invisible, yet annoying all the same. While Zej wasn't bothered by Rett (he was as mysterious, though as consistent as Seyfer), Sif's character threw Zej in for a loop. One minute, it would seem like she detested and looked down on Zej, and the next, she would speak to him as if he were a friend.

Zej raised a questioning eyebrow at what she said, but she just shrugged in a cryptic manner. He followed along without any more questions and was soon floored by the unbelievable sight in front of him.

Fluorescent white light, like the kind in his cell, flooded the space, which stretched as far as he could see. The ceiling was several storeys high. Conveyor belts ran in an organized yet haphazard way around the space.

Zej followed Sif to one of the tables where there were two trays, each filled with nuts and bolts. Without prompting from the guards, Sif began to show him what he was supposed to do. The guard standing closest to them, who had been eyeing them since they entered the premises, gave a grunt once he saw Sif teaching Zej how to assemble a certain part and take his place in the factory line.

Zej's gaze travelled to the contraptions on his wrists. *It's amazing what fear can do to people.*

In this cavernous factory, there wasn't even a whisper heard from the prisoners once the conveyor belts started moving. The guards didn't have to do much, although it was clear that they were super alert and on the lookout for any signs of unrest. Their eyes were covered by protective gear, but it wouldn't be far-fetched to imagine that if he could see their eyes, every pair of them would reflect a level of madness so complete that they would look calm to those who didn't know better.

As Zej performed the simple task that Sif had shown him, he observed whatever he could from the periphery of his vision. He soon realized everyone else seemed dead intent on the work that they were doing. A few moments later, he noticed a guard taking a step towards him. The thought of having his hands and feet cut off had him immediately casting his eyes downward. His obedience earned him a moment of reprieve from the watchful eyes of the guard, and he would have heaved a sigh of relief had he not thought that any movement beyond a minute shrug would earn him his death.

Zej didn't know how long he kept at the work assigned to him. In the beginning, he had to focus to make sure that he assembled every part correctly. After a while, he found himself losing focus, though he was still able to keep up with his task.

Time flew by. Yet it dragged along. The monotony of what he was doing allowed Zej's mind to wander. Was he supposed to do this every day? How many days—or weeks, months, even years—would he be stuck doing this? Until ExA had enough machines to rule the world? Until he decided that enough was enough and he tried to make an escape only to be made an example of? He thought back to the footage replaying on every screen plastered in this prison. What was that for? It was gruesome. But was it an effective scare tactic? Zej couldn't decide. He mentally ran through what the rest were probably doing. Seyfer, Dace, and Alric—statuses unknown. There was a high probability that they were at another facility, doing this same job as him. *If they aren't already dead.* Zej's throat closed up. Vin should still be at Tilsor, producing weapons and amassing troops for their cause (Zej almost smiled at the parallel between themselves and ExA). Maii had gone with Iv't to track down the Ifarls. How much help would they be when the actual battle happens, Zej couldn't judge. Perhaps if they all got their powers, they could command ExA to freeze—like what Maii did in Tilsor—while all the fighters went around killing them or tying them up? Just thinking about it was ridiculous.

And Keix . . . She would most likely have already arrived at Yurkordu with Jūn. Putting aside his complicated feelings for her, Zej knew that getting the Kulcans on their side was their best bet at winning this war. Sighing, and determined not to mope, he tried to shift his thoughts elsewhere.

Moments later, a commotion drew his attention to a corner of the room, where a man was frantically shaking his head, eyes pleading with a guard standing in front of him. Because they weren't situated very far away from where Zej was, and because all the conveyor belts had stopped, silence fell in every part of the room and the man's voice carried over to Zej.

'No! No! I swear, I wasn't! I was just bent over because I was feeling unwell!'

The guard remained impassive. 'We'll know once we check the footage,' he said without a hint of emotion.

Zej resisted the urge to crane his neck and look around. His time as a spy had taught him, more than anything else, to guard his true feelings—because to reveal them was to hand over his life to his enemy. Of course, there would be surveillance footage covering every inch of this space. He kept his eyes fixed on the situation unfurling in front of him. He figured that it was safe to at least do that, because everyone had stopped what they were doing and turned their attention to the argument.

The acoustics of the enclosed space let sounds carry throughout the hall, ensuring that conversations, official or otherwise, wouldn't escape anyone's notice. But more than that was the fact that this anomaly caused the wave-like momentum of the workers assembling the machines to break—and that, in itself, was blasphemous.

As soon as the guard turned away from the man to speak into his intercom, the man pounced at the guard and tried to grab something off his utility belt, causing him to stagger and lose his balance.

The next moment, three things happened in quick succession. A click echoed through the hall. Something red seeped out from under the man's metal contraptions as his eyes widened and he opened his mouth. Tension drained from the man, and he slumped forward.

Blood. The last vestiges of the man's life. It spurted, poured out of him.

Meanwhile, the guard who was attacked straightened up.

Zej heard himself gasp even as the rest of the prisoners around him remained stoic. So much for his poker face. A wave of nausea hit him as his mind drew parallels between the man and his best friend, Pod, a blade skewered through his chest, his blood spilling out from him, his eyes widened in shock, his head lolling forward.

Zej gripped the edge of the conveyer belt in front of him to prevent himself from doubling over. *No, I can't faint now.* He knew his face was likely as white as the knuckles of his clenched fists. He took a stuttering breath. The conveyor belt started moving again. He tried to focus. He had to resume his work if he didn't want to end up like the man who had just been killed, but he couldn't see anything except his best friend's face.

At the back of his mind, what Seyfer had said to him at the rooftop echoed repeatedly.

You're in this state because you lack conviction. If you were committed enough, you wouldn't feel this way.

Muddling Seyfer's voice was Dace's contemptuous one.

You have no right to wallow in self-pity! You brought this on yourself!

The voices blurred together even as the image of Pod's dead body sharpened in Zej's vision.

Was he falling over? Had someone grabbed hold of him to break his fall? Did someone just yell at him?

His senses were fading into oblivion. His vision was darkening. The jumble of Seyfer and Dace's voices in his head were gradually getting softer. Then . . .

Click.

He slipped into oblivion.

10

Maii | Overtures and Concessions

Maii had never been more anxious in her life. She snuck a glance at Iv't. The two of them had been on the road for weeks now. By her estimate, Zej's group should have reached Atros, and Keix should be in Yurkordu. There was no way of knowing. Sending a signal into the sky would be one of the most foolproof ways to communicate their progress with each other; it was also the easiest way to run the risk of exposing their whereabouts and put ExA on alert. Besides, even if they had a set of signals, Maii couldn't bring any of them along; they—meaning Maii, Dace, and Keix, in particular—were hiding their contingency plans from Iv't. They wanted Iv't to think that he had control over the entire situation, and that everyone was dancing to his tune.

'Are you okay?' Iv't's melodic voice, soothing and just the right pitch, cut through the night air.

Maii couldn't get over the same minuscule degree of anxiety that would seize her every time he spoke. She forced herself to unclench her fists. 'Just tired,' she said as convincingly as possible. Once again, the uncertainty about whether they should have split up gnawed at her insides. She knew being paired with Iv't added to her apprehensiveness. He wasn't just an Ifarl, but a powerful one—so mighty that he was able to kill hundreds of ExA soldiers by just muttering a chant and clenching his fists.

Ifarls had powers of compulsion, but this was only ever used on living beings. Even then, there were limitations. Ifarls couldn't use their powers to cause harm to others, and when faced with different races, the effect differed. For example, compelling other Ifarls was challenging, unless the victim was taken by surprise; Kulcans had a natural resistance to compulsion compared to Atrossians (she herself had felt the strain in trying to bend Keix, who was half-Kulcan, to her will some time back); and Odats were even harder to convince, probably due to the fact that they were ruled more by their instincts than rationale. Now that Maii knew that Iv't created Tilsor, she wondered how exactly he did it. The image of him toiling away physically to build each and every structure within the city wasn't only unimaginable, but it was also beyond impractical. The only other explanation was that he had bent all things, living and non-living, to his will—moulding dirt and water into buildings to create an entire mystical town, then splitting it into Sections with the same paths leading to different parts of the town as these pieces rearranged themselves every dusk and dawn.

'We should be a day away from home. Why don't we take a rest here?' Iv't gestured to the surroundings.

Home. The word felt strange coming from Iv't. Maii nodded and swept her gaze around. The woods that they were in didn't look any different from the ones that surrounded Tilsor and Atros, but if they were within the vicinity of the Ifarls' home—her home—she knew that they would *feel* different. If she still had her powers, she would be able to notice the shift in the atmosphere because the trees around the Ifarls' homeland felt more 'alive', as if they beckoned and welcomed her back when she returned and wished her godspeed whenever she left. But she had lost her Ifarl powers after she participated in the ritual to close the portal between the living and the dead, like all the Ifarls who had been involved in it. Only those who weren't present at the rites had retained their powers.

Maii closed her eyes and tried to recall the sensation that she had once taken for granted, but she knew that even if she had her powers back, everything would still feel different now. Because what used to be her home had become just a stopover that she had to make to confirm her suspicions.

Before she left Atros—or was forced to leave Atros, more accurately—she had run into Shin, an Ifarl who was as mysterious as they got. He had passed her a note, written in a script that Maii knew belonged to Zenchi, her mentor and the leader of the Ifarls. No one knew the true contents of the note except her, unless Shin managed to open and reseal it without her noticing.

When she showed it to Zej and the rest, she had told them that Zenchi had written, 'The light of stars shows the path'. It was the truth. But it wasn't the entire truth. The cryptic message not only warned that massive changes were afoot, but it was also the code phrase that she and Zenchi had agreed to use in the worst-case scenario when the fate of the entire Ifarl race was at stake. If her home had been attacked by ExA, Zenchi would have made sure that everyone who could flee would head to the sacred grounds of their ancestors to hide. This was a piece of information that she had refused to share with anyone—even Keix.

The only reason why Maii hadn't rushed back home to aid the Ifarls was because Shin had mindspoke to her after he passed her the note. 'Zenchi said to stay on your mission. There would be no peace otherwise,' he had said.

So, Maii had remained to assist Zej in eliminating ExA, even though that was the last thing she wanted to do. But she had failed her task miserably. Zenchi would be disappointed in her. *Will I ever get the chance to set things right?* wondered Maii.

'Something is weighing on your mind,' observed Iv't, sounding genuinely concerned. 'I could help if you would just have a little trust in me.'

Trust? Maii almost scoffed. Who would be naive enough to place their faith in someone who had thrown open the gates to the netherworld when confronted with rage and grief? Not to mention, this same person had also created a town to confuse and trap everyone who set foot into it.

'You're scared of me.'

Indignation rose in Maii at Iv't's latest statement, but she remained stubbornly silent. She was wary of him, definitely. But she wouldn't go so far as to say that she was *scared* of him. It was just that her thoughts had been all over the place since she left Tilsor, although she knew that it was more important now than ever to ground them. She blamed it on the fact that she was figuring out how to face someone who was supposedly a legendary figure in the history books on the daily and trying to treat them as equals.

'There's no need to,' continued Iv't. 'Just so you know, I have nothing against you. My enemy is ExA. If the Ifarl elders prove that they had no hand in the death of my wife and the disappearance of my daughter, my fight is not with them either.'

The air remained unmoving as words churned in Maii's head without making any sense. *If only Pod were here with her . . .* The thought of the Atrossian made her eyes sting. Her aura must be all over the place now; Iv't would be able to see that since aura-reading was another power that the Ifarls had. Still, she took comfort in the fact that even though he could tell that her mood was fluctuating, he wouldn't know what emotions she was going through since he didn't know her well enough. She wondered if and when Iv't would compel her to tell him what she was thinking or feeling, but she got a sense that he wanted to prove he was more ethical than the Ifarls who had betrayed him, so he wouldn't pull such a stunt on her—not yet, anyway. She also suspected that he was doing his best to gain her trust and get her on his side, so she would tell him all their secrets willingly.

Maii promised herself once again that she wouldn't fall for anything Iv't said, so she remained steadfast in her silence, shutting down any hope Iv't had of holding a conversation with her.

The night flew by and by first light, Maii and Iv't had set off on the last leg of their journey to the Ifarl's homeland. Iv't didn't attempt to engage Maii today, as he looked wearier and caught up in his own thoughts too.

Surreptitiously, Maii observed Iv't. His neon pink hair seemed to have lightened several hues and gotten duller. It had also grown rapidly since they first met and was now pulled back haphazardly into a short ponytail at his nape, diminishing the vibe of polished lethality he used to exude.

Maii shifted her gaze to the horizon apprehensively. They should be nearing the boundaries of her home now. She kept her eyes peeled, trying to catch a glimpse of her homeland as she picked up her pace. To her horror, she was hit with a rotting stench before her home even came into view. Breaking into a run, her stomach lurched and she fought to keep down the meagre portion of the biscuits that she had eaten for breakfast.

'Maii!' shouted Iv't.

But Maii didn't answer or look back. She didn't care what Iv't thought of her sudden reckless behaviour, or if he could catch up with her. All she wanted to do was to get to her home to see what ExA had done to it.

By the time she stepped foot into the village, she was panting from exertion, and her head was spinning from anger and dejection at the sight in front of her. A small voice in her head told her to stop now that she had concrete proof that the Ifarl village had indeed been destroyed; there was no need for her to witness more of this atrocity. But she kept going, placing one foot in front of the other, picking through the wreckage that used to be her home. The harsh glare from the sun put every last bit of destruction in stark detail, searing the morbid images into her head.

Lifeless, rotting bodies of Ifarls strewn on the ground, numbering in the hundreds—perhaps thousands—some of whom she recognized. Abandoned houses with gaping holes where doors had been thrown off their hinges. Burnt patches as well as overgrown weeds where gardens that had been carefully cultivated by the Ifarls once stood.

Maii uttered a word of thanks to the stars every time she came across a corpse that didn't belong to her parents. There was only so much loss she could take in such a short amount of time. She had to know if they had escaped. Finally, when she had gone through every corner of the village and found no signs of life or her family, she heaved a temporary sigh of relief. *I'll be able to see them at our sacred grounds. They must have made it out*, she reassured herself. Then, she looked at Iv't, who had been silently trailing her.

His expression was inscrutable, but there was no mistaking the hard, intense glint in his eyes. His anger was palpable too, but whether it was because ExA had razed the Ifarl village to the ground or if he was upset that he now had to travel more to reach the surviving Ifarls, Maii wasn't sure. One thing she was certain of was that the same steely resolve he had in his eyes was reflected in her eyes too. As if he had been waiting for this moment, he said, 'I can restore your powers.'

Maii had prepared herself for this possibility—she and Keix had agreed that Iv't would be willing to try out anything to gain her trust, and this was one of the scenarios that they had discussed.

'If he offered to help you get back your Ifarl powers, you should take it,' Keix had said.

Maii pressed her lips together and looked away from Iv't. Of course, she wanted her powers back. But what was the trade-off?

She heard Iv't sigh, then say, 'I'm trying to help you. And your friends.'

The next thing she knew, he had put a hand on her shoulder. Shocked at the sudden show of familiarity, she spun around and almost fell trying to scramble away from him.

'What are you trying to do?' Maii bit out her words to mask her fluster.

Iv't, who had frozen up at Maii's reaction, retracted his hand and sighed again.

Because Maii was facing him this time, she was sure that he was putting on a show.

'I thought that I'd restore your powers so you would believe me,' he said placatingly. 'I know you want them back. So why are you resisting?'

Maii flushed, thinking back to that time in Tilsor when she had felt the crack in the atmosphere after reaching out for her lost powers. That troubling feeling that something was wrong still bugged her because that thread of power, which had been drawn from her surroundings, never felt like it truly belonged to her. She would never forget how difficult it had been to mould that foreign power. How much it took from her to wield it and shape it into a command. If she let Iv't restore her powers, would it feel the same way too? More importantly, would she be bound to do his bidding?

For Iv't, revenge against ExA was personal.

For Maii, the war against ExA had taken on a different face since Pod was killed. But while she had felt a deep sadness at losing Pod, there had never been a burning intensity radiating from the core of her being—until now, after seeing more than half of her race decimated. The vicious need to drive her fist into an ExA soldier's face. The undeniable want to tear each and every one of them from limb to limb, to dismantle all their machine parts and burn everything to dust.

Something had shifted in her, replacing the need to know—which made up the entire reason of her existence—with the need to do. Eventually, she gave Iv't her answer. 'I'll think about it.'

* * *

Maii took a deep breath as she approached the entrance to the Ifarls' sacred grounds. It had taken them another full day of walking to get here. Iv't, who was right beside her, was staring at a cluster of trees in the distance with furrowed brows.

'Are you sure this is the spot?' he asked.

'What's wrong?'

'It's . . . different from how I remembered it.'

'Who did you—' Maii closed her mouth when she realized how invasive her question would have sounded. 'Never mind,' she muttered hurriedly. Any Ifarl who had lived long enough would have been to this spot at least once in their life. This was the final resting place for the ashes of an Ifarl. The corpses of the deceased were transported here by their surviving family members for a final farewell. A pyre would be set up to burn the body, and after that, each of the family members would take turns to carve words of wisdom that the departed had imparted to them into the bark of any one of the older standing trees on the grounds. This rite of passage could be extremely brief, if the deceased had unfortunately met their demise early, or if they didn't have many family members. For Ifarls who lived to a ripe old age, however, the ritual could drag for days.

Maii remembered falling asleep halfway through her maternal grandmother's rites, because there were just too many people and too many things to say. When she woke up from her nap, her family had already planted the tree sapling to signify the end of the ceremony. The significance of planting these saplings was to ensure that later generations would have huge, sturdy trees to continue this Ifarl tradition.

But as far as Maii knew, Iv't had been an orphan since he was born, and after he had lost his wife and daughter, he had torn apart the veil separating the world of the living and the dead in search of them. Then, he had descended into madness and imprisoned part of himself in an alternate dimension in a town that he had built. So, whom exactly had he lost to warrant a trip here?

'Moi,' said Iv't wistfully, answering Maii's half-spoken question. Then, he scoffed and shook his head, before hiccupping awkwardly. 'The trees have aged.'

Maii wasn't sure what to say to that. She did a quick calculation in her head. 'Um, yes. It's been over seventy years since your . . .' *loved one died.*

The stony resolve that Maii had previously seen in Iv't's eyes slid back into place at the reminder. To put an end to further awkwardness, Maii walked straight into the cluster of trees, weaving through them, following the subtle glint that would appear on the tree trunks to lead the way into the Ifarls' sacred grounds—glimmers that Maii could see even though she had lost her powers.

The light of stars shows the path.

And the path now led them to emerge from a tree maze into a clearing thrumming with an uneasy silence. The serenity of the burial grounds in Maii's memories was replaced with a frenzied tension and the space had been transformed beyond recognition. The trees and the carvings on them remained—some aged, some fresh. But the pockets of clearing where the pyres used to be built were now outfitted with rectangular sheets, which Maii figured were doubling as beds, and makeshift shelters. Ifarls were moving around in a sluggish and robotic manner, gathering up the cloths on the ground and folding them up to pile at a corner.

No one seemed to have noticed that two strangers had appeared in their midst. Maii was searching for her parents and Zenchi, or a familiar face to approach, to make her arrival known when she heard a voice call her name.

She turned in the direction of the voice and found her mum looking at her. *She's alive*, was the first thought that came to Maii's mind. She was certain her mum must have thought the same because disbelief and relief reflected in both their faces in quick succession. Then, her mum looked around and, without putting down the cloth that she had folded halfway, pattered towards Maii.

'Where's Father?' asked Maii.

'He's out gathering supplies with a group.'

He's alive. My parents are alive. Maii sent what seemed like her thousandth thanks towards the sky.

'Did you bring good news?' Ruii asked in a low, uncertain tone.

'I . . .' Maii started, then clamped her lips together. Could she classify the information that she had to convey to Zenchi as such? How was she going to summarize everything that had happened since she left for Atros? No one knew what kind of mission Zenchi had sent her on—not even her own parents. And while she hadn't expected an enthusiastic welcome home, the dejection she felt from Ruii's lukewarm response hit her right in the gut. Had hanging around Atrossians changed her? Ifarls never wore their hearts on their sleeves, and the unshed tears in Ruii's eyes was proof that her mother cared. Still, Maii felt herself longing for any hint of physical affection—a brief hug, a stronger-than-usual grip on her shoulder . . . She even tried to imagine that she was the cloth that Ruii was gripping.

Maii recalled the night she had spent with Pod under the stars in Tilsor, just chatting. He had put his hand over hers. It was the first time she had let someone other than her parents and Zenchi hold her hand. The warmth and comfort she had felt from such a simple touch spurred her to promise him that she would think about his proposal to one day leave all this 'fighting for the greater good' behind them, and to 'write their own narrative'. A promise that had no chance of being fulfilled now . . .

'Things have . . . changed,' said Ruii, banishing Maii's straying thoughts.

'What do you mean?' asked Maii, her widened eyes searching her mother's face.

Ruii's hesitation spoke volumes, and it was then that Maii realized her mother had been contending with her own complicated thoughts. Maii chided herself for being so caught up in the agenda of stopping ExA—an agenda that wasn't even her own to begin with—that she hadn't even stopped to consider that what happened to the Ifarls was as bad as—or worse than—what she herself had faced.

Even though Maii wanted to pull Ruii to a corner to have a long overdue catch-up chat, she knew she had to get Iv't to Zenchi. She also noticed that their little gathering was attracting stares from other Ifarls, who had now almost finished packing up in the camp. Disquiet was rippling through the grounds.

'Where is Zenchi, Mother? I have'—Maii glanced back at Iv't, who was appraising everything within view—'someone I need her to meet.'

Ruii looked dismayed. 'Zenchi is—' she began before switching her tone to one of deference. 'Elder Pa-shin.'

Maii turned around. A wiry man in a loose, grey robe was approaching them. It was Pa-shin and he looked no different from how Maii remembered him—his head shaved, showcasing the maze of bright pink lines on his scalp, and his eyes, wise and gentle. Pa-shin was Zenchi's right-hand man, poised as her successor. He was probably only half as old as Zenchi, but his abstract thinking and wisdom made him ascend to the rank of Elder, back when his bright pink hair had barely greyed. Maii suspected that he had shaved off his hair to appear older, and to bring further attention to the bright pink lines on his scalp. The more obvious the maze of lines, the stronger their powers.

'Elder Pa-shin.' Maii inclined her head as she greeted him. Then, she asked, 'Where's Zenchi?'

Pa-shin's eyes, containing a hint of curiousity, flicked to Iv't. Then, he glanced around before replying in a low tone, 'Come with me.' He nodded to Ruii, who returned the gesture and then threw Maii an indecipherable look before she turned on her heel to leave the group.

Maii was sure that Pa-shin and her mother had communicated through mindspeak, but she didn't want to draw further attention to their exchange, knowing full well that if she had caught it, Iv't would have had too.

Maii barely noticed her surroundings as she let Pa-shin lead her and Iv't deeper into the forest as they walked through a series of smaller clearings. In her preoccupation to guard against Iv't, she hadn't really considered how she was going to convince Zenchi to trust—or, at the very least, work with—him.

Finally, the group reached a spot that was so heavily shaded, it looked like night had fallen. The only illumination in the space was a string of lanterns draped on the lowest tree branches. Canvas sheets, like the ones she had seen the Ifarls packing up, were tied to the trees to create an enclosed space. Even though the material concealed the tree trunks, Maii could tell that they had expansive girths and appeared like a bunch of cords twisted together.

Set in the centre of this sheltered space was a petite figure laying atop another sheet of cloth. The Ifarl's frailness was emphasized with the intermittent rise and fall of her chest. The neckpiece that was synonymous with her identity lay beside her head, confirming Maii's worst suspicions.

'Zenchi?' gasped Maii. She turned to Pa-shin. 'What happened to her?'

'Her health deteriorated rapidly after closing the portal. By the time we reached home, she could barely stand upright. Then, not long after, she said something big was about to happen, so she directed all of us to come here to hide. And she also sent out messengers to all the Ifarls who were not home, so that they would know to head here at the earliest possible time.'

'How about the rest of the Ifarl elders?' interrupted Iv't.

Pa-shin's wise eyes stared unblinkingly at Iv't. 'I didn't want to bring attention to you just now, when there were so many others around,' Pa-shin said, then turned and addressed Maii. 'Did Zenchi ask you to bring him?'

'He's—I—' started Maii. It didn't escape her notice that Pa-shin hadn't asked for Iv't's identity. But even if Pa-shin had guessed who Iv't was, where could she even begin her tale? 'No,' she answered Pa-shin eventually. 'Zenchi didn't ask me to bring him. But . . . where are the rest of the Ifarl elders?' Maii repeated Iv't's question because it was relevant to what she was going to reveal. If Zenchi was indisposed, these would be the people she had to convince besides Pa-shin.

'They . . . I . . . I don't know.' Pa-shin cast his eyes downward.

'You don't know?'

'They stayed back to buy us time to escape.'

Maii's heart dropped. 'I thought you said Zenchi directed everyone to come here to hide?'

'She did . . . but the other Ifarl elders wanted to discuss further.'

'What's there to discuss further?'

'Whether or not it was necessary to take such a drastic move.'

'Why?' Maii was flabbergasted.

'Because messages that we read in the stars are sometimes vague.' Pa-shin looked like he was on the verge of tearing his non-existent hair out.

Maii swallowed. 'So, you're telling me that the rest of the Ifarl elders stayed back to be slaughtered because they were too stubborn to believe Zenchi's words?'

Pa-shin took a deep breath, as if he was the one who needed to brace himself for what he was about to say. 'Not exactly. The ExA soldiers arrived in the vicinity of *teseg* field before we started moving out. The elders who had their powers decided to stay to try to stall the advancement of the soldiers. But . . . their charm didn't seem to hold. Zenchi would have stayed behind if I hadn't convinced her to flee with us.'

Maii was familiar with the field that Pa-shin was talking about. It was where she used to train her fighting skills alone, because she felt that being physically fit was as important as gaining knowledge. 'Just how many ExA soldiers stormed our home?' Maii didn't want to appear hysterical, but she couldn't help but be in disbelief at what she was hearing. How could a bunch of elders who had their powers be unable to stop the intruders?

'Does it feel like your powers have weakened?' interrupted Iv't.

Pa-shin cast an appraising glance at Iv't. A good length of time passed before he replied, 'Yes. Our powers have weakened since we closed the portal.'

Maii's jaw dropped. Pa-shin was one of the elders who had stayed behind while Zenchi led the portal-closing ritual, so Maii had felt that he was one of the 'lucky' Ifarls who didn't lose his powers. 'How did that happen?' she asked, her confusion at this new revelation apparent.

'The ritual should never have been performed because there was no way to do it correctly. That's why there was a brief moment in Tilsor when you could access your power despite having lost it after the ritual,' said Iv't.

As Iv't's words sank in, Maii searched her memory. There was this pair of ancient rhymes, 'The Night of Legends' and 'Act of Repentance', that every Ifarl had to learn. History told of a child who was born when the nine dimmest stars in the sky formed a line and glowed the brightest. This child was rumoured to be powerful but would create a problem for the rest of the Ifarls to solve by doing something unpredictable. As far as every Ifarl of this generation knew, Iv't was this miracle but problem child, and the complication he created was opening the portal between the living and the dead.

Ifarls were supposed to undo the knot that this child made and restore balance to the universe. This was why Zenchi had led a group of them—Maii included—to conduct a ritual to close the very same portal. They only had one chance to do so, when the nine dimmest stars lined up again. To be frank, it was through sheer luck that the Ifarls managed to gather all the hybrids that Atros had created and offer them up as sacrifice to close the portal. But now, Iv't was saying that all that had been for naught? How could it be? Zenchi had done everything within her power to make sure that the ritual was done correctly!

'*I* had to be present in order for the ritual to work,' said Iv't, answering Maii's unspoken question.

Maii's mind blanked even as Pa-shin looked enlightened by Iv't's explanation. As if asking for something as inconsequential as what Iv't had eaten for breakfast, Pa-shin said, 'There is a way we can undo this curse, right? Even though the night where the stars were the dimmest has passed?'

At moments like these, Maii could almost appreciate why Pa-shin had risen to his status despite his young age. His astuteness and ability to remain unfaltering even in the face of someone as powerful as Iv't weren't something that came naturally to anyone—at least not to Maii.

Looking at Maii meaningfully even though his words were addressed to Pa-shin, Iv't said, 'That depends on whether or not you'll accept my help.' Then he paused for effect before continuing, 'And render yours in return.'

* * *

An Ifarl's powers are what distinguish them from the rest of the races. Who are you without your powers? Nothing. So, there was never a choice, was there?

Iv't's mocking voice echoed in Maii's head. It was as if he had used his Ifarl powers to communicate with her through mindspeak. But the difference was that this 'conversation' was possible not because of his power, but that he now had full access to her thoughts. It was the one 'side effect' that he had conveniently forgotten to mention when he had proposed to Pa-shin to restore *every* Ifarls' powers to their original state in exchange for them to aid him in his revenge.

'You're wrong,' replied Maii now. Even though the words had formed in her head, and Iv't could sense them, she purposely said them out loud as a form of protest. 'We, Ifarls, are not defined by our powers.'

Every single Ifarl who was present spun their head around to look at Maii. Some of them looked confused at her sudden outburst, but there were also others who regarded her with contempt. *Either they disagree with me on the importance of our powers, or they blame me for their current plight*, thought Maii.

To restore their powers, Iv't had asked them to empty their minds and to let him take the lead in re-establishing the connection they had had with nature—since an Ifarl's powers were attributed to their unique sensitivity to their environment. Maii had blanked out for what felt like a couple of seconds. Then, when she regained consciousness, instead of the worst-case scenario where the power felt foreign, she had felt a familiar well of Ifarl power within herself. But her elation was short-lived when Iv't, after having carried out this same process with all of them, revealed that he had not only restored their powers, but also established an individual connection with each of them. And this let him farm their powers for his own use, making himself even more powerful than before.

'If your powers do not define you, then why were you so eager to get them back?' asked Iv't. His eyes were dancing with a fiery intensity that reflected his unstable state of mind. He had kept it in check previously, but having achieved his goal of getting all the Ifarls under his thumb, he didn't seem to care about maintaining that affable front any longer.

Maii was outraged. And even though she might be a pariah to the rest of the Ifarls now, they hated Iv't even more for taking away their privacy and free will. But there was nothing any of them could do. Because Iv't could read their thoughts and had access to their powers, he could paralyse them before they even made a move against him. Some Ifarls who had been the most vocal about forcing Iv't to reverse the process were made examples of; Iv't had rendered them unconscious immediately and left them back at the sacred grounds as hostages to ensure that the rest of them would obey him without question.

I thought you said that it's common sense to never go to war with soldiers who are unwilling to fight it for you, thought Maii, recalling the last conversation Iv't had had with Keix and the group before they had left Tilsor to go on their separate missions. *So why are you doing this right now?*

Maii could hear Iv't's humourless laugh in her head before he said, *Pa-shin has ordered everyone to follow my instructions. The hostages back at your sacred grounds will be more than sufficient to ensure everyone's willingness.*

Yes, Pa-shin wouldn't want to see the annihilation of the Ifarls on his watch. Maii glanced at the Ifarl elder, who was standing next to her, and hoped that he held some wisdom or knowledge that could get them out of this dead-end situation.

Well, you can certainly hope, came Iv't's voice again. *But you'd better wish that he comes up with something fast because we're going to be back at Tilsor really soon.*

Wh-what? It had taken them weeks to reach the Ifarls' sacred grounds. Now that they had just set off, how could they be back at Tilsor so soon?

Iv't chose to ignore Maii's thoughts this time around. But soon, it was clear that he was manipulating their surroundings—like how he had moved the Sections in Tilsor. The manoeuvre made Maii nauseous as everything in sight—the path, trees, and even the tiniest bit of gravel on the ground—seemed to whisk past this huge platoon of almost five hundred dumbfounded Ifarls.

Maii could sense how Iv't was doing this because of the connection that he had established. It wasn't as one-way as Iv't wanted them to believe. He was pulling from her well of power firmly and making the energy flow towards him like a stream. It also became clear to Maii that Iv't hadn't been able to do this manipulation of their surroundings after they had left Tilsor because he didn't have enough power at that time.

Maii wanted to deny what was happening, but as the boundary of Tilsor appeared on the horizon, she was struck speechless, horrified at the amount of power that they had naively placed in Iv't's hands—and with minimal resistance at that.

11

Vin | Set-up

'How many people do you think will turn up today?' whispered Vin, nudging Mohgen's shoulder with her own.

The two of them had spread the word that they were organizing a meeting to speak to those who would like to know who exactly invaded Tilsor and how the massacre in Square Thirty-two happened. Now, they were hanging out at a corner of one of the top-floor rooms in Ma.erdene's bathhouse for this gathering, watching as people filed into the room.

'After the stunt ExA pulled here, I'd say everyone we managed to reach out to, and more,' replied Mohgen, her lips drawn thin. 'But whom to trust—that's what's key.'

Vin nodded in agreement. Before she and Keix, and the rest of their original gang split up to carry out their own parts in this mission to take down ExA, they had agreed that to stand a chance at winning against ExA, especially if their opponent launched an attack before any of them succeeded in bringing back reinforcements, they had to drive their enemy into an area filled with booby traps. So, before Iv't left Tilsor, he had 'fixed' some Sections in Tilsor to make them direct everyone into the same Square at intermittent intervals.

Vin, Mohgen, and Ma.erdene, whose task was to coordinate and gather fighters, immediately set to work.

Their first 'recruit' was the bald, middle-aged man who was the owner of the weapons shop where Jūn had gotten Vin her twin blades. Vin didn't get his name, because he had never properly introduced himself. Mohgen didn't know his name either, despite him being the most well-known weapons trader in Tilsor. Vin thought she heard Ma.erdene address him as Falc, so she and Mohgen had taken to calling him that in private. Every time they mentioned him, they would giggle a little because his name sounded like a curse word in Atrossian.

After Falc joined them, he and Ma.erdene had then drawn on their extensive network and connections to reach out to those who called Tilsor home. As the room got more crowded, Vin noticed that almost a third of those who had turned up were injured in one way or another, and that all of them were armed. She stood up a bit straighter and paid extra attention to everyone's mood, in case anyone decided to set a spark to ignite the flammable tension in the room. With their individualistic attires and variety of weapons on display, this was the strangest hotchpotch of people she had ever seen in her life.

Once it looked like everyone had settled in—all the seats were taken and every inch of space was occupied by those who were standing—Falc stepped up to the centre of the room. He began, his baritone voice echoing, 'I know everyone's curious to know what really happened in Tilsor a few days back, so I'll cut to the chase. The soldiers whom you fought were not Atrossians.'

A murmur rippled through the audience.

A tall man with a buzz cut stood up and levelled his gaze at Falc. He was surrounded by a handful of figures who looked suspiciously like the bloodthirsty group of outlaws who had slashed Jūn with a poisonous blade when Vin first arrived in Tilsor with him and Keix. 'Damn right they aren't,' the man said in a booming voice. 'How do we know we can trust you?'

Vin and Mohgen exchanged glances. Despite his menacing bearing, Vin could hear a hint of fear in his angry words. The fact that no one did anything except run their mouths, even though all of them were on edge, also spoke volumes about their keenness to understand what was going on.

'You're looking for answers. And this is the one that I have,' said Falc without any change in his composure. 'They are Atrossians, technically. But they're not the ones that we've come to know. The ones who minded their own businesses, you know?'

'Damn right the Atrossians mind their own business. Who doesn't know that they hire Odats to guard their borders?' said Buzz Cut even more loudly.

'Yes, you said it yourself. They hire Odats to guard *their* borders. But they've never launched an attack on us before. The ones whom we fought are ex-Atrossians—and the Atrossians we know call them ExA.'

Chatter exploded as everyone turned to those around them in disbelief.

Vin tensed up and reached for the blades slung on each side of her hips. Drawing weapons in this packed room would definitely result in casualties. But that was the last thing on her mind. She needed to protect herself and Mohgen too. In her peripheral vision, she saw two figures gesturing aggressively at each other and was about to step towards them to prevent a fight from breaking out when a metallic clang ran through the air, halting everyone in their tracks.

Vin spun in the direction of the noise and saw Ma.erdene glowering at everyone. Whenever had she brought a metal plate into the room?

'Perhaps we should start at the beginning?' Ma.erdene's tone was mild, but no one could misread the threat in it. It was obvious that her reputation in Tilsor outstripped Falc's when everyone complied and settled back down. She turned to the corner of the room where Vin and Mohgen were standing. 'Vin?'

Vin's jaw dropped as everyone turned to her. With difficulty, she ground her teeth together and swallowed. Puzzles, she could solve. Parties, she could go wild. But speeches? Ma.erdene could have at least given her advance notice that she would be called upon to convince the crowd!

'Damn right we're going to listen to a little girl speak,' shouted the hot-headed man as he stood up once more. But when Ma.erdene threw him a scathing look, he immediately shut his mouth and sat down awkwardly.

Vin hid her smile at the strange turn of events as she sucked in a deep breath and channelled the only person of authority who came to mind: Oron. He was one of her mentors back in Atros and his lecture to the platoon about keeping their guard up during their patrols was the last thing Vin remembered before her life changed drastically because of the ghost attack that put her in Atros's laboratories. She straightened her spine and pulled back her shoulders. Just to calm her nerves, she cleared her throat and looked to Mohgen, who gave her an encouraging nod.

'Hi,' began Vin. She was glad that her voice came out strong and steady. 'My name is Vin, and I used to be an Atros trooper.'

To her surprise, the group seemed more willing to listen to her than Falc; Ma.erdene's influence was not to be underestimated. But why had she used it on Vin and not Falc? Vin didn't have time to wonder as she focused on telling everyone present about the story between ExA and the current Atros, and their differences. After she finished her tale, she answered a series of clarifying questions. For those to which she had no answers, she honestly replied as such. Laying everything out in the open seemed like the best way to convince these people of the gravity of the matter.

When the murmurs subsided, a young woman whom Vin recognized as one of Ma.erdene's staff spoke up. 'So, you're saying you need our help to prepare Tilsor as a trap for ExA when the war arrives at our doorstep. And you also want us to help you fight these ExA soldiers, and that if your friends manage to convince the Kulcans and Ifarls to join our side, we have a good chance of eliminating ExA and bringing true peace to the world?'

Vin weighed her answer. She didn't know if saying they had a 'good' chance was overstating the fact, much less guaranteeing 'true peace'. But before she could open her mouth, another voice spoke up. This time, it came from a man hidden in the shadows.

'Why is fighting the only option? Why can't we all just pack up and go into hiding?' he asked without derision or fear.

Vin looked down and let out a long breath. For the umpteenth time since Keix had agreed to help Seyfer find Iv't, Vin had asked herself the same questions. Why couldn't they go into hiding? Perhaps if they had done so at the beginning, Pod would not have met his untimely death. It was only because Keix and Zej had been stubborn enough to feel that they should bear the weight of the world on their shoulders that it had come to this.

But even as Vin tried to convince herself this was the case, she knew it was not. When a force as ruthless as ExA was set on ruling the world, they would leave no stone unturned. It was like what Maii had said. They would not rest until they had everyone at their feet. And those who went on the run would be running for the rest of their lives, or until they had no place to run to. And that wasn't something Vin was keen on doing.

She met the man's gaze straight on. 'A predator who hunts for sport will not merely be satisfied with filling its tummy. And I'm sure you know that hiding will only whet the hunter's appetite, especially if the hunter's got a bloodthirsty streak.' She knew her words had had the intended effect when the rest of the participants shifted their weight nervously.

'How do you know ExA will attack Tilsor? They've already tried, and they failed. So why would they take the risk again?' piped the young woman once again. 'If they wanted to launch an attack on the Kulcans, they could go for Yurkordu right away. Why make a detour?'

'First of all, ExA didn't have the intention of attacking Tilsor so early. They only did so because my friends and I chanced upon them, and one of us'—Vin had to take a steadying breath at the mention of Pod—'one of us got caught by them and we fought back. And with some help from an Ifarl, we managed to kill every last one of the ExA soldiers who were deployed here. Because of this, we believe the news that their unit was decimated has yet to reach their headquarters.

'Also, Tilsor is not a detour for them. In fact, it's a convenient shortcut. What do you think are the chances they'll take the roundabout route to Yurkordu? Lastly, Tilsor would make a much better base compared to Atros, don't you think? Atros is wide open, and its borders are a pain to guard and defend.'

The woman frowned as she considered Vin's words while the mysterious man chimed in again. 'Ever since the battle in the Square, there has been no news coming out from Atros at all. It's as if the city has become a black hole. Everyone who had been headed in that direction has gone missing.'

Vin's heart pounded at the man's words—not because it was new information, but because it underscored her suspicions that Zej, Dace, and Seyfer, along with Dace's father, had likely been caught by ExA. She had no way of knowing. Not unless they sent a distress signal into the air—a signal that they agreed they would only use if the situation got dire. There was also the possibility that they had managed to sneak into Atros and were trying to not draw attention to themselves. No news seemed to be good news at this moment in time.

Mohgen squeezed Vin's hand in reassurance, as if she could tell what was going through Vin's mind. 'We know of the disappearances,' interjected Mohgen. 'Which is why we called this meeting. Figured it was time we shared our plan on how to bring down ExA—once and for all.'

* * *

Vin had never been a worrier. If a problem presented itself, she would analyse it, fix it, then move on. There was no point painting all kinds of scenarios only to make herself anxious over something that she could do nothing about. Yet, here she was, with her stomach all tied up in knots after a meeting that was considered successful by every measure.

Everyone who came had left seemingly convinced—although to varying degrees. Some of them even raised suggestions to refine the plan to trap ExA soldiers, making Vin feel heartened because each of those folks knew things about Tilsor that no other did. It was as if

Tilsor had presented itself with slight differences to every individual. In the end, almost every aspect—from evacuation plans for those who could not join the fight, to the setting of traps in the Squares, should Iv't not return in time—was considered.

'Tell me we're right to sit and wait for ExA to come to us,' said Vin. Now that everyone had left the room except for Mohgen and Ma.erdene, Vin felt comfortable enough to voice her doubts.

'You know we're right,' said Mohgen reassuringly.

Ma.erdene shot Vin an empathetic look, but her voice was stern when she said, 'Don't you go losing your patience on me now. Sometimes, the hardest thing to do is to sit on your hands and do nothing. We've agreed that no news means good news. Have faith in your friends.'

Vin sighed. Perhaps this earful from Ma.erdene was what she needed to get her head back in the game. 'I'm just worried that Zej and Dace had been caught, and they didn't have enough notice to send over a signal to let us know they've failed.'

'They knew what they were getting into, and we've considered that the possibility of this worst-case scenario happening was high,' said Ma.erdene without inflection.

Mohgen squeezed Vin's hand again, just like how she had done at the meeting when she sensed Vin's distress. 'Whether they were caught by ExA or not, it's inevitable that ExA will bring the fight to us. Come, let's go. It's about time for us to take over the shift.'

Vin nodded. She and Mohgen were due for a two-hour shift right outside Tilsor, where they would sit and gaze at the sky to check if anyone had sent a signal. Every single day since the others left, Vin and Mohgen had been setting out at dusk to Tilsor's boundary. They had to get out of the city to be able to see the signals that the scouts stationed at intervals along the route that Maii and Iv't had taken would shoot into the sky once they saw the Ifarls returning. Vin looked forward to this part of her day the most because she and Mohgen would have a length of uninterrupted time to chat about everything under the sun. But it was also the part of her day that she dreaded the most because of the apprehension involved in the duty.

Like Ma.erdene said, no news was good news. But no news also meant just that—no news. Vin had no other way of knowing what was happening.

As she headed out, she promised herself she would stop whining about her circumstances. Walking through Tilsor felt infinitely different from when she had first arrived here. The streets used to be filled with a palpable excitement, yet now, what was palpable was trepidation instead. ExA's massacre had destroyed many people's belief that Tilsor was a safe place to settle in. That, in turn, had resulted in many people fleeing the city. Those who stayed on had also become wary. But Vin reassured herself. Preparations were underway. Hopefully, the group that they had convinced today would go on to reach out to more people. The additional help would bolster the countermove that Vin and the rest had planned, rendering it more powerful and debilitating, the longer ExA took to launch an attack.

As Vin and Mohgen squeezed through a barely visible gap between a stack of haphazardly arranged crates, they took extra care not to disturb these boxes because they contained combustible balls filled with highly flammable and corrosive liquids. Mohgen had developed these mini bomb-like weapons and started mass producing them in preparation for the inevitable battle with ExA. The idea for this trap was multifold. The first was to stall ExA's progress by making them think that each Section had only one exit by blocking the rest of the routes with these crates. And the second was to use these incendiary balls as a last resort to burn Tilsor down if the ExA soldiers looked set to be victorious.

Of course, the best scenario was if Iv't returned as soon as possible. The Ifarl was the only one who could manipulate the streets of Tilsor to direct everyone where he wanted them to go—a death trap. And then, someone would be assigned to ignite these crates on the tail of the last batch of ExA soldiers, signalling to others that their strategy had worked.

'Would we even be able to hold them off, much less run them into a corner to get rid of them once and for all? What if they just keep coming in waves?' wondered Vin out loud.

Mohgen paused in her tracks and sighed. Looking into Vin's eyes, she asked, 'Vin, do you wish that you had accompanied Keix or Zej, or even Maii, instead of staying here?'

Vin scrambled to refute Mohgen's words. She knew it sounded like she was constantly complaining about her choice to stay back in Tilsor instead of being fully committed to it. 'No! I've just never . . . had to hang back and wait for things to happen.' As the words spilled out, Vin realized that the sense of loss that had driven her to follow Keix out of Atros and the feeling that had made her *not* follow Keix to Yurkordu were one and the same. Vin wanted to be where she felt she would be most useful.

Mohgen's gaze softened. 'I know Ma.erdene said the hardest thing to do is to sit on our hands and do nothing. But that's not what we're doing. You're not hanging back and waiting for things to happen. We're making sure everything is in place, so we achieve our goal of taking down ExA.' She looped her arm around Vin's and tugged her back into a walk.

'I know. I just . . . haven't been away from Keix for this long since we met at the orphanage,' admitted Vin, hanging her head. Keix was her best friend and her only one constant since they first met. Vin couldn't help but feel antsy without her presence.

'Oh. You miss Keix.'

Vin's eyes snapped to Mohgen's face. She thought she had heard a wisp of jealousy in Mohgen's statement, but the apothecary proprietress' shrewd but gorgeous features kept her true emotions hidden from Vin.

After a beat, Mohgen said, 'You know she's interested in Jūn, right?'

Vin couldn't help but laugh at that. 'I think anyone who's hung around the two of them for longer than a second can see that. Keix is oblivious though.'

'Ah . . .' Mohgen sounded a little more neutral now. 'I thought . . . you shared a special relationship with Keix.'

Vin suppressed a smile as they stepped into another Section. They should be reaching Tilsor's boundary, and yup, Mohgen was most definitely jealous. 'We do. Share a special relationship,' said Vin as she picked up her pace. 'Keix has been a close friend since we met. More like, I decided that she would be my close friend the moment I met her.'

Mohgen turned to her with a raised eyebrow as they continued walking.

'Because I grew up in an orphanage without knowing who my parents are, it took me a while to figure out how and why I was different from the other kids in Atros—you know, pink hair and all?' elaborated Vin.

'I always felt overwhelmed visually. Because I could see auras around everyone. But Keix stood out the moment I saw her because her aura was muted. I just wanted to be around her to rest my eyes. And that gave me the space to start looking at myself instead of being distracted by other people all the time. Later, I found out that the reason why her aura was less visible to me was because she was half-Kulcan.'

Mohgen nodded and her soft gaze grazed Vin's visage. 'I'm glad you found her then.'

Vin smiled and confessed. 'I don't miss it. My Ifarl powers.'

As they entered the last Section that would lead them out of Tilsor, Mohgen said with a faraway look in her eyes, 'There are some things that are better not having. And better not knowing.'

Vin gazed at Mohgen, whose mahogany hair looked set ablaze by the setting sun's rays. Mohgen had always given off the vibe that she never had any inclination of getting involved in affairs that were not her own, although she seemed to owe some sort of debt to Ma.erdene, or at least had some mysterious trade relationship with her. Yet, after the massacre in Tilsor, Mohgen had developed a kind of edge to her usual carefree and easy-going personality. Vin itched to probe Mohgen's history, which had always been inaccessible to her. She didn't know if she was reading too much into Mohgen's words, but it felt like Mohgen really didn't want to share anything about her past with anyone, Vin included—and that left her feeling a little downcast.

The air shifted the moment the two of them stepped out of Tilsor. The weather was gradually cooling down, but that didn't stop sweat from beading on Vin's forehead. The landscape on this side of Tilsor was markedly sparser. Unlike the more heavily wooded areas between Tilsor and Atros, there was much more distance between the trees here. And instead of dense branches that tapered to a point, these trees had spread-out crowns, which made it harder for the scouts to conceal themselves. But Ma.erdene and Mohgen had reassured Vin that their scouts were experienced and knew the lay of the land like the back of their hands, so there was little chance of them getting caught. Besides, they had developed a signalling system and network that would ensure that there would be no loss of information even if one of the scouts should fail.

The sun had almost fully set now, and the two people whose shift Vin and Mohgen were set to take over were climbing down a small hill of boulders. As they passed Vin and Mohgen, they inclined their heads in acknowledgement and made their way into Tilsor without a word.

'Still nothing then, I guess.' Vin gave Mohgen a tight smile.

Together, they ascended the boulders and settled into their spots in silence until Mohgen spoke and rendered Vin speechless by suddenly asking, 'Have you ever thought of what you would be doing if your circumstances were different?'

Vin turned to Mohgen and blinked. She considered for a moment before answering, 'I don't know. I've never thought of it before. Just seems like a waste of time, thinking about the what-ifs.'

Mohgen let out a soft laugh at that, and the way her eyes crinkled sent a little jolt through Vin's heart.

'All right. I get it,' said Vin, cracking a wide smile. 'What you were asking is, if I were a different person, what do I think I would be doing—I'm understanding you correctly, right?'

Mohgen nodded.

'Yeah, I've never thought about it,' repeated Vin. 'But I'll do so from now on and let you know once I have an answer. How about you? What would you be doing if you were a different person?'

'Hm . . . I guess I might be doing the same thing—concocting solutions and manning the apothecary. I think a peaceful, no-drama life suits me.'

Vin burst out laughing at the mock-serious answer and Mohgen joined in because both of them knew Mohgen was half-joking. Seeking out exciting and fun experiences was her definition of peaceful. Being embroiled in a war that no one asked for was not.

For the rest of their shift, they bantered back and forth about nothing of consequence. Even when they spoke about some of the more colourful people who had attended the meeting, it was to make the wildest guesses about what these characters would be doing if they weren't here in Tilsor. These discussions were frivolous, but they were the perfect balm for Vin's frazzled nerves.

By the time the sky darkened, the temperature had dipped. Before long, both Vin and Mohgen were standing up, ready to change shifts.

'Another day down,' murmured Vin as she brushed the dirt from her clothes.

Mohgen let out a long exhale and said, as if she were reminding them both, 'No news is good news.'

* * *

Vin didn't know what time it was exactly when Mohgen barged into her room and woke her up. It felt like she had just closed her eyes after yet another exhausting day of prepping for a battle that seemed to be taking its own sweet time to reach their doorstep. Mohgen pulled her out of bed, and from the streaks of grey seeping into the section of inky sky that was visible from her room's balcony, Vin figured it must be almost light.

'Vin, we need to hurry,' said Mohgen without attempting to hide her excitement.

Vin's brain went into overdrive. 'Are they back? Or is ExA arriving?' she asked in a voice still husky with sleep.

'Maii's coming back,' answered Mohgen a little breathlessly, grabbing Vin's hand, half-pulling, half-supporting her wobbly run out of her room.

This was tremendous news. At the very least, a piece of their plan had fallen into place.

As they ran out of Ma.erdene's establishment, Vin asked, 'How many Ifarls do you think they've brought along?'

Mohgen shook her head. 'We can't be certain. But from what I gathered, the first scout along the route seemed to have missed the group, so only the next signal went up.' Seeing Vin's look of horror, she added, 'No, I don't think the scout was compromised. Probably fell asleep and didn't catch the group heading in their direction. Besides, from the frequency of the signals, it seems like the Ifarls are moving really quickly.'

Vin, who was a trained Atrossian soldier like Keix, tried to not balk at the fact that a scout had missed an entire group of Ifarls heading their way.

'See, I told you to have faith in your friends,' continued Mohgen as they rushed towards Tilsor's boundary, hand in hand.

Vin nodded, even though she didn't think that she was familiar enough with Maii to consider her a friend. Nonetheless, hope surged in her for the first time, soothing the anxiety that had wrangled her nerves raw in the past few weeks.

By the time she and Mohgen reached the edge of Tilsor, she could see a ripple of pink in the horizon. From the looks of it, she must have grossly underestimated the number of Ifarls that Maii and Iv't could convince. Surely this boost—even if the Ifarls didn't have their powers and couldn't really fight—should tip the scales of winning this war quite substantially in their favour, right?

But a split second after the possibility of salvation came into sight, a small, sparkling golden ball of glitter exploded silently in the sky. Vin gasped as the ramifications of this new development struck her. This wasn't a signal that Zej and Dace were supposed to send up in case things went south for them. This was what their scouts posted along the route from Atros to Tilsor would deploy if they spotted ExA advancing. The only reason the warning was made as inconspicuous as possible was so that anyone who wasn't watching the sky intently for it would have written its significance off.

Vin turned to Mohgen immediately and said in an urgent whisper, 'We need to get word to Keix.' Yurkordu was too far off for Keix to have seen these signals. The only way to let her know of the latest development was to send a messenger over. Perhaps Ma.erdene had a better and faster way to get this done.

Seconds later, another set of golden sparkles appeared in the sky.

Without a doubt, ExA was on the move. And judging by the frequency of the signals, and the distance between them, Vin estimated that ExA was likely sending more than two battalions over. She mentally calculated how much time they had left before ExA reached them and cursed out loud when she concluded that it would be roughly the same amount of time for her message to reach Keix—unless Keix was already on her way back here. But the possibility of that was zero to none, because if that was the case, Vin and Mohgen would already have spotted Keix's signal to indicate that she had succeeded in her mission.

'I'll head back first to inform Ma.erdene,' said Mohgen, letting go of Vin's hand and patting her shoulder. 'You wait here for Maii and Iv't, so you can catch them up.'

Vin nodded and said, 'Don't worry. I know what to do.' She gave Mohgen a tight but reassuring smile and watched as Mohgen spun on her heels to race back to Tilsor, her signature red ponytail whipping back and forth from the momentum. Once Mohgen had disappeared from sight, Vin rushed to meet up with Maii.

The moment Maii and the Ifarls came into view, Vin felt a prickling sensation at her nape. Fatigue was to be expected in these Ifarls since they had been on the road for so long. But Vin thought she sensed this fleeting and bizarre robotic quality to them that made her do a double take. Maii greeted Vin in her usual cold and detached way, and at Vin's questioning look, she gave an imperceptible shake of her head. Vin thought she caught Maii's eyes darting to Iv't, who was standing right next to her. The powerful Ifarl looked like he had aged half a decade in the past weeks, but his eyes were shrewd as usual. When he turned his gaze towards Maii, she looked away, her eyes blazing and jaw clenched, as if biting back a litany of curses.

The relief that Vin had felt at the news of the Ifarls' return was replaced with alarm in an instant. Something was wrong, and even if she only had half a brain cell, she knew she had to keep her suspicions under wraps for now—since they were under Iv't's watchful eye. She made a mental note to catch Maii alone at the earliest instance, so they could speak freely. But her gut told her that even then, she might not get the whole truth out of Maii.

As the three of them, together with the rest of the Ifarls, made their way into Tilsor, and Vin updated Iv't and Maii on the progress of the preparations, Vin's discomfort intensified. How could they face ExA and expect to win when they couldn't even establish basic trust in each other?

12

Keix | Judgement and Incursion

Days in Yurkordu were cold. But the nights were even chillier. Yet, the frosty environment was starting to grow on Keix. There was something about waking up in the arms of her lover, warm and cosy, then peeling off the covers and letting the cool air skim past her rosy cheeks to coax her to alertness.

It had been three days since Jūn was allowed to leave the icy peak where he was serving out his punishment. As it turned out, Basch had greater authority than Keix had initially thought. Her estranged father was not only able to get Daman to agree to let Keix visit Jūn, but he had also managed to convince Daman to lighten Jūn's sentence—albeit in an under-the-table manner. This meant that while Jūn didn't have to be exposed to the elements, he was to remain out of sight and away from the main area of Yurkordu where most of the Kulcans lived. So, after two days of staying out in the wild, Jūn—and Keix, by extension—had now moved into a small, makeshift tent; they had been given permission to set up the tent somewhere in the vicinity of where Sandom left Keix to make her way up to the peak.

'It's past daybreak. Shall we head out?' Jūn's breathy whisper caressed Keix's ear.

The two of them had been waking up around this time to make their way to a clearing nearby to practise sparring since their swords hadn't been returned to them. The exercise kept them warm, and they had nothing better to do anyway. Other than the fact that they had taken a huge step in their relationship, everything had reverted to how it was when the two of them left Tilsor to make their way to Yurkordu. Even the niggling feeling at the back of Keix's mind urging her to focus on her mission, refusing to let her fully enjoy her time with Jūn, had returned. But now, unlike before, she mitigated her guilt by telling herself that Basch was on her side. He could get Jūn off the hook for what was considered a serious offence, according to Mujin. Surely, he would be able to convince Daman of the gravity of the situation and get the Kulcan chief's buy-in for the war? What she was requesting Daman and the other chiefs to consider was a no-brainer to her—save the world and be a hero, or hide and wait to get destroyed.

Also, Keix knew that her days in Yurkordu were numbered. The scout that she promised Jūn she would wait for should be back with news any day now. By then, regardless of Daman's decision, she would be leaving Yurkordu. The thought brought forth conflicting feelings. Though she had spent just less than a week here, she could somewhat understand Daman's resistance to getting involved in a war that had nothing to do with his community. Yurkordu was cut off from the outside world. It felt safe. Self-sufficient. Yes, both Jūn and Basch had told her that this tranquillity was tenuous, that any whisper of unrest could destroy this facade in an instant. But if anything, this brief respite taught her two things. The first was that she couldn't bring herself to fault Daman for being one of those people who lived to protect their loved ones, not the world. She had tried to do the latter—and look at just how miserably she had failed. It pained her to admit it, but she had become distinctly aware that she was just one of those people who didn't have the capacity to undertake such a grand task. She wasn't noble enough. But her second realization was at complete odds with the first. Even if she didn't have the ability to save the world, did that mean she shouldn't try? Not out of ambition, but rather due to how it had never been in her nature to sit back and watch as disaster unfolded. This glimpse into what the world could be like if peace prevailed reinforced her choice to persist in the goal of eradicating ExA. The hardest thing was not dying for the cause. It was having to constantly resist the temptation to discard the last shred of her conscience, so she could stay closeted with Jūn in the comfort of their little bubble.

She nuzzled against Jūn and buried her face into the crook of his neck as heat crept up her cheeks. When had she developed this clingy behaviour, and how had it come so naturally to her? As she tightened her arms, which were wrapped around his waist, the answer came naturally to her. Jūn made her feel safe and accepted. Even when he didn't agree with her decisions, he had stood by her because he respected her choices. She could be as self-absorbed as she wanted to in front of him because he had given her the reign to feel comfortable enough to show her vulnerable side to him.

'I'm going to take that as a yes,' said Jūn, answering his own question that Keix had already forgotten.

Keix didn't move an inch. Sighing, she said something she had never expected herself to confess in a thousand years. 'I wish I could stop time. Then we could stay like this forever.'

Jūn's chest fell as he kissed her forehead. 'Me too.'

* * *

A surprise in the form of Sandom and a majestic-looking shih greeted Keix and Jūn when they reached the clearing.

'Zorig!' exclaimed Jūn, rushing forward to hug a huge, furry beast with a distinguished mane and a pair of piercing yellow eyes. Its lithe body was covered in light, bluish-grey fur that graduated into a darker shade at the tips of its bushy tail and its mane.

Meanwhile, Keix was gaping—and she didn't even try to hide it. It was the first time she had seen this creature, which was considered extinct and legendary by Atrossian standards, up close. Was this the same one that Jūn had ridden when he came to her after the Ifarl ritual? Her memory of that moment was still hazy.

Sandom, who was wearing a set of pastel green robes that matched her eyes today, said something in her native language. She sounded like she was grousing.

'Keix,' said Jūn, leading his shih towards Keix. 'I want you to meet Zorig, my shih.'

'Sure, you don't see me. I'm not here,' mumbled Sandom in Atrossian, crossing her arms. She looked towards Keix, as if switching languages would make her presence here more prominent.

Keix couldn't decide if she should laugh at Sandom's annoyance or greet the shih first. Eventually, she decided that showing her amusement would be bad manners, and saying hi to Zorig would be polite, so she said tentatively, 'Um . . . hi?'

'Zorig, this is Keix. You've met her before, remember?'

The beast's intelligent eyes scrutinized Keix and self-consciousness washed over her. Somehow, she felt like she had stepped into a full-body scan and the person—creature, in this case—reviewing the results was Jūn's closest friend. She could have sworn if Zorig opened its mouth, it would speak as eloquently as Jūn. *But shihs can't speak, can they?* She stood frozen, a tense smile plastered on her face, as the shih continued to take her measure. She racked her brain to recall if there was some etiquette to greet these creatures that she couldn't remember at this moment; she came up with zilch.

After a length of time, Zorig made a snorting sound and threw a slow blink in Keix's direction. Then, it locked eyes with Jūn.

'That's her,' said Jūn somewhat sheepishly in reply to the shih's questioning look.

What was this—some kind of innate talent of communicating with beasts? thought Keix. When she had first met Jūn, he had had a way with the haagi they had come across too. This species of furry, palm-sized creatures that lived in the woods outside of Atros were great at navigating, but would lose their sense of direction in captivity. Recalling the grey furball that she had once saved, Keix thought that she definitely felt an affinity with it. Perhaps the Kulcans had a power that let them speak to animals—a power that she had yet to discover in herself.

'All right, if the both of you are done,' said Sandom, clearly irritated that she was being ignored, 'I caught wind that Daman and the other chiefs have reached a decision regarding *your* request.'

Keix and Jūn snapped their heads around to look at Sandom, who looked like she wanted to shout, *So, now you see me, eh?* But instead, she said in an even voice, 'I don't know the outcome. But if I were you'—she stared directly at Keix when she said this—'I wouldn't place too much faith in this bunch of *schwots* who can't even agree with each other.'

Keix stared wide-eyed at Jūn's sister. She didn't know the meaning of the Kulcan word that Sandom had used, but it sure didn't sound flattering. Apparently, Keix's original assumption that Sandom would be on Daman's side since she was hanging out with Mujin was wrong.

'Don't look so surprised. I'm just stating the facts.' She then glared at Jūn, who was looking at her with a mix of gratitude and love, and chided him in the Kulcan language. Then, she added for Keix's benefit, 'I just figured that Zorig might want to have a moment with you. His eyes were following me the entire time I was at their pasture riding Katmaa yesterday. Even if Daman agrees to join this war, they wouldn't let you bring Zorig along. We both know that.'

Zorig turned an accusing eye towards Jūn, but the Kulcan looked unfazed. 'Thanks,' he said instead, before turning to Keix. 'Want to go for a ride?'

'Me?' Keix pointed to herself as Jūn climbed atop the shih in one swift movement. She glanced at Zorig, whose eyes had lit up in . . . anticipation? Since Sandom had referred to Zorig as 'he', Keix wondered if there were any differences in appearance between male and female shihs.

Jūn extended his hand to her. 'Here.'

'Is it really okay?' she asked tentatively, unsure of whom she should address—the shih or the Kulcan.

At Jūn's encouraging nod, and the lack of reaction from Zorig, she took Jūn's hand.

'Do you want to sit in the front or back?'

'Er . . . front?' She might get thrown off Zorig if she were seated at the back.

With his widest smile, Jūn lifted her up onto the shih. He helped her adjust to a comfortable position on the saddle, then enclosed her in a gentle embrace as his hands gripped the pommel. Keix placed her own hands between the gap that Jūn had left for her and heard him whisper right next to her ear, 'Don't worry. Zorig's really stable when he runs, so just grip his body gently with your thighs and keep your hands where they are. Ready?'

At Keix's nod, Jūn nudged Zorig into a trot. To Sandom, he said something in their native language—a first for him, since he had been considerate all this time about speaking Atrossian whenever Keix was around.

Before Keix could demand to know what he had said, Sandom rolled her eyes. 'Just go,' she urged. 'You don't have much time.'

The next instant, Keix felt Jūn's thighs, which were set flush against her own, squeeze Zorig's body a little more tightly. The shih picked up speed obediently, and Keix lurched backward at the sudden change in momentum.

Jūn's arms tightened around her. 'Sorry, I should have warned you. Are we going too fast? It takes a little getting used to.'

'It's okay,' said Keix, a little breathlessly, as she got used to this weird feeling of riding on an animal. The only rides that she had ever gone on back in Atros were in metal vehicles or on hoverboards.

As Zorig broke into a full-on run, galloping steadily through the snowy landscape and weaving through the trees silently like a ghost, the cold bit into Keix's face, stinging her nose and cheeks. Soon, an exhilaration that she hadn't felt since her ATI days exploded from the core of her being. She found herself grinning, then half-laughing, half-whooping as Zorig brought her across the vast lands of Yurkordu. She saw houses—diminutive at this distance—sometimes spread out, sometimes in clusters. Clearings that looked like crop fields. But mostly, she saw heaps upon heaps of trees filling in the gaps between vertical rock faces—a landscape that imparted conflicting, welcoming yet forbidding, vibes.

Between the thrill of her ride and the unexpectedly laborious task of having to grip on to Zorig's powerful body with her thighs to remain in her seat, sweat started beading on her forehead. When the shih finally broke through a clearing, Keix found herself robbed of words as she dismounted with Jūn's help.

Standing in groups around her was a herd of shihs. They came in various colours, from light brown to one which even had hints of green. Together, they looked like a patchwork of forest colours that had been lightly dusted over with snow. Keix did a quick count. Ten. Fifty. Eighty. Over a hundred shihs were standing or sitting with their legs folded under their bodies. Most of their eyes were closed, but at the sound of approaching footsteps, a handful of them had perked up their ears and looked at the two humans who had appeared in their midst.

The shihs' eyes harboured neither fear nor anxiety—as if this was a common sight.

'I guess Zorig wanted to show you his home,' said Jūn with an impressed smile. 'I think he likes you.'

'Really?'

Jūn nodded. 'He took you on a quick tour of Yurkordu and then brought you here. Also, Zorig and I tend to see eye to eye when it comes to our preferences for company.'

Keix grinned as her heart did a silly little dance. If what Jūn said was to be believed, she had just gotten the stamp of approval from not just any shih—a historic beast by all accounts—but *Jūn's* shih.

Zorig, free of his riders, ambled away to join a group of his own kind nearby. Jūn, meantime, led Keix to a soft patch of grass under a tree, then sat down and gestured for her to do the same beside him. After she complied, she leaned her head against his shoulder and the two of them sat silently, observing the shihs.

After filing this away as yet another moment of peace to look back on fondly, Keix decided to face the thoughts that she had been avoiding for the past few days. 'I wonder how Vin and the rest are doing.'

'Have faith in Vin. She can handle herself. And with Mohgen and Ma.erdene, I'm sure that they've gotten everything set up.'

'How about Maii? Do you think Maii can handle Iv't?'

'Iv't's hard to read,' confessed Jūn.

Keix picked at the grass. 'You saw how he killed the ExA soldiers. And the way he said he wanted revenge. I think he's shown that he's pretty easy to read. That's why you were guarded against him, weren't you?'

'His intentions are clear. Like you said, he wants revenge. And to do that, he will likely stop at nothing. But that has got nothing to do with whether Maii can handle him. So long as our end goals are aligned, there is nothing much to fear from Iv't. Yet.'

Keix sighed in frustration. 'But I keep feeling that we've wasted our time coming here. And we've been . . . just enjoying ourselves for the past few days instead of returning to help them the moment Daman dismissed our request.'

Jūn cupped Keix's face in his hands and looked into her eyes. 'I won't allow you to guilt-trip yourself into thinking you could have done more. Daman *did not* dismiss our request. He said he would consider it because he has to discuss it with the other chiefs. And you did good by speaking with Del and the rest of them,' he added, his eyes full of pride. 'We need to give them time to think it through. Imagine being in their shoes and a stranger came to your homeland and asked you to fight alongside them in a war that has nothing to do with you. You'd need to weigh the risks too.

'And how much help do you think the two of us are going to be if we returned straight away without getting any of the Kulcans on our side? Or do you think that we should have stood outside the Council Hall like statues and mentally tortured ourselves while we waited for Daman's answer?' Jūn's tone was far from harsh but it was obvious that he was upset. He dropped his hands to his sides and Keix closed her eyes in resignation.

'Why do you drop truth bombs on a person who just wants to indulge in some self-pity?' she asked. When Jūn didn't answer, she caved and opened her eyes to find him still staring at her.

'It's okay to throw yourself a pity party sometimes. But I don't like it when you say you regretted spending time with me.'

'What? I did not say that!'

'You said you should have returned to Tilsor instead of enjoying your time with me.'

'You know that's n-not what I meant. I can't believe you're sulking over this!'

'Well, I'm doing it. How are you going to appease me?' asked Jūn, pouting. He was obviously fishing around to see what Keix would do to coax him. Impulsively, she grabbed his face with both her hands and gave him a loud smack squarely on the lips. 'Now, are you appeased?'

Jūn didn't bother hiding his smile. 'I will be, if you give me a proper kiss.'

Keix leaned in until their lips were almost touching. She held still until she heard his breath becoming heavy. His eyes, with their molten gold pupils, burned into her and the want in them drew her in. The kindling fire in the pit of her stomach flared and she finally closed the distance between them. Just like before, every coherent thought left her body, and she found herself melting into his embrace as they kissed each other hungrily. His arms tightened around her torso, and then his hands made their way to the exposed skin on her neck. The touch elicited a groan from her.

When they broke apart, Keix was still bubbling with giddiness. They took in each other's swollen lips and laboured breathing, their willpower to look away from each other's eyes out of reach until a snort brought them back to their senses.

It was Zorig, staring at them with what Keix assumed to be a judgemental look.

'It's bad manners to butt in on a private moment,' chided Jūn without much conviction as the shih continued staring at him unblinkingly.

Then, a cluster of footsteps from afar made Keix and Jūn jump to their feet.

Keix's good mood vanished in an instant when she saw a figure approaching. When she felt Jūn tense up beside her, her scowl deepened.

'Well, well, well. Look,' said Mujin, tutting. 'If it isn't Basch's esteemed *guest*.'

Keix ignored the malice in his tone.

'My father and the other chiefs have reached a decision, you know?' continued Mujin when he failed to rile Keix up. 'And just so we're clear, you played no role in the decision-making process.'

Keix's hopes soared. Did Mujin just confirm that the Kulcans would be fighting alongside them? She clamped her lips together. She wasn't going to give him the satisfaction of seeing her reaction—elation or otherwise. Besides, he could just be pretending to be in the know. Forcing herself to remain detached, she said, 'I would thank you for your advice, but I have no regard for a bully's words.'

Mujin opened his mouth, but no words came out. When he finally found his voice, he said incredulously, 'I'm a bully?'

'Self-awareness is the first step to self-improvement.' Keix knew she was being petty, but she wanted to get back at Mujin for what happened during their first meeting. She had seen enough people like him back in the orphanage. Regardless of their age, finding joy in taunting people was just what they did to distract themselves from their own insecurities.

Jūn, who had stood by as this unfolded, coughed to cover up his laugh and Mujin turned on him, scathingly spitting out what sounded like a grave accusation.

When Jūn's face blanched, Keix stalked towards Mujin. She had never been a patient person, and she never had the habit of walking away from a fight too. 'Leave him the hell alone.'

Mujin scoffed and switched back to Atrossian. 'You don't even know what he's done and you're *defending* him? Just goes to show how deluded and incompetent the both of you are.'

Jūn's hand, which was covering Keix's clenched fists, was the only thing preventing her from throwing a punch at Mujin. No one had ever called her incompetent before.

'Let's walk away,' whispered Jūn.

But of course, Kulcans being Kulcans, Mujin could hear Jūn loud and clear.

'Walk away?' said Mujin. 'Sure, you can walk away from me. But you won't ever be able to walk away from the fact that you murdered your own brother!'

Jūn's back stiffened and he let go of Keix's hand. The temperature around them took a nosedive. Even the shihs looked restless as many of them stood up and stalked away. Only Zorig, who had been standing beside Jūn this entire time, refused to budge. Instead, he nudged Jūn's shoulder and growled at Mujin.

Meanwhile, standing rooted to the spot, Keix's first response was to reject Mujin's words. But another voice spoke up inside her. *How do you know it isn't true? How well do you even know him?* She cast a tentative glance at Jūn, who looked pained. Uncertainty stabbed through her heart. She reached for his arm, but she wasn't sure if it was because she wanted to comfort him or if she wanted him to refute Mujin's words.

He turned to her and started, 'I can—' But before he could finish his sentence, his eyes widened and flew to Mujin, as if something had interrupted his thoughts.

Confused, Keix too, looked at Mujin, and saw that he was as shell-shocked as Jūn.

Zorig snorted while Keix asked, 'What's going on?'

The argument that had been set to blow up between Mujin and Jūn was forgotten as Mujin said something to Jūn, whose only reply was to mount Zorig at a striking speed before reaching out to Keix.

Despite not understanding Mujin and Jūn's exchange, she wasn't stupid enough to not get the urgency of Jūn's actions. Like before, she took his hand and let him hoist her up onto Zorig's saddle.

'Yurkordu is under attack,' said Jūn the moment she was mounted.

Terror seized Keix. From her peripheral vision, she saw Mujin running towards a silver and brown-coloured shih and mounting it, then taking off at top speed. 'How do you know?' Keix's question was a whisper as Zorig ran to catch up with Mujin and his shih.

'The warning signal at the bottom of the cliffs was set off.' Jūn's tone was matter of fact, and his steady presence helped ground Keix a little, even as she lost sight of Mujin.

'You can hear it?'

'Yes, you can too. Try it. Go to the farthest point that your sense of hearing is, then focus on pushing that invisible boundary beyond that bit by bit.'

Keix tried to tune out the quiet padding of Zorig's paws on the ground to do as Jūn directed. Eventually, she heard a soft but shrill whistling. At first, she wasn't sure if it was because Zorig was getting closer to wherever the battle was taking place, but once she pulled back her focus so she could ask Jūn if she had heard correctly, she found that she couldn't hear the noise any longer. Was this what Sandom meant by 'practising more' to improve her sense of hearing?

'Do you think it's ExA?' she asked, turning her head to the side. She didn't dare to move too much since she didn't want to get thrown off Zorig. But she couldn't see Jūn's face, even at this angle, so she looked in front again. They were now emerging from the forest into the main path that ran through Yurkordu.

'We can't be sure . . .' said Jūn, the worry apparent in his voice.

'How did these intruders get in?' Keix's knuckles were white from holding on to the pommel. Even with Jūn's arms enclosing her, she felt like she was going pitch forward any time as Zorig raced downhill.

Mujin reappeared beside them all of a sudden, with Sandom riding pillion on his shih.

'Here!' called Sandom as Mujin's shih drew closer to Zorig. She held out Keix and Jūn's swords.

Jūn didn't miss a beat as he received the weapons from Sandom. Keix took her sword from Jūn with one hand and held it at an awkward angle in front of her because she didn't want it to become a hazard.

'Who are they and how did they get in?' Jūn addressed his question to Sandom as she seemed to be the most updated on the situation.

Keix threw Sandom a grateful look when she answered in Atrossian. 'We think it's the ExA's advance party, because there aren't many of them. And we suspect that they somehow managed to get a hold of our charms.'

Mujin's voice was hard and contemptuous when he said, 'It must be from those Kulcan scouts who had gone missing.'

Keix bit the inside of her cheek. Basch had told her the Kulcans were seeing signs of people moving towards Yurkordu, but he didn't mention anything about their scouts disappearing. Was Yurkordu's situation more precarious than what Daman and Basch had led her to believe?

The unmistakable sounds of battle were obvious to Keix now. They must be getting really close to the fight, which seemed to be happening near the foot of the cliffs.

'Can you dismount from Zorig when we get to the edge of the battle?' asked Jūn. 'I think you'll do more damage on the ground than riding on Zorig since you're not used to it.'

Keix nodded in reply. Perhaps joining the Kulcans in this battle was a way to prove to them that they were on the same side—that is, if they didn't mistake her for an enemy and kill her first. But Jūn had faith in her, so she decided she would trust his instincts.

Dismounting from Zorig, she said with determination to Jūn, 'Do what you have to.'

13

Keix | Cross Junctions

Keix watched as Jūn rode Zorig straight into the thick of the battle and slashed through the ExA soldiers with an elegant and practised ease. She would have been content to just stand there and admire him if not for the fact that she was worried sick that Tilsor had fallen to ExA without any word having been sent to the Kulcans. Ma.erdene had reassured Keix before she left Tilsor that there was no way the system she had created to send word to Yurkordu would fail. She refused to divulge anything else, so everyone just had to take her word for it. Jūn had shrugged as if he had utmost trust in Ma.erdene, and Keix had decided to do the same. But now . . .

Even if Keix wanted to rush back to Tilsor right now, she would have to get through the waves of ExA intruders first. These ExA soldiers were dressed like the ones that she had encountered outside Atros—black, shimmery unitards, with gloves, hoods, and goggles. Even as they were engaged in a heated battle with the Kulcans right now, they moved as silently and quickly as Keix remembered they did. Of course, the Kulcans themselves were unparalleled masters of stealth. So the only sounds ringing through the air were the clashing of weapons.

Keix looked around. At present, there seemed to be an equal number of Kulcans and ExA soldiers. Basch was nowhere to be seen. Mujin and Jūn, who were the only ones on shihs when they had arrived, were suddenly joined by dozens more of the majestic creatures and their riders.

There was no better time than now to join the fray, so Keix drew her sword and filed a mental reminder to thank Sandom later for bringing it for her. When she encountered her first ExA soldier, she swung her weapon upward in a backhand arc to cut through its midriff. The soldier's unitard ripped and a sharp screech sounded but . . . how could it be?! Instead of blood gushing out from the soldier's body, a metallic-looking exoskeleton was revealed.

The soldier, who also had a blade built into their arm, seemed unaffected by Keix's blow. Dodging a counterattack from the hooded figure, Keix tried to recall the last time she had fought these soldiers. Back then, she was unarmed and had only managed to take down one of them. How had she done it, exactly? At that point in time, she had been running on pure adrenaline after starving for days. Now, she was no longer emaciated. She also had a weapon that she was familiar with. This should be an easy fight.

She pivoted to the side and cast a quick glance around to see what the other Kulcans were doing. But all she could see was a chaotic mass of blurred figures and flashes of weapons.

At that very moment, a shih came into her view. She caught a glint of metal in her peripheral vision. Reacting instinctively, she raised her sword to deflect the blow from the ExA soldier that was aimed at the creature. Whether her intervention was required, she would never know because her weapon clashed with the attacker's blade a split second before they were knocked out by the Kulcan riding the shih.

When the ExA soldier crumpled to the ground and stayed there, the memory that Keix had been seeking came rushing back. She glanced up and was shocked to see that the rider of the shih was Daman.

The Kulcan chief threw her an odd, indecipherable look and said, 'Strike them—'

'In the temple,' interrupted Keix.

Daman raised a reappraising eyebrow. 'I was going to say head, but temple works too.' As he finished his sentence, he hit another ExA soldier in the head with the flat of his blade. With a flick of his wrist, he deftly switched the way with which he was wielding his weapon and took down another intruder.

Yet another ExA soldier appeared in front of Keix, and she stepped back so that she would have enough space to bring her sword down forcefully on the head of her opponent. As it turned out, hitting them in the head wasn't as easy as she had expected. The figure parried her blow and Keix was almost thrown off her feet by the force. But her training with Jūn paid off, as she not only managed to stay on her feet, but also channelled the momentum into a counterattack. Her reaction speed took her opponent by surprise, and she landed a strike right above the hooded figure's temple, taking it down.

Keix fought swiftly as another group of three came at her. The freezing weather stopped bothering her as she took on the ExA soldiers. While this type of ExA soldier seemed easier to take down, compared to their bigger and bulkier comrades, their ability to counter Keix's moves as if they were learning to read her mind by the second made the task trickier.

But Keix was nothing if not tenacious, so she kept at it until the Kulcans had taken out every last one of these eerie-looking opponents. The Kulcans not only had the home-ground advantage, but the riders on the shihs were also best positioned to hit the intruders on their weakest point to render them unconscious with a single, hard blow.

In the end, this turned out to be possibly the shortest—and quietest—battle that Keix had been in. While some Kulcans were breathing heavily, she herself was panting from exertion. She saw Jūn make his way back to her, and she put her sword back in its scabbard.

Bodies of ExA soldiers were strewn around the clearing. Among them was just a light smattering of similarly unconscious bodies clad in the Kulcans' usual garb. The ratio was pretty staggering.

Yes, if this could convince Daman to deploy the Kulcans and shihs to fight ExA, Keix and her friends would have victory in the bag.

* * *

'WHAT?' yelled Keix. She couldn't believe the déjà vu that was striking her right now.

It seemed like nothing had changed as she stood in the Council Hall once more.

The other chiefs were back on their throne-like seats, with their guards beside them. Mujin had taken up his previous position beside Daman, and Jūn and Basch were flanking Keix. The only differences this time around was that everyone looked weary from the battle, and the Council Hall was packed with other Kulcans.

Keix forced her spine straight. There was no way in hell she would allow herself to look intimidated or dejected at Daman's rejection. Obviously, she had misjudged the effect of ExA's invasion of Yurkordu. She had thought Daman would realize the risks of not striking first. Instead, the attack seemed to have concretized his decision to stay out of the fray.

'We'll spare you as many Kulcans as those who volunteer for your cause. No more, no less,' repeated Daman. 'And those who are leaving with you will have to surrender their charms.'

Keix was rendered speechless.

In the aftermath of the battle, the Kulcans had set about examining the ExA soldiers' corpses. Contrary to Keix's wild prediction that these soldiers were droids, they were just humans wearing exoskeletons. Still, Keix was weirded out because even though half of them had just been knocked out and not killed, their breaths were shallow and they didn't react to any external stimuli.

The Kulcans threw hostile and querying stares in Keix's direction as she tagged along and witnessed these discoveries alongside them. Yet, nobody protested or whispered anything behind her back. They could have done it in their native language, and she wouldn't have understood any of them. Perhaps that was the only good thing about being an outcast in Yurkordu—the Kulcans only showed their discontentment in their behaviour and not through words, because they had been conditioned to the risks of being overheard.

But even *they* couldn't contain their chatter when they had retrieved from the bodies of the ExA soldiers gemstones that Keix supposed were Kulcans' charms. Recalling what Jūn had told her about how Kulcans were taught to guard this 'key' to their home with their lives, she concluded that the ExA soldiers must have achieved the feat of ambushing or capturing the Kulcans by surprise to get their charms.

And Daman's solution to this was to get the Kulcans who volunteered to join the war against ExA to leave this piece of gemstone—something that had been part of their identity since they were eleven—behind? He was practically throwing them out of their homeland!

Sure, that will definitely convince everyone to join me, thought Keix bitterly. She wanted to throw up her hands—or throw a punch in Daman's face. There was no point in staying here any longer. She and Vin, and the rest of the Tilsorians, were just going to have to make do with whomever they managed to convince. The battle at Tilsor might be their last hurrah, but they would at least die with their conscience intact, knowing they had tried their best rather than hiding here in Yurkordu while the rest of the world was slaughtered. She gritted her teeth and was about to turn to leave when Mujin spoke rapidly to his father, looking outraged. It sounded like they were having a disagreement. Her guess was probably right because Daman's eyes narrowed dangerously, and he put up a hand to silence his son. The rest of the chiefs also looked scandalized by Mujin's outburst.

To Keix, Daman said, 'We will not be asking anyone to fight your war for you, if they don't want to.'

Jūn spoke up then. 'How many Kulcans will be joining us?'

Daman, whose facial features had remained inscrutable, looked at Basch.

'Two thousand,' replied Keix's father.

Having finally caught on to what each of them meant, Keix stared aghast at Daman. 'Two thousand? How do you think two thousand Kulcans are going to fare against an enemy that has who-knows-how-many troops and that is making use of machinery and odd weapons to conquer the world?'

Daman remained unaffected by Keix's plea. 'I cannot force my people to fight a war that they want no part of,' he said simply.

Keix was too incensed to continue speaking in circles with Daman right now. She turned to Basch and asked without any sense of propriety, 'You'll be leading the contingent?' He had promised her previously that Daman could be swayed. But look at where they were right now.

Basch shook his head. 'Jūn and Mujin will be leading it. I'll be staying back in Yurkordu.'

'What?' Keix couldn't stop herself from blurting out the same response over and over again. But what else could she say? Basch, who was some sort of commander, was trusting Jūn and Mujin with two thousand who-knows-what-kind-of Kulcans? Nothing made sense. It wasn't that Keix had a problem with this arrangement, but that Jūn looked as confused at this new information as her. And then there was the matter of Mujin. Since when had Mujin agreed to or gotten involved in this? Nothing in their interactions so far had suggested he was interested in helping her. So why would he lead the Kulcans back to Tilsor for Keix? Why would Basch get Mujin to do this?

'I've already discussed this with Mujin. He and Sandom will fill the two of you in later,' said Basch, signalling an end to the conversation.

Keix blew her top. Why should she agree to a plan that she had no part in finalizing? Sniggering, she said caustically, 'Yeah, I'm sure *you* tried your darnedest to convince the other Kulcans that the world's fate is at stake. And you!'—Keix glared at the Kulcan chiefs whom she had met privately, holding her gaze the longest when she met Del's eyes—'Each and every one of you! You know if we don't band together to fight ExA, they *will* invade Yurkordu and you guys are going to have to fight this war all the same! Except this time, you'll not have the advantage of being prepared for it—just like today!'

The Kulcans collectively drew in sharp breaths. But Keix couldn't care less. To hell with not offending the chiefs. Or any other Kulcan for that matter. There was nothing more for her to lose now anyway—except perhaps the two thousand Kulcans who would likely have reconsidered their decision after the ultimatum issued by Daman.

The Kulcan chief's eyes were contemptuous as he glared at her. 'We're *always* prepared for war. But only for wars that we have a stake in. Wars that are *worth* spilling Kulcan blood for.'

Before Keix could react, Mujin had stepped away from his father's elaborately carved chair and taken off his charm. Keix had to blink rapidly. She must be seeing things. When Mujin declared something to his father, she turned to Jūn and made it clear through a querying look that she needed an explanation. Right now.

So, Jūn whispered in her ear, 'He just told Daman to keep his charm safe and await his return.'

Keix's eyes bulged out of their sockets. Jūn wouldn't lie to her. So, Mujin was really on her side . . .? Was it because of Sandom? Or had Basch convinced him to do so? Regardless, Mujin's status as the son of the head Kulcan chief and his willingness to surrender his charm to join the battle spoke volumes about how confident he was about winning. Keix didn't want to talk herself down, but whichever way she looked at it, she couldn't figure out how Mujin was calculating these odds. But she knew what he just did would have swayed many of the Kulcans present.

Still, Keix refused to lay her doubts to rest. She would not let her guard down around Mujin until she got to the bottom of what he was playing at.

* * *

'Someone remind me again why he's here?' said Keix irritably. She was sitting with Jūn and Sandom in a large clearing, on the fringes of the two-thousand-strong contingent of Kulcans. It had been a week since they left Yurkordu, and Keix could no longer stand the apprehension building up within her. Perhaps because she was travelling with Kulcans, or she was now more anxious to get back to Tilsor, Keix felt that they were making faster progress compared to when she and Jūn had been heading to Yurkordu. As Sandom had predicted, Daman hadn't allowed anyone to ride the creatures out of their homeland. But even at the breakneck pace with which they were journeying, Keix estimated that it would still take them another three to five days to reach Tilsor.

Keix fixed her gaze on Mujin, who was walking around the temporary camp that they had set up tonight, diligently checking on everyone's well-being, then looked back at Jūn.

Jūn tried to hide his smile. With his usual patience, he replied, 'Well, he was the first to turn in his charm in the Council Hall.'

Sandom just shrugged.

Sighing in exasperation, Keix hissed as softly as she could, 'I still don't trust him.'

'And you trust me?' prodded Sandom jokingly, earning a mock glare from Keix.

'I don't, but your brother's here to keep you in check,' said Keix on purpose. She grinned in satisfaction when Sandom scowled at her. The truth was, Keix's gut feeling told her Sandom was on her side, especially after she had brought both her and Jūn's swords to them when Yurkordu was attacked. But in Mujin's case, just his hostility towards Jūn was enough for Keix to blacklist him.

'Mujin's not *that* bad once you get to know him,' said Jūn, trying to soothe Keix's anger. But his words had quite the opposite effect.

'Not that bad?' repeated Keix, her eyes widening to the point they almost swallowed up her face. *How could you vouch for his character so sincerely when that pest accused you of murdering your own brother?* Keix wanted to ask. But she bit her tongue because she had faith that Jūn would explain everything to her in due course when he was ready. So she changed tack instead. 'Don't you remember what Iv't said? He said it's common sense to never go to war with soldiers who are unwilling to fight it for you!'

This was the rationale that the Ifarl had given previously, when they had asked him why he didn't head straight to Yurkordu to compel all the Kulcans to fight for them. His words seemed like a premonition now.

To Keix's surprise, Sandom replied without a hint of malice, 'Then you have nothing to worry about, right? Every one of us present here volunteered for this.'

'But what if he's going around putting *ideas* in other Kulcans' heads, sabotaging us?'

Sandom frowned. 'Why would he do that?'

'Mujin won't do anything to jeopardize the lives of the people whom he's fighting alongside,' said Jūn, shaking his head for emphasis.

Keix fought the urge to grab him by the shoulders and shake some sense into him. 'You two can't seriously be defending him right now.' There was only one word to describe these Kulcans (yes, Jūn included): weird.

'I am,' said Jūn, reaching out to pat Keix's clenched fists. 'Mujin's not an evil person. He can hate me, and he can still want to help because he thinks it's the right thing to do. These two issues don't have to be mutually exclusive. He's . . . an opinionated person and his feelings are valid because they are his.'

The right thing to do . . .? thought Keix. She was reminded of Zej, who had done everything he did because he thought it was for the greater good. Then, she recalled how she felt about this entire situation and why she was here instead of escaping from ExA with Jūn and she fell silent. They were all victims of their circumstances . . . Still, she couldn't help but think that her lover might very well be stupid or naïve—or both. Even if the hatred that Mujin harboured for Jūn wasn't deep, no one in their right state of mind would be so unconcerned about fighting alongside someone who would think twice about saving their life on the battlefield.

At this point, Mujin strode up and made a show of sitting down beside them. Then, he bent towards Keix and whispered in her ears, making sure that he was loud enough only for Jūn and Sandom to hear. 'You know that everyone can hear you, right? Us being Kulcans and all. And it's bad manners to gossip about someone who's putting their life on the line for you. At the very least, we need to present a united, cordial front to the other Kulcans. Don't forget for a second that they are here—not for you, not for me—but for what they think is the right thing to do.'

Keix chewed the inside of her cheek. She looked like she was biting back a retort when, in fact, she had been surprisingly chastised by Mujin. He was repeating Jūn's words on purpose, but he was right. The least she could afford was respect for these two thousand Kulcans who had agreed to help her out.

Mujin turned to Jūn and added, 'Thanks for the vote of confidence, but no thanks. I don't need you to defend me.' Then, as if the conversation had just started, he said in his normal volume, 'So, now that we've more or less acclimatized to each other and the dreadful weather, do you want to tell us what kind of ExA soldiers you've come across—other than the ones who entered Yurkordu? Are all of them puppets? Do they *all* have weapons built into their bodies?'

Keix hesitated as she tried to sort out the mixed signals conveyed by Mujin's actions. He still looked ready to tear out Jūn's jugular, but he was behaving as if he genuinely wanted to take down ExA. She decided to give the clearest vague answer she could think of. 'It's more like they've fused themselves with the weapons.'

She thought she saw a calculated glint in Mujin's eye at her reply, but she told herself not to overthink it. If playing nice with Mujin could further convince the other Kulcans that the threat was real, she was prepared to put her personal revulsion for him aside. It also appeared as though Mujin was offering her a stage to speak to the rest of the Kulcans, who were definitely listening in on their conversation. Once she started listing out the different types of soldiers that ExA had sent after her, she realized it was surprisingly easy to speak to Mujin. In addition, the more questions he asked—all of them shockingly relevant—the closer the other Kulcans moved to them to listen openly to what she had to say.

By the time Keix finished explaining the entire complicated history of Atros versus ExA, she had the undivided attention of everyone in this party. No one had interrupted her, although she was sure they probably already knew more than half the things she was telling them—or, at the very least, the Kulcans' version of this history. Yet, they had let her go on without mocking or diminishing her tale. Keix felt a tenuous but odd sense of comfort and belonging with this realization. Regardless of her less-than-pleasant run-ins with Daman, the rest of the chiefs, and Mujin, she shouldn't lump all Kulcans together. She registered afresh the faces of those who had left Yurkordu with her—and for the first time, she didn't consider them as mere pawns in this war, but rather as people with their own individual stories instead.

There were more than a third of them who looked to be Basch's age—which meant they should be seasoned fighters. And it was this group who had their compassionate eyes trained on her. The rest of the contingent were made up of younger fighters around Jūn's age, determination and idealism etched into their faces. Male. Female. Long hair. Mid-length hair. Short hair. Bald. The one thing they had in common was their towering statures—even the shortest of the group was half a head taller than her.

Dressed in their battle gear layered over lighter robes—now that they had left the chilly temperatures of Yurkordu behind—each one of them looked as impressive as the other. A sudden sense of pride surged in Keix at the thought of being able to fight alongside them, as did a steely resolve to turn her mindset around.

I won't go into battle ready to be defeated, she thought. *I won't die trying to take down ExA. I will eradicate them so that no one needs to live in fear any longer—whether they are Ifarls, Kulcans, or Atrossians.*

Jūn caught her eye and gave her a proud smile that warmed her up from the depths of her heart.

And I will grow old with this Kulcan. We will go to bed together and wake up in each other's arms every single day for the rest of our very long lives.

14

Dace | Unravelling

It had been ages since Dace ran out of patience. He had never had to tiptoe around anyone—not even his parents—since young. But now, he had to do that every single second of every day. It was torture. Make a wrong move. Piss off one of those pesky ExA guards who were always hovering around. Bad luck to him. Because they would then take out that small remote they kept in their left pocket, punch in his number, and *click*. Goodbye to his hands and feet—and life, essentially.

Days were bleeding into weeks and Dace had begun to wonder with increasing frequency why he shouldn't just hurl himself over the edge. His estranged father was missing, likely killed or imprisoned by ExA. Lana was . . . gone. There was little to live for. Hatred and helplessness washed over him at the memory of her smile, the sadness in her eyes when she had said her last goodbye, and the gruesome image of her impaled on an ExA soldier's weapon. Mixed into this bloody sludge was the face of another girl, her determination shining through the gloom that threatened intermittently to envelop and drown him.

He sighed. Of course, it would be the thought of Keix that would pull him back from the temptation of casting his soul into oblivion. He wondered how she was faring, and his thoughts naturally strayed to Zej. Dace wished that Zej had better luck evading the unfortunate fate of getting caught by ExA. He knew the chances were slim, yet he held on to that sliver of hope because he hadn't seen any trace of Zej at the facility where he had been living like a well-fed slave.

How far have I come, to now wish for the safety of the person I fantasized about murdering countless times before, he thought to himself. He decided to turn his attention to what he was supposed to be doing presently—assembling a metal part. He worked on different parts every day, and today's project looked suspiciously like the fingertip of a mechanical fist for a three-storey-tall robot. He supposed the theory that ExA was resuming the production of droids held some water. These machines had been rendered inoperable when the portal between the living and the dead was opened because they malfunctioned whenever they came within the vicinity of spirits. But now that the portal was closed, it seemed safe to use them again. Well, as safe as whatever fallout ExA could handle with the destruction a mammoth robot could cause.

'How much longer do you think we will be stuck here doing this?' Dace uttered the question out of the corner of his mouth to the person beside him.

'Why do you like to ask questions to which you have no answers?' muttered Seyfer before sighing. His actions were clean and efficient, as he assembled his own set of mechanical parts. He had been silent the past couple of hours—or at least that was how long it felt like to Dace—that they had been at work. If one could call slavery 'work'.

Dace interlaced his fingers and straightened his arms to stretch them out. Then, he rubbed his hands together. He was getting calluses on his fingers, and his eyesight was deteriorating because of the menial labour that ExA was making them do. Even when he used to monitor security footage back when he was with Oka—it was disputably one of the most boring jobs within the rebel group—he had never felt like his brain was turning to mush. Now, he couldn't even keep track of the days.

Dace had to take his hat off to Seyfer. Not only did the soldier not bat an eye when they had woken up in the same cell after getting caught by ExA, but he also seemed to have an infinite amount of patience for mindless work that dragged on for hours on end.

'I was wondering if you had a different answer today, seeing as you've stopped sneaking away the parts you're handling.' Dace's whisper was conspiratorial, but Seyfer's eyes flew to him. 'Thought I wouldn't notice, eh?' Dace smirked. Although Seyfer's head was always bent and his hands never stopped moving, he exhibited an alertness that kept Dace on edge. That was the reason why Dace hadn't let his guard down and probably how he saw Seyfer pocketing one of the metal rings that they were supposed to weld to the board that were brought to them via conveyor belts. Too bad ExA didn't let them handle sharp objects. Dace was confident Seyfer would be able to break out of this prison if they could get their hands on a weapon.

One of the ExA guards walked towards them just as Seyfer opened his mouth. He clamped it shut and threw Dace a warning look.

Dace shrugged. The warning was redundant. Now that he had gotten hold of a thread of the cocoon that enveloped Seyfer's mysterious actions, he was determined to unravel it. He continued his task as he considered Seyfer's next move. The soldier definitely knew some people in this facility. They would acknowledge each other with the barest nod of their heads, but beyond that, they never spoke. Yet, every time they walked past each other in one of the narrower corridors, when their shoulders *had to* brush past each other, Dace would get the sense that some message or item was being exchanged, but he had never been able to confirm his suspicions.

In the past who-knows-how-long they had been stuck at this facility, the two of them had strengthened their rapport and uneasy alliance. In a sense, his father was right. The enemy of your enemy is your friend. Zej was gone. So was his dad. And Dace figured that the best way to survive was to latch on to the next best person, who, in this case, was Seyfer.

Dace was worried Seyfer had an escape plan that he wasn't sharing. He would strangle the elite soldier before he let him leave him behind, especially after everything that they had gone through. Out of the corner of his eye, he saw Seyfer slip another piece of metal into a fold in his prisoner's uniform.

'Wha—'

'Not here,' interrupted Seyfer.

Dace sighed in resignation. They both had to stay alive if he wanted to find out what Seyfer was up to. So, instead of making a commotion, Dace got back to work. But he couldn't stop himself from glaring at the side of Seyfer's head. Through telepathic powers that he knew he didn't have, he tried to deliver a promise that he would ask the ex-elite soldier about his latest steal the next chance he got.

* * *

The atmosphere felt tenser than usual that night when Dace and Seyfer were making their way back to their cell after dinner. Dace couldn't put his finger on it, but he could swear that something was clearly about to go down. The number of ExA soldiers patrolling the corridors had been diminishing gradually in the past week. The frequency of patrols had also dropped, though neither of these developments were obvious. The soldiers also seemed more uptight—and that was saying something, seeing how stuck up they had been from the very start.

There was no way that Seyfer, being the observant soldier he was, hadn't noticed this. But none of them said a word about it to each other, as if they had reached an unspoken agreement to prioritize self-preservation. Who knew how fast the guards would pull out their remote to dismember someone who dared criticize them.

But Dace was itching to ask Seyfer about what had happened in the dining hall. Seyfer had once again brushed past someone while they were returning their food trays, and when Dace had looked closely at his cellmate's sleeve afterwards, he could swear that there was something hidden in it, right next to the deadly metal contraptions that they had on.

Once they entered their cell, Seyfer gestured for Dace to get into a corner.

Dace's reply was a confused frown. What was Seyfer up to? There were surveillance cameras all around.

Dace had enough experience with Oka to know that there were no corners in this facility that did not have cameras pointed at them.

He had always exercised caution when speaking to Seyfer because he didn't know how soft a conversation had to be so that it would not be picked up by the devices. 'What do you want?' he mouthed in response.

'Just come here. Now,' Seyfer hissed.

Bewildered, Dace finally gave in to his curiosity and did as Seyfer asked. He got a rude shock when Seyfer invaded his personal space, stopping short of pressing the lengths of their bodies together. Dace's back snapped ramrod straight. Part of his brain ceased to function because this was one of the few times anyone had gotten so close to him, physically; Lana was the first, and in a momentary lapse of judgement, Zej had been the second.

A logical voice in Dace's head insisted that Seyfer must have an indisputable reason for wanting to appear as if they were making out in their cell. He tried to stay calm, but the moment Seyfer ran his hands along the length of Dace's arm, he lost it. He jerked his hands, which were itching to shove Seyfer away, straight. 'What do you think you are doing?' whispered Dace through gritted teeth.

'This.' Seyfer brushed his wrists against Dace's and a soft clank rang out as their manacles came into contact. 'Move your right hand between us.'

Dace blinked. 'What?'

'Right hand. Move it to your stomach. Hurry.'

Nothing made sense—he and Seyfer whispering into each other's ears, the way they were standing, Seyfer's out-of-nowhere instructions. But the part of Dace that was sold on its theory of Seyfer's 'indisputable reason' made him obey Seyfer in spite of the awkward tension in the air. This time, when Seyfer brushed his wrist against Dace's . . .

Dace's eyes widened. 'You're . . .'

'Deactivating your cuffs. Yes. You're welcome.'

See, indisputable reason, said the voice in Dace's head.

Then why couldn't he have said so instead of acting all mysterious? Dace argued with this voice of his.

He must have been worried about the cameras. This might be the most ingenious way to avoid arousing the suspicion of anyone who was assigned to observe the surveillance footage. Even though there are no dead angles here, the way you two are standing makes both your movements less obvious, replied the voice.

Dace looked to the ceiling. He couldn't believe he was having a conversation with himself—in his head. The things being imprisoned here was doing to him.

His silence must have made Seyfer uncomfortable too, because Seyfer knew Dace just well enough to sense that he was bursting with a million questions. 'I'll explain later,' offered Seyfer voluntarily. 'But listen up now. When the chime to indicate that it's five minutes to lights out goes off, we're going to run out of here. And you're going to follow exactly everything that I say, understood?'

Dace rotated his wrists in reflex. 'Are you sure they don't work any more?' The deadly metal bracelets didn't feel any different. Had he imagined the soft clicks from before? Now that the probability of escape seemed within reach, the thought of dying felt much more abhorrent compared to earlier in the day, when he had been toying with the idea of letting one of the guards put him out of his misery.

'They should.'

'Should?'

Seyfer raised a snarky eyebrow.

'How about the ones on my ankles?' He jumped when Seyfer's hands touched his hips.

'I'm going to kneel down now to deactivate both yours and mine, so you'd better not move a muscle until the chime sounds.'

Dace choked. But beyond that, he had no time to respond because Seyfer did exactly as he said he would.

Seyfer's estimation of when the chime would ring was perfect too. He had just deactivated all their ankle traps—gosh, Dace sure hoped it was true because there was no room for error—when the moment they were waiting for came.

The ExA guards patrolling the corridors, expecting their captives to return to their cells as they did every day, had their weapons all sheathed. So, when Dace and Seyfer rushed out of their cell, the first ExA guard they came face to face with was taken by surprise. He fumbled to unhook his gun, but Seyfer beat him to it. With a precision that Dace had become familiar with, Seyfer snatched the weapon from the guard's waist and swiftly fired a bullet at that thin line of exposed skin on his neck.

Dace turned his attention to another guard who was rushing towards them with his weapon out. Just as the soldier's finger tightened on the trigger, Dace slid towards him and knocked him off his feet. Seyfer finished the guard off with another bullet.

Giddy from clinching a win right off the bat, Dace wondered if they should have disregarded the fear of getting killed and just mobbed the guards earlier. The two adversaries that he and Seyfer had taken down hadn't even had the chance to activate the deadly contraptions—or thought to do so!

Scuffles had broken out everywhere by the time the two of them got halfway through the corridor. There were flashes of bright orange colliding with spots of grey that marked the ExA guards. Dace caught glimpses of his fellow prisoners as he ran past them and saw their hardened, determined expressions. None of them looked shocked that this was happening. Had they been informed of this rebellion just moments before, like him?

Though Dace had no answer to that question, one thing was for sure. The inmates had expended the advantage of their surprise attack. Dace and Seyfer found themselves fighting harder to take down subsequent ExA soldiers that they came across. A man with straight, shoulder-length black hair joined them, bringing their party count from two to three. Dace recognized him! He had brushed past Seyfer several times.

'What's the latest update?' Seyfer asked as he chucked aside his gun, which had run out of ammunition. Without missing a beat, he picked up another gun from one of the fallen ExA soldiers and continued heading down the corridor. Long-haired guy followed close on Seyfer's heels, and so did Dace.

Seyfer's question was left unanswered because the fighting had intensified.

Just as their group emerged into the wide, open space that branched out into other corridors to the cells, as well as a wider tunnel leading to the dining hall, Dace heard the crisp click that everyone dreaded. With the racket going on around him, it was a miracle that the sound had been audible.

Dace saw a petite figure crumple to the floor right in front of him. Her hands, feet, and the cuffs separated from her body. Her mouth gaping, frozen in the scream that she had been about to let loose that had died in her throat.

It was only because he had seen enough of these scenes recently that he managed to raise his gun and fire it at the culprit who had hit the kill switch without hesitation. Seyfer had done the same and their bullets hit the guard one after another, causing him to stagger before falling to the ground, motionless.

'Let's go. We're running out of time.' Seyfer directed them into the dining hall.

Dace fought the urge to tug at his cuffs as he swallowed hard. If his deduction was right, they should be heading towards a pair of doors guarded by ExA soldiers. That door led to an emergency stairwell that would take them out of this building . . . He opened his mouth to ask Seyfer what exactly was their plan but was interrupted by Long-haired guy. 'Staircases by the north and west sides of the buildings have been barricaded, as we suspected.'

As we suspected? Dace almost ground to a stop mid-run to stare at the man and Seyfer. How had the two of them managed to communicate? Dace had been stuck with Seyfer almost every waking second and he didn't recall them having had any conversation at all.

'We head for the east stairwell,' said Seyfer, taking out another guard.

Two other people—a man and a woman—joined their group now. The newcomers looked like they knew both Seyfer and Long-haired guy.

'I've seen you before,' said Dace to the only woman present. He guessed that she must have had a pixie cut before she got caught, because her hair had now grown out into an uneven shoulder-length style. He huffed as he sidestepped another unlucky soul who had been dismembered—the young man's bloodshot eyes were staring blankly at the wall. Dace almost slipped on the thick blood pouring out of his extremities. 'How did you guys manage to plan this?'

The woman blatantly ignored Dace.

Instead, Seyfer was the one who answered him. 'There are many ways of communicating besides talking.' It sounded like he was scolding Dace for being talkative.

Dace huffed in irritation and exertion as he shot dead another guard, then patted himself on the back mentally for his marksmanship. 'Okay! I'll give it to you. But I do prefer to talk. No need for second guessing, right?'

Seyfer didn't deign to reply, and surprisingly, ExA soldiers didn't overwhelm their group even when they got to the emergency stairwell. Armed with keys and weapons that they had snatched off the fallen ExA guards, Dace's group burst out into the open and was greeted by a blast of cool yet humid air that was characteristic of nights in Atros.

Dace looked around. How was ExA's security so lax? The soldiers whom they encountered in Tilsor hadn't gone down so easily. Then, he frowned as a faint acrid smell assaulted his nose. He tried to get his bearings. The building from which they had just escaped was one of the factories in Sector K, recognizable for its incinerators. This Sector was also one of the outlying ones in Atros that was the furthest from Tilsor. There were only two routes they could take to head back to Tilsor—*if* they wanted to. The first was right through Atros's city centre, which Dace presumed would be the most highly secured area; the second was to get out of the city and circle around Atros's boundary, which would take much longer.

'Are we heading back to Tilsor?' asked Dace.

'Yes,' answered Seyfer. 'But in order to get there fast, we'll need some mode of transportation . . .'

'So, we're headed to that building first,' said Long-haired guy. He pointed to a neighbouring structure and ran towards it.

Dace frowned, confused. As far as he knew, the structure was a storage facility. Could they find any transportation tools—hoverboards or cars—inside it . . .?

'We have intel that the droids that ExA has been building are located in that building,' said Seyfer to a wide-eyed Dace, answering his unspoken question. 'I'm sure you've noticed that we've been assembling different parts of these droids.'

Dace nodded, though he still couldn't figure out how and from whom Seyfer had gotten all this information. Tentatively, he asked, 'If you guys know this much, then do you know the whereabouts of . . . Alric and Zej?'

Seyfer froze momentarily. Then, in an even tone, he said, 'The last we heard, a guard hit the kill switch on Zej.'

Shocked, Dace stopped in his tracks and stuttered, 'Wh-when did you find out?'

Seyfer motioned for him to keep moving because the two of them had fallen back and away from the rest of the group. 'It happened right after we got caught. And the news reached me only about a week ago.'

'Why didn't you tell me?'

'I . . . I didn't want the news to affect you, since it was so close to the takeover day today. Besides . . .' Seyfer trailed off, a troubled frown on his face.

Dace narrowed his eyes and prompted, 'Besides?'

'He might not be dead . . .'

'What?!' Dace had seen the 'kill switch', as Seyfer called it, being activated. There was no way anyone could survive the rapid loss of blood from getting their hands and feet cut off.

The others in their group glanced back at Dace's outburst but continued heading towards their destination. Even if ExA still hadn't sent a backup to hunt them down—yet—they shouldn't dally.

Dace pictured coordinated rebellions happening across Atros's facilities like the one he had been trapped in. It was something Oka had dreamt of: overthrowing the organization that called the shots in the city. But he supposed Atros had more experience when it came to revolutions like this; they had chased ExA out of Atros once, after all.

'I'll explain later,' hedged Seyfer. 'But as for Alric, he is safe. He'll be moved to somewhere safe for hiding, until we come back for him.'

'Did he know about today's plan?'

'No, he didn't,' replied Seyfer. 'He was taken out of the loop after he tried to protect you from the other Atros leaders who put you on the "Wanted" list for breaking into ATI and releasing all the hostages who were supposed to become part of our hybrid army.

'Then, after we found out the Ifarls had been successful in closing the portal, we knew that ExA would return with a vengeance, and that it was highly likely that Atros might fall to them this time around. So, we started planning for the worst. Long story short, we managed to smuggle spies into ExA's ranks, which is how we could pull this off today.'

Dace only understood about half of what Seyfer was saying, but he nodded all the same. It wasn't important to know exactly how they got here. What was more crucial was how they were going to move forward. 'Does this mean we're going to try to control the droids that ExA built and take back Atros?'

'That's the gist, yes. Remember what we said about ExA only caring about keeping people *in* Atros and not out of it?'

Dace nodded again.

'That's because ExA thinks it doesn't have to defend its rear. They had already swept the entire landscape barren when they advanced to Atros. This is why they're confident that no one's going to attack from behind them because of these cuffs that they snapped on all their prisoners,' explained Seyfer, raising said cuffs for emphasis. 'All they have to do is to maintain that status quo by pushing forward in order to get to Tilsor and Yurkordu.'

'So, we're going to try to attack them from their rear, and trap them in between ourselves and Keix's group?'

'Yes. And take back Atros,' concluded Seyfer.

The group was at the entrance of the storage building now, and whoever was inside was opening the doors, gesturing for them to get in.

When Dace and Seyfer stepped through the door, a group of people dressed in the same orange uniforms hurried forward.

'Come,' called one of them, rushing to slam the heavy doors of the storage facility shut. 'The Odats are here.'

Dace turned to see a troop of the foul creatures marching into view from the narrowing gap of the doors. How could he have not noticed these mercenaries following hot on their heels?

A deep, resonant voice echoed around the huge space at this moment. 'Let's hurry and get up into the chambers of the droids,' said the voice. 'We'll make better and faster progress than being on the ground. Rett will lead the rest to retake Atros and ensure that we don't have to watch our backs as we proceed to Tilsor.'

There was something familiar about this man's voice, but Dace couldn't figure out what it was. The man was out of his line of sight at the moment, and he didn't think too much about it. He was too stunned, craning his head up to look at the huge, metallic statue-like droids that were casting stark shadows on them. There were dozens of these machines, and he couldn't even see past their legs.

Where are the 'chambers' and how are we going to get into them? Dace's questions bounced around in his head because he had lost his ability to speak. *Just how deep into ExA had these elite soldiers gone to have seized control of this space and the droids? And if ExA was launching an attack on Tilsor and Yurkordu, why hadn't they brought all these machines with them—when it would guarantee their victory? Could Seyfer and the others really wrestle Atros back from ExA so easily?*

As Dace looked around for some answers, a group of people stepped out from the shadows. When the light hit their faces, his thoughts scrambled further into an even huger and more tangled mess because he recognized two of them.

'Oron? J?' he gasped as soon as he found his voice. He hadn't seen either of these two men since the night the Ifarls closed the portal. Oron was one of the top commanders of Atros who had joined Oka, the rebel group, because he didn't agree with Atros's plan of creating a ghost-human hybrid army to defend themselves against ExA. Dace wondered how Oron felt about his decision now, since the closure of the portal had caused Atros to fall back into ExA's hands. Meantime, J, like Zej, was one of the who-knows-how-many spies Oka had had in Atros. Dace had crossed paths with him a couple of times before, and he seemed like a friendly guy, but Dace wouldn't even consider him to be an acquaintance. What were the two of them doing with an entire group of Atros's elite soldiers? Shouldn't they be on the 'Wanted' list, just like him? Why did it seem like they had been in on this plan since the very beginning?

Oron and J's responses gave nothing away as they only inclined their heads in acknowledgement.

A shadow descended over the group then, cast by one of the droids that was reaching its fist towards them. Dace's first instinct was to duck and get out of danger, but Seyfer grabbed his hand to stop him.

To Oron, Seyfer asked, 'How many of these did we manage to create?'

Dace's confused gaze swivelled between the two men as Oron replied, 'Only about fifteen. That's the best we could do within the short span of time that it took ExA to move out all their droids. But this number should be sufficient for us to get out of here.'

The fist came to a stop in front of them and its fingers uncurled.

Dace watched in astonishment as the soldier nearest to it climbed up into the droid's gigantic palm. Around them, other soldiers and survivors were also mounting the palms of the droids who had reached down to retrieve them. Seyfer gestured for Dace to do the same as Long-haired guy asked Oron, 'How many soldiers did we lose?'

Oron shook his head, his expression grim. 'Not many. About ten of them didn't survive the fusion process, but it's already a good ratio compared to the number of civilians ExA sacrificed trying to get these droids working.' He climbed up the droid's palm nearest to them and continued, 'We lost more than thirty trying to figure out how to turn off the controls to that Ifarl chant they put in place.'

Oron's words sent the cogs in Dace's brain turning, but his head hurt from the sheer effort he had to make to connect the dots. All he got from the conversation was that ExA was somehow controlling the people in the droids with an Ifarl chant, and many people—mostly civilians—had died when ExA tried to fuse their bodies with the droids. Then, the fist that Dace was sitting in moved upward and it took all his willpower not to freak out and fall off from this exposed 'lift'.

When the fist stopped at the droid's chest, a panel swung outward and everyone stepped through it.

The sight that Dace saw was mind-boggling, enlightening, and horrifying in equal parts. Standing in the centre of the 'chamber' that Oron had mentioned was a woman strapped to what looked like the back half of a human-shaped exoskeleton. Her hands and feet had been cut off, and her limbs were strung up by thick wires to the corners of the small, squarish space. But instead of looking helpless, determination shone in her eyes.

A ringing filled Dace's ears as he stepped into the 'chamber' and the panel slid shut behind him. Was this what Seyfer meant when he said that Zej might not be dead . . .? Before his horrified thoughts could spiral, the woman's bored voice rang through the small space.

'Come on, quit dallying,' she said. 'I didn't volunteer to chop off my hands and feet to watch you guys chit-chat.' And with that, she frowned in concentration and swung her arms and legs, and Dace, who had finally managed to put two and two together, was barely surprised to see the droid stomping forward.

Interlude II

I don't know how long this has been going on. I know that time is passing. Just not for me. Time seems to have everything yet nothing to do with me.

So, when the first pull of desire strikes, I'm overtaken by a thirst I've never experienced. It calls out to me from a subtle ripple in the tranquil environment. I turn towards the source—so do the other souls. And we do so in unison. The draw is irresistible. Come, *it seems to say.* It's time to do what you need to. To do what you've been meaning to.

We pause to ponder the call, but only for a split second. Then, we rush towards the cracks in the dimension. There are several fissures. I surge towards the one closest to me and fly through it without a second thought.

My senses return the moment I land in the other dimension. Buzzing life energies call to me from all directions. I hear something in my mind.

Take it. Chase it down. Absorb it.

I barely registered that I had become a small, glowing orb. All the better to speed to my first destination—the nearest source of life energy. I touch it and it electrifies me. For the first time, I feel truly alive. Alive in a way that I had never felt even before I died.

The sensations I feel are like blood rushing to a numb limb—every touch is amplified to the extreme. I don't recoil from the prickly sensation. I relish it. There is something familiar—no, friendly—about this. It makes me hunger for more.

But the exhilaration is snatched from me as suddenly as it appeared. I am jerked back into the weird dimension and the fissure has sealed itself up.

Deep silence returns.

A desperation that's worse than desperation sets in. I feel like a child who had been given a candy only to have it taken from me after I got a brief taste of it. Something had pried my mouth open and taken my treat from me. Yet, there is nothing I can do except rage and grieve over this loss.

No. This anguish I'm feeling cannot go on. I need to empty my mind. I should not think. I should not know. I should not feel. Not anything. Nothing.

This is what death should be like.

15

Disruption

The massive droids crumbled stones and crushed grass as they stomped one foot in front of the other, making the ground shudder with every step that they took. Alongside them marched soldiers outfitted with machine parts. The droids recognized them as kin—inasmuch as machines and robots could be considered related. The melodious chanting in their system told them they were all on the same side.

The soldiers conversed with each other as they proceeded towards their destination. Unlike the humans encased within the metal shells in the droids, the soldiers' humanity was unaffected by the machine parts embedded in their bodies. They also needed regular breaks to rest and regain their strength before continuing to march forward. The droids would stop too and stand guard until their army was ready to proceed again.

During one such break, one of the soldiers—a young man who looked like he still hadn't shed the baby fat in his cheeks—nudged his comrade and jerked his chin at the droids standing behind them. 'Kinda creepy, aren't they?' he said, sitting down on the gravelly ground of the forest.

The man he addressed, an older, seasoned soldier, shrugged. He adjusted the weapons slung around his waist with one hand and took a seat beside the boy, sighing in exhaustion. The battalion had been on the move since daybreak. There was a limit to his physical abilities, even if he had been a soldier all his life. His left leg was aching, especially when compared with his right leg, which had been replaced with a mechanical limb. For a fleeting second, he toyed with the idea of replacing his left leg too, but the memory of getting his leg cut off resurfaced in his mind. *Forget it*, he thought. *I'm not putting myself through that type of pain again. And age is catching up with me.* Taking back Atros City had knocked the wind out of him, even though it had been done with minimal fighting. They had infiltrated the city and dismantled it from the inside instead of launching a frontal attack. The ease with which they had taken over Atros surprised him, and it made him wonder how absurd it was that these were the very people who had thrown them out decades ago. How and when did the rebels become so weak? They must have gotten complacent.

Still, the thought of launching a full-scale battle to conquer other areas tired him out. Perhaps he should have stayed back in Atros to guard the prisoners whom they were using to build more weapons.

'But I've been thinking of replacing my entire arm, or leg,' continued the young man, oblivious to the fact that his older counterpart had no interest in engaging in conversation with him. He raised his left hand, which was cut off at the wrist. With a sharp click, a blade extended out of the stump, and he started polishing it with a cloth he had whipped out with his right hand, which was still intact. 'This is great for battle,' he said, flourishing the blade. 'But not so much for my daily chores. It took me a long time to get used to being able to use only one hand.'

Young people nowadays have no sense of self-preservation, do they? thought the man. To the boy, he said, 'Oh, it's going to take much more than getting used to any type of inconvenience, if you want to replace various body parts.'

'What do you mean?' asked the boy in confusion.

The man looked around to ensure no one was paying attention to their conversation. The leaders didn't want to broadcast the fact that doing what the boy was contemplating might have serious repercussions. 'Haven't you heard stories of people who died just replacing a finger joint with a machine part?'

The young man frowned. 'Why would anyone do that? What's the point of having just one small joint being replaced with metal? How's that going to help you in battle?'

Suppressing the urge to shake his head, the man gestured to the droids and asked, 'Do you know that there are real humans inside them?'

'Yeah, of course. Otherwise, how would they function? But they're able to get out after the battle, right?'

The man let out a humourless laugh at the boy's naivety. This fresh-faced soldier would not last a fraction of a second if he were to get another machine part embedded in him. People with weak wills could succumb and die if they weren't able to withstand the fusing process. The more the machine parts, the stronger the will of the person required. That was the main reason why the leaders didn't have an entire battalion of droids; it wasn't solely because of the lack of materials and structures to build and house them. Now that they had taken back Atros, they could construct many more droids, but the biggest challenge was to find people to inhabit these machines and provide them with the life power that they needed to function. And at this point in time, they couldn't risk too many of their people dying because they didn't even have that many to begin with.

But they seemed to have reached some sort of optimal ratio when they developed the soldiers that they sent out mainly for reconnaissance. The weight of the exoskeletons and machine parts were easier to balance, which was why those recon soldiers made up a large fraction of their army. The only issue was that you couldn't fight a war with just a single type of soldier. Recon soldiers were stealthy and lightweight, but they had nothing on the droids when it came to destructive power.

When the man pulled himself out of his musings, he realized that the boy was still gazing at him expectantly. But instead of answering the boy's question, he glanced at a glittering star in the sky, then patted the boy on the shoulder and said, 'Rest early. You can think about augmenting your body with machine parts when we take over Tilsor.'

***

A tall, old man with hair shining silver against the backdrop of the rising sun gave the command to march on towards Tilsor at daybreak. He was one of three commanders leading this charge, and his co-commanders—one male, one female—were standing on either side of him. Their troop's unmatched discipline could be seen in the decisive and efficient way that they fell into step one after another following the order.

The soft stomping of the soldier's boots, together with the droids' loud one, drowned out other ambient noises in their surroundings.

Without warning, a strange jolt of energy filled the air.

The soldiers, who were still marching in unison, didn't miss a step. But they did cast glances around as their bodies tensed in preparation of an ambush.

A whisper broke through the ranks, stopping the entire army in its tracks. 'But . . . It can't be!'

The one who uttered the words was the young man who had been talking to the seasoned soldier the night before.

Colourful, glowing orbs had flashed in front of his eyes for a split second. But when he blinked, the flickering, floating lights were gone. There was nothing else accompanying this anomaly except for that seemingly pre-emptive shift in energy—no loud noise, no weather changes. Nonetheless, the terror it inspired rippled through the ranks. If these were what everyone thought they were . . .

The young man wasn't certain if he had hallucinated because he was feeling weary. After all, it was broad daylight. Besides the fact that ghosts rarely appeared in daytime, the rays of the sun could also be playing tricks on them. No one had sighted any spirits since the whole lot of them had disappeared completely a few months back.

But when the young man turned and saw the shock and disbelief reflected in the faces of his comrades around him, especially the experienced soldier whose face had paled, dread set in. The presence of ghosts could prove fatal to those who had machine parts fused into their bodies. Still, years of training meant these soldiers were able to hang on to their discipline and rationality—even if by a thread—to stay still and wait for their next command.

Thousands of eyes darted around as minutes passed and . . . nothing out of the ordinary happened—though disturbance had started rippling through the battalions as speculations about the return of ghosts spread. Engrossed in their own whispered conversations, not many of them noticed that the three commanders were discussing the situation in urgent whispers too.

Just when everyone thought things had returned to normal, a strangled scream filled the air. The glowing orbs had flickered back into existence. Some soldiers broke ranks. It wasn't just a small cluster of ghosts this time, but dozens, scattered throughout the group. Several soldiers came into contact with the spectres and started convulsing as the machine parts embedded within their bodies reacted to the electromagnetic pulses of the ghosts.

'Keep them away from the droids!' shouted the other male commander, a short, stout man with hair that was so black, it couldn't possibly be natural. His mellifluous voice carried through the air effortlessly while he ran to the droids who were at the rear of the battalion.

The soldiers moved to obey his order immediately, fighting the primal need to escape, running to try to shield the droids from the glowing orbs even though they knew there was nothing they could do. What use were machinery and weapons—and even their own bodies—against spirits that could incapacitate them with a single touch?

The veteran soldier called out, 'Kid.'

The young man turned his wide eyes towards the man, who continued, 'There's no point going head-to-head with them because what they're after is your life energy. When you see them coming, duck and lead them away from the droids. You have to be fast. 'Cus these spooks are.'

The young man nodded and thanked the older man for his advice, as he readied himself for the onslaught.

But once again—thankfully—the spirits disappeared mere seconds after their reappearance. The co-commander with the too-black hair who had been making his way to the droids heaved a short sigh of relief. He was ranked the highest, and one of a handful of Ifarls, among this group of ex-Atrossians. Most of the Ifarls who joined this troop had been spurned by their own kind for being 'stupid' and 'lacking in talent'. He himself had done so out of personal greed and a secret feud. It was his life goal to see the pretentious Ifarls cower in front of him. *They'll see that knowledge stands no chance against sheer, brute force, and they would regret ostracizing me.* He scoffed now. If he were really as inept as they said he was, he wouldn't have felt this shift in the atmosphere. Could it be that something had gone wrong with the Ifarls' ritual? Or was someone attempting to reopen the portal? In any case, he thought it would be better to exercise caution and slow down their advancement. He would advise the commander that they needed to regroup and make sure that the troop remained focused on their end goal. An occurrence like this was an unwelcome distraction. The soldiers would understandably be disconcerted, but it wasn't anything that he couldn't handle. He thought about how his powers had diminished since the disappearance of the spectres. It had been an unexpected development, but he had convinced himself that it wasn't something significant enough to convey to his co-commanders. He wondered if it was the same for the rest of the Ifarls, although those on the same side as him hadn't mentioned anything about their own powers weakening. But if the Ifarls back home lost these powers that fed their sense of misguided superiority, they would be pretty much useless, wouldn't they? Thinking thus, he cast his senses towards the droids and found everything to be intact—the endless chanting that he had put in place to ensure the placidity of their life force was untouched.

Reinforce the charms on the droids, he directed through mindspeak to the rest of the Ifarls who were under his command. It was better to play it safe. Then, he circled back to take his position with his co-commanders, congratulating himself for what he thought had been a flawlessly executed charm.

Yet, little did he know that in his complacency, something had completely slipped his notice. A man who was fused with one of the droids was frowning in his enclosure within the machine. One of the ghostly orbs had brushed against the massive bot for a brief second before disappearing. The droid had shivered at the touch; so had the man within it. The melodious chanting within the system had also been disrupted and the man's eyelids had fluttered even as he remained suspended in a state of unconsciousness. Images flashed through his mind, but they flickered away too quickly for him to make sense of them. The briefest touch of self-awareness had returned, and the man struggled to recall what he had forgotten—his name, his mission, his . . . everything. But the one word that had echoed through his mind hinted at something else that he had lost—conviction.

16

Keix | Disquietude

It was dusk when Keix and the Kulcans reached Tilsor.

Ma.erdene, who looked as stern as Keix remembered, though much more harassed, had taken it upon herself to help the Kulcans settle into a building provided by one of her contacts. To Keix's surprise, Mujin and Sandom had decided to follow Ma.erdene's lead instead of tagging along with Keix, who wanted to return to the bathhouse to look for her friends.

'I'll be with Keix,' said Jūn, looking at Sandom and then Mujin. 'We should get as much rest as we can, seeing as ExA could be here at any moment.'

Mujin sniffed, as if offended that Jūn had had the cheek to tell him what to do. 'I'll see to the Kulcans. And you'd best make sure everything else is in place for a smooth victory.'

Other than an exasperated shake of his head, Jūn didn't deign to retort. To Sandom, he added, 'In case anything goes wrong, remember what we discussed. Remind the others too.'

Sandom nodded and waved him off.

The thing that they had discussed was the contingency plan that they had come up with on their journey. In case things went south in Tilsor, Sandom—whom Keix had recently found out was one of the swiftest Kulcans—along with a dozen others was tasked with taking the news to Yurkordu.

Keix thought back to when Ma.erdene had reassured her that she had a 'foolproof' way of getting news from Tilsor to Yurkordu.

Was that method as simple as sending messengers between the two places . . .?

'All right,' chided the elderly woman, as if she had read Keix's critical thoughts. Pursing her lips, Ma.erdene continued impatiently, 'Let's stop wasting time here. You two'—she frowned at Mujin and Sandom—'come with me.'

Without protest, Mujin and Sandom fell into line after Ma.erdene, as did the rest of the Kulcans.

Keix was about to turn and head through the other exit in the Section, towards the bathhouse as directed by Ma.erdene, when she halted for a moment and looked at Jūn as if she had something to say. But then she realized she had said enough about her distrust in Mujin, so she shut her mouth and continued on her way.

Jūn, who was walking right behind her, ruffled her hair affectionately.

Tilsor's Sections were surprisingly straightforward to navigate today, and in no time, they had reached Ma.erdene's bathhouse. Once they entered, a figure with brown hair tinted with neon pink roots flew towards Keix and engulfed her in a tight embrace.

'Vin,' gasped Keix as an invisible band around her heart loosened.

'I'm so glad you're fine,' said Vin when they finally broke apart. She nodded at Jūn in acknowledgement. 'And the two of you are just in time. How many Kulcans did you manage to recruit?'

Keix looked down in dejection as she answered, 'Just two thousand.'

'Hey, two thousand's better than nothing,' said Vin, giving Keix a one-armed squeeze.

'They're just so stubborn! And selfish!' Keix burst out. The tears of frustration that she had been keeping under check suddenly threatened to spill over.

Jūn put his hand on Keix's shoulder, since Vin was still hugging her from the side. With a patient smile, he said, 'They are. But let's hope that Basch will manage to convince them to join us soon. That's the reason why he stayed back in Yurkordu. Otherwise, I'm certain he would rather have come with us.'

'You don't know that,' retorted Keix, glaring at Jūn. She knew he was telling the truth, but what he had said didn't pacify her in the least.

'All right. You two can continue your lovers' quarrel later,' teased Vin with a knowing look. 'We should head on up to the top floor.'

While the three of them were making their way upstairs, Keix noticed Ma.erdene's establishment had been emptied out. The opening and closing of doors, as well as the low hum of activity that Keix had associated with the bathhouse, were all absent.

'Are Maii and Iv't upstairs?' asked Keix.

Vin nodded. Without turning around, she replied, 'They arrived with four hundred other Ifarls just a couple of days ago. It was around the same time that we saw the signal that ExA was advancing towards us.'

'We ran into the messenger you sent about a day ago, and we made our way here together,' said Keix.

'Yes, we sent her as soon as we could,' responded Vin. 'But . . .' She stopped dead in her tracks and turned back to Keix with a complicated and worried expression. 'You know, I just—I-I can't help but feel that the timing is all too coincidental . . . for you and Jūn to arrive right after Maii and Iv't . . .'

Keix, who had almost bumped into Vin, frowned in confusion. 'What do you mean?'

'There's something wrong here that has got nothing and yet everything to do with this upcoming battle. I just can't put my finger on it. And Maii is . . . I don't know her to begin with, but something about the way she's behaving just feels . . . wrong.' Vin's eyes implored Keix to comprehend the feelings that she couldn't put into words.

'Do you think that Iv't has her under his control?' asked Keix. She and Maii had spoken about the possibility previously, but Maii had reassured her it wasn't that easy for Ifarls to compel one another. Still, with Iv't, all bets seemed off.

Vin chewed her bottom lip. 'I can't say for sure . . . But there was this strange look that she gave Iv't when she just arrived . . . I keep second-guessing myself and thinking I may have imagined it because she seemed normal after that. Detached, you know, in her usual way.'

'I'll observe her more closely later,' promised Keix, casting a glance at Jūn to get him to do the same.

'If she's under Iv't's influence, what do we do?' asked Vin.

Jūn was the one who answered this time. 'Then we'd better hope that his goal of taking down ExA is still aligned with ours, and that he has no other agenda. Otherwise, we'll have to take him down to stop him from dragging us all to wherever he wants to go.'

The hard glint in Jūn's eyes was reflected in Keix's, and Vin nodded in agreement.

'Do we know how far away ExA is now?' asked Keix.

Vin's expression was grim. 'It's likely they'll arrive any day now. We've been sending scouts out every day, but most of them have not returned.'

Keix frowned at the underlying meaning in Vin's words. Those scouts must have either been killed or captured. Keix tried to estimate the might of the ExA troops to no avail. Without the scouts' intel, any conclusions that she could draw were pointless at best. 'How's the evacuation going for those who don't want to leave Tilsor?' she asked instead.

'They're safe in a handful of Squares,' answered Vin, as she continued ascending the stairs. 'Iv't said he will make sure all the paths that lead to these Squares will be shut down once ExA's forces enter Tilsor. There should be enough supplies stocked to last them a little over a week.'

'And . . . Zej and Dace?' Keix had left this question for the last because she knew that the answer was not one that she wanted to hear. But this was a conversation that had to be had. Otherwise, it would be hanging in the air unresolved when they went into battle.

Vin hesitated for a moment before she shook her head. 'We haven't heard from them at all.'

The last wisp of hope that Keix had been hanging on to evaporated at Vin's words.

Jūn slipped his hand into Keix's and squeezed it.

No one said anything more until they reached the room on the top floor of the bathhouse. It was the same one that they had stayed in the last time they had been in Tilsor.

Vin slid open the door and Keix's eyes swept through the spacious room.

'You're here,' said Maii by way of greeting.

'Mm,' replied Keix. If she hadn't been watching Maii closely, she wouldn't have caught Maii's eyes darting apprehensively towards Iv't. The middle-aged Ifarl was currently seated cross-legged on a raised platform set to the side of the room. His eyes were closed, as if he was meditating. His neon pink hair was several shades lighter and less lustrous, and deep lines that had formed between his brows made him look a decade older.

Maii, who was standing next to a table set up in the centre of the room, backlit with the setting sun's golden rays, also looked like she had aged years in the past few weeks. The hard edge, which Keix had grown to associate with her, had also sharpened since they parted.

Keix reasoned that Maii's jumpy behaviour wasn't unfounded. *All* of them should be on their toes around Iv't; not only was he a crucial figure in their war against ExA, but he was also a loose cannon.

'What do we have so far?' asked Keix, giving Vin a subtle shake of her head to indicate that she couldn't tell for sure whether Maii was under Iv't's control—yet.

Catching Keix's drift to pretend as if nothing was amiss, Vin moved towards Maii. Keix followed her while Jūn stood guard next to the door.

'Besides the fact that we have a bunch of ExA soldiers arriving at any moment,' replied Vin, pointing to a map on the table, 'we believe they have expanded their boundaries beyond the original borders of Atros. The scouts from earlier runs who returned said the huts outside Atros had been torn down, and even trees in the vicinity had been chopped off. But all the debris had been cleared.'

Keix, who was following Vin's finger as she traced out the areas on the map, recognized it as the one that Pod had drawn when he was trying to figure out the layout of Tilsor and its location relative to Atros and Yurkordu. A pang of pain struck her heart, and she wondered how Maii was coping. She tried to make eye contact with the Ifarl, but Maii seemed dead set on evading her gaze. Vin was right. Something was most definitely wrong with Maii.

'What is the point of this destruction?' asked Keix, frowning. Taking over the unclaimed woods outside Atros was one thing. Why was there a need to turn it into a barren land too?

Jūn's voice came from the doorway. 'They're not expanding their boundaries. They're building something.'

Vin nodded solemnly while Maii stared at the map, a stoic expression on her face.

'That's our best guess,' said Vin. 'We believe they cut down the trees for tinder to mould metal. From what we've seen, that's what their weapons and machines are made of. Another point that corroborates our theory is that our scouts—not the recent ones who have gone missing,' she emphasized with a perturbed sigh, 'also reported that there had been a constant burning smell in the air. But a few days before we received the signal that ExA was on the move, the smell had abated.'

'So, you're saying they've managed to build whatever they needed to? That's why they're launching an attack on us, right? They're ready for full-on war,' said Keix, her uncertainty clear. She looked to Vin to see if her inference was accurate. But Iv't was the one who answered her.

Iv't, who hadn't moved a muscle since Keix entered the room, spoke with his eyes still shut. 'You young people keep referring to this as a war, but is it really? From ExA's point of view, what this really is, is a conquest. They will keep building and sending out troops in waves because it's a sustained effort for them. Without ample preparation, it's almost impossible to hold out against a drawn-out attack.'

Keix noticed Iv't's voice carried a slight tremor that hadn't been present previously. Was there a possibility that he was ageing rapidly now that part of him wasn't imprisoned, frozen in time, in a dimension that he had created for himself?

'Yes, you're right,' Vin piped up, agreeing with Iv't. To Keix, she explained, 'Because the smoke only subsided, we think they're still building whatever it is they're building, but at a slower rate.'

Maii chimed in, surprising Keix. 'Because of their advancement, it's near impossible to send scouts to go past or around them to figure out what exactly is happening in Atros.'

'But an optimistic assumption is that they lack manpower, which is why they're scaling back production,' deduced Vin.

'Logically speaking,' said Jūn, his brows knitted tightly together, 'one would send out an advance party to gather intel about the place they're attacking. In this case, this advance party would be the ExA soldiers that we've eliminated here, in Tilsor.'

Keix caught his eye and knew he was thinking about the ExA soldiers who had infiltrated Yurkordu.

'But it's safe to assume,' he continued, 'that while we managed to delay any sort of information from getting back to ExA by killing all of them, ExA would have caught on that something had gone wrong after they didn't hear back from their troops.'

After Jūn's elaboration, Keix finally managed to tie together the different threads of the conversation and understand what was on everyone's mind. 'This means they're sending over more troops now because they guessed they're up against a more powerful force than they expected?'

Jūn nodded in affirmation. 'What would you do if you were ExA?'

Keix was stumped. She had been trained to defend Atros, not attack other places with the aim of conquering them! But she hazarded a guess. 'I might send out another party to gather information . . .?'

Iv't's sharp and condescending laugh assaulted Keix's ears, and she turned red as he said, 'What's the point of sending out another small group of soldiers to gather information? The first wave of troops that you deploy *is* your first show of force. This means ExA would be sending their best and strongest soldiers to ensure a quick victory, even if it means leaving weak spots open back at their base.'

Keix gulped at the thought of facing an even bigger group of ExA soldiers than the one that they had previously fought here in Tilsor. But then her resolve to defeat ExA kicked in. Her brain went into overdrive trying to work out the best way for them to come out victorious should these assumptions which they were making be correct.

The scouts couldn't get past areas where ExA had advanced. Her side didn't have enough people to split up for a pincer attack on the ExA troops while trying to take them down in Tilsor . . . but ExA had left Atros, or their 'base' as Iv't called it, open. And Tilsor was set up to their advantage. 'So . . . if we can take down this entire group here, like we did their advance party, that means we've effectively crippled their forces! And after that, we can move towards Atros to eradicate ExA once and for all!' exclaimed Keix hopefully.

Iv't, regarding her with a patronizing smirk, said, 'That's the spirit. And you're going to hold on to that thought, all right? Because this group of ExA soldiers that we're going to eradicate just stepped foot into Tilsor.'

* * *

On the way to the Square where they were supposed to ambush the ExA soldiers, Keix kept wondering, *How did Iv't sense the arrival of the ExA soldiers? What was his other agenda, if he had one?* She didn't say anything to Jūn, who was right behind her, but she knew he must share her queries. She could only hope they would be able to figure out Iv't's endgame soon. But right now, she had to channel all her energy into this imminent fight.

As they weaved through the Sections, Vin and Mohgen updated Keix with more details of the plans that they had come up with during her absence.

'These are filled with combustible and corrosive balls which Mohgen developed,' said Vin, pointing to a stack of crates.

Keix nodded, noting the substantial damage they could cause. She recalled the uncontrollable screams of the ExA soldiers who had had these balls thrown at them, as they had spontaneously burst into fire or gotten their skin melted off.

'We've stationed one person in each Section,' continued Vin, gesturing to the tallest building in the area. 'They have a direct line of sight to the crates and will ignite them once the ExA troop exits the Section. This way, we'll cut off all their escape routes. If we set them off too early, we run the risk of not being able to corral them into the Square.'

Keix could make out a shadowy figure lurking near the open window of the structure. 'Will the person setting off the fire be able to evacuate after that?' she asked.

Vin's expression was grim as she admitted, 'We've mapped out a route for them. But . . . it may be challenging to leave once the fire starts.'

Keix fell silent. Knowing that yet another group of people was ready to sacrifice themselves to bring ExA down added to the increasing burden on her shoulders. She didn't know how she had ended up as the person with whom these people decided to put their lot. After giving a nod of appreciation and sending her wordless thanks in the direction of the person at the window, she turned to Iv't and asked, 'Where are the ExA soldiers now?'

'I'm making them go around in circles at the moment,' replied Iv't without missing a beat. He led them through the Section's unblocked exit, and they emerged into a Square where crates of booby traps were piled up.

A stroke of genius hit Keix—or so she thought. 'Is it possible to continue doing that until they die of exhaustion or starvation? Then, we could win this war without fighting!'

Iv't narrowed his eyes at her, as if what she had just suggested was the most absurd plan he had ever heard. 'I would have done that long ago if it was an option. Even though I created Tilsor, there are laws of nature that I can't bend. There's only so much of the city I can manipulate without something giving.' Then, he stalked to the exit on the opposite side of the Square as if he had had enough of Keix's nonsensical ideas.

Keix swallowed an indignant huff. She would turn in her sword and fight this battle with her bare fists before she would believe that the Ifarl who created Tilsor couldn't mould every aspect of the city to his whims and fancies. Every Section they had passed through so far was different—a sure sign that Iv't was rearranging them, so their group didn't have to make any detours. Even if she were to trust Iv't's words, wasn't it a bit too late for him to inform her of such a significant limitation only now? Everyone here had placed their faith in her plan—a plan that Iv't had a hand in coming up with!

Keix kicked herself mentally. She turned to Maii in search of an answer . . . only to have it delivered in the most unexpected way—projected straight into her head in Maii's melodious voice.

It's complicated. But things will turn out fine.

Keix's eyes rounded in surprise, and it took all her willpower to stop herself from blurting out loud to Maii, *You recovered your powers?* Maii must have a compelling reason for keeping this development a secret from her until now. Keix's gaze flicked to Iv't as Jūn's hand wrapped around hers. He had been walking in step with her all this time and, having caught her wordless exchange with Maii, gave her a querying look. But whatever he wanted to say was eclipsed by Iv't's announcement.

'We're here,' said the Ifarl, with a feverish look in his eyes. This was the moment he had been waiting for.

The Square that he had chosen for the battle was Square Thirty-two—the very same one where they had their first face-off with the ExA soldiers.

For all that Iv't said about not being able to fully control Tilsor's elements, he did manage to get everyone to their destination in record time.

Mujin, Sandom, and the rest of the Kulcans, were here too, dressed in full battle gear and standing in single files. The Kulcans looked like an island of statues set amidst a body of gently flowing water, formed by the fighters whom Ma.erdene, Vin, and the rest had gathered.

'The Ifarls are situated in the higher levels of the buildings around the Square,' said Maii emotionlessly. She was behaving as if she hadn't handed Keix a shocking yet mysterious revelation just moments before. 'We aren't the best fighters,' she continued, 'so we equipped everyone with guns.'

Keix's doubtfulness about the Ifarls' shooting skills must have been apparent from her expression because Maii immediately said, 'Don't worry. We'll make sure the bullets find the right targets.'

Maii's words gave Keix a hopeful, yet ominous feeling. It sounded like the Ifarls could control a bullet's trajectory, but the thought of letting a group of untrained people fire into a densely packed battlefield still didn't strike Keix as the wisest idea.

'How about you? Where will you be stationed?' asked Keix. She had fought alongside Maii and she knew that despite being an Ifarl, Maii could definitely hold her own against ExA soldiers.

'I'll be at the lower floors to stop anyone from getting to the rest,' replied Maii. She gave Keix a determined look before turning on her heel to move into position.

Without preamble, Iv't announced that he was going to start channelling the ExA soldiers into the Square too.

For a moment, Keix thought of asking him to hold off for a bit longer, but she knew that postponing the inevitable would only prolong the anxious anticipation of the impending fight. Better to get it over and done with. She had to trust what Maii said: that everything would turn out fine—even if they didn't have sufficient information about the battalion of ExA soldiers marching into their trap.

Mujin, who had stalked up to them, cast a sideways glance at Iv't and asked Keix, 'So, this is it?'

Keix nodded despite not being fully certain of the 'it' Mujin was referring to. She grew suddenly self-conscious as it dawned on her how amateur their set-up must seem to Mujin and the rest of the Kulcans who had spent almost their entire lives in battle. There was no overall commander, no master plan. Save for a whole lot of guts, as well as the stubborn belief that ExA would burn down the entire world if Keix and her friends didn't stop them, their side basically had nothing. But the underlying goal was clear as Iv't let the first wave of ExA soldiers into the Square. They were fighting for survival.

17

Keix | Clash

The chaos, when it intensified, took Keix by surprise. One second, she was confident of their chances of eliminating the ExA soldiers filing into the Square. The fighters on her side had ample time to prepare, lying in wait and picking off their enemy as they were ushered into the Square through Iv't's manipulation of Tilsor's layout. Even though their enemies were hardier than they had expected—which led the number of ExA soldiers to gradually increase despite their disadvantage—everything was unfolding as Keix and her friends had planned.

Then, without warning, ExA soldiers started pouring into the already-packed Square Thirty-two, clambering over each other as if rushing to get away from invisible demons that were hot on their heels. It took Keix a full second to figure out why ExA had suddenly become disorganized; the crates containing balls of combustible and corrosive fluids had been set ablaze and those touched by the rapidly spreading fire were getting consumed alive by it. Frantic screams and the smell of burnt flesh filled the air.

This must mean that we're facing the last wave of the ExA troops, since those standing by in the Sections were supposed to ignite the crates once their enemies had passed through, thought Keix. Her faltering confidence returned, and she hoped that those who had stayed back to seal off ExA's escape routes had managed to get out of the Sections alive. *Just a bit more to go*, she told herself as she sidestepped an ExA soldier charging at her and drove her sword into her attacker's side. If Keix's side managed to eliminate this last wave of opponents, they would be able to regroup and advance to Atros to put an end to ExA's senseless conquest—that is, provided their assumption that this group of soldiers made up the bulk of ExA's military might was correct. If they were wrong . . . Keix shuddered and shook her head. Now was not the time to have such defeatist thoughts. She pulled her attention back to the present and let her instincts, honed from the intense training with Jūn, take over. Falling into a familiar rhythm, she dodged weapons and blows that came her way, and thrust and slashed her sword at her enemies. Her opponents were easily identified, with their dark-coloured uniforms and protective gear, including helmets that covered every inch of their faces and heads. Unfortunately, this also made it more challenging to find and attack their weak spots accurately.

The line of defence that Keix's side had held suddenly broke as ExA soldiers swarmed them.

'Keix, to your left!' shouted Jūn, who had been right beside her this entire time.

Keix turned just in time to see a uniformed figure, whose body was engulfed in flames, barrel towards her. She gripped her sword tighter, ready to slash through the soldier's midsection before knocking them out. The distance between them closed. Keix caught sight of a bullet flying towards her. She didn't dodge because she was sure it would change course and strike her opponent, just like the rest of the bullets that had been fired by the Ifarls so far. The shots never wounded the ExA soldiers fatally, but they provided momentary distractions, giving Keix and Jūn the chance of delivering fatal blows to their enemies.

Just as she thrust her sword forward, Keix realized the bullet had remained on its trajectory and was going to hit her. She didn't have enough time to pull back, and the lack of warning proved catastrophic as the bullet struck her right shoulder and embedded into the bone. She lost her balance and almost dropped her sword. What was worse was that she made contact with the ExA soldier and a red-hot sensation engulfed the back of her hand.

Jūn called for Keix, but she couldn't croak out a response. One of her arms was on fire, and her other shoulder was burning from the bullet wound. It took everything in her to drop to the ground and roll around to put out the rapidly spreading fire—all the while praying she wouldn't get stomped on or killed by other ExA soldiers. She bit her lips, drawing blood in a bid to distract herself from the monstrous, flaming pain coursing through her body. Thankfully, she managed to put out the fire before it burnt her arm to ashes. Still, the damage was done and her skin started blistering. She stood back up and readjusted her grip on her sword to help Jūn, who was fending off enemies that had closed in on them. That was when she realized she couldn't see Jūn!

'Jūn, where are you? I'm all right!' She tried not to let panic seize her as she searched for him. Crippling pain radiated from her wounds with every move she made. Her sword was also slick with her blood, affecting her grip, so she had to dodge more than counter the strikes coming at her. With difficulty, she skewered an ExA soldier through the neck and whipped around to parry a blow. It felt like her sword was going to slip out of her grip at any moment. She needed to find her friends. Otherwise, her delayed responses would do her in before long. 'Vin!' she yelled. 'Jūn!'

It was impossible to spot any of her comrades—even the tall Kulcans—through the pandemonium. The onslaught of ExA soldiers was relentless and bouts of dizziness struck her with increasing frequency and intensity. Why wasn't the number of ExA soldiers dwindling even though so many of them had been dispatched?

Two bullets flew towards Keix, and she flinched in response. She thanked her lucky stars when they struck the ExA soldiers nearest to her. Instead of finishing them off, like she had done before she got injured, she took the chance to run away because she wasn't sure she would be able to take them out. To get temporary respite from the fighting, she ran towards the buildings bordering the Square, where the Ifarls were stationed. She kept to the edges of the structures and crouched to make herself as small as possible to avoid attention. Panting from the exertion, she reassessed the situation.

Dozens of bodies had piled up in the Square. The blood rushing and seeping out of the corpses was dyeing the cobbled ground a dark red. There seemed to be equal numbers of casualties from both sides—which wasn't a good sign, seeing as Keix's side had started this battle with the upper hand. Many of those on her side who had been killed were Tilsorians. Even though Keix had had run-ins with some of the bandits and wouldn't think twice about tearing off the head of the one who had slashed Jūn with a poisonous blade when they first entered Tilsor, she couldn't shake off the sense of guilt that had been bugging her from the very beginning of this doomed war.

Unsurprisingly, the Kulcans were faring much better. Keix saw one of them take on a handful of opponents as if the fight was just routine practice. Mujin and Sandom were nowhere to be seen. And Keix still couldn't spot Jūn.

An ExA soldier jumped in front of her. She stepped back and countered the attack, striking the flat of her blade against her opponent's temple and knocking them out. Luckily, this lone attacker seemed to be the only one who had noticed her. Casting her eyes around the Square to see if anyone else had crept up on her, Keix saw something odd. A group of ExA soldiers was moving swiftly towards the same destination as her. Even fools could deduce there were gunmen stationed at vantage points of the buildings—what with the bullets raining down on the Square—but the sheer number of ground forces that ExA had to face should make these snipers the least of their priorities.

Hell, even Keix had miraculously escaped notice, darting between pillars and hiding behind them as she skirted along on the fringes of the Square, while the battle raged on. And yet, this specific group of soldiers seemed to have made it their mission to take down the snipers.

It then struck Keix that a couple of the buildings had become deathly quiet, and the shooting had gotten much less intense compared to when the battle had just started. These soldiers must have already taken out some Ifarls! As the group turned a corner, Keix backed up to avoid landing in their line of sight and found herself bumping into a warm body. She whipped around, ready to impale the intruder with her sword, only to find a familiar face fraught with worry looking at her.

'Jūn!' she gasped. If they weren't in the thick of a battle, she would have thrown her arms around his neck and given him a long kiss.

'I've been looking all over for you,' whispered Jūn, relief flooding his face. He looked like he wanted to give her a hug too. But he stopped short when he registered her injured shoulder and blistered arm. 'What happened to you?' He ripped off one of the sleeves of his robe to form a makeshift bandage for her gunshot wound.

'I'm all right, but the Ifarls . . .' She tried her best not to wince as he tied a knot to hold the cloth in place.

'Let's go check in on them. Just don't leave my side again, all right?' Jūn pushed Keix gently behind him and helped her carry her sword as they followed the ExA soldiers from a distance.

Keix was glad that she could rest her arms for the time being. She would have to take care of the burn later on. But at least the throbbing pain from the gunshot wound didn't feel as intense now that the 'bandage' was exerting pressure and stemming the blood flow.

When the ExA soldiers entered a building, Keix and Jūn hurried forward to stop them. But suddenly, deafening sounds of stomping reverberated throughout the Square. Shocked by the thundering noise, the two of them froze. The ExA soldiers that they were about to engage, however, didn't look surprised at all. The leader of the group moved so quickly he almost managed to slash Jūn's hand with the blade attached to his stump of an arm. Thankfully, the Kulcan's reflexes were nimbler, and he dodged the weapon and countered with a fatal blow.

Despite her injuries, Keix managed to get her weapon back from Jūn and put down two ExA soldiers. By the time she and Jūn had cut down the entire group, the stomping sounds had gotten louder. Had ExA's reinforcements arrived?

Keix glanced around anxiously as she made her way up the stairs to check on the Ifarls. Where was Iv't? And where was Maii? Hadn't the last of ExA forces been channelled into the Square, screaming and burning? Haven't the Sections been closed off after that to trap ExA here? Why did it sound like ExA's reinforcements were on the way?

When another ear-splitting stomp rang through the air, Keix and Jūn, who were on the fourth storey of the building they were ascending, made their way to one of the windows overlooking the Square. Dread filled Keix when she saw the source of the noise.

A bulky, humanoid machine as tall as the clock tower had made its way into the Square. Everyone—regardless of their race and the side they were fighting for—was scrambling to get out of its path.

'That's a droid,' said Jūn from beside Keix, sounding awed yet disgusted.

Droids. Keix had learnt about them in textbooks. But she had always had the impression that these machines were 'life-sized'—or, approximately as huge and tall as the average person. But this one in front of her was a giant robot—at least ten times her height and a hundred times as heavy, by Keix's estimation—and similar to the one she had fought during the second trial of Taavar. If this droid was as difficult to take down, this Square, where they had set the trap for ExA, might very well be everyone's burial ground today.

Keix opened her mouth to ask Jūn what they should do, but before she could get a word out, another series of stomps echoed through the air. That was when the ugly truth struck her like a resounding slap across her face. ExA didn't only have one of these freakish machines that could effortlessly tear apart her and the motley crew that she had assembled. ExA had a *fleet* of them.

18

Maii | Dust to Dust

Maii almost took a knife to her gut when the machines appeared. The shock had left her momentarily frozen, and the ExA soldier whom she was fighting saw his chance to eliminate one of the obstacles standing in his way of getting to the Ifarls on the upper levels of the building. Out of the five ExA soldiers who had barged in to kill the Ifarls, he was the last one standing. His comrades had all been taken out by Maii, the harmless-looking and petite Ifarl he was facing.

Maii came to her senses quickly and, at the last minute, managed to pivot out of the way of the blade, which was attached to the soldier's arm and pointed at her midriff. She readjusted her grip on her daggers and leapt at her opponent, sinking one of her daggers into his neck and the other into a vulnerable spot between his armour.

As the ExA soldier fell to the ground, Iv't's voice rang clear in her head. *It's almost time to go*, he announced.

Maii cast a look around and realized from the uncertain expressions on her fellow Ifarls' faces that Iv't must have broadcasted the message to all of them.

It had been more than a week since Iv't had hooked up all their consciousnesses to his own and started drawing on their powers to exact his revenge. Maii had been obsessively observing Iv't's every move through the one-way 'connection' that he had formed with her to see if he had any other goal besides vengeance. That was how and why she knew he wasn't privy to her thoughts every second of the day, especially when he was focusing his attention on something else—

like now, when he was in one of the other buildings manipulating the layout of Tilsor. The Ifarls were like open books to him, but he could only read them if he actually spent time and effort to do it. The only thing was, Maii never knew when he was listening in. There had been a couple of times when she had been thinking of getting back at him only to have him scoff at the futile ideas in her head.

I need everyone to hold the ExA soldiers back in this Square, came Iv't's voice again.

Every command that he issued was a threat because he could make all the Ifarls go into a coma if they disobeyed him. Unless they were okay with dropping to the ground like puppets with their strings snipped off, they were effectively at his beck and call.

On Iv't's instructions, Maii had pretended that he wasn't in control of her when they arrived in Tilsor. She had also reassured Keix through mindspeak that things would be fine eventually. And throughout the entire battle, she and the other Ifarls had worked to keep as many of the Kulcans and ExA soldiers alive as possible—because Iv't told them to. Maii was certain he was setting up an ultimate showdown between the two groups; he couldn't care less about the Atrossians or Tilsorians. But every time she tried to probe to find out why he was doing this, he would either ignore or sidestep her questions, whether she voiced it out loud or in her head.

In the end, Maii had decided to play the role of the obedient foot soldier (well, as obedient as she could bring herself to be) because she knew she would be of little use to Keix if she were to fall unconscious. Thankfully, despite toeing the line that Iv't had drawn several times, he hadn't cut her off yet. Either Iv't had a soft spot for her, or he needed the Ifarls more than he had led them to believe.

Why are we holding back the ExA soldiers? How about the Kulcans and the others? asked Maii in her head. She didn't know where Iv't was exactly, so this was the only way to communicate with him right now.

As fate would have it, Iv't was listening this time as he replied immediately, *I need the Kulcans to retreat home to ask for help. Yurkordu's our final destination. So, why don't you go ahead and look for your friends to get them to leave Tilsor now?*

Maii shivered at his sinister tone. *Yurkordu? Why?*

You'll see, came Iv't's reply.

After the cryptic remark, Maii couldn't hear Iv't in her head anymore, so she sheathed her daggers and pulled out the gun she had strapped across her back. She stalked to the open window, aimed the weapon at one of the ExA droids within view, and pulled the trigger. She needed to test a theory . . . Like how Iv't had taught them, she directed a burst of command at the bullet, leading it to her target's neck because she suspected it to be one of its most vulnerable spots. She watched in dismay as the bullet bounced off the droid as if it were a rubber ball. She fired off another series of volleys. But none of them made a dent in the metal. How were the people on her side going to fare against these indestructible machines? She did a quick count. There were eighteen of them crowding in the Square now. And she wasn't sure if there were more coming.

'We should go,' Maii called to the Ifarls who were with her. From the looks of the situation right now, ExA would be able to turn the tables soon. Just having the droids stomp around the Square was sending everyone into a frenzy.

Maii rushed out of the building into the open space and noticed something odd; the ExA soldiers were miraculously spared being flattened by the robots' clumsy yet deadly steps. Most of the other fighters had retreated in fear because everything they did seemed puny under this display of strength. Only the Kulcans persisted, leaping from all directions to try to find a weak spot on the droids to exploit. But even they, blessed with all their athleticism, weren't able to land a critical blow.

Keix . . . Where's Keix? Maii ran around frantically while fighting ExA soldiers. Her petite size worked in her favour as she was able to weave between other soldiers and use them as temporary shields. But in the midst of the chaos, she lost track of the Ifarls who had followed her down from the building.

She was going to give up looking for Keix and just start getting people out of the Square when a familiar voice called out her name from behind her. She spun around to see Keix and Jūn running towards her.

'Maii, we need to get out of here!' said Keix, whose face was as white as a sheet.

Take the north exit out of the Square, Iv't's voice sounded in Maii's head before she could respond to Keix. *I'm going to rearrange all the Sections, so you get to the edge of Tilsor that's the closest to Yurkordu.*

What about after that? asked Maii. The way Iv't had managed to take all the Ifarls on the shortest route from their sacred burial grounds to Tilsor was still fresh in her mind. If his end goal was to get everyone to Yurkordu, was he going to channel everyone, including the ExA troops, over in the shortest time possible?

Ha . . . You don't have to know that, replied Iv't.

He sounded a little winded. Maii scanned the Square to try to find him, as she considered coming clean with Keix. Perhaps they could join forces to take down Iv't first, then turn their attention back on ExA after that.

Iv't's humourless laugh rang in her head. *I'm sure you'd be ecstatic if I died now. But if I die, so would all the Ifarls who are connected to me. You can go ahead and tell Keix or anyone else I'm bringing the war to Yurkordu, and I'll make sure to destroy Tilsor immediately and bury everyone here.*

Maii swallowed her nervousness. She had come too far to be taking any uncalculated risks. Perhaps it was better to take one step at a time—get out of the Square, then Tilsor, then decide what to do next. She wouldn't put it past Iv't to lock them all down in this Square and keep them here until they were all dead.

Smart girl, praised Iv't.

'Maii!' repeated Keix, looking at her in concern. 'Did you hear what I said? We need to get out of here! If we continue to contain the battle here, the droids are going to pick us off one by one.'

'Yes,' said Maii hesitantly, coming back to her senses. 'To the north exit.' She picked up her pace, leading the way to the exit she had indicated. It was diagonally opposite where they were, and the fastest way to get there was to cut through the Square.

Maii, Keix, and Jūn formed a small ball with a bunch of other Tilsorians and Kulcans, and advanced towards the exit. They took down one ExA soldier after another, and gathered those who were on their side as they moved. The only issue was that, as their group got bigger, they became a more visible target for the droids.

When they were almost three-quarters through to their destination, the droids' stomping got more furious. Maii whipped her head around to check to see what was happening, only to find one of the droids . . . hobbling? Rationally speaking, she should have continued heading towards the exit, or at the very least, in the opposite direction of the stomping. But her gut told her to get closer to the commotion instead.

'You guys go ahead first,' she said to Keix, Jūn, and the others in her group. 'I'll catch up soon.'

Keix's protest was immediate. 'No. I'm coming with you.' She looked to Jūn, who nodded in agreement and whispered for another Kulcan to continue leading the group towards the exit.

Together, the three of them moved closer to the stomping droid. They encountered little resistance in that short distance, probably because everyone, including the ExA soldiers, had moved away from the gigantic machine.

Then, Maii spotted Vin and Mohgen, surrounded by a protective circle formed by several Tilsorians. Vin and Mohgen were throwing small green balls at the machine and the reason for its unusual behaviour became apparent to Maii. She watched in fascination as the metal exterior of the droid, which didn't even yield to the bullets, started emitting wisps of white smoke and corroding where the balls made contact.

'Do you have any more of the balls?' shouted Vin.

'That's the last I have with me! The rest are stashed across various Sections,' came Mohgen's reply. 'But the corrosion is contagious!'

That means that if the corroding metal touches another surface, it will spread? thought Maii.

There is no point, interrupted Iv't again. *There are more droids coming this way. You guys won't be able to take them down. Just get everyone out of Tilsor. I'll hold ExA back.*

But you're going to unleash them once the opportunity strikes! protested Maii. Was letting Iv't bring the war to Yurkordu really her only choice?

I was wrong to call you a smart girl, Maii. The war will reach Yurkordu's doorstep regardless. Have you forgotten ExA's aim? asked Iv't.

But if we can take all of them down right here, then they won't be able to proceed! retorted Maii.

With that, Iv't finally ran out of patience with her. Clearly frustrated, he said, *I didn't want to do this, but you leave me no choice. Get all the Kulcans out of Tilsor and back to Yurkordu.*

Maii didn't even get the chance to gasp as Iv't's compulsion weaved its way into her head. Then, she heard his broadcast through mindspeak to everyone in the Square.

Everyone has to get out of here now. Through the north exit. Maii will lead the way.

These words didn't have a hint of an Ifarl's charm in them, but everyone still heeded them because it was the most sensible course of action now. Meantime, Maii had caved to his compulsion. 'This way!' she shouted.

Keix looked at Maii as if she had something to say, but then she shook her head and moved along with the rest of the crowd, leading them out of the Square and disappearing from Maii's sight within seconds.

While the Kulcans, Tilsorians, and Atrossians escaped, the droids and ExA soldiers in the Square seemed to have been suddenly bound by invisible ropes, shuddering and vibrating as they stood in their spots, unable to move even half a step.

Ifarls who rushed past Maii gave her odd looks; she wasn't sure if they had been compelled like her, but no one in the right state of mind would stay back in the Square. Some Atrossians and Tilsorians murmured their thanks, while the Kulcans simply gave her acknowledging nods as they fled the Square.

Almost half the crowd had escaped when a loud, creaking noise rang through the air. The clash of metal against metal followed. Maii spun towards the noise to see the metal exterior of the droid that Vin and Mohgen had attacked caving in on itself as the corrosion spread.

'Run, everyone!' someone shouted, jolting into action those who were standing still, looking wide-eyed, slack-jawed at the droid.

But the droid didn't fall, as everyone had expected it would. The only thing that happened was that its leg became bent, reducing its mobility.

All of a sudden, Maii felt an eerily similar sensation—that break in the dimensions that she had encountered the last time she was in Tilsor. Back then, she was being held captive by ExA and she had pulled at the thread of power to escape. Iv't had told her later on that the portal between the living and the dead hadn't been closed properly and fully, which was why cracks sometimes appeared. But there was nothing they could do to 'repair' these fissures, or so he had said. He had also warned that if they pulled at the energy, like she did, the crack might become bigger, and the closed portal might just collapse.

Still, days ago, Iv't had made the call to tamper with this fragile partition. Maii had felt him use as much unnatural energy as he dared to try to delay the advancement of the ExA troops that were heading to Tilsor. The Ifarls themselves—as well as the Kulcans—were on their way back to the city and Iv't didn't want ExA to get there before any of them. If Iv't hadn't used this dangerous tactic to slow down the ExA troops, Tilsor might have been razed to the ground or fallen to ExA before either the Ifarls or the Kulcans stepped foot back into it.

Glowing orbs started appearing in the air now.

Maii, who was struck with an idea, jumped when Iv't, whom she thought had retreated from her mind, said, *No. We're not going to reopen the portal. We can't. Not when the Ifarls on ExA's side have just arrived.*

Maii didn't fully register Iv't's words as the crack closed back up and the orbs disappeared. Ifarls? On ExA's side?

Iv't's voice sounded both sympathetic and disgusted when he said, *I'll let you see for yourself.*

And just like that, he turned the one-way bond between Maii and himself into an open channel.

Maii's senses were suddenly overwhelmed as the sheer scale of Iv't's power hit her. She could see in her head—no, Iv't's head, to be exact—how he pulled up a mini replica of the Tilsor map, rearranging the Sections mentally to cage and free the people in the city. The activity in every part of Tilsor could be felt in detail if she focused enough on that area.

Iv't directed her attention to a group making their way through some Sections that were supposed to be burning or had burnt down. Were those the Ifarls whom Iv't was talking about?

Awestruck by how Iv't was juggling all these events, she belatedly noticed he had popped up next to her—physically. Was his aura faltering? When he had restored her powers, she was finally able to see the glow surrounding him. While everyone else's auras changed colours with their mood, Iv't's one thrummed with a quiet ferociousness, as if it were a beast that he could hardly keep under control. When he drew on the other Ifarls' powers, his aura turned blinding.

Maii wondered if his powers were unstable because he had trapped himself in his own nightmare for too long. But now that she knew how Iv't wielded his powers, she wondered why this act of rearranging the Sections in Tilsor, which seemed so simple, was taking such a toll on him. He was the city's creator, after all.

Since Iv't had turned the connection between Maii and himself into a two-way street, her sense of the energies around her were also amplified. Now, she could discern a distinctive melodious Ifarl chant emitting from . . . the droids? She cast her attention towards the machines, and was shocked to realize that there were actual, living people inside them . . . who were being controlled by this Ifarl chant! How was that possible? Surely, no Ifarl would betray their heritage this way?

This is not who we are, thought Maii.

'Why are you so surprised?' asked Iv't out loud, his voice strained. His brows were furrowed. He was panting slightly too. 'There are bad eggs everywhere. Your heritage doesn't define you, nor ensure that you won't head in a certain direction in life. Your choices do. Has it not crossed your mind that there were Ifarls who left the village because of their greed, ambition, or beliefs that differed from your elders' teachings?'

Maii, who had been ushering people out of the Square's exit in autopilot mode all this time, paused mid-action. Was this really a good time for Iv't to give her a lecture on heritage and choices?

Beads of perspiration had gathered on Iv't's forehead and were trickling down his face. He wiped his brow and took a deep breath. 'All of us need to get out of here,' he said, his voice breaking up a little. He held his ground until the last of the fighters on their side were filing out of the Square.

Just as Maii thought they would be able to get out of the Square without incident, the crack in the dimensions appeared again.

Glowing orbs flickered into existence everywhere.

A deep rumbling coupled with a screeching noise sounded behind Maii. She looked back to see that the damaged droid was flailing its limbs. The corrosion had spread. The droid's limp had turned into a full-blown wobble. It bumped into another droid and, as luck would have it, its corroded part touched this other droid.

The corrosive effect was slow but potent; and the hissing of metal as it melted doubled in volume. Maii toyed with the idea of imprisoning these droids within this Square. If she could do it, all of them would slowly but surely turn to smoke!

But then, the one unimaginable thing happened. Iv't was prying open the crack in the closed portal. Just minutes ago, he had told her that reopening the portal wasn't an option!

'What are you doing?' she shouted.

But Iv't was concentrating too hard to respond. His face was red with exertion, and his aura was not only flickering now, but it was also getting dimmer. Even the pull he was exerting on Maii's powers had weakened.

'I . . . need to disable these droids. I can't bind them . . . using just our powers,' explained Iv't haltingly. Then, he cut off the two-way connection between them.

Now that Iv't had kicked her out of his head, Maii could feel the entire foundation of Tilsor vibrating. Was the city aware that its creator was at his limit?

The stomping noises that had stopped when Iv't brought the droids under control resumed suddenly.

Maii's sense of foreboding intensified. She knew she had to flee. Immediately.

A handful of the droids that Iv't had rendered immobile staggered towards them. Maii's first instinct was to run through the archway of the north exit and call for Iv't to do the same. *If he dies, we die.* That's why Maii turned back to check if Iv't was behind her the moment she stepped out of the Square. But what she saw made her mind blank out.

Square Thirty-two was caving in on itself. The force of the implosion made her lurch forward. She fell, and the foot of a droid landed right in front of her. From the periphery of her vision, she watched the diameter of the implosion grow in slow motion. Survival instinct took over and she clambered onto her feet. Even Iv't's safety and whereabouts were driven from her mind as she did the one and only sensible thing she could do. Run.

She crossed Section after Section. The streets looked deserted, so everyone else must have evacuated successfully, right? She was nearing the boundary of Tilsor when heavy panting came from behind her. She turned, only to come face to face with the person she had least expected to see.

'Elder Pa-shin,' she gasped in relief. She hadn't seen him since the battle started. Iv't must have split them up on purpose because he was afraid that they would put their heads together to overthrow him. But she was glad he looked none the worse for wear.

'Maii!' yelled Pa-shin in reply. 'I know how to put an end to this!' he said, his eyes ablaze with frenzied energy.

'B-but—what? How? Iv't—Iv't's trapped! And he said if he dies, all of us die with him.'

'Yes, I know—' Pa-shin grabbed Maii's hand and urged her to continue moving forward.

'You know?'

'Yes, I heard. But—'

'You heard?'

Pa-shin finally stopped running and ditched his gun, which he had been holding on to this entire time. He grabbed Maii by her shoulders and shook her. 'Listen to me. We don't have much time. So just focus on what we have to do!'

Maii's eyes widened at his reprimand, and she forced herself to nod in acknowledgement.

'Good,' said Pa-shin, loosening his grip on her shoulders to wipe the sweat off his brow. 'When Iv't opened up his mind to yours, I managed to butt in. And it's true that if he dies, we'll go down with him. But he's not going to die!'

Maii blinked, confused. She tried to parse through the recent events. What Iv't had told her. How he looked to be folding under the pressure of holding the ExA droids back while facilitating everyone's escape from Tilsor. The way his aura had faltered . . .

'It's all a ploy,' Pa-shin rushed to clarify. 'Did you think he would let himself die just like that—when he's been planning his revenge for decades?'

'B-b-but . . . How . . .?'

'My guess is he's trying to take control of the droids—a definite possibility since they're being controlled by Ifarls who are on ExA's side now. But I figured out how to stop both Iv't and ExA, and to close the portal once and for all . . .'

As Pa-shin laid out what they had to do in the most concise manner he could, Maii was dumbfounded. She was still processing what Pa-shin had said when he asked breathlessly, 'Do you understand me?'

'Yes . . . One of us has to go and stop Iv't, while the other has to die,' she summarized without inflection.

'Cross over to the other side of the portal!' corrected Pa-shin.

'Which means to die,' insisted Maii.

'If the Ifarl who's here can't bring them back in time, then yes, they die. I wouldn't ask that of you, Maii. I'll go. All you have to do is to stop Iv't and leave the rest to me,' said Pa-shin, his eyes filled with understanding and kindness.

Maii knew rationally she should just do as Pa-shin had instructed instead of wasting everyone's time debating with and doubting herself. Her question slipped out before she knew it. 'How can you trust that I will be able to bring your soul back after you cross over?'

Pa-shin's gaze was unwavering as he stared at Maii. 'Because Zenchi trusts you. And she has always had high hopes for you.'

Tears stung Maii's eyes at the mention of her mentor, whose life was teetering on the edge. If Zenchi were to die . . . 'No,' she said suddenly. 'I'll go. I'll cross over. The Ifarls need a leader, and I can't be that. So I'll go, because I'm not confident I'll be able to stop Iv't or bring you back from the realm of the dead.'

Pa-shin did a double take at the conviction in Maii's tone. He must have known it was impossible to change her mind, because he nodded and gently took her hand in his. A warmth radiated through Maii at the contact, then she felt a strange tether form between Pa-shin and herself. *Let's go*, he said through mindspeak, and the two of them turned and ran back in the direction of Square Thirty-two.

After passing through several Sections, a gigantic cloud of dust appeared and started rolling towards them. The stomping had gotten increasingly louder in the past few minutes, indicating that the droids must be nearby now.

Maii and Pa-shin exchanged determined glances, and she said, 'I'm ready.'

Then, the Ifarl elder chanted something under his breath that sounded like an ancient version of the Ifarl language.

Maii felt a jerk in her consciousness. A sudden lightness overtook her as she floated away from her physical body and rushed to find the first person she could think of.

Final Interlude

The fissure has opened again. I am drawn to the call again. Come, *it calls again. Hunger overtakes me again. Rationality leaves me again.*

But the duration is brief this time around. I don't even get a taste of that sweet life energy before I am pulled back to this suspended dimension . . . again.

To be absolutely frank, I'm sick of this. I snap into a raging ghost when the call beckons. But it takes me much too long to return to a state of apathy that makes existing in this endlessness bearable.

I will myself to take deep breaths to calm down.

Oh, that no longer works because I don't need to breathe any more.

I recite the mantra I created: I should not think. I should not know. I should not feel. Not anything. Nothing. This is what death should be like.

I should not . . .

I curse, though I don't make a sound.

The crack has reappeared. But . . . it's weird. I am not overwhelmed with hunger this time. I can pause and think. I am pausing. Have I gotten immune to this?

The call beckons once more. It sounds different from previous times. It's more . . . tangible. Strained. I think I can put a face to this voice. I should satisfy my curiosity. I float through the crack, and I see buildings, built in a mishmash of styles. They're odd and . . . familiar?

Tilsor!

Tilsor . . .?

How could it be?

Memories rush at me. Missing pieces of the puzzle click in my mind. I was . . . killed here . . . A cry resounds in some deep recess of my mind. Maii . . .

I remember her now. I search the surroundings for her. But before I can find her, the voice commands, Bind them.

The command weaves its way into the core of my spirit. I can't stop myself from flying straight into one of those massive machines I now see in the Square. Clinging to them as I obey the command, I can sense someone channelling some sort of energy that is helping me maintain my mental clarity now, holding back the urge embedded deep into my soul to revert to a mindless creature with an insatiable thirst for life energy. These two sets of forces are warring in me. I feel my rationality slipping. I feel the man's energy wavering.

Snap.

I've lost my grip on the machine that I'm supposed to hold back.

Darkness sets in, but it is gone in the blink of an eye.

When everything comes back into focus, my eyes widen. I'm no longer in Tilsor. Not the 'real' dimension, anyway. I'm back in the endless realm . . . aren't I? But yet again, it feels different.

'Pod . . .?' A voice calls out.

I know this melodious voice all too well.

'Maii?' It is the first time I've spoken out loud in this dimension.

A figure materializes in front of me. It is her. Her pink hair has grown longer, and she looks wearier.

I am at a loss for words. How—why—?

Maii gives me a bittersweet smile that confirms the worst. 'It's okay, Pod,' she says. 'We have all the time in the world to catch up later.' She pauses for a moment as if she's re-evaluating what she said, then corrects herself. 'We m-may. But now, I need your help.'

'My help?'

Maii nods, and her face lights up as she says, 'I know how to kill Iv't, bring down ExA, and close the portal for good.'

I had to blink. Wasn't expecting that. 'H-how?' I manage to croak out. I swallow and continue a little more steadily, 'I mean, how did you figure all this out, and what do we have to do?'

Maii smirks and her answer makes my jaw hang.

'That's another whole long story, but the first step is to gather everyone.'

'Everyone?' I ask. 'You mean the ghosts in this realm?'

Maii's smile turns wide. 'Every last one of them.'

19

Keix | Retreat

'Maii! Vin!' shouted Keix as she ran back in the direction of Tilsor. Initially, it hadn't taken much convincing for her to heed Iv't's words when he asked everyone to get out of Tilsor. The appearance of the droids was something they had not foreseen, and any fool would know if they continued to contain the battle in the Square, they would all be trampled to death by the massive machines.

Her priority at that moment was to get everyone out of the Square, and then Tilsor. She had thought Maii was going to bring up the rear. So, together with Jūn, Keix had gone ahead to make sure the escape route was clear. Because of the chaotic situation, she had lost track of Vin and Mohgen.

Still, Keix had been confident that her friends would join her eventually, and that Iv't had the situation in the Square under control—otherwise, how could she and Jūn have made it out of Tilsor without much of a hitch? But now that the two of them had been at the field outside Tilsor's borders for what seemed like a lifetime, and it looked like the last of the survivors were trickling out of the city, Keix started to panic because her friends were nowhere in sight!

'Keix, where are you going?' shouted Jūn, rushing after her.

'I'm going back in to look for Vin!' She showed no signs of slowing down even though the pain from her injuries was reverberating through her body.

'Hold up, I'll come with you.'

Keix stopped and turned back to face Jūn in surprise because he didn't attempt to stop her. Without hesitation, he adjusted the sword strap slung across his shoulder to make sure his weapon was secure, then turned to Bakuro, who had joined them at some point during their escape. After Jūn was done speaking to Bakuro, he told Keix, 'Bakuro's going to make sure the rest of the survivors get to Yurkordu. Mujin and Sandom should have gone right ahead to update Daman on the situation here, and they should be able to return with at least a small group of Kulcans to help with those who are injured. If Daman agrees to let them ride out on their shihs, they'll be here sooner than we know.'

Keix's eyes were filled with gratitude as she stared unblinkingly at Jūn. She didn't know what to say. It felt like all their planning and work had come to naught. How long could Iv't hold the droids and the ExA soldiers before they were unleashed again? Would Daman even allow them to seek refuge in Yurkordu? She was about to ask Jūn for his thoughts when the ominousness in the air intensified.

A muffled bang sounded in the distance. It seemed to have come from one of the inner Sections of Tilsor. The next second, Keix felt the ground vibrating. She exchanged glances with Jūn, and they ran in tandem towards the source of the rumbling.

'Vin! Maii!' Keix called out as she pumped her legs under her and pushed her way past a crowd of people who were running out of Tilsor. She scanned the faces of everyone passing by, but try as she might, she couldn't spot any familiar faces.

The next thing she knew, a cloud of smoke was rising into the air. She tuned her hearing to the highest sensitivity. It sounded like most of the people had managed to escape. Besides some shouts and screams, she could make out a dull, somewhat rhythmic thudding that sounded like the stomping of the droids. This must mean Iv't had lost control of the situation in the Square!

'Vin!' Keix sprinted harder towards Tilsor. There was no way she was going to leave this place without finding her best friend. She was about to step into the city when a vice-like grip closed around her arm and jerked her to a stop.

'Tilsor's collapsing, Keix.' Jūn looked rattled by her disregard for her own safety. The veins in his neck were popping out. Through gritted teeth, he said, 'You're only going to send yourself into death's jaws!'

Keix looked down at Jūn's hand and blinked. No, how could he not understand that she couldn't lose another friend? Not after Pod. Not when Zej and Dace's whereabouts were still unknown! She shook off Jūn's hand and let the pain that shot up her arm fuel her anger as she continued into Tilsor. Keeping in step with her, Jūn crossed past the city's threshold, sparks flying from his eyes at her stubbornness. Keix wanted to tell him to leave her be, but she understood him well enough now to know he was just as obstinate as her. Regardless of whether he agreed with her actions, he would stay right beside her. In the end, she swallowed her protests and they both ran forward wordlessly.

They had barely approached the exit of the first Section when the distinctive stomping of the droids became deafening.

Keix's jaw dropped when a behemoth machine wobbled into the Section from the exit she was heading towards, blocking it off. How did it get here so fast?

'I'll distract it.' Jūn's eyes narrowed dangerously as he unsheathed his sword with a hiss.

Keix didn't even have time to protest before Jūn leapt towards the droid. Determined to not let his good intentions go to waste, she immediately ran towards the space in between the droid's legs; it was the shortest distance to her destination. But the droid, which was sporting an 'injury'—a corroding limb courtesy of Mohgen's invention—stumbled backward instead of leaning forward to counter Jūn's attack.

'Keix, look out!'

Keix hadn't even registered Jūn's warning before an explosion went off in the distance, and she felt the ground shaking from the impact of the blast. Concurrently, she was shoved from the back and sent flying forward. She couldn't put up her injured hands quickly enough to break her fall. Jarring pain shot through both her arms and face as her cheek scraped against the cobbled ground and she tasted blood. Something huge and heavy also crashed down behind her and the ground shuddered once more.

Though she was shaken to her core, Keix pulled herself together and turned her head around. Her heart stopped. 'Jūn!' she screamed as she scrambled to her feet. *No . . .*

Jūn was lying motionless on the ground, blood gushing out from a huge gash at his temple. It was a sheer miracle that the droid hadn't fallen on him. For the time being, the machine was no longer a threat because one of its legs had corroded to the point where it couldn't support its weight any more. Keix just had to make sure that both Jūn and herself were out of range of its thrashing limbs.

I can't leave him here, Keix thought, looking frantically around for help. But the handful of stragglers whom she had seen just minutes ago had already fled from the area.

Keix forced herself to move. *I can do it. I am strong enough to carry him out of here.*

'Jūn,' she called out as she knelt beside him. The droid must have hit him as it was falling. Was he hurt anywhere else besides his head? Keix ran her hands all over his body to check for other injuries. In the meantime, she tried to reassure herself, *Vin will be fine. Maii will be fine. They will be able to get out of Tilsor. Maybe they'd left by another exit. I just need to get Jūn out of here now.*

She reassessed her own condition. It felt like her body was coming apart. The gunshot wound on her right shoulder was still hurting and she needed to hold on to her sword at the very least, in case they ran into their enemies. *Left side it is, then.* The skin on her left arm had not only been burnt off, but also scraped off when she had fallen down, but there was no other alternative. Biting the inside of her cheeks to prevent herself from screaming out loud, she grabbed Jūn's hand as gently as she could and hoisted him to a standing position, then looped his arm around her neck.

Barely seconds had passed since Jūn got injured, but it felt like an eternity to Keix. The combination of him being unconscious and her being injured made it near impossible to move even an inch. Sweat poured down every inch of her skin, and it was with extreme difficulty that she maintained her grip on her weapon.

When she heard more stomping noises, she snapped her head up and saw that the cloud of white smoke from earlier was getting closer and bigger now. Jūn was right; Tilsor was collapsing. The rumbling and vibrations that had been growing in intensity and volume was from falling debris of the buildings collapsing within the city.

Keix's determination left her then. She didn't know Vin's whereabouts. She didn't know if Jūn was going to survive this, not when she didn't even know where to bring him to get his wound cleaned and dressed. Not when the world was disintegrating in front of her.

But when Jūn's weight was suddenly lifted from her shoulders, she was pulled out of her daze as her instinct to protect Jūn at all costs kicked in.

'Come on,' called a voice next to her.

She blinked away the blurriness in her vision. It was Bakuro, and he held Keix's despondent gaze with his own determined one and said, 'Let's get out of here.'

* * *

Keix was beyond exhausted now. All she could do was to muster up enough energy to place one foot in front of the other as she trailed behind the rest of the survivors who were making their way to Yurkordu. In front of her were those who were injured but could still move forward independently, albeit at a much slower pace compared to the rest. Among them were Ifarls who had mysteriously fallen into a comatose state after Tilsor fell and were now either being carried on the backs of those who were uninjured or on makeshift wagons. Bakuro was beside her, piggybacking a still-unconscious Jūn.

Days had passed since they left a crumbling Tilsor behind. Still, sounds of what Keix presumed were stomping droids and marching ExA soldiers persisted behind them. Their enemies sounded close enough to make them hasten their retreat to Yurkordu, yet somehow, the ExA contingent wasn't moving fast enough to close the gap between itself and Keix's group.

Night had just fallen, and the temperature was dropping. But the survivors pressed on because of the pressure the ExA soldiers kept on them.

Was ExA toying with them, deriving sadistic pleasure by keeping them alive, yet not letting them rest? Keix wanted to turn around to confront them. But what right or ability did she have right now?

You're only going to send yourself into death's jaws! Jūn's reminder kept replaying in her head.

She fought to keep her tears at bay as she looked at Jūn. Bakuro had helped her stem the bleeding on Jūn's head and bandage the wound, but the massive loss of blood had turned Jūn's complexion ashen. If not for his shallow breathing, which Keix had been and was keeping a close eye on, she would have really thought he was dead.

Please hang on, Jūn, pleaded Keix silently. If only they could get to Yurkordu faster . . . She didn't know how she would have the courage to continue facing the world if Jūn died. All her friends were gone. Because of this vendetta between Iv't and the people who killed his family, and ExA's greed to conquer the world.

The group entered yet another clearing when Bakuro suddenly spoke up. 'They're here,' he said breathily, the relief in his voice apparent.

Keix perked up her ears and looked around. She recognized this part of the woods. They were more than halfway through to Yurkordu, and even though Keix had been drowning in despair, she couldn't help but notice how much shorter the journey seemed to have become. A feeling of déjà vu registered in her head, but there was barely time for her to consider the odd phenomenon clearly, because a soft rustling was approaching them. Within minutes, the party came into view and Keix thought she must be hallucinating.

Leading the group of over three dozen or so Kulcans were Mujin, Sandom, and Basch. All of them were mounted on shihs, looking like avenging guardians.

Keix was suddenly riled up. Jūn had mentioned the possibility of Daman allowing the Kulcans to ride the shihs out of Yurkordu. And she should feel heartened that Daman had softened his stance. But all she could think about was why—why hadn't the Kulcan chief come to his senses earlier?! Jūn was dying. She had lost her friends. All this could have been prevented if Daman had put the full force of the Kulcans behind them in the first place!

Sandom, who was riding Zorig, approached Keix. The creature cast woeful eyes at Jūn and nudged him with a whimper, and Keix's heart, which already felt like it had been cut a thousand times, contracted, sending a wave of pain throughout her body.

'I'm sorry, Zorig . . . I couldn't keep him safe . . .' she murmured, swallowing the tears of frustration and desperation threatening to spill out of her downcast eyes.

A man's voice called out then. 'Here,' he said.

Keix recognized Mujin's voice and looked up to see that he was in the midst of helping Bakuro gently transfer Jūn to the shih that he was riding. The fact that Mujin wasn't making snide remarks just underscored in Keix's mind how dire the situation must be. Once Jūn was securely strapped, Mujin rode off without a word. Bakuro also climbed atop another Kulcan's shih and set off.

Throughout all this, Keix had stood frozen. Around her, riders pulled up survivors who were more critically injured onto their shihs, presumably to rush them back to Yurkordu for treatment. Those who were more mobile and could still walk without excessive hobbling carried on their way.

Sandom's voice cut through Keix's paralysis. 'You ride with me,' she said emotionlessly.

Meanwhile, Zorig was sniffing impatiently, as if he, too, wanted to go after Jūn. So, Keix wasted no time in taking Sandom's extended hand to hoist herself up the shih. Unlike previously, when Jūn had enveloped her in a back hug while she rode Zorig with him, Sandom let Keix sit behind her. Sandom nudged Zorig into a run without warning and Keix, not wanting to fall off, grasped at the Kulcan's robe and held on tightly as they sped off in the direction of Yurkordu.

Before long, the momentum had lulled Keix into a semi-conscious state even as she kept her ears peeled to see if they were leaving ExA in the dust. Logically speaking, they should. Yet, the stomping and marching sounds never dropped off, as if the distance between them had remained unchanged.

But Keix's brain was so burnt out, it didn't even register that this situation spelled impending danger. Subconsciously, she had also stopped caring. She was tired of this world, these people—ExA, Ifarls, and even most of the Kulcans. Those whom she loved and cared about kept getting taken away from her. She was at the precipice of choosing oblivion because she just didn't see the point of going on this path alone any more . . .

Caught up in her own thoughts, Keix was silent on the ride back to Yurkordu. So was Sandom. And even though Keix had turned in her charm that allowed her to enter the Kulcans' homeland, she didn't have problem crossing over the protective barrier; she figured it was probably because she was holding on to Sandom, who must have retrieved her pendant when she had returned with Mujin. The other survivors must have been brought in by Kulcans who had their accessories on them too.

Despite vowing to care less about everything, Keix still couldn't believe her eyes when she set foot back into Yurkordu.

Thousands of Kulcans in full battle gear were standing in single files at the very first clearing past Yurkordu's protective barrier. To the side of this battalion was a makeshift first-aid spot, where survivors were getting their wounds treated and dressed.

Keix remembered her burnt arm and shoulder. She should get them looked at too. But Jūn! She searched the clearing for Jūn, only to see Mujin riding away from her. The Kulcans had parted to let Mujin pass, but moved back into position immediately, making Zorig stomp his feet in displeasure. Keix, like the shih, wanted to follow along, but Sandom interrupted her imminent outburst.

'Jūn's going to need more help than what this,'—Sandom gestured to the makeshift post—'can do. And you, too. But before that, Daman wants to speak to you.'

'Daman?' echoed Keix, confused.

Sandom dismounted from Zorig and gestured for Keix to do the same. The moment Keix's feet landed on the ground, the stubborn shih charged forward in the direction where Mujin had taken Jūn. The Kulcans, out of either shock or respect, moved aside immediately to let him pass.

Keix hadn't even managed to gather her wits about her before the Kulcan chief stepped in front of her, his expression complex and indecipherable. 'You—' he began before stopping short, his eyes widening and turning dangerous in an instant. 'H-how did th-they—' he stuttered.

The Kulcans behind Daman snapped to attention and unsheathed their weapons in unison.

Keix would have been bewildered to no end at this reception had she been unfamiliar with the Kulcans. But because she had spent some time in Yurkordu, she knew that Daman—and the rest of the Kulcans by extension—must have heard something alarming.

Instinctively, Keix drew her sword too. She cast the range of her hearing further. Her heart dropped when she heard that distinctive stomping yet again. ExA's droids must be approaching. Not only that, but it also sounded like there were dozens of them.

Keix trained her eyes on the horizon, and she saw a blurry figure appear just beyond Yurkordu's invisible barrier.

How had ExA caught up with them so quickly?! And how had the Kulcans missed the droids' approach?

It was all too sudden. There could only be one conclusion. Keix's suspicion that ExA was toying with them was right! ExA had chosen to wait until everyone had arrived in Yurkordu before making an appearance. But how did they do that—and why? To catch the Kulcan unawares? They must be planning to conquer Yurkordu too! Still, wouldn't it have been more effective if ExA had killed everyone in Keix's group before this? Then, they could ambush the unsuspecting Kulcans . . .

Just when Keix thought the situation couldn't get more mind-boggling, the person leading the charge on ExA's side stepped into a gentle beam of moonlight filtering through a sparse layer of clouds. As the figure came into focus, a gasp escaped Keix. The reason as to why everyone—her group, as well as the ExA troops—had made such rapid progress to Yurkordu dawned on her and she stammered, 'I-Iv't?'

20

Keix | The Dawn of Reckoning

With the sudden appearance of Iv't, as well as the droids and ExA soldiers which were flanking him, Keix had momentarily forgotten that there still stood a protective barrier concealing Yurkordu from outsiders. There was no way Iv't and the ExA army (or should she call it Iv't's army now?) could have gotten their hands on the Kulcan charms, right? Which means they *shouldn't* be able to see into Yurkordu, nor know that Keix and the rest of the Kulcans were right in front of them.

Keix tried to summon some optimism, but she came up empty. This Ifarl standing in front of her was the most powerful of his race. He had walked out of a crumbling Tilsor with nary a scratch on him, and with the entire fleet of his enemies' droids and soldiers at his command, it seemed; Keix didn't believe for a moment that he, of all people, would be hoodwinked into thinking he was merely looking at an ordinary stretch of cliffs and not the entrance to Yurkordu—even if he did not possess an accessory that could let him see past the illusion.

Keix's realistic conclusion was proven right when Iv't walked forward and stepped through the boundary between the outside world and Yurkordu as if it didn't exist. The clouds had dissipated now, and the unobstructed moonlight threw the Ifarl's features into sharp relief. In the short span of time since she had last seen him in Tilsor's Square, Iv't had aged yet another decade. Even so, every cell in Keix's body was on high alert. Instinct told her she shouldn't underestimate Iv't no matter how frail he looked. And there was no way he had arrived on Yurkordu's doorstep with good intentions—not when he had been stalking them like a predator waiting for the perfect moment to pounce on its prey. Still, could there be a chance that this inevitable confrontation she sensed would be resolved peacefully? After all, the droids and ExA soldiers had remained in their positions, lined up outside the barrier. Keix estimated there were at least fifty of the massive machines at Iv't's command. The soldiers were too numerous to count.

Other than the Kulcans who were standing in formation for battle on Keix's side, a circle of them had also formed around the makeshift first-aid area to protect the wounded. Keix, Daman—who was standing diagonally behind her—and Iv't were the only ones who seemed out of place.

'Where is he?' Iv't asked, his voice ringing through the clearing, loaded with menace and arrogance.

'Where is—who?' asked Keix, her confusion apparent.

Iv't ignored Keix and addressed Daman. 'Where is he? The Kulcan who killed my wife.'

Keix must have misheard. *Wasn't the culprit who murdered Iv't's wife from ExA? Has Iv't lost his mind after subduing ExA and turning them into his lackeys?* She looked at Daman, fully expecting him to refute Iv't's words but—

'He's dead,' said the Kulcan chief without emotion.

Keix almost staggered back in shock. Did Daman just admit that a Kulcan *had* murdered Iv't's wife?!

Iv't snarled. 'I know he's not. Hand him over and I'll spare everyone else's lives. Don't take my goodwill for granted! I can still kill every last one of you. So, I'll ask you once more. Where is the Kulcan who killed my wife?'

'I'll answer you once more. He's dead,' repeated Daman.

Anger flooded Iv't's eyes as the tension in the air reached its breaking point. He thundered scathingly, 'Then you leave me no choice!' With that, he raised his arm in an arc.

Keix's sense of foreboding turned to horror when the air rippled in response to Iv't's action. At the same time, the droids and ExA soldiers stomped forward. Other than the excruciating pain in her injured arms, Keix's head also started to hurt as she wondered, *If Iv't now has full control over this army, does it mean ExA has been successfully eliminated?* She didn't have time to ponder if the implication was worth celebrating though, because the droids were making short work of the distance between the Kulcan army and themselves.

Keix had to give it to the Kulcans, who stood their ground and didn't even flinch as their massive opponents neared. Tightening her grip on her sword, she willed herself to numb the pain she was feeling. Her breathing quickened. For her, there was only one simple goal: Prevent the advancement of her opponents at all costs. The fate of Yurkordu aside, it was Jūn's survival that she needed to ensure.

The moment the droids came within striking distance, a shrill whistle cut through the air. The ringing of swords leaving their scabbards followed as the Kulcans struck first.

Keix, however, had a different strategy. She charged forward and ducked a blow from one of the droids. Then, she weaved between the legs of the machine to rush towards the first ExA soldier who came into view. She might not be able to take down the massive droids—she hadn't managed to back in Tilsor—but she could pick off the ExA soldiers, so the Kulcans could focus on bringing down the big guns.

Taking aim at the thin, exposed line on her opponent's neck, Keix thrust her sword forward. But her injury made her action sluggish, and she missed her mark. Her blade struck the ExA soldier's shoulder, which turned out to be a metal limb. The impact sent a shot of pain up Keix's arm. She hissed and skipped backward to dodge her opponent's counterattack. Using the pain to sharpen her focus, she gritted her teeth and slashed again. This time, her blow managed to land true.

But the next second, ExA soldiers, who seemed to think they had found an easy target, rushed at her. Keix's exhaustion and pain compounded as she had to expend the bulk of her energy dodging the droids' feet even as the mob around her got larger. She shouted in frustration when she missed her target yet again. Her opponents were lithe figures, experts at side-stepping her blows. As they chipped off the last vestiges of her endurance, a familiar figure appeared beside her.

'Sandom?' said Keix, shock and relief apparent in her voice.

The Kulcan leapt forward and took out two of their opponents in a single blow. 'Stay back,' directed Sandom as she knocked out yet another ExA soldier with ease.

Even though Sandom was engaging an entire group of opponents in battle, Keix didn't have the luxury of rest. One of the droids in the vicinity had homed in on the pair. Keix leapt at it and aimed her sword at a slit between two connecting plates in the mammoth's legs, which she thought could be a possible weak spot. Her aim was true, but her assumption was wrong as she struck yet another hard surface.

Stars appeared in her vision as a new wave of pain overtook her. She jerked her sword back, intending to retreat only to find that her weapon was stuck. While she was considering sacrificing her sword for her life, Basch appeared beside her and dislodged her blade with a quick stroke of his sword. Then, he struck the machine's leg, causing it to stagger backward.

Keix was awestruck at the amount of strength Basch had managed to pack in his strike.

'These machines are impenetrable,' complained Basch. He adjusted his position beside her. Then, the droid dropped a blow that sent the two of them flying in opposite directions to dodge it.

Keix fell back on her instincts.

Thrust. Duck. Counter. On and on it went until . . .

'We can't go on like this,' she called out to Sandom and Basch, both of whom had stayed close to her all this time. Huffing, Keix added, 'The droids may not tire out, but we will.'

Basch's reply was a grunt, while Sandom said sarcastically, 'Thanks for the vote of confidence,' before knocking out another ExA soldier.

The bodies of their enemies were piling up around them, yet it was apparent that the Kulcans were not making any progress whatsoever with the machines.

A shout rang through the air just as Keix was about to ask Basch what they could possibly do to win this battle.

'We have the person you want, Iv't! Cease the attacks now!' came a woman's voice.

Keix's head whipped around to locate the source of the interruption.

Del and three other Kulcan chiefs (only Daman was missing from the group) were escorting an emancipated figure at sword point into their midst.

A hush as deafening as the chaos that reigned before it fell because everyone had frozen—the droids and ExA soldiers stopping in eerie tandem—at the appearance of the newcomers.

'What have you done?' came Daman's shout. He pushed past Kulcans and ExA soldiers alike in a bid to get to Del's group, but he was intercepted swiftly by Basch.

Keix was bewildered. Hadn't her father been just beside her seconds ago? But her insignificant question was forgotten when Basch grabbed Daman's arm and said, 'You can't keep protecting him.'

Basch had lowered his voice when he spoke, but he hadn't exactly whispered. And his tone, though quiet, held a clear ring of authority and command. To all the Kulcans present, Basch had as good as shouted out loud his reprimand of Daman.

'Y-you . . . I-I . . .' Daman stuttered, his eyes wide as if this was the last thing he would have expected from his commander.

'He has to be held accountable for his own actions.' Basch sounded pained, as if reminding Daman of this elderly Kulcan's crime was the last thing he wanted to do.

Keix appraised the subject of this distressing conversation, whose presence alone had put a stop to this seemingly endless battle. He was tall, like all Kulcans, but could easily be considered the most fragile Kulcan Keix had ever seen. Hunched over, he was wearing what looked like a huge piece of rag, tattered and torn in places. Patches of his long and unkempt hair had fallen out, resulting in bald spots all over his head that revealed sections of scalp dotted with age spots.

'He is!' shouted Daman, affronted by Basch's accusation that the elderly Kulcan had not paid for his wrongdoings. 'He's nothing but an empty shell now. He's as good as dead!'

'He would have died ages ago if you hadn't been helping him since the previous council sentenced him to roam the peaks,' said Basch in exasperation. 'Look around you! Do you want to see Yurkordu, which you've worked so hard to stabilize, destroyed because you're shielding a murderer?'

Before Daman could come up with a reply to what Basch had said, Iv't, who had all but disappeared from the scene of the battle, resurfaced near Del's group. He still wasn't holding any weapon, and the distasteful thought that he might have retreated to the sidelines to watch while his henchmen tore down Yurkordu occurred to Keix. Anger sparking in his eyes, Iv't pointed at the person whom he had sworn to kill and exclaimed with a voice shaking with barely contained ferociousness, 'You!'

Keix, like everyone else present, was transfixed on the scene unfolding in front of her.

'Tell me. Why did you have to kill her?' Iv't's voice trembled with emotion.

But the Kulcan didn't respond. He just stood there, tottering his feet like a toddler and wringing his hands as if he was overwhelmed by his current predicament.

Daman rushed forward and tried to drive his sword through Iv't. But the Ifarl sidestepped the blow easily. Shocked by his quick reflexes, Daman froze for a split second before slashing at Iv't again. Despite his speed, he still failed to strike the Ifarl. More than a handful of failed attempts later, Daman settled for planting himself between the anguished Ifarl, whose eyes were glowing passionately, and the dreadful-looking Kulcan, whom he seemed dead set on protecting. 'He's not in the right state of mind!' shouted Daman. 'No matter what you ask him, he won't be able to answer you!'

But Daman's words were immediately invalidated because the Kulcan standing behind him suddenly fell to his knees, crying and murmuring, 'No . . . no . . . I'm sorry . . . We shouldn't have been so greedy . . . We shouldn't have coveted your power . . .'

The elderly Kulcan's distress set off something in Iv't, and the Ifarl shoved Daman out of his way. But in an unexpected turn of events, the old Kulcan suddenly reached for Daman's sword and managed to get a hold of it. He brandished it in front of himself and cried, 'G-get away from me!' His eyes darted from Daman to Iv't, then his shoulders drooped as he repeated, 'I said I'm sorry . . . Sorry . . .'

Iv't snapped then. He roared in frustration, and the droids and ExA soldiers reanimated.

Keix barely managed to get out of the way of a droid that started stomping forward. In the midst of dodging it, she saw Iv't making strange hand gestures. But her observation was cut short when a massive fist came at her. Keix dropped to her side and rolled away just in time. Struggling to get to her feet, it crossed her mind that even if she were lucky enough to survive this war, one of her arms would very well be deformed while the other might just be rendered completely useless.

But she would worry about that later—*if* there was a later. Because the battle around her had resumed in earnest. The adjournment had re-energized the Kulcans' opponents, and they pressed forth now with a vengeance.

Keix searched her surroundings for Iv't. If she could take him down now, perhaps she could end this madness. But the Ifarl had disappeared into thin air again. That was when she knew that even if Iv't could get his hands on the Kulcan that he had said he wanted, the Ifarl would not stop until Yurkordu was razed to the ground. What was worse was that not only had Iv't set his army amok, but he had also turned the natural fortifications that made Yurkordu into a fortress into a free-for-all open field!

The narrow, winding path that led to a uniformly dense forest, then to more snaking paths and dense forests—layers and layers of obstacles that made Yurkordu almost impossible to penetrate—they were all gone.

Riders on shihs were charging down this new open slope.

Iv't's advancement had to be stopped. Now.

Keix worked past the extreme pain assaulting her as she dodged a blow from a soldier and parried a strike from another one. They would only get past her dead body. She heard Sandom call out for her and responded with a huffy 'What?'

'There are'—Sandom ducked to her side as an ExA soldier slashed at her—'more'—she countered with an attack of her own—'droids coming our way!'

'WHAT?!' shouted Keix in disbelief. She took out her current opponent and perked up her ears for telltale signs that Sandom was right. When Keix registered the sound of stomping in the distance, she gasped.

Did Iv't have backup arriving? Or was this a new battalion of ExA soldiers and droids that was advancing on Yurkordu?

Keix didn't have to wait long to get her answer, because like Iv't and his army, these newcomers appeared all at once, as if they had been teleported to the edge of Yurkordu. And besides dozens of droids, there were also soldiers dressed in . . . orange?

While a part of Keix tried to figure out why these newly arrived troops were wearing something other than the all-black outfits she had come to associate with ExA soldiers, another part of her was struggling to find ways to keep these machines and soldiers from taking over Yurkordu. Then, before she could even formulate a solution for either of these situations plaguing her, a droid ran headlong into another of its kind and a deafening metallic clang rang through the clearing. The machine that had been rammed into fell on its back.

Keix couldn't believe her eyes. Why were the droids under Iv't's control attacking one another? A tiny column of white smoke spouting out of the legs of the fallen droid caught her eye. She squinted at the sight. Was that what she thought it was? Keix sucked in a breath. Could it be that somehow, by some mysterious and fortunate turn of fate, these droids and soldiers in orange who had just arrived were on her side? If not, how had they managed to get their hands on the corrosive substance that Vin and Mohgen had been using against ExA back in Tilsor?!

Hope surged in Keix. Vin and Mohgen *must* be here, in the group that was attacking Iv't's droids! Keix wanted to call out to her friends, but all she could do was watch dumbfounded and slack-jawed as the juggernauts went at each other.

Keix gasped when one droid punched through the chest plate of another machine and tore it out as it pulled back its fist. Then it reached towards its opponent's head and . . . ripped. It. OFF. The decapitated droid's body, which had parts that were still corroding, folded to the ground. Its attacker tossed away the head as if it were a piece of crumpled foil.

Sandom rolled out of the way of the discarded head, but Keix hadn't responded as quickly. She would have been hit by the ball of metal if someone had not pulled her out of danger at the very last second. That someone turned out to be Mujin.

'You can't even dodge something this big?' he chided in a tone dripping with judgement. His shih was nowhere in sight and neither was Jūn.

'Jūn! Where is he? And how is he?' asked Keix, her desperation and concern clear.

'He's somewhere safe, but . . .' Mujin let his sentence hang. Even though his tone was tempered now, betraying zero hint about whether he was gleeful or gloating at Jūn's predicament, it was obvious to Keix that his deliberate omission meant Jūn's survival wasn't guaranteed.

Another lump of metal came at them, and Mujin pushed Keix out of the way again. She stumbled into yet another chunk of metal torn from a droid's body. And there was . . . something flesh-coloured embedded in it? Was that . . . a human limb? But how could it be? The extremity didn't have a hand or foot attached to the end of it. Instead, it ended in a stump capped with a piece of moulded metal, just like the ones she had seen on the ExA soldiers who had retractable blades as hands.

Keix's horrified but transfixed gaze traced the limb from its stump and landed on an actual human body. And when her line of sight moved even further up and she saw the face of the person, who was unconscious, the noise around her was sucked out of the air . . .

'Zej?' said Keix, the word a bare whisper. Fractured memories of their last talk crossed her mind. She struggled to understand why Zej was here. She had somewhat accepted that he had likely been captured by ExA. But she had held out hope that she would be able to find him after this war was over. Never once could she have imagined she would see him here, embedded in a block of metal from a droid's body. But was it Zej, really? No, it couldn't be . . .

Keix's thoughts were in a jumble. Where was Dace? And Seyfer? Alric?

A jolt of pain in her arm pulled her out of her head and the sounds of battle resumed their roar in Keix's ears.

'Who is he? Do you know him?' came Sandom's voice. She was the one who had grabbed Keix's arm because all her calls had gone unheeded. 'Keix! Can you hear me?'

'Sandom!' yelled Mujin. 'Just drag her along! We can't let them advance any more.'

Keix's eyes refocused just in time for her to register the cause of Mujin's panicked shout. In the seconds that she had lost track of what was going on, the droids and soldiers under Iv't's control had managed to push back the Kulcans' line of defence!

And Keix didn't know if she was imagining things, but the main area of Yurkordu that housed the short, polygonal structures that the Kulcans called home, looked to have been brought closer.

'Iv't . . .' she muttered. 'We need to find Iv't!' It was the most logical thing to do—kill Iv't and end this. She cursed and kicked herself mentally for not running her sword through the Ifarl when she had the chance to do so.

'This way,' said Sandom, leading Keix up the slope. Mujin was right in front of them, clearing a path.

Keix searched her surroundings as she moved along with Sandom and Mujin. But no matter where she looked, Iv't was nowhere to be seen. What if he had fled after killing the Kulcan he was after? Had he even managed to get his hands on his target? Keix had lost track of both of these people who were key to ending this war when the fighting had restarted. But a figure standing in the midst of this maelstrom, his shaved head emitting a flickering, reddish glow, caught her eye now.

Without a second thought, Keix ran towards this Ifarl, ignoring Sandom's desperate call for her to stop. Perhaps this would go down in history as the second stupidest decision she had ever made in her life; she had made many, many, huge and stupid decisions, and the last one that got Jūn injured was her dumbest one yet. But the idea she had in her head seemed like the only plausible one. If there was anyone who could find Iv't, it would be another Ifarl, right? And from the bright maze of lines on this Ifarl's head, he seemed like the perfect candidate to help Keix do so.

'Can you find Iv't?' Keix asked without preamble the moment she reached the Ifarl. This close, Keix could tell that his eyes had a frenzied look, and she felt it deep in her gut that this Ifarl might well be the key to untangling this messy war.

'I'm—I'm trying to,' he replied, sweat beading above his tightly knitted brows. 'But I need more . . .' He looked like he was concentrating on fighting an invisible force.

Keix looked around. She didn't know if she was imagining things, but some of the droids' movements had begun to look a bit erratic, like they were second-guessing their own actions, throwing a punch only to jerk it back before their fist made contact with their target. An improbable—though not *that* far-fetched—thought struck Keix. Was this Ifarl trying to seize from Iv't the control of the ExA soldiers and droids?

'More what? How can we help?' Keix asked because Sandom had caught up to her and was glaring at her in an accusatory manner. Mujin was nowhere to be seen.

The Ifarl opened his mouth, as if to answer Keix's question. But the next instant, glowing orbs had appeared all around them. Instead of looking shocked, a look of triumph shone in his eyes. 'Finally,' he muttered, as if he had been waiting for this moment.

Keix's jaw dropped. Since the closure of the portal, she hadn't come across any ghosts—except when Pod's soul left his body—at all. Did this mean the portal had reopened?

Neither Keix nor Sandom made a move to attack the ghostly orbs. Recent developments, namely, the appearance of the fighters in orange and *their* droids, had made them aware of how volatile alliances and loyalties were. These spectres could be on their side, for all they knew.

In Keix's peripheral vision, some droids, which had come into contact with the ghostly orbs, had malfunctioned, their movements jerky and completely out of control.

Sandom eyed the Ifarl warily while maintaining a tight grip on her sword. The Kulcan probably had less reason to fear these glowing orbs compared to Keix. Jūn had mentioned before that Kulcans' weapons were able to strike ghosts, unlike Atrossian ones.

Before Keix could interrogate the Ifarl, a melodious chanting filled the air. She raised her blade instinctively to defend herself as one of the orbs flew at her.

'Wait,' said the Ifarl. 'They're here to help.'

Yet, at the very moment Keix hesitated, the orb picked up speed. She only had enough time to flinch as the glowing ball reached her and a familiar pain shot through her. Just like before, when she had touched ghosts, flashbacks that didn't belong to her played in her head. The images streaked by, too fast for Keix to make sense of them. But amidst the blur, she thought she saw her own face and the faces of Pod, Maii, and even Dace and Zej.

Then, it felt like the spirit was settling into its host, fusing itself with her, similar to the time when Maii had chanted the Ifarl charm to bind a ghost to her. But this time, instead of pure hatred and an overwhelming thirst for vengeance as the transition came to an end, Keix retained her faculties and was fully aware that another consciousness was right there, in her head. And it belonged to . . . *Rold?*

A laugh rang in her mind. It was indeed the Ifarl who had sacrificed his life to save her from hybrid-Seyfer, way back when Zej and Pod had been hiding her from Atros! He was also the very same ghost that had occupied her body when she had been turned into a ghost-human hybrid.

Yes, it's me, answered Rold. *Our affinity is strong.*

But how?

It's a long story, said Rold. *But suffice to say that we're putting things right.*

Keix noticed then that besides the fact that this conversation with Rold was happening in her head, she had also lost control of her body. Even though it was her who was turning to face the Ifarl with the shaved head, she had not directed the action. And when she said, 'Pa-shin', it was her voice that came out of her mouth, but it wasn't her saying it. Rold was the one dictating her each and every move.

And Sandom was . . . suspended in animation as if time had stopped for her?!

We're in the realm between the living and the dead, explained Rold. Then, sensing Keix's confusion, he added, *Where only those who've been on both sides can exist.*

Keix processed his words. So, he meant ghosts and hybrids—since they had been killed and brought back to life numerous times—like herself? She didn't get an answer from Rold, but a familiar figure walked to her side and smiled at her, as if to confirm her deductions.

Vin! Keix could cry in relief. All she wanted to do was to give her friend the tightest and longest hug, but her body wasn't hers to command.

There will be time later, Rold reassured Keix, who was now wondering why Vin had smiled at her; did the ghost who was possessing Vin know her?

This time, Rold did not answer her questions but instead, said to Pa-shin, 'He's in the mountains.'

Keix didn't have to ask whom they were referring to. There was only one person whose whereabouts they could possibly be interested in right now.

Pa-shin nodded, and more figures appeared beside Keix. When Rold looked around, Keix thought she recognized some of the Atrossians who had been turned, or had been in the process of getting turned, into hybrids. And . . . Seyfer! The elite Atros trooper-turned-reluctant ally was here too! He must have arrived with the second wave of droids because he was wearing an orange uniform. Keix longed to call out to him to ask about Zej, Dace, and Alric—how did they even manage to get here and in this state? But Rold didn't budge.

Glowing orbs, which Keix took to be ghosts without hosts, nudged themselves into gaps between the hybrids, which barely numbered one hundred. Then, Rold looked to the sky. It was a striking purplish-blue now because of the faint orange glow from the rising sun that was bleeding out from the horizon.

Pa-shin, who had also tilted his head up, started chanting in his melodious voice. And everyone—Keix (or should she say Rold) included—followed his cue. Keix couldn't understand the words coming out of her mouth, but she could make out nine stars streaking their way across the sky, aligning into a single line, before they dimmed to the point of becoming black dots.

Keix was reminded of the twin Ifarl rhymes, 'The Night of Legends' and 'Act of Repentance'—the first told to her by Rold, and the second, by Maii.

Keix never forgot the words after she heard them.

The Night of Legends

Nine of Stars,
Cut sky's bars.
Traces line,
Make ties bind.
Bae born,
Mae worn.
Bae be bound, powers—unbound.

Evil dwells,
Where fear swells.
Evil thrills,
Where joy fills.
Teach right,
Tread light.
Bae be born, of Nine Stars bond.

Act of Repentance

Stars of nine,
Forgo shine,
Line the skies,
Break the ties.
Condemn,
Repent,
Bae we renounce in assent.

Failure stains,
Power wanes.
Deadly dance,
Single chance.
Chant right,
Tread light.
Plunge anew into the night.

And though Keix never quite grasped the meaning of these rhymes, she knew deep in her heart they were relevant now. Perhaps the Ifarls' ritual to close the portal hadn't gone as planned the first time round because they had interpreted the words wrongly. That's why Rold had said they were putting things right now . . .

Keix could sense that the natural elements around her were different. Rold seemed to be casting some sort of energy outward while the chanting intensified. Then, she felt it—a particular person's presence in the vast landscape.

Iv't.

Keix saw him in her mind's eye—a flickering dot. His movements were sluggish as he picked his way through a maze-like area in the peaks. Was he lost or was he searching for something—or someone?

Rold sought out another presence. It was old, tired, full of guilt, and deranged. It was the elderly Kulcan whom Iv't was looking for. The two of them had somehow embarked on a game of hide-and-seek in the peaks, where the Kulcan was at an advantage because it had been his home for decades.

Targets acquired, Rold sent out a thread of energy.

All at once, Keix's senses went into overdrive as she felt dozens and hundreds of other similar threads shoot towards Iv't, weaving themselves into a web around these two figures, then tightening, pulling them somewhere . . . Then—

A chill so freezing deep set into Keix's very core. And a darkness so completely hollow took over her existence.

* * *

The first thing Keix noticed when she regained her senses—the pain shooting through her body once more, the ambient noises filling the air, and the stench of blood, sweat, and burning flesh and metal—was that it was as if no time had passed.

Sandom was still next to her, though she was now frowning in confusion at all the people who had suddenly appeared around her. To her querying look, Keix said with finality, 'Iv't is dead. So is the Kulcan who murdered his wife.

'It is over.'

21

Keix | Closure

Keix stared at Jūn and fought back hot tears that were pooling in her eyes. 'Hey,' she started with a shaky voice. 'It's over, you know.' She was sitting in Jūn's home located in a rather quiet area higher up in the hills. Like all Kulcan homes she had seen, it was polygonal and didn't have any partitions separating the different living areas. Jūn was quite the minimalist; the only noteworthy item was his sword, propped on a stand right next to the door flap. Displayed with it was a small, wooden toy sword that Keix imagined a little boy with golden eyes had once wielded while running around.

The grown-up version of that adorable boy was lying on a platform bed in front of her now, betraying not a single hint that he had heard her or was privy to her wistful thoughts. His face was deathly pale. The caked blood on his head had been cleaned up, revealing a stunning purplish bruise and a cut that ran from the arch of his right brow straight to the top of his head. To treat the wound, the hair around the cut had been shorn off. The exposed stretch of scalp was stained brown by an ointment that had been applied to prevent the cut from getting inflamed. The rest of his wavy hair, which he had always kept tied up in a messy knot, was spread out like an unruly halo—some of his hair had matted in clumps—around his head.

'Iv't's dead. So is the Kulcan who killed his wife,' said Keix, trying to rouse Jūn again. 'Sandom didn't believe me at first, like you. And Pa-shin had to step in to lead Basch and Del to the bodies while everyone else stayed back to sort through the bodies of the casualties.

Turns out, Dace and Seyfer had managed to escape from Atros after they were caught because of some genius plan—possibly the backup of the backup plans, or as Pod would call it, Plan Z—that Atros had in place.' A corner of Keix's lips quirked up at the thought of her friends' witty commentary, but her face fell immediately.

Taking a steadying breath, she continued, 'So, anyway, the two of them—or should I say the rest of the elite Atros troopers like Seyfer—managed to take control of some of the droids and arrived in Tilsor just in time to save those who were trapped, like Vin and Mohgen. And—' She sucked in a deep breath and was about to continue with her recap when a dangerous thought popped into her head. What if Jūn never regained consciousness?

He's ignoring you because you didn't listen to him, chided a voice in her head.

Almost immediately, another voice countered, *No. Jūn would never do that.*

Why is he not waking up then? He hasn't even twitched an eyelid at what you've said. Even the Kulcan physician had said the reason why he hasn't woken up is more psychological than physiological.

An anger sparked in Keix then. 'You know what? I'm not going to tell you anything else until you wake up,' she said as sternly as she could. But when Jūn still refused to stir at her sudden threat, the fire inside her died just as quickly as it had kindled.

Shoulders drooping, Keix picked up Jūn's limp hand and held it between her cool, shivering palms gingerly.

'I can't really feel your hands,' she murmured as her tears finally leaked out of her eyes and trickled down her cheeks. Choking back a sob, she said in her most aggrieved voice, 'I wanted to rush here right after we ended the war, but Sandom insisted on forcing me to drink a numbing concoction that tasted and looked like dirt mixed with water. And she said I had to clean up and dress my wounds because she wasn't going to let anyone track blood and dirt into your house.'

Neither pleas nor threats had worked. Perhaps complaints might, thought Keix. 'But my arms hurt so much I can't even wash myself properly.' She added a hint of whine to her voice just to play it safe. She raised her heavily bandaged arms to supplement her point.

Then, it occurred to her that since she had gone this far, she might as well try seduction too. She leaned forward and whispered into Jūn's ears thoughts she had never imagined she would verbalize, giving him the play-by-play of their most intimate moments. By the time she finished speaking, her face was flushed.

But Jūn was still the epitome of calm.

Keix cried freely then, letting her tears fall on Jūn's cheeks. 'I'm sorry. I'm sorry for being so stubborn. If I hadn't insisted on heading back into Tilsor, you—you . . .' she said before racking sobs took away her coherence and the last bit of energy she had left.

Eventually, Keix fell into a deep sleep at the bedside of the person who had embraced her true self before she herself did—and the only person who could cure the deep, intense ache at the core of her being.

* * *

'How's he doing?' Sandom asked the moment she stepped into Jūn's home. Dawn had just broken, and she was here to reapply Jūn's ointment and bring a new dose of medicine for Keix, just like she had done for the past couple of days.

Keix's wounds were now covered with a thin layer of bandages to protect the new skin that had grown over them, and the pain from the gunshot wound in her shoulder had diminished mostly to a dull throb. At times like this, she was grateful for her enhanced physicality and rapid healing courtesy of her Kulcan blood.

It had just been three days since Iv't's death. In that time, Yurkordu had become noisier than Keix remembered it to be. The Kulcans had been trying to figure out how to house the injured and the groups of fighters who were gathered here. Sandom said that the Kulcans were at a loss because they had never had to be hospitable, and it was apparently hilarious.

Keix wouldn't know. She had refused to leave Jūn's side except for two instances—once to visit Vin, who had her hands full trying to nurse a seriously injured Mohgen back to health while helping Ma.erdene look after the rest of the injured Tilsorians; and the second time, to check up on Dace, who had arrived in Yurkordu with Vin and was, surprisingly, working seamlessly with Seyfer on reorganizing the Atrossians and prepping them for the journey back to Atros.

At this moment, the only thing Keix knew for sure was that the medicine she was taking from Sandom was *foul.* After downing it in one gulp, she replied, 'The same.' She didn't want to tell Sandom there were a few, short minutes last night when Jūn's breathing seemed to have gotten shallower. Keix was convinced she was just being paranoid. Her thoughts were all over the place because she was forcing herself to fight the drowsy effects of the medicine and stay up all night at Jūn's bedside. This was the best explanation for why she kept alternating between reassuring herself that Jūn was going to pull through and blaming herself for his condition right now.

'I would tell you to get some sleep right now,' said Sandom disapprovingly. 'But Del has summoned you to the Council Hall.'

'What—why? Now?' Keix asked, flummoxed. Then she paused and considered. 'I'm not going.' She glanced at the evermore peaceful Jūn.

Sandom made her exasperation clear as she expelled a breath. 'Keix,' she called, as if she were scolding a misbehaving child. 'You have to stop blaming yourself. Jūn won't want to see you this way. And I'm sure he's glad that he's the one lying there instead of you.'

Keix's lower lip trembled. 'But . . .'

'No buts. I'm his sister. I know him better than you.'

Not knowing what to say to that, Keix pressed her lips together. She recalled how bewildered she had been when she first found out Jūn and Sandom were siblings. While Keix had always banked on Jūn telling her more about why his relationship with Sandom was strained someday in the near future, she felt immensely dispirited now that the chance might never come. 'How is it that you two are siblings, yet I sometimes feel like you're enemies?' she asked. Perhaps a distraction was what she needed to get all the nasty hallucinations of Jūn's current condition out of her mind.

To her surprise, Sandom's response was a short laugh. And instead of telling Keix off for trying to delay her meeting with Del, she settled herself down as if she were in the mood for a long session of storytelling. 'We're . . . twins, did you know that?'

Keix's eyes widened. That was truly unexpected.

'And I'm older.'

The indignant way in which Sandom said that made them both burst out laughing. It seemed petty yet significant at the same time. Perhaps it was because Jūn had always appeared immensely mature to Keix that she had always assumed Sandom was a couple of years younger than him.

'Yeah, we don't see eye to eye on many things, so we're not exactly best friends,' elaborated Sandom. 'But we're blood. So that's that.'

Keix nodded as if she understood Sandom's dilemma, though being a single child, she had never experienced anything like that before. She didn't know how to keep the conversation going, and Sandom reverted to her usual laconic self, so an awkward silence fell.

'And about your brother . . . who's not Jūn?' ventured Keix after a beat. She knew it wasn't her place to probe, and it just made her seem rude, but her curiosity had been piqued ever since Mujin accused Jūn of being a murderer. Now, this mystery suddenly felt like an overwhelming itch in her head she needed to scratch.

Thankfully, Sandom didn't look offended. Instead, she gave Keix an appraising look, as if evaluating if she was worthy of receiving this valuable piece of information about Jūn's past. After a long while, Sandom's eyes took on a faraway look and misted over. Then, she shifted her gaze to Jūn. 'It was an unfortunate incident. But it might have been prevented if Jūn had listened to me in the first place. I'll let him tell you his side of the story, but what's past is past.'

A tinge of disappointment struck Keix, and she let out the breath she had been holding. In a way, she could relate to Sandom's reluctance to talk about something so painful, so she didn't press for more even though she was dead curious to know what Mujin's role was in all this.

As if she could read Keix's mind, Sandom added, 'Mujin was Wex's best friend. He just hasn't worked through his loss. He's really not that bad.'

Keix clamped her lips together. Perhaps Sandom was right. After all, Mujin was the first one who had surrendered his charm in a show of support for Keix's cause. And Keix supposed he had played an integral role in convincing Daman and the rest of the chiefs to agree to let the survivors take refuge in Yurkordu—including getting a group of shih-riding Kulcans to transport them back to their home—after the disastrous battle in Tilsor. Despite all these, Keix still couldn't bring herself to see Mujin in anything but a less-than-positive light because she continued to hold a grudge against him for constantly looking for ways to make Jūn's life difficult.

'And just so you know,' added Sandom, interrupting Keix's thoughts. 'Jūn's rebellious phase was . . . intense. His angst had always been the type that simmered without causing a ripple on the surface. No one knew it was scorching unless they touched it and burnt themselves.

'Yet somehow, something changed in him after he met you.'

Keix thought back to what Jūn had said to her that night in the peaks of Yurkordu, about how his perspective shifted after watching her process her grief. Until now, she still didn't understand how it was possible for her to have such an influence over someone she hadn't even spoken to.

'Sometimes, there are mysterious forces in the world that surreptitiously shape our lives, whether we like it or not,' said Sandom, holding Keix's gaze. 'But never underestimate the strength of one's will to take charge of their own destiny.' She turned to glance at Jūn, who looked to be still in a deep sleep, unperturbed by the fact that his sister and lover were talking about him right to his face.

The lifting of the door flap made Keix's eyes snap to the entrance, and she saw Mujin standing there with an unreadable expression. She hadn't heard Mujin approach and she wondered if he had stood outside to wait for them to finish their conversation before entering, or if he had just arrived.

'Del sent me to get you,' he said, glancing at Keix before his eyes flicked to Sandom.

Sandom waved to him and gave him a small smile. To Keix, she said, 'Go. I'll stay here until you get back. If Jūn wakes up, you'll be the first to know.'

Seeing as there was no way out of this meeting with Del now that Mujin was here, Keix nodded to Sandom and left with him. Like Sandom had said, Yurkordu was bustling in a way she had never thought was possible. Back when she first arrived at these peaks, she had been met with suspicion, curiosity, and hostility. Now, the Kulcans she was bypassing spared nary a glance in her direction.

Even Mujin was uncharacteristically silent as they made their way down the slopes.

Keix supposed it was because of his dad. Come to think of it, despite all the updates about Yurkordu she had gotten from Sandom, Daman's name was never mentioned. Keix wondered what had become of the Kulcan chief. No one found him during the sweep of the grounds after Iv't died—at least not to Keix's knowledge. The last time she had seen him, he had been defending the old and slightly mad Kulcan who had murdered Iv't's wife. Just what kind of relationship did they have for the Kulcan chief to defend a madman at the expense of the fate of the entire Kulcan race and their homeland? There was no way Keix could pose this question to Mujin, so she bit her tongue as they reached the Council Hall.

'I leave you here,' said Mujin at the entrance to the hall before turning on his heel to stalk away.

Without sparing two thoughts for Mujin's peculiar behaviour, Keix made her way into the large hall to find that only Del and Basch were present. She stopped a distance away from the foot of the raised platform where Del was sitting in the elaborate, high-backed chair that Daman used to occupy. Keix hadn't seen her since the showdown though Sandom had implied that Del had taken over the role of the lead Kulcan chief. Basch, who was standing next to Del, had briefly dropped by Jūn's, muttering something about having to put things in order.

Keix's first response was one of irritation. Why couldn't they have met her at Jūn's if it were just the two of them? She folded her arms and asked, none too politely, 'Why did you drag me all the way here?'

A muscle in Del's jaw twitched while Basch remained stoic.

'I would like to make your acceptance at Yurkordu official,' said Del, holding out a jagged purple gemstone strung on a silver chain.

Staring at the charm that she had left behind because of Daman's ultimatum, Keix considered rejecting Del's gesture of goodwill out of spite. There was no reason for her to stay in Yurkordu or live here if Jūn wasn't comatose. Although she doubted Del would chase her out if she refused to take back her necklace, she walked forward to receive it from the new Kulcan chief's outstretched hand. Forcing herself to swallow some choice words of how needless she thought this was, she muttered, 'All right. Thanks.' *You could have just gotten Sandom to pass it to me*, she couldn't stop herself from adding in her head.

'We prefer to formalize these significant moments,' said Del, uncannily guessing Keix's thoughts. 'Old habits die hard, as you can tell. But we Kulcans should change our perspectives if we want to move past the bubble that we've kept ourselves in, don't you think so?'

Keix gave a shrug that could be interpreted as 'whatever' or 'yeah, I suppose I understand' and considered the risk of appearing rude if she said she was going to take her leave now. So, she started in as neutral a tone as she could manage, 'If there's nothing else . . .'

'Aren't you interested in what happened to Daman?' Del's gaze was sharp. 'Because the last time we met, you sure had a lot of opinions.' She was referring to when Keix had visited her house and tried to convince her to let Kulcans help out in this war which had just concluded. 'But I think you can see now that the war was always destined to reach Yurkordu—as long as Yurkordu stood, and as long as Al remained here. Daman knew that, which was why he would never have agreed to letting a big-enough force follow you to Tilsor. He just hadn't expected Atros or Iv't to turn up at our doorstep.'

Keix wanted to ask, *What's the point of telling me all this now?* But she felt Del would not let her go until she had said her piece, so even though Keix had no interest in anything except Jūn's survival, she gave in and asked, 'So who is this Al to Daman?'

A satisfied smirk replaced Del's usual detached and shrewd expression. 'Al is Daman's grandfather, and he was exiled for killing another Kulcan chief and conspiring with outsiders to seize power.'

Something about this narrative rang a bell to Keix. It sounded like the story Jūn had told her at the peaks when they heard the howling sounds. Looking back, she realized the ghostly calls could well be made by Al.

'Ah, yes. I can see that Jūn has told you the story,' said Del, nodding. 'And in case you're wondering, Daman has been exiled to the peaks, and Mujin will see to it that his father's punishment is meted out accordingly.'

Mujin's stoic face crossed Keix's mind then, and she felt a hint of sympathy that Mujin was being cruelly punished, even though Daman was the one who was sentenced.

Then, after a dramatic pause, Del added, 'I wanted to—what is it the Atrossians say?—put all my cards on the table so we don't get off on the wrong foot this time around. I trust you will let your friends know the Kulcans are looking forward to forming a better and mutually beneficial relationship with the Atrossians and Tilsorians.'

Keix stared numbly at Del. *This* was Del's main purpose of summoning her to the Council Hall. To be the ambassador for the Kulcans? Scoffing, Keix said, 'I think you've overestimated my influence.'

Del made a tutting sound at Keix's denial. 'I think you're *underestimating* your influence, Keix. Never forget that you convinced me to step up.' At Keix's look of shock, she added, 'Yes, your little spiel about how combining forces can end the fight more quickly was sound. Though I still think it's up for debate whether evil can be eradicated.'

When Del realized Keix wasn't going to respond to her statement, she waved her hand and said, 'Well, I shan't hold you back longer.

Basch will walk you back to Jūn's. I'm sure the both of you have lots to talk about.'

Following Del's dismissal, Keix spun on her heel and stalked out of the Council Hall, making sure to only roll her eyes after she was certain Del couldn't see her doing so. What a waste of her time. And how dare Del assume she would have anything to say to Basch anyway?

But Basch seemed to agree with his new chief as he strode right up next to her and said, 'The Ifarls left yesterday.'

Great, now he wants to start a conversation, thought Keix, keeping her eyes on the path, her legs moving, and her mouth shut. Sandom had already told her Pa-shin and the rest of the Ifarls had left Yurkordu to journey back to their home, taking with them a handful of Ifarls who had been on ExA's side, helping them create and control the army of droids. But the only Ifarl whom Keix was concerned about was Maii. And she had learnt from Pa-shin right after the battle that Maii had volunteered to cross over to the realm of the dead—in other words, died—to coordinate their efforts to stop Iv't and reseal the portal for good. Pa-shin said there was a chance Maii's soul had been returned to her body, but he couldn't be certain of her revival. Despite wanting to head back to Tilsor to search for this reluctant-ally-turned-friend, Keix's priority was Jūn. In the end, she agreed with Vin and Ma.erdene that the best course of action now was to wait for news from the first group of Tilsorians who were heading back to the town to assess the damage. Keix's presence was of little consequence.

'I stayed back in Yurkordu so I could help Del search for Al,' explained Basch, seemingly determined to get through the mental wall that Keix had thrown up around herself. 'If Iv't wasn't in the picture and it was just ExA attacking, I'm sure the Kulcans could have taken them any time. But when we found out Iv't was back, we knew the battle was going to end up in a three-way fight, and Al was crucial in stopping Iv't.'

Keix wasn't having any of Basch's attempts at reconciliation. After all that she had been through, she wasn't going to sit through yet another talk about the greater good or doing the right thing. And she had grown disgusted with everyone harbouring secrets that they thought others couldn't handle. 'Right. I'm glad it all worked out for you. And the Kulcans,' she said sarcastically, picking up her pace.

'Keix,' said Basch with a sigh, as if he was disappointed she couldn't see or understand the big picture. 'There are times when we need to choose between what we want to do and what we *need* to do. I compromised by sending Mujin and Jūn with you, and I had faith they would ensure your safety.'

If Basch thought mentioning Jūn would soften Keix's stand towards him, he was sorely wrong because she stopped dead in her tracks and rounded on him. 'You know what? I am sick of everyone using "the greater good" as a shield for their inability to see beyond deep-seated prejudices. Yes, you heard me right. All this talk about what's right, what needs to be done—it is just your blatant refusal to see that what's morally correct is determined by the very ones who had set this system in place!

'Was Atros wrong to want to create a ghost-human hybrid because they wanted to defend themselves against ExA? Was Iv't wrong to seek revenge for the death of his wife when a small group of Kulcans and Ifarls coveted his power?'

'Which was why we brought Al to him,' interrupted Basch just as Keix was taking a breath so she could continue her rant.

'That is beside the point!' shouted Keix. She almost stomped her feet in frustration, and she was past the point of caring about any Kulcans who could overhear them even though there was no one in the vicinity. Continuing in a raised voice, she said, 'What I'm saying is that what anyone thinks is right will differ from someone else, especially if their experiences are different. And we're shaped by our own experiences that are unique to ourselves. And ultimately, if we subscribe to beliefs set in place by someone else without thinking thoroughly about whether it's a belief that aligns with what our heart tells us, we're just going to be pawns in these people's games!

'*You* don't get to tell me how to live my life. *You* weren't there when Mum died. And you will never know that for a few years after that, I'd been living for a cause set by those in power and I was too blind to see it—no matter how much you want to believe that you do, just because of those fragmented reports you got Jūn to convey to you!

'And you're not the one who got turned into a host for ghosts. And you weren't sacrificed because the Ifarls thought that it was necessary, and you just happened to be collateral damage. But you know what? It's okay. Because I don't need you now. I've figured out myself for myself. And I don't need anyone's acceptance except from those whom I love. So, just for the record, I will throw the invitation that Del extended back in her face once Jūn wakes up,' spat Keix, referring to the charm the Kulcan chief had returned to her.

Basch looked shocked at her long tirade. After all, she had never spoken more than what was necessary in conversations with him so far. He opened his mouth to explain himself, but she wasn't going to give him a chance to do so. Huffing, she turned away and walked back up the sloping path fast enough to make it clear that the conversation was over.

She wasn't surprised when Basch continued to trail her half a step behind her. What she didn't expect was that after a length of silence, her father muttered, 'I'm sorry . . . for Jūn, for everything . . . and Layne.'

Keix's heart squeezed at the mention of her mother's name, but she still refused to respond to Basch's apologies. In a way, she had concluded that there were some relationships that couldn't be mended—and there were those that *shouldn't* be mended. The kinship between Basch and herself probably sat somewhere in between these two situations, even if she had set out to reconnect with this person during her darkest moments. Sandom's words about her own relationship with Jūn and how they were connected by blood ties came back to Keix then. But Keix couldn't fully agree with Sandom, maybe because her non-existent relationship with Basch was fragile to begin with, and no one had ever spared enough effort to deepen it. Yes, Basch had reached out several times since they'd met, but it just seemed . . . facile. Maybe one day, if she were to feel benevolent, she might allow him into her space. But for now, her capacity to accept people into her life was filled, and whether Basch accepted that boundary made little difference to her.

22

Keix | Family

It had never crossed Keix's mind that the temperatures in Yurkordu could dip even further than what she had experienced with Jūn during their short time spent in 'exile' at the peaks. But the highlands seemed to relish surpassing—in this case, in the reverse—all her assumptions about it. Because Keix had to throw on several additional layers of robes now, even as she caged herself in Jūn's home. She only left once every two days, to go to the spring that Sandom had once brought her, to wash up.

In a sense, it felt like the Atrossians and Tilsorians who had gradually left Yurkordu after recuperating from their injuries in the past two weeks had taken with them the warmth that their presence brought to the Kulcans' homeland—both literally and figuratively. But Keix didn't send any of them off. She had been glued to Jūn's side, trying to regale him with stories of her trainee days at Atros, waiting for him to wake, refusing to let her hope slip out of her grasp, no matter how hard the days seemed to want to snatch it away from her.

'Hey, Jūn. When are you going to wake up?' asked Vin jokingly, prodding the Kulcan's shoulder. She had been joining Keix in the evenings, and they would take their meal together while she updated Keix on the latest happenings on the Tilsorian side. Today, she had brought Mohgen along with her. 'Even Mohgen's recovered,' she added, nudging the subject of her sentence in a conspiratorial manner.

'And I'm not a Kulcan, like you, who is supposed to heal rapidly,' Mohgen piped up.

Keix considered taking her best friend's side but decided it would be unfair to Jūn for three of them to gang up against him, so she said placatingly, 'He'll wake up when he's ready.' Then she let out a soft laugh when Vin threw a mock-disgusted look her way.

'Anyway,' continued Keix, changing the topic. 'You guys are heading out to Tilsor tomorrow, right?'

Vin nodded and took Mohgen's hand into her own. 'Yes, Mohgen's well enough to travel, and we want to head back to Tilsor to see if we can rebuild it. Even if it has lost Iv't's magic, Tilsor is still where many had put down their roots. It's where I think I want to put down my own roots.' She glanced at Mohgen meaningfully then, and it was clear to Keix that her best friend's plan had everything to do with the burgundy-haired beauty with the most piercingly sharp brown eyes she had met. Vin had never been a planner—until this blossoming and deepening connection that she had struck up with Mohgen.

'Ma.erdene's latest note says the journey between Yurkordu and Tilsor had reverted to its original layout. No one can be sure if this is because of Iv't's death or if Pa-shin and the rest of the Ifarls decided to reset the landscape,' supplemented Mohgen.

Keix's nod was curt. Word had spread since the note arrived this morning via one of Ma.erdene's qiues. As it turned out, the stern old woman's 'foolproof' way of getting information from Tilsor to Yurkordu was through qiues that she had trained. And these little birds, which had electric green feathers and red beaks, could only carry short messages since they were no taller than Keix's pinky finger. At least that was one mystery solved for Keix.

'Basch told me the same thing this morning, but I'm pretty sure Iv't's death undid the magic he held in this realm. The clearings and their connecting paths in Yurkordu that vanished due to his charms were reinstated the moment he died too,' said Keix. Basch had been popping in for a couple of minutes in the afternoon every day since that fateful day when she had shut him down. But he didn't say much except to ask about Jūn's condition and check if Keix had eaten. It was a good thing he was respectful of her wishes, even though she could tell he was holding out hope that she would soften her stand against him.

'Figures,' said Vin. 'So, once we're back in Tilsor, I'll make it a priority to look for Maii. Perhaps she's on her way here as we speak.'

Keix mustered a small smile at Vin's reassurance, then sighed. The reversion of the landscape also meant it would take much longer for the people to get back to Tilsor, which was why there had been no news of the Ifarl so far. 'Let's hold out hope until we have something concrete,' said Keix. She didn't want to voice out the possibility that Maii was likely buried under the rubble when Tilsor had crumbled.

'I'll send news as soon as I can,' said Vin with a nod. Standing up, she said, 'We'll get going so you can rest.' Then, she glanced at Jūn's prone form and added, 'Don't worry about sending us off tomorrow. Just come as soon as you can, all right?'

Keix stood up too and she engulfed Vin in a tight hug that lasted longer than any of the hugs they had had before. Blinking away tears swirling in her eyes, she nodded into her best friend's shoulder. She brushed away the pang of regret at her best friend's impending departure, but she resolved to be happy for Vin, who had come into her own in the time they had spent apart. 'I'll be with you before you even know it,' she promised. When they broke apart, Keix turned to Mohgen and held her piercing gaze. 'Take care of her for me, won't you?'

'You can count on it,' said the apothecary's proprietress with a wink. 'We'll master all the recipes of the most delicious food we've eaten and prepare them for you when you catch up with us. Bet you'll put on all the weight you lost here, eating—or rather, not eating—all the flavourless food that the Kulcans are weirdly partial to.' She wrinkled her nose for effect.

A hearty laugh escaped Keix, and she smiled gratefully at Mohgen who had managed to lighten the mood of this farewell.

After the two of them left—following one more long, tight hug with Vin and a brief one with Mohgen—Keix returned to Jūn's side. 'Mohgen's not wrong, you know,' she said. 'It's a strange diet of boiled-anything-and-everything that you guys have. Is it because it's healthier? Or because no one's really bothered to understand the culinary arts?'

Staring at Jūn's unmoving form, Keix's eyes unfocused. She was about to turn in for the night when footsteps approached. She jumped up and moved towards the door flap because they didn't sound like they belonged to Sandom; her habit was to visit early in the morning and sit with Keix for a couple of hours, mostly in silence.

But when a familiar voice called Keix's name, she gasped. 'Dace?'

'The one and only,' said the cheeky Atrossian, stepping through the door flap that Keix had held up. Then, he extended his arms for a hug.

'Why are you here so late?' asked Keix, indulging him by giving him a brief but tight embrace. She hadn't seen him since after the battle, but she knew from Sandom and Vin's updates that he had been busy with Seyfer figuring out the logistics of getting everyone under their charge back to Atros.

'To whisk you away with me to Atros,' he teased, the dancing light in his eyes reflecting his amusement.

Keix's reply to his joke was a smile and a roll of her eyes. 'No, I mean seriously,' she said, leading him to sit down on one of the stools that Vin and Mohgen had been perched on.

'I'm serious. We're leaving Atros tomorrow morning with Vin's group,' he said, as Keix took a seat opposite him. 'It was just decided, and I went to tell Vin about it before I came for you.'

'I see,' said Keix, her happiness at seeing Dace vanishing in an instant. *Another goodbye*, she thought, looking at Jūn and wondering whether they'd get a chance to bid farewell to someone, anyone—together.

'Seyfer and some others have been talking about it for a while, since we've managed to make sufficient carts to transport . . . you know—Zej and the rest.' His hesitation spoke volumes about the state of Zej, as well as the other Atrossians who had had their hands and feet cut off and survived that fusion with the droids. The group of them had regained consciousness not long after the battle ended. But they were shells of themselves, unresponsive, staring soullessly into thin air. Sometimes, a flicker of emotion would cross their faces, but this awareness never lasted. 'Pa-shin said it was likely due to the clash of Ifarl charms between the ones who were working with ExA and Iv't's power, and it might take a little longer for them to recover mentally from this stress,' continued Dace.

Keix bit her bottom lip and nodded. She had heard that only the elite soldiers who had sacrificed their hands and feet to power the droids had retained their mental faculties because their minds hadn't been addled by Ifarl compulsion. Even though these troopers were disabled now, they took the loss of their body parts in stride. *It had to be done. It is done. We won*, Keix could picture them telling themselves.

'How about the droids?' she asked. The machines had ceased to function after Iv't's death and last Keix heard, the Atrossians had been trying to repair them.

Dace shook his head. 'They're fried. We considered dragging them back, but we haven't figured out what we'd use the scrap metal for. And there are no tools here we can use to turn them into something more useful. I mean, it's like the Kulcans survive on sword-fighting and bland food.'

Keix had to force herself to frown so she wouldn't burst out laughing. 'You shouldn't judge others just because they live differently from you,' she chided.

'Well, you're right. I am chastised, but my tongue—it has a mind of its own.'

Keix, who had almost forgotten how much nonsense Dace could spew, waved off his comment off-handedly and asked, 'So, back to Atros, huh? What are your plans? Or should I say Seyfer's plans?'

Dace's answer was his signature shrug. 'We're going to try to rebuild Atros,' he said. 'Seyfer's group of elite Atros troopers should have been able to hold on to the city since most of ExA's army were deployed to Tilsor. And Atros—both the city and the organization—are in shambles, so it might be the best time to give everyone a fresh start, you know?'

'Huh,' said Keix appraisingly. 'I never pegged you for someone who was into structures and systems.'

Dace tilted his head. 'I mean . . . I joined Oka, right? And a true rebel fights to enact positive change, yeah? I figured that rather than let someone else dictate how we should live our lives, I should play a more active role in getting people to realize that *they themselves* should be the ones deciding their own paths.'

A bubble of laughter escaped Keix then. 'So then, you're helping to set up the system that lets them get out of the system . . .?' She pretended to muse over the convoluted concept.

Dace tapped his chin with his forefinger, as if he was mulling over Keix's words. 'Maybe think of it as creating a society that functions less like a machine that treats the civilians as just another cog, and more like individuals with the capability to think for themselves? Because I swear, the first one is just infinitely *dull*.'

'All right, all right. I get it,' said Keix with a chuckle. 'Who am I to refute the great Dace's wisdom?'

Dace's shoulders shook with mirth, and he flashed Keix a satisfied smile. 'So, what say you? Come with me tomorrow?' he asked, standing up and pulling Keix by her hand from her seat to face him.

Even with the low lighting in the room, Keix could see Dace was up to his usual mischief at this proximity. But when she opened her mouth to ask him what exactly he wanted, he silenced her with a look and mouthed, *Let me try something*. Then, he jerked his chin at Jūn meaningfully.

Caught by surprise, Keix blinked and tried to decipher Dace's actions.

'I've always liked you, Keix.'

Keix almost choked at Dace's out-of-nowhere confession. But she caught on quickly. Dace was trying to see if provoking Jūn would make him break out of his weeks-long coma. She shook her head and mouthed back, *It's no use. I've tried everything.*

But Dace was knee-deep in his role-play mood now and the sparkle in his eyes told Keix there was no way he was going to stop this little dramatic skit of his. 'I should have figured it out,' he continued. 'While Lana was my first love, you're the one whom I'm attracted to. Your fire, the way you face everything that life's thrown at you . . . I just know that you're the one for me.'

Keix didn't know if she should laugh or cringe at Dace's absurd soliloquy. She compromised by letting out a choked cough. *This would definitely give the game away*, she thought, *if the stilted monologue hadn't.*

Say something, mouthed Dace again. Then, he nodded at Jūn, hinting to Keix that he wanted her to say something about the unconscious 'third-party' among them.

Keix chewed hard on the inside of her mouth and, before the pain subsided and she laughed out loud, she began, 'But Jūn—'

Dace's interruption was swift. 'The Kulcan doesn't care for you. If he did, he wouldn't be ignoring your pleas. Or the fact that you've been waiting on him hand and foot the past weeks. Or that you've lost so much weight because you can't stomach the *tasteless food* here,' he said, sounding as if the Kulcans not having a glut of delicious food was the most sacrilegious act they could commit. Then, he continued, 'Trust me, Keix. Come with me and I promise you won't regret it.'

Keix would have lost her self-control, if not for the fact that Dace had cupped her face in his hands and drawn her close after his tirade. His amber eyes bore a stark resemblance to Jūn's golden ones. Then, in the breathiest and most seductive voice she had ever heard him use, he asked, 'Can I kiss you?'

The outrageous question brought Keix back to reality. *Okay, this has gone overboard*, she thought, even as her heart skipped a beat. Dace was so good he could probably make a hybrid forget its thirst for the energy of a living soul. Maybe they should have sent him to convince Iv't that he didn't need to massacre everyone to get his revenge, or to get Daman to hand Al over to Iv't from the very beginning. She was about to raise her hands to push Dace away when she felt a featherlight brush on the tips of her fingers.

This time, she gasped for real because both of Dace's hands were still holding her face, and there was no way he was the one who had touched her hand! Her eyes flew to Jūn, and she saw his eyelids fluttering open. 'Jūn!' she called, kneeling beside him immediately.

She took the hand that he was raising feebly and grasped it between hers as Dace's smug laugh sounded above them.

'I'm a genius,' he said unabashedly.

Keix looked up at him with eyes shining with appreciation. 'Yes, you are,' she breathed. 'You're *the* genius. Thank you . . .' She would have jumped up to hug Dace right now if Jūn had not tightened his grip on her hands.

Waving off Keix's compliment, Dace said airily, 'All right, I'll leave you two to your little reunion. But you'—he gestured to Jūn—'you'd better haul your lazy ass out of bed to send us off with Keix tomorrow. I think you've had quite enough rest. And the next time you pull a stunt like this again, I'm whisking Keix away from you. You can bet your life on it.'

Instead of getting upset at Dace's threat, Jūn said in a voice husky from lack of use, 'I know. But you won't get the chance because I'll make sure that this doesn't happen again.'

Dace's response was a snort as he walked towards the door flap and lifted it up. And because he *had* to have the last word, he muttered something under his breath about how Jūn would do better to ensure that Keix had better food, rather than making a promise that was out of his control. Then, he stepped out and dropped the flap loudly behind him to punctuate his grievances.

Smiling, Keix helped Jūn up into a sitting position and brought him a drink. After he sipped on the cold water, he pulled Keix into his arms and buried his head in her hair. It felt like he was breathing in all the reasons why he wanted to live.

Yet, when he spoke, of all the things he could have said, he asked, 'Were you really going to let Dace kiss you?'

Keix laughed at that, brushing away the happy tears falling down her cheeks with her fingers. 'Yeah, and that would serve you right for staying unconscious,' she said half-jokingly.

Jūn's response was to nuzzle his head into the crook of her neck and bite her.

Keix gasped at the half-painful, half-ticklish sensation. 'What would you have done if I had kissed Dace?' she teased.

A long beat passed before Jūn replied, 'Then I'd strive harder to become the better choice.'

Keix sighed and shook her head. How could he be so steadfast after she had almost caused his death? 'I'm sorry,' she said, fighting back a sob. 'I should have listened to you . . . I shouldn't have been so stubborn and rushed into danger without thinking . . .'

'Don't be,' said Jūn, tightening his arms around her. 'Because you wouldn't be you if you weren't stubborn. And Sandom's right. I would rather be the one lying here than you.'

Keix pulled back in shock. 'You heard us?'

'Everything that has been said in this house, yes,' answered Jūn.

'Then why did it take you so long to wake up?'

'I was . . . stuck in a nightmare with . . . W-Wex.'

'Your brother?'

Jūn cast his eyes downward. 'It was the same mirage of Wex as the one that we . . . in Tilsor.'

Keix understood what Jūn was trying to say even as his sentence was incomplete. During the third trial of the Taavar tournament in Tilsor, they had each been trapped in their individual living hell. Keix's personal purgatory was meeting her mother, which she eventually overcame. But when she had escaped from the nightmare, Jūn was there, appearing a little troubled but none the worse for wear.

'And somehow,' continued Jūn. 'It just felt much more real . . . and I couldn't extract myself from it, no matter what I tried . . .'

'Would it help if you told me what happened?' asked Keix tentatively. She had always wanted to ask him about what he had encountered then, but she thought it was rude, considering their relationship at that point in time. However, things were different now.

Peppered with hesitant pauses, Jūn told her about how a misjudgement during one of the skirmishes that had happened between the tribes, combined with his rebellious phase, had snatched away the life of Wex, who was two years younger than him. The details were chaotic, vivid, and distressing, but Keix knew Jūn had to get this out of his system—especially after his ordeal.

'I had come to the conclusion long ago it wasn't my fault he died,' he concluded eventually. 'But part of me held on to the guilt because if I had let it go, then the self-reproach would feel more intense when it came back. If it makes sense.'

Keix nodded but didn't do anything except remain in his embrace.

'And I guess the head wound just addled my mind and I got sucked into this downward spiral that I couldn't get out of . . .'

'Until Dace threatened to—what did he say—kiss me and whisk me away to Atros,' said Keix with a laugh.

Jūn groaned and took Keix back in his arms. 'Don't remind me of that,' he murmured, burying his face back into the crook of her neck.

Keix patted his back in long strokes and said, 'Thank you for telling me.'

'Thank you for listening,' came his reply. 'I wish we could stay like this forever, but I think it's time to go send Dace off. Don't want to give *the* genius any more reason to tempt you from my side.'

Startled, Keix realized that time had flown by, and it was almost dawn. 'Are you sure?' She pulled back and examined Jūn with worried eyes.

In reply, he nodded and moved to get off the platform bed. 'I may need a bit of help, though,' he said as he struggled to stand.

Keix rushed to find a thick overcoat to drape over his shoulders before looping his arm around her shoulders to stabilize him. After much wobbling, the two of them finally made it out of the house.

The freezing pre-dawn air hit Keix's cheeks, snapping her to full alertness even though she hadn't slept the entire night. As they made their way down the path, Jūn said, 'Give me about a week or two to regain my strength and we'll leave Yurkordu to go wherever you want to go, all right?'

Keix's gaze was soft as she smiled at him. 'Just take the time you need. We're not rushing anywhere—not any more. And Vin and Dace can hold their own. I trust them.' Now that Jūn had woken up, there were only two things weighing on Keix's mind. Whether Maii was still alive, and Zej's recovery; her friends had stepped up to take responsibility for these two tasks. She had to have trust in them, in the bond they had formed, and that all of them would find their way back to one another because they had chosen each other. In every sense of the word that mattered, they were family.

Jūn | Epilogue

Jūn didn't like ruckuses. They were taxing on his heightened Kulcan senses. But he didn't mind this one because it was clear his lover was thoroughly enjoying herself. Keix was seated with him around a circular table. They were in a rectangular room in the tallest building in Atros, and surrounding them were all the people whom Jūn knew had become an integral part of Keix's life—Vin, her best friend; Dace, the eccentric Atrossian; Zej, her ex-lover; and Maii, the Ifarl who had miraculously survived the crumbling of Tilsor. Then, there was himself, Keix's plus-one; Mohgen, Vin's lover; and Seyfer, the ex-Atrossian elite soldier who had upgraded in status from reluctant ally to associate. All of them were whooping at Dace's announcement that the last of the ExA leaders had been tracked down and were now imprisoned in Atros's most secure facility.

'Though, I mean, how can you be sure it *really* is secure?' asked Keix, her expression full of mischief. She was sitting between Jūn and Dace because the Atrossian had insisted on plastering himself to her side the moment she entered the room. 'I was broken out of ATI,' she continued reasoning, 'and you and Seyfer broke out of that factory where ExA was holding you guys.'

Dace tsk-tsked and pretended to look annoyed. 'You said it yourself. It's a *factory*—which means security is shoddy at best. And as for ATI, we're the ones who broke in, so of course we'd be the best candidates to plug all those security gaps that we uncovered, right?'

Keix raised her glass in concession, and Dace did the same in acknowledgement. The rest, however, were content to just sit back and witness their banter.

After taking a sip of the deep brown liquid from his glass, Dace asked, 'So, you and the Kulcan'—he wiggled his eyebrow at Jūn—'are leaving tomorrow to go travel around without a destination in mind, huh?'

Jūn inclined his head. He and Keix had spent about a month in Yurkordu after he had woken up from his coma. Amidst his recuperation, he had brought Keix to all the places in Yurkordu that held his memories—both good and bad. They went on carefree rides with Zorig, which had very quickly formed a bond with Keix. Then, they had bid Sandom and Basch a polite, albeit awkward, farewell.

'Feels like the right thing to do,' replied Keix, shrugging. She turned to Jūn. 'Right?'

Nodding, Jūn gave her a warm smile. Of course, he would agree with her. There was nothing he would like more than to spend the rest of his life with her, now that the world seemed to be in a good place. But her interactions with her friends had brought forth a twinge of odd longing in him. Perhaps he should open up more to the people in his life. After the death of Wex, he had avoided all sorts of emotional attachments because of the crushing loss he experienced—until he met Keix. She had been, in a weird way, a safe harbour for him.

'Hey, what I said that night in Yurkordu still holds, all right?' Dace said, meeting Jūn's gaze and holding it.

'What did you say to him?' asked Vin, leaning forward to prop her elbows on the table, her eyes swivelling between Dace and Jūn.

Dace waved off her impertinent questioning. 'That's for me, the Kulcan, and Keix to know. Don't be nosy.'

Keix's smile was shy when she looked at Jūn.

Reaching out to grip Keix's hand in his own, Jūn said, 'I've been on my toes.'

'Good,' came Dace's satisfied reply.

The ebb and flow of the conversation took over after a short lull, as Vin and Mohgen talked about how their business had been booming recently. The two of them had initially wanted to try to rebuild Tilsor, but they didn't even know where to begin to pick through the rubble. Many survivors had also ironically fled to Atros, so it was decided they would move there. Needless to say, Seyfer and Dace had welcomed them with open arms, though it was made clear to the survivors from Tilsor that looting and murder plots were outlawed; Ma.erdene and Falc had been roped in as part of Seyfer and Dace's new committee to take charge of this aspect as the rebuilding of Atros began in earnest. The two wily elders would be able to keep any unruly Tilsorian bandits under check.

As dinner drew to a close, Dace brought up random topics such as the weather (he made his dislike for Atros's humidity and Yurkordu's freezing temperatures clear), and how the food at Atros had levelled up since the Tilsorians arrived (to which Mohgen and Vin nodded their heads smugly, as if they had been the main contributors to this development, and Keix laughed heartily).

Jūn's deduction that Dace had had a little too much to drink was soon proven right when the Atrossian joked with a slight slur, 'You know, I think someone somewhere must love us very much.'

Everyone laughed at his sudden and nonsensical declaration.

'And whom do you think this "someone somewhere" loves the most, huh?' said Seyfer in a faux-challenging voice. 'Out of all of us at this table.'

Without hesitation, Dace replied, 'Me, of course.'

'And if you could enlighten us plebeians why you think so . . .' said Zej, smiling. He had been silent the entire dinner, and everyone present had respected his reticence. It hadn't been easy for him to regain a fraction of himself after what he had been through.

And while Jūn had mixed feelings about this misguided Atrossian, he was relieved to see a hint of genuine amusement dancing in Zej's eyes now.

When Zej folded his arms, it looked so natural no one would have guessed that under his black leather gloves were machine parts that Dace, Seyfer, and a group of Atros's elite soldiers, together with the help of Vin and Mohgen, had managed to develop. Maii's contributions were also significant, as she had been helping Zej and the rest of the people who had lost their limbs implant and bind metal prostheses to their bodies. Her Ifarl powers made it possible for them to control the metal limbs as if they were their own. The only thing that she hadn't managed to do was to replicate the tactility of real skin.

'Well, I'm the most good-looking one here,' said Dace in answer to Zej's question. 'And if Jūn could leave the table for a moment, I would be the tallest one here. I'm also the cutest, fun—Ouch!'

A spoon had flown at Dace and its trajectory made it clear Maii was the one who had chucked it at him. Laughter filled the room once more, and the banter continued deep into the night, as everyone's reluctance to put a stop to this intimate session was apparent.

Eventually, they said their goodbyes, and Keix and Jūn headed back into the room that Dace had prepared for them. The two of them were leaving early the next morning, and Keix had told her friends that she had had enough of them, so she didn't want them to send her off. But Jūn knew the real reason was because she had gotten way more emotional recently (in a good way, of course), and she didn't want her friends to tease her for crying.

The next morning at daybreak, Zorig came running to them the moment they stepped out of Atros. Del had loosened the rules about not letting shihs out of Yurkordu. Too many people had witnessed their existence after that battle, and it was unlikely word hadn't spread. Since keeping the species' revival secret wasn't an option, the new Kulcan chief had said that if any Kulcans were to bring their shih out of Yurkordu, they would be responsible for their safety. Jūn thought this was a superfluous warning since the Kulcans' attachment to their shih (and swords) were indisputable.

But Jūn had still left Zorig to roam when he entered Atros because he knew and trusted that his shih was more than capable of fending for himself. He had told Zorig when he and Keix would be leaving, and the shih's well-timed arrival proved these majestic creatures were more cognizant than people gave them credit for.

While Keix proceeded to throw her arms around Zorig, Jūn patted his furry companion and said, 'Right on time, Zorig.' The shih nudged him with his nose and Jūn realized Zorig was holding something furry in his mouth.

'Caught a prey, have you?' asked Jūn as Zorig dropped something into his outstretched palm. Jūn hooted in surprise. Unless there was another haagi out here that was grey and had a white triangular spot at the tip of its right ear, this would be the very same one that had crossed paths with Keix and him before.

'Look, Keix! It's our little haagi.' He held out the creature to Keix, who had just let go of Zorig's mane. Glancing at this furry ball, he switched to a lower, and even more gentle tone as he scratched it on its head and said, 'You missed us, didn't you?'

As Keix leaned forward to examine it, Jūn teased, 'So, reconsidering keeping it as a pet?' The last time they had met this little creature, he had asked if Keix wanted to keep it as a pet. She had declined and said the haagi belonged in the wild—probably because she knew these creatures would lose their sense of direction if they were caged up.

'It could follow us around and we wouldn't have to cage it up,' said Jūn hopefully. He had felt an affinity for the creature ever since he saw Keix scoop it up from the forest ground when she had been chased by ExA soldiers. And truth be told, he wanted to keep the little furball close, if nothing but to watch over it.

Keix scrunched her nose and considered his proposal. Finally, she compromised by saying, 'If it does follow us around.' She looked at Zorig and added, 'And if it can catch up with Zorig.'

The shih gave her a proud look at the implied praise while Jūn laughed.

'All right, little one,' said Jūn to the haagi as he put it down on the ground gently. 'If you want to be part of our little family, you're going to have to work for it.'

This time, Keix was the one to chuckle, though she blushed when she caught Jūn's eye. With their challenge for the haagi issued, they mounted Zorig and set off at a leisurely pace. And as Jūn's arms tightened around Keix's waist and she leaned back against him, he couldn't help but think about how they fit—in every sense of the word—because a peculiar, serendipitous stroke of fate had brought them together, to heal the broken bits of themselves that they had kept hidden for the longest time.

END

Acknowledgements

By the time this book is published, I would have spent eleven years in the imaginary world of *The Night of Legends*. It's been a hell of a journey, and I have a whole list of people to thank for helping me get to where I am.

Firstly, to Dave Chua, my mentor. Thank you for being the first one to believe in me. My memory of the interview for the Mentor Access Project (MAP) is fragmented, but I am pretty sure I said something along the lines of 'because I like to write and tell stories' when asked about my motivation for applying for the mentorship. And somehow, that was a good enough answer for you to take me under your wing. Without this trigger event, I might not have discovered that writing is my calling.

Of course, that means thanks is due to the National Arts Council of Singapore, for coming up with the MAP initiative to develop aspiring Singaporean writers. *The Night of Legends* might not be a typical 'Singapore story', but it's still one written by someone who's Singaporean, through and through.

My thanks to Nora, Publisher of Penguin SEA, for taking a chance on *The Night of Legends* and, subsequently, allowing it to become a trilogy.

To Thatchaa, my structural editor for *The Light of Stars* and *The Dawn of Reckoning*: Thanks to your big brain and direct feedback, the stories reached their maximum potential. I really appreciated your patience and understanding as we worked on this book. Hoping for many more future partnerships!

To the author friends I've made on this journey: There are too many to name, but a special shout-out to my Scribe Sisters, Joyce,

Cat, Eva, and Marga, for being my super safe space, and my Singlit MG queens Vivian and Ying Ping, for your constant support. This author journey would have been much rougher without all of you.

To the Singapore bookstagram community: Your enthusiasm for *The Night of Legends* is the reason why @lesliewwrites decided to embrace her true identity to become @kayceteowrites and take pride that the trilogy is classified as Singlit.

To my sister and my closest friends, Aries, Banny, and TY—I know y'all never read my books, but your unwavering faith in me and your consistent presence in my life means the world to me. Thanks for being my rock(s).

To my 2Gs—you two can't even read my books yet, but you still go around proudly telling people 'Google my mummy!' and that 'My mummy is an author!' I always feel very *paiseh* when your teachers come to me and tell me you two said that, but of course, I'm very moved. I love you two more than my life, and my writing life.

Lastly, to my dear readers who have journeyed with Keix and me over the past six years. Thank you for staying till now. People don't usually want to wait this long for a trilogy to be completed unless the author's a big shot, and I know I'm not. So I feel heartened and always want to thank you by delivering the best story that I can.

This is the end of an era! Till next time! ☺